WHITE ELEPHANT

WHITE

a novel

ELEPHANT

CATHERINE
COOPER

Freehand Books gratefully acknowledges the support of the Canada Council for the Arts for its publishing program. ¶ Freehand Books acknowledges the financial support for its publishing program provided by the Government of Canada through the Canada Book Fund.

 Canada Council   Conseil des Arts
for the Arts   du Canada   Government

Freehand Books
515 – 815 1st Street SW   Calgary, Alberta   T2P 1N3
www.freehand-books.com

Book orders: LitDistCo
100 Armstrong Avenue   Georgetown, Ontario   L7G 5S4
Telephone: 1-800-591-6250   Fax: 1-800-591-6251
orders@litdistco.ca
www.litdistco.ca

Library and Archives Canada Cataloguing in Publication

Cooper, Catherine, 1982–, author
White elephant / Catherine Cooper.

Issued in print and electronic formats.
ISBN 978-1-55481-303-2 (paperback).
ISBN 978-1-4604-0582-6 (html).
ISBN 978-1-77048-623-2 (pdf)

Title.

PS8605.O654W49 2016   C813'.6   C2015-908583-7   C2015-908584-5

Edited by Barbara Scott
Book design by Natalie Olsen, Kisscut Design
Front cover image adapted from "Charles Copeland Morse mansion, Santa Clara, California," photographed by Eugene Zelenko. https://commons.wikimedia.org/wiki/File:USA-Santa_Clara-Morse_Mansion-4.jpg
Author photo by Jonáš Koukl
Printed on FSC® recycled paper and bound in Canada by Friesens

For Sammy

WHITE ELEPHANT (NOUN): *a possession that is useless or trouble-some, especially one that is expensive to maintain or difficult to dispose of.*

Origin: from the story that the kings of Siam gave such animals as a gift to courtiers they disliked, in order to ruin the recipient by the great expense incurred in maintaining the animal.

— Oxford English Dictionary

Her face looked ugly in the attempt to avoid tears; it was an ugliness which bound him to her more than any beauty could have done; it isn't being happy together, he thought as though it were a fresh discovery, that makes one love — it's being unhappy together.

—GRAHAM GREENE, *The Ministry of Fear*

CHAPTER 1

AS ANN RAN DOWN the front steps of the British High Commission cradling two thick, brown envelopes addressed in Tony McCann's loopy handwriting, a sense of panic rose within her. They were late. The boy was waiting at the wharf, the store would be closing any minute, and Maggie still wanted to go to the fabric market. Something would have to be left out.

"How long does it take to get to Choithram's?" she asked as she climbed into the truck.

"I cannot know now," said the driver.

"What time is it?"

"Four o'clock."

"Ugh. And how far is it from Choithram's to the wharf?"

"I think this boy is not there."

"You said he would be there."

"At eleven o'clock he was there. He is a good boy. Now it is four o'clock."

Ann turned to Maggie. "Why don't we leave you at the fabric market while I quickly go to Choithram's and the wharf, and we'll pick you up afterwards?"

"Why do I get the feeling I'll never see you again if I agree to that?" Maggie said, and Ann wished she hadn't invited her to come.

It was partly her fault they were late, she hadn't even offered to help pay for gas, and now she was going to be angry if Ann didn't arrange for her to get to the fabric market, but there simply wasn't time.

Ann turned over the package. Tony's elegant, feminine script formed soothing curves that wound over each other economically, as if the surface of the envelope were something precious that shouldn't be wasted. How strange, she thought, that such an ordinary, familiar thing should seem so exotic.

She looked out of her window at the neat hedges and walls, the palm trees, and people under colourful umbrellas selling fruit and sweets. They were still close enough to the ocean to smell the salt air, and Ann wished they weren't in a rush. She was feeling relatively well for once and longed to sit on a terrace at one of the hotels, eat good food, and breathe for a while, but instead she had to go directly into the furnace of downtown Freetown with Maggie pouting in the back seat.

Another pang of anxiety. She couldn't miss Choithram's. She'd been washing her hair with soap for two weeks after having an allergic reaction to the chemical shampoo Jusuf bought at the junction, and she had to get Tor his candy. He had so little to look forward to, and although at thirteen he was too old to be making lists of treats, she wanted him to have at least some comforts, despite Richard's insistence that suffering built character.

How had it become four o'clock? The driver had been late to pick her up, as always, and when they'd finally arrived at the orphanage, Ann had waited for at least half an hour while Maggie and Pastor Mark prayed over one of the kids, who was having an epileptic fit or something. Then there was the road, which was even worse than usual because of the heavy rain, and they'd been held up at every single checkpoint along the way, where Maggie insisted on preaching to the soldiers and giving them Bibles if they asked for bribes.

They had to go to the High Commission first because it had recently moved and the driver wasn't sure exactly where it was or what time it closed, and they'd arrived just as the gates were being locked. The janitor asked Ann not to tell anyone that he had let her in, so when the rude man at the desk barked, "Who let you in?" as she rounded the corner at the entrance, she'd said, "I couldn't say," because she didn't like to lie. He tried to tell her that he couldn't release her mail because they were closed, and he made an obnoxious comment about how it was highly irregular for people to use the High Commission in this way and it was only meant to happen *in extremis*. She'd had to smile and try to be charming even though she was furious, knowing that there was no way he would have been so rude to her husband, who was English and a doctor. In the end, he'd given her the mail, and she'd been as quick as she could, but now it was four o'clock, and the boy was probably gone, and Richard would blame her for everything, because he always blamed her when things went wrong.

She opened the first envelope from Tony and took out the contents. There were some bills marked PAID, some medical magazines for Richard. Flipping through the pile, for a moment Ann thought Tony hadn't written to her, and she felt wounded until she saw, near the bottom, an envelope addressed to her in his handwriting, which she slipped into her purse.

In the second package she found two envelopes bound with an elastic band and a note from Julia — *"Looks IMPORTANT!"* — stuck to the top. Ann hated it when people used capital letters. It was so alarming.

Re: Request for Records

Dear Dr. Berringer,

Audit of income tax for the period of 1990–1992.

Your account has been selected for audit for the period noted above. Please contact me before 15 days from the date of this letter to arrange a date, time, and place for the audit to begin.

Subsection 230(1) of the Income Tax Act requires that you keep records. Subsection 231.1(1) allows authorized auditors of the Canada Revenue Agency to inspect, audit, and examine the records. Your prompt reply is appreciated....

Ann flipped to the second letter, which looked the same as the first.

Re: Request for Records

Dear Dr. Berringer,

Regarding the audit of income tax returns for the period of 1990–1992.

We are auditing your records for the period noted above. Section 231.1(1) of the Income Tax Act gives us the authority to inspect, audit, or examine your records. You are required to provide all tax records for the period above. Please mail or fax this information to my attention at the tax service address shown below.

If you do not comply, we may issue a requirement notice to provide the documents under subsection 213.2(1) of the Income Tax Act. Please contact me at the number listed below before 15 days from the date of this letter.

THE FIRST LETTER, which must have arrived at their house in Canada just days after they left, was already over two months old. Ann's first thought was that she should do what Rita Bergman had done and use the war as an excuse to convince her husband to go home early. She wasn't about to ask Julia and Tony to go through all the boxes of receipts she had packed in the basement back in Nova Scotia, because they would never understand her system. When she got back she could manage everything, but she had to put it off until then. This meant she would have to write one of her letters, and that wouldn't be easy, because her mind wasn't as clear as it used to be, although she was feeling clearer than usual after a day away from the Foundation House.

Living in that place was like living in a swamp. No one had told her that they would be arriving in the middle of the rainy season, and their first two months had been relentlessly wet. Everything was damp all the time, and her lungs felt constantly swollen and inflamed. She thought of the Foundation House not as a house, but as a pulsating mass, a throbbing white body of liberated spores and perpetual oozing. She had tried for a while to fill holes and stop leaks, she had tried insisting that they move, but nothing had worked, so eventually she had given up. Then Jusuf, that idiot, had brushed off the black mould that ran along the base of the living room walls without even closing the door first, so Ann and Tor had had to run through the house like a SWAT team with their T-shirts over their faces spraying a diluted bleach and Dettol mixture on every surface, but even that, she knew, was hopeless. The Foundation House was free, and Richard didn't believe it was making her illness worse any more than he believed that the house in Nova Scotia had caused it.

ANN COVERED HER NOSE with her blouse as the truck crept down a gridlocked street. She caught sight of herself in the side mirror, the bags under her eyes highlighted by the afternoon sun, and she had to turn away.

"How much further?" she asked. The driver shrugged. Maggie sighed loudly.

Ann had never met a Texan or a missionary before she came to Sierra Leone, but Maggie was exactly what she would have imagined if she'd been asked to conjure an image of either: overweight, badly dressed and full of aggressive certitude. She had short, feathered white hair and always wore one of two shapeless outfits — a long sleeveless floral dress over a faded yellow T-shirt or a short-sleeved denim dress with mismatched metal buttons down the front. She was loud and bossy, always trying to get things for free and criticizing people and denouncing their beliefs. When Ann made the mistake of talking to her about Richard, Maggie had quoted the Bible,

Judge not, or you too will be judged, but she was the most judgmental person Ann had ever met.

Perhaps what bothered Ann most about Maggie was that Maggie had sacrificed her relationships with her own children and grand-children for people she didn't even know. Ann couldn't understand that. As difficult as he was, Ann would find it unbearable to be sep-arated from Tor, but Maggie hadn't even seen any of her children or grandchildren in over fifteen years. She said she couldn't justify the expense of flying to the States when they were so short of money at the orphanage, but Ann was sure there must be more to the story than that. Maybe her children didn't want to see her. Maybe she was trying to make up for all the mistakes she had made with them by taking care of her orphans, who would be grateful for any kind of care.

Ann checked her reflection in the side mirror again, and again she had to look away. She wondered why she was being so negative. Maggie was a good person, and despite her pushiness and funda-mentalism, Ann did admire her in a way. She was giving up a lot to take care of those kids, most of whom had been abandoned because of some disfigurement, and she was doing it because she wanted to serve God. There was something about that which Ann couldn't judge, even if Maggie was indoctrinating those kids, even if Maggie was a self-righteous American, and even if Maggie was judging her.

Some boys selling toothpaste stood next to the car chanting, *"Oporto, oporto,"* so Ann had to roll up her window. She hated it when people did that. Richard said it was something to do with the Portuguese, because they were the first white people there, and she shouldn't take offence. This was the same man who didn't like her calling black people black people and said she was clueless when she asked what else she was supposed to call them. It was true that she'd never known a black person before she went to England as a teen-ager. When she was growing up in Nova Scotia, black people were a mystery to her. They lived at the extreme south end of town and didn't go to her school, and although you sometimes heard about someone marrying one, she didn't know anyone who had. But people were people, as far as she could tell, and it was just as weird to pretend you didn't notice something as obvious as skin colour as it was to shout about it for no reason.

By the time they reached the part of Freetown Ann recognized, it was pouring. She put her head out of the window to find out what was making the traffic move so slowly, but she couldn't see through the rain. When they stopped moving altogether, she became frantic. "Why have we stopped?" she shouted at the driver. She felt an urge to take the wheel, but there would have been no point. No one was moving.

"We are very near," the driver said. He was sucking something from a bag he'd bought from a vendor the last time they were at a standstill.

"How near?"

He yawned and waved vaguely to the left. "Choithram's is there, and the wharf is there."

"Can you draw me a map?" Ann looked through her purse for some paper. She had only been to Freetown once before, and she had no sense of where anything was. She was also afraid that she might have one of her breathing attacks while she was alone out there.

She gave the driver an old receipt to draw the map on and straightened out her skirt, noticing that she had dried food on her chest. She looked in the mirror again. Her face was red, the pores enormous; the skin under her eyes was swollen and her hair was sticking up wildly. She looked like her mother, she thought with horror. She turned to Maggie.

"You two go to the market and meet me at the wharf as soon as you can, okay?"

"That's up to John, isn't it?" Maggie said brightly. She patted the driver on the shoulder, clearly pleased that she had her way, and gave Ann her umbrella. "Be careful out there," she said. Ann took the umbrella from Maggie and the map from the driver and stepped out of the truck into a puddle of mud and garbage.

"Shit," she said. She had to limp to scrape her shoe against the street as she walked, and she had trouble getting Maggie's cheap umbrella to open, so it wasn't until the driver was out of sight that she looked at the map and saw it was written in some kind of code and half soaked, the lines bleeding into each other.

"Excuse me, where is Choithram's Supermarket?" she shouted across the street at a man in a suit holding a newspaper over his head and running in the opposite direction. He stopped and crossed over between two cars.

"Pardon?" he said.

"Choithram's," she shouted. "Please."

"There." He pointed at a building on the corner.

"And the wharf? Where is that?" She wanted to get all the directions she needed now, so she didn't have to stop and talk to any more strangers.

"Keep going to Gloucester Street, turn left and walk to the waterfront," he said.

"Thanks," she said.

"I can escort you," he said, but she was already off, leaping over puddles toward the store.

Most of the pedestrians had moved inside or under awnings to get out of the rain, and Ann was aware of people laughing at her as she ran down the now empty sidewalk, one hand on her purse, the other gripping the umbrella. She couldn't tell yet if the shop was closed. No one was coming in or out. At the entrance, she passed a man sweeping, and he held the door open for her.

Inside the store, the air conditioning hit her like a cold slap, and she stood in the doorway gasping. "I'm sorry, we're closed," came a voice from behind the counter.

"I'll be one second," Ann said. Tor had given her a long list, but she'd only promised to do her best, and she didn't have time to look at it. She took some Smarties off the shelf and did the math. The prices were outrageous, and she was glad she hadn't brought Tor, because he would have driven her crazy with wanting everything.

Hurrying through the aisles, she picked up three bottles of gin, some shampoo, two bars of soap, a jar of raspberry jam, some Dettol for Billy's wound, two cans of tomatoes, two boxes of spaghetti. She was trying to add it all up in her head, but she'd started to lose track after the jam, and she couldn't remember how much cash she had with her. She had to keep something for the boy at the wharf, to pay him for his time and for his ferry tickets to and from Lungi, where he'd picked up the package from the airport.

When she had everything she needed, she took another box of Smarties and put it in her purse, reasoning that at those prices, whoever owned the store was stealing from *her*.

There was a Middle Eastern-looking man closing up the till. "We're closed, Madam," he said.

"Please," she said, and her voice broke, because by that point she was feeling quite desperate about Richard's package. The man shook his head and started to unload her basket.

After paying for the food, she only had one thousand leones left. She had no idea how much she was expected to give the boy, but she imagined it would be more than that. Then she remembered he might have had to pay for his transportation from the airport to the ferry and back as well, and she knew there was no way she had enough.

Outside, it had stopped raining. She looked around for a bank, but there was none in sight, and the street was once again chaotic with pedestrians and vendors. She wondered if she could return some of her purchases, but the store was closed, and she hadn't bought any-thing extra — she needed it all. She decided to go to the wharf and see if the boy was still there. The money thing could be sorted out later. The driver could probably lend her some, or maybe Maggie could, if she hadn't spent everything she had on fabric.

There wasn't enough space on the footpath, so Ann walked on the tiny bit of street between the gutter and the oncoming traffic, and she was repeatedly knocked by side-view mirrors and splashed with filthy water. By the time she got to the wharf, one of her bags had split open, and she was cradling it in her arms. The ferry had just left. Apart from a few people collecting their luggage outside the main building, the terminal was empty.

She turned to catch her reflection in a window. In the sunlight, she could see only the outlines of her face and body, her long neck, the shape of her breasts, the curve of her full lips in profile. There were no details in the reflection, no wrinkles or huge pores or dull, uneven skin.

"Are you Mrs. Berringer?" said a man in a dark blue uniform.

"Yes," she said.

The man held out a piece of paper. "This boy was waiting to give you a package. He was here for several hours, but finally he had to leave. He left you his particulars."

Ann put down her bags and sat on the steps. The note was a limp square of graph paper ripped from a school notebook. She stared at a math problem written in the top corner for a full minute before realizing that she was looking at the wrong side. Turning it over, she found a neatly printed address and the boy's name written in pencil.

Why hadn't he had the sense to leave the package instead of this note? Now they'd have to pay to send the driver back to get whatever was so important. And why was a schoolboy delivering the package in the first place? Why hadn't it been sent to the High Commission with the rest of the mail?

Ann took Tony's letter out of her purse and opened it. It was only the second letter she had received from him, but already the repetition was annoying. They should come home. Don didn't hold a grudge. Things had blown over. No one had even looked at the house, let alone made an offer on it. They weren't safe in Sierra

Leone. He'd heard that some relief workers had been killed by rebels. *I drive by your house every day,* he wrote. *I tell myself I'm keeping an eye on it, but really I do it to feel close to you. I miss you, Ann.*

Reading Tony's letter made Ann feel so tired and so, so ugly. Neither of her parents had been beautiful, and sometimes she took comfort in this when she felt cheated. She wasn't owed her beauty. It was an accident. Her father had been as warm and generous as her mother was cold and withholding, and their faces had reflected this — his broad and open, hers pinched and hard — but by some trick of nature Ann got just the right combination of their features, resulting in a face so lovely that it had come to define her more than anything else. That face, she had been told by her Classics professor when she arrived one afternoon in his office, flustered and late, could have launched a thousand ships and burnt the topless towers of Ilium, but now it was collapsing, and she had no idea what would be left when it was gone.

She lowered her head and finally let herself cry out the tension and exhaustion that had been creeping up on her all day. She was dizzy and nauseated. Richard would shout at her about the package. He would say it was typical. Tor would complain that she hadn't bought everything on his list. She'd forgotten Maggie's umbrella somewhere. And now she had to drive on those roads again, go back to the Foundation House, which she hated, which was killing her.

As she sat sobbing on the steps of the ferry terminal, Ann's thoughts inevitably returned to the two torments that would always supplant any other, lesser pains — the house, her own, perfect house, the physical manifestation of her life's dream, and Richard's affair, which had ruined everything.

She remembered the day the house was moved from its original location near the public swimming pool to the riverfront property where there was a new basement waiting for it. Everyone in town came out to watch. The children were allowed out of school. A photographer from the newspaper even showed up. But Ann didn't fool herself that they had come to support her. They were hoping to witness a disaster.

"What if it don't fit?" asked her neighbour, the only person who said out loud what Ann was sure everyone else was thinking.

"What if it *doesn't* fit." Ann hated to think of Tor growing up, as she had, in a place where people talked like this.

"I'm asking you."

"And I'm telling you, you've said it incorrectly." Richard didn't like her correcting people, but Ann felt it was her duty, somehow.

Watching her house being driven toward its new foundation, she felt an acute sense of exposure, as in a nightmare of nudity. She knew that there was a moment in life when everything congealed, and whatever you were and whoever you were with, you were stuck with. You turned out. And although it wasn't ideal, when she considered the dwindling scenarios for how she might turn out, Richard and the house were by far the best bet. It was such a profound risk, building your life around another person, but if she was going to do it, she had to go all in. And if Richard was happy at work, as he promised he would be, and if they had this beautiful house to live in, and if she could have one more baby, one more chance to get it right, they might all still turn out okay.

She'd walked backwards on the road in front of the truck, guiding the driver with the kind of gestures mothers use to encourage their babies. Around her, children in gaudy fluorescent clothing dug their greasy hands into bags of chips. Men in dirty coveralls and baseball caps smoked cigarettes and scratched their genitals. Women in synthetic blouses and cheap jewellery whispered to each other. Those women were the most wanton bunch of gossips Ann had ever met. When Ann and Richard first arrived in town, Paige, a receptionist at the clinic, had invited Ann to an afternoon tea where she and her friends spent the entire time talking about someone named Maria whose boyfriend had abandoned her with three young children. As the women told stories about the gross things Maria bought at the store and how bad her kids smelled and her pathetic attempts to make money by painting animals on rocks, Ann was filled with empathy and outrage.

"That poor woman is on her own and really struggling by the sounds of it," Ann said. "And instead of helping her you make fun of her? You should be ashamed." The women didn't say anything, so Ann put down her cup and left. Later, she found out where Maria lived and went to her house, which reeked of pee and hot dogs, to offer her a housekeeping job. She had always tried to help people who were down on their luck, because she felt for people who were struggling, probably because she had struggled so much herself.

When the house made the final turn onto its new street, the driver came too close to a maple tree, and a heavy branch scraped against the side of the building, whipping back when it was released. There was a brief panic as people tried to get out of the way, but nothing broke or fell. With the sunlight now hitting it from the side, the house seemed to be lit up internally, as if it were a being with eyes that glowed, its front door a red mouth.

That was the last, tense stretch.

Ann cupped her hand toward herself to coax the driver forward. The crew were waiting on the lawn in front of the open basement. The air smelled of wet concrete and gasoline, and something about it gave Ann such cheerful thoughts for the future. She had a vision of the house in its place, covered in Virginia creeper, framed by apple and peach trees behind a high lilac hedge. *It will fit,* she told herself. *It will fit and my family will thrive and I will have another baby, and it will be a girl.*

HUNCHED ON THE STEPS of the ferry terminal, Ann was aware of two schoolgirls standing hand in hand and watching her in silence. She smiled at them weakly, but they didn't smile back. Suddenly she remembered the letters, the audit. "What have I done?" she said to the girls, whose stares seemed to confirm her guilt. She'd ruined everything, and she had no idea how to fix it. She was terrible, dishonest, a liar. But as soon as she had these thoughts, she buried them. She'd done nothing wrong. She would write one of her letters. She would explain. Everything would be fine.

By the time Maggie and the driver showed up, Ann felt too ill to be worried about anything. She rose to get into the truck and dropped the note on the ground. *I'll tell Richard the boy wasn't there,* she thought. It was the truth, after all.

CHAPTER 2

RICHARD PEERED OUT of his office window to see if he recognized any of the women waiting in the courtyard. At 9 a.m. his shirt was already soaked with sweat, and his trousers had a streak of grease across the left leg from the emergency bike repair he'd had to do after John failed to pick him up in the hospital truck. He scanned the line once more, but no one stood out, and this allowed him to hope that the women might not come.

His colleague, Osman Sandi, was away from the hospital for the day, which was just as well, since Richard was not in the mood to have another debate with him. He hadn't slept. The night had been incrementally surrendered to the sounds of the rats, the music from the checkpoint, and Ann's incessant pleas for grapefruit juice. She'd spent half the night moaning, "Tor, Richard, one of you, please, I need grapefruit juice," and no amount of stern insistence that there wasn't any would shut her up.

When she came home from her trip to Freetown without the package that was half the reason for her going, Richard wasn't surprised, although whether it was her fault or John's, he would never know, since neither of them could be trusted. The medication in the package had been donated by an English NGO, who'd had it flown in with some other supplies, but said that Richard would have to have it picked up at the airport. Richard had been foolish enough to let John arrange for his teenaged nephew to bring it on the ferry from the airport to Freetown, where Ann was supposed to have collected it. John insisted that the boy had waited for them all day, but John was completely unreliable. Richard suspected that he was stripping the hospital truck of parts to make some money on the side, and he would have liked to fire John for that, but he couldn't prove it, and besides John was Sandi's brother or cousin or whatever.

When Ann came home without the package, Richard hadn't even had a chance to tell her how much she had inconvenienced him, because as soon as she came inside she started vomiting all over the entranceway. He was used to the coughing and griping, the constant complaining about mould and rain, but this was different. This seemed to be real.

It turned out she had malaria — hardly a surprise, since she'd refused to take Lariam after Rita Bergman told her it could cause hallucinations and suicidal ideation. Richard might have approved of his wife's concern about her susceptibility to psychotic manifestations, but the problem was that she was incapable of protecting herself in any other way — too absent-minded to cover up or light coils, too paranoid about chemicals to wear repellent, too disturbed in her sleep not to kick away the net, which always ended up bundled around her head and arms like a shroud, her bare legs thrown over Richard's side of the bed and covered in red welts, having won their nightly battle with the sheets Richard had tucked in with military precision.

Of course, her being ill somehow became his fault. He wasn't sympathetic enough. He wasn't giving her the right treatment. But he simply couldn't keep up with all of the illnesses she had invented on top of the ones she legitimately had. He would have liked to point out to her that it would be much easier for him to shoot her full of painkillers or whatever else it took to get her to sleep through the night, and the fact that he didn't was proof that he *did* care about her well-being, but in order for her to see that, she would have had to accept that, apart from malaria, all of her ailments were figments of her imagination.

Ann was the type of patient known as a heartsink, because your heart sank when you saw their charts on your office door. Don Williams, Richard's co-practitioner in Nova Scotia, had a less kind name for them. When Richard first began working in Don's practice and asked what the letters PF at the top of some charts meant, Don told him that it stood for Pissfart, and it was how he identified, "You know, the hypochondriacs, the worried well, the list bearers, the shoulder criers, the insufferable moaners with multiple symptoms in multiple systems for which there is no explanation and no cure." If these patients were also belligerent, assertive, or just overly chatty, Don wrote PITA, which stood for Pain In The Ass, next to the PF.

RICHARD CHECKED THE LINE AGAIN. At the back were the despondents, who didn't move except to wipe their tears, and at the front were a couple of loud complainers, who shut up when Richard told them that if they were well enough to complain they were too well to be at the front of the line. He didn't see any of the women he was expecting.

It had been a feat of coordination, but he'd managed to get all ten women to agree to be at the hospital at the same time to receive their first doses of injectable contraceptives. They needed doses every three months, and the logistics of staggering their appointments would have been too complicated, so when he told them to come he'd stressed that this would be their only chance. Now when they did show up he would have to tell them that the drugs weren't there because his wife had decided that it was more important to buy Smarties for her son.

Richard stepped outside and saw Osman Sandi bustling toward him from the nurse's station. When they'd first met as medical students in London, Sandi had been thin and self-conscious, but now, almost twenty years later, he was chubby and confident with an elegant wife, four daughters, and a household that exemplified, from the outside at least, the kind of warm, effortless family life Richard had once imagined for himself.

"What are you doing here?" Richard said.

"What do you mean?"

"I thought you were doing community visits today."

"Joyce needed me at home," Sandi said. "Her brother arrived today." Sandi's wife was from Liberia, and it seemed as though every week she and Osman had a new family member coming to stay with them because of the conflict there.

"Are you staying long?"

"I'm checking on a few patients."

"Well, don't feel that you have to hang about...if Joyce needs you."

Sandi looked at the people in the line. "Before you start here, I wonder if you'd mind having a quick look at a hernia and telling me what you think you would do."

Richard had heard it said that to be a true African hernia it had to be down to the knees, but he hadn't seen any that big yet, and his curiosity made him forget, temporarily, about the women. He also wondered if Sandi's request might be a subtle acknowledgment that Sandi knew what had happened when, earlier that week, Martha asked Richard to look at one of Sandi's patients who had come back to the hospital because he wasn't doing well.

Martha was the hospital's newest employee, a clever and distractingly pretty young nurse who had attached herself to Richard right away, following him on his rounds and taking notes on whatever he told her. Richard had nicknamed her "Matron" because when a box of uniforms came from England, the nurses had chosen theirs without knowing that they each carried strong messages of rank, and she, a junior nurse, had chosen the highest rank of all.

Richard had been pleased that Martha wanted his opinion on Sandi's patient, but he couldn't give it to her behind Sandi's back.

"Where's Sandi?" he said. She shook her head. "Well, find him. Tell him that the treatment he's given isn't working and ask if he'd like to have a second opinion from me." Richard knew that Sandi wouldn't like that at all, but he liked the idea of Martha suggesting it.

"I've already looked for him, Doctor Berringer," she said. "I think he must be away from the hospital now, and the situation is very serious." Richard had been doing everything he could to avoid causing professional rivalry between himself and Sandi, but it was his duty to look at the man if Sandi wasn't there.

Sandi's experience and the fact that he was Sierra Leonean clearly put him in a position of authority, but it was obvious to Richard that his colleague's skills and thinking had narrowed after years of doing the same things over and over again, and the hospital's development was stagnating under his conservative leadership. Since Richard had been in Sierra Leone, he had tried several times to make small changes or start new initiatives, but Sandi seemed determined to maintain the status quo, and it had been the source of some conflict. Still, Richard's willingness to submit to the role of apprentice in their current professional relationship meant that they got along for the most part, despite the fact that each of them thought himself the better physician — Sandi because he had better qualifications and Richard because he had better ideas.

"Make sure and tell Sandi when you see him next," Richard had said as he followed Martha to the men's ward. "Tell him I told you to try and contact him, and you did try, but you couldn't find him."

"I will, doctor," she said.

"That's important, Matron," Richard said. He studied her face and she nodded earnestly.

It was immediately obvious what was wrong with the patient. The man was lying rigidly on his back, and there was extreme tenderness in the right lower quadrant of his abdomen. On the chart, Sandi had written, *Abdominal pain several days, no localised tenderness, parasites. Rx Mebendazole.*

"He needs to have his appendix removed," Richard said.

"Dr. Sandi said it was worms," Martha said.

"He probably did have worms, but he has appendicitis as well." Richard wasn't going to let Sandi look bad, because he knew how easily he could have made the same mistake. "It's simple for me to diagnose it now that it's advanced," he said. "But it's extremely difficult to diagnose appendicitis at an early stage without any scanning ability."

"What should we do?" Martha said.

"You need to find Sandi," Richard said. "Send John to his house. Tell him that his patient has taken a turn for the worse and you — *you,* Matron — suspect appendicitis." If this worked, it would earn Martha Sandi's respect. "If you can't reach him within one hour, come and tell me, and I'll do the surgery myself."

Within fifteen minutes Sandi had been scrubbing up to operate, and Richard had enjoyed the thought that Martha might have been lying about not being able to find him in the first place. Now that Sandi was himself asking Richard to look at one of his patients, Richard wondered if Sandi somehow knew about all of this and wanted to show that he was ready to be more open to Richard's suggestions in the future.

IN THE MEN'S WARD, eight metal cots draped with blue mosquito nets faced each other under the open windows. Sandi led Richard to the bed of a thin, elderly man, who was eating with his hands from a tin bowl. The man was wearing a white shirt unbuttoned to his navel, and his legs were covered with a sheet, through which Richard could see an unnatural bulge.

"Mr. Conteh, this is Dr. Berringer. I've asked him if he would give us his opinion on your condition," Sandi said. The man clearly hadn't understood a word.

"Aw di bodi?" Richard asked. *Di body fine* or *I tehl God tenki* was the standard reply, but the man said nothing. "How long you dae get dis problem? You get am bohku tem?" Richard had been trying hard to speak Krio, the lingua franca, but for the most part people either pretended not to understand him or simply responded in English until he stopped.

Sandi spoke to the man in Temne. "A long time," he said after the man had responded.

"I don't know what that means. Years?" Richard didn't have time for this.

"Yes, years."

"It dae grow, or it dae always di same size?" Richard knew this wasn't perfect, but it was good enough. Why, then, didn't the man answer for himself? Why did he look at Sandi and wait for him to translate?

"It was the same size for many years, but in the past days it has grown," Sandi said.

"It dae pain am?"

"Yes, it causes pain."

"Vomiting?"

"No."

"Let's have a look then," Richard said. He pulled back the sheet, exposing the mass extending from the man's groin. It wasn't as big as he had expected, but bigger than anything he had ever seen in Canada. He had known before he set foot in Sierra Leone that conditions would be more extreme than what he was used to, and that had been one of the great appeals of going — a chance to witness the natural history of untreated disease. He turned to his colleague. "Have you tried to reduce it?"

"No."

"Why not?"

"Would you like to have a go?"

Richard knew that it would take a fair amount of sustained pushing to rule out the possibility that the hernia could be forced back into the body, and he knew that he should get back to the line, but he had been able to reduce almost all of the hernias he had seen in Canada, and he imagined that it might work in this case, although it would take much more effort.

"I'll give it a shot," he said. "See if you can find a couple of blocks to raise the foot of the bed, or else we can use pillows to raise his hips before we start."

"It will never work," Sandi said. "It's too big."

Richard was confused. "Why did you ask me to try if you've already made up your mind?"

"Do you think you can repair it surgically?" Sandi said.

"Yep."

"He's not obstructed, and we don't operate on these people unless they're obstructed, because they do badly," Sandi said.

What kind of mind games was this guy playing? "So why did you ask me?"

"I thought it would be a good example of the sort of case we have to deal with. It's not the same doing a massive one as it is doing the small ones you've been used to. You get halfway through and you can't get the bowel back inside."

"So what are you going to do?" Richard said.

"Nothing. *Primum non nocere.*"

"Well, thank you for sharing this with me. Now I need to get back to my patients." Richard was about to leave when a nurse came in with a woman he recognized as one of the contraceptive patients.

"Dr. Berringer," the nurse said, "This woman say you have something for her."

"Yes, hello sister. Please come with me." Richard tried to usher the woman out of the room, away from Sandi, but she crossed her arms and stayed put. "Okay, tell her I'm sorry, but the medicine didn't arrive," he said to the nurse. "Medicine no dae," he said to the woman.

"What medicine?" Sandi said.

"I arranged a donation of Depo Provera for some women who asked for contraceptives. Ann was supposed to pick it up when she was in Freetown yesterday, but she didn't manage...."

32

"You should have discussed that with me first," Sandi interrupted.

"She say she had to hire a motorcycle to come here," the nurse said.

"Why?" Richard said to Sandi. "My patients asked for birth control. I arranged to get some free of charge. If there hadn't been a mix up with collecting it, it would be here now."

"You should consult with me before you go ahead with things like this," Sandi said.

"She asked for this," Richard said to Sandi. "I'm not imposing it on her. This is a good, discreet way to help her to control her fertility."

"Can you give her something to cover the cost of the travel?" the nurse said.

Richard had four thousand-leone notes in his pocket. He gave the woman one and the nurse another two, saving the last one for his after-work beer. "There will be nine other women with the same complaint," he said. "This is all I have."

Richard turned away from Sandi and the nurse and went back to his office, where the loud complainers were once again griping about the wait. It didn't occur to them that he could be back in England or Canada sleeping in a comfortable bed, earning a comfortable income, working reasonable hours, having time to relax, instead of being surrounded by people who didn't even appreciate what he was doing. They had no clue what his life was like. But then again, he reminded himself, he didn't know what their lives were like either, just as he didn't know how many of the cheerful nurses and orderlies he worked with went home to domestic disasters every night. Before calling in his first patient, he tried to calm down by telling himself that he didn't know what Sandi was going through either, not really, and anyway, there was a bigger picture, and any petty difficulties they were having now were a natural part of their relationship working itself out.

They hadn't been great friends in medical school, but after Richard told Sandi he wanted to spend his career serving the poor, they had started to form a partnership, and that partnership had grown into a friendship, or at least the kind of relationship Richard associated with friendship, which he had never been very good at.

After they had finished their training, they both sat the fellowship exam for the Royal College of Surgeons in Edinburgh. Sandi passed and Richard failed, which was extremely demoralizing, and for a while Richard was full of doubts about himself and his abilities.

He could have gone to Sierra Leone anyway and started the hospital with Sandi as they had planned, but he felt it was unethical for him to work in Africa without the qualification he would have needed to practise in England. He also wanted the security of knowing that he could practise his profession somewhere *other* than Africa, so he took the advice of Joan, his Canadian girlfriend, and applied for some surgical residencies in Canada. This meant starting his training all over again, but he didn't want to live in England anyway, and this plan would allow him to build up his experience and confidence and, once he'd passed the Canadian exam, give him something to fall back on if things didn't work out in Sierra Leone.

When he was rejected from all of the Canadian residencies he applied for, he seriously considered giving up on his surgical dreams and working as a general practitioner. Then he received a phone call saying that someone had dropped out of one of the residencies and he could have a space if he could be there within two weeks, so he and Joan left behind almost everything they owned in their flat in London and moved to Nova Scotia.

The plan was that Richard and Joan would set up the Foundation with the help of friends in Canada and England, Sandi would establish the hospital in Sierra Leone as soon as they had raised enough money, and Richard would join Sandi once he had finished his training in Halifax. Instead, about three months before Richard was due to leave Nova Scotia for Sierra Leone, he wore all black to a party in a house with no furniture, and Ann walked in, also wearing all black, sat next to him on the floor, and said, "Who died?"

When he looked at her, he immediately forgot his witty response. If she'd been a blonde, she would have been a knockout, but with her green eyes and thick black hair pulled back in a severe ponytail, she was astonishing, and suddenly he was extremely aware of the effort it took for him to swallow. He was also aware, as he was sure she was, that everyone in the room was watching her, and that they looked at him differently because she was next to him.

He was asking where her accent was from when Joan appeared in front of them and passed him a drink. Ann looked up at Joan and then back at Richard. "I'm a gypsy," she whispered, and he realized she hadn't even considered the possibility that he and Joan might be a couple. He took the drink from Joan, and Joan walked away.

He wasn't sure exactly how it came about that he ditched Joan at that party and jumped headfirst into a relationship with Ann. He liked to think that it wasn't only Ann's beauty, though, or her confidence, which he realized too late was a flimsy front for her strange combination of snobbery and self-hatred. Maybe it was that she'd seemed to want more out of life than other people. More than Joan, certainly. She wanted some mysterious thing that had to do with adventure and being extraordinary, and at the time he thought that what she wanted might be the same thing that he wanted.

Her mother was dying, which was why she had come back to Nova Scotia from England, where she had been living, and Richard started going with her to visit her mother in the hospital. By then he was due to leave for Sierra Leone in two months, and it was becoming clear that he would either have to ask Ann to come with him or say goodbye to her forever.

He proposed to her one night after they saw *Airplane!* at the cinema. He was genuinely happy, though somewhat surprised, when she said yes, and he did enjoy the wedding, which was an incredibly last-minute thing in an art gallery, and then everything was in order except that they had to wait for her mother to die.

They took a short honeymoon to Cape Breton, but Ann was so terrified that her mother would die while she was gone that they came back after two days. Then, two weeks before Richard was scheduled to fly to Sierra Leone, Ann discovered she was pregnant. Richard had tried to make the best of it, even though the timing was terrible and he was becoming increasingly concerned about what he'd gotten himself into. He cancelled his flight and pretended to be happy, but a big part of him wished that he could rewind to just three months earlier, when he was quietly reading by the wood stove while Joan made one of her stews in the kitchen and there were still unlimited possible lives before him.

Joan had told him once that she was an Acadian witch, and if he ever left her she would put a curse on him. Sometimes he wondered if there wasn't some malevolent force involved in how things had unfolded, and he found it morbidly amusing to think of it as Joan's revenge, but it was far more realistic to imagine Ann as the witch. She had looked at him and seen all the things she needed — a father figure, financial security, status — and somehow she had coerced him into doing what he did, which seemed so incredibly reckless in retrospect that he couldn't believe he'd done it in a normal state of mind. Suspended between the unacceptable self he had been before and the ideal self he was planning to become, he was vulnerable to someone like Ann, who seemed so strong and capable, but who was really just another weak person desperately looking for someone to hook all her dreams on.

The truth was that he had done Joan an enormous favour when he unceremoniously dumped her and married Ann. It was easier to get over someone who had treated you shabbily, and he wanted her to find someone who would love her and take care of her the way she deserved — the way he knew he never could have. It was a shame their friendship had been destroyed in the process, but that was just the way it went, and it was no one's fault. Ann would have disagreed, of course. She believed everything happened for a reason, that good things happened to good people. Karma. All that bullshit. But what Richard was sure of, and what he saw other people coming to accept every day through his work, was that shit happened, and it was pointless trying to find a greater meaning or create an ennobling experience out of it. Beliefs to the contrary – beliefs like Ann's – were just ways for obscenely fortunate people to salve their petty disappointments or justify their ridiculous luck. And they weren't benign beliefs, either. They were abhorrent. Because if things happen for a reason and good things happen to good people, then people who suffer must deserve to suffer. This was the logical extension of the tidy world view championed by people like his wife, who had never really suffered at all.

When her mother finally did die, which took months, Ann was already saying she didn't want to take a small child to Africa, and by the time Tor was born, it was clear to Richard that she had never seriously intended to move to Sierra Leone in the first place, and what she actually wanted was to go back to England and live some fantasy life of ginger beer and rose gardens. He refused to move to England, and his refusal made it possible for her to refuse to move to Sierra Leone, and as they started to make other plans – plans that would ensure they would both be equally unhappy – from time to time he thought, *my God, what have I done,* but it was too late.

What they had agreed on, in the end, was that he would find work as an old-fashioned GP surgeon in a small town in Nova Scotia, Ann would build her dream house, and when Tor was older they would go to Sierra Leone for a longer period, maybe permanently. In the meantime, they continued to help raise money for the hospital in Sierra Leone through the Foundation, and Richard made a few short trips to Sierra Leone over the years so that he could feel like he was doing fulfilling work, even if he wasn't.

He and Sandi had cooperated well from a distance, and when Richard visited he was made to feel like a valued partner, even though he suspected that he was being shielded from a lot of the realities of the day-to-day running of the hospital. But now that Richard was finally in Sierra Leone long-term, able to inject some of the energy he'd been bottling up during a decade as a small-town GP in Canada, Sandi was putting up roadblocks every day. Richard saw so many ways the hospital could improve the services it was providing and reach more people, but when he told Sandi his ideas, Sandi consistently shut him down. There wasn't enough funding, there were other priorities, it would be too hard to get the drugs, it couldn't be done in Sierra Leone....

When, one month into his contract, Richard found out that one of the most popular herbalists in the country lived a two-minute walk from the hospital, he couldn't believe no one had mentioned it earlier. Many of the patients they saw at the hospital had already been to some kind of traditional healer, so it seemed obvious to Richard that partnering with this man might make it possible for them to intercede before too much damage had been done, but Sandi immediately vetoed the idea.

"Can we just say it's not a good idea and leave it at that?" he said, the implication being that Richard wouldn't understand so there was no point wasting time explaining it to him.

"Our patients go there, so we should at least know what he does, and if we could get him to trust us enough to refer patients here, we could probably save a lot of lives."

"Richard, I appreciate your input," Sandi said. "But you're only here for six months. I'm the one who will have to live with any changes you make. And I know the man you are talking about. He is not someone we want to give more credibility to."

"What we don't want is people coming to the hospital as a last resort, because it means we have more complicated problems to deal with and people will think of the hospital as a place you come to die. We need to get them coming here first, and it seems obvious to me that the best way to do that is to partner with the person they *do* go to first."

"I agree with you in theory," Sandi said, "but if we did want to work with a herbalist, we would have to know much more about what he does before we could associate ourselves with him. We would have to carefully look at his practices, his dosing, and we would have to understand how his treatments would interact with ours. We don't have the resources for that."

"But surely it's better to risk an interaction than have people dying of treatable diseases within a two-minute walk of the hospital because he's rubbing herbs on them instead of giving them antibiotics."

"Richard!" Sandi was almost shouting. "Our resources are stretched to the limit here, in case you haven't noticed. Many of the staff aren't properly trained, so I have to constantly supervise and monitor them. In the past we had volunteers, but now it's just you, and we are short of everything. I know it can be difficult to priori-tize when there is so much need, but we have kids dying of diarrhea, malaria, measles…that's what we have to focus on."

"Yes, and people are taking those kids to the herbalist instead of here, that's the problem!"

"Which is why we were promoting the vaccination and health education programs, because if we can teach people some basic things and get them to vaccinate their kids then they will be less likely to get sick in the first place. If we provide quality services, people will come to us first. That's already happening. But mixing our treatments with his only creates confusion, because people don't know who is responsible if someone gets better or dies. And if you start trying to get him to send patients here he'll probably assume that you want to steal his business, which is actually true, isn't it?"

"I am beginning to feel like you don't want my input at all," Richard said.

"I do, but you haven't thought it through." Sandi was shaking his head. "Can we talk about this later?" he said. "I have to go."

Richard decided to drop it for the time being. Like most people, Sandi was afraid of change, and with Richard around he wasn't going to be able to make all the decisions on his own any more. Richard understood that this made him a threat to Sandi, so he was willing to yield, but only to a point.

IN THE AFTERNOON, a young girl was carried into Richard's office by her mother. She was obviously in shock, sweating through her clothes and breathing rapidly. Richard had Martha ask the mother what had happened, but the mother said she didn't know. The lower half of the girl's belly was extremely distended and tender to the touch, and when tapped it made a dull sound consistent with urinary retention. Richard wondered if her condition was caused by trauma to the urethra, perhaps a result of circumcision.

"I need to examine her," Richard said. "Ask her to relax and separate her legs." Martha translated, but the girl's legs stayed firmly together. When Martha put a hand on each of the girl's knees, the child started to scream and resist. Martha spoke to her gently, and the girl calmed down a bit, but her legs stayed locked together.

Richard knew that female circumcision was very prevalent in Sierra Leone, and he saw evidence of it all the time, but this was the first time he'd had someone come in with complications, if that was what this was. Martha had shared with him that she herself wasn't circumcised — something he had wondered about privately many times — and that she had faced a lot of criticism and ridicule as a result, but he didn't know if she was as opposed to the practice as he was. "Do you think she's been circumcised?" he asked.

"The initiations normally take place after the harvest," Martha said. "But it's possible. Normally if people have problems with that they will be treated by the *sowei* or by a traditional healer."

"Okay, tell her I'm not going to touch her, I'm just going to look," he said. "Tell her we want to help her. She can trust us."

The girl wouldn't calm down, so Richard decided to sedate her so they could drain her bladder and examine her properly without causing her any more trauma. He wrote a prescription and asked Martha to tell the mother to fill it at the pharmacy.

"She says she no get money," Martha said. She was the only one at the hospital who tried to encourage Richard's Krio.

Richard wanted to tell the woman she should have thought of

that before subjecting her daughter to a dangerous and unnecessary mutilation, but he knew he had to be careful if he didn't want her returning to her community and telling them not to go to the hospital.

People often asked Richard for money, directly or indirectly. He generally didn't mind, unless he got the impression that they expected it. People in Nova Scotia probably assumed, as he once had, that the work he did in Sierra Leone would be received with unqualified gratitude, but he was surprised by how often he had to deal with demands and complaints — from employees asking for "tips," from patients wanting him to buy them food, from John asking for money to repair the truck. Sometimes it seemed as though everyone wanted something from him.

Richard chided himself for thinking this way. On the whole, he found people in Sierra Leone incredibly generous, and he had always admired how they seemed to get on with their lives without constantly moaning about their childhoods. He reminded himself how much of his own success had to do with an accident of birth, when it came down to it, and how much he preferred to be asked than to be the asker. With this in mind, he usually gave some small sum to whoever requested it, although sometimes he was tempted to share how desperate his own financial situation was becoming.

"We have some ketamine left over from a man who died this morning," Martha said.

"Fine," Richard said. "Give her that and catheterize her. I'll come back and check on her later."

Martha sat next to the girl to explain what was happening, and Richard admired how she managed to conceal any feelings she might have without seeming to have no feelings at all. He liked to imagine she was showing the same restraint in her relationship with him, but after over two months of having her follow him around with her notebook and her questions, he had accepted that her appreciation was purely professional, enjoyed it for what it was, and felt grateful to know her. She was a good nurse, he thought. She was utterly humane.

RICHARD SPENT the rest of the day between his office and the operating room, a dark concrete chamber lit by a single central light and four barred windows. Before he left, he checked on the girl. Her condition had improved since she'd had her bladder drained, and he was able to examine her, but there was so much swelling that it was difficult to see her anatomy. He didn't need a microscope to see that there was pus in her urine and she needed antibiotics, so he gave Martha a prescription and asked her to tell the pharmacist that he would pay for it the following day.

Richard was collecting his briefcase when Sandi poked his head in the open door of his office. "Everything okay?" Sandi said.

"Still here?" Richard said.

"I won't be able to join you and Turay this evening," Sandi said. "I told Joyce I'd be home hours ago." He smiled, and Richard was pleased to see that things seemed to be alright between them.

"Okay," Richard said. He picked up his bike and hooked his briefcase over the handlebars. "Tomorrow then. No excuses."

He knew he should go directly home. He needed to work on his proposal and check on his rat traps, and one drink with Turay, the hospital's nurse anaesthetist, would only lead to more. There was also Ann to consider. She was still sick, after all. But when he passed Nene's, Turay flagged him down by waving the fingers of his left hand, which hung over the concrete half-wall of the bar, and this gesture so appealed to Richard that he stopped.

Inside, a group of police officers sat in the shade sipping soft drinks and listening to a football match on speakers set up at either end of the bar.

"Kushe," Richard said to Turay. He ducked under the roof and leaned his briefcase against a white plastic chair across from his colleague, who already had three empty beer bottles in front of him.

"Kushe, Doctor," said one of the police officers. Richard had forgotten yet again to greet everyone.

"Una kushe," Richard said to the policemen. He walked around and shook each of their hands. One of the men held out his wrist instead of his hand, and Richard, who wasn't sure what this meant, touched it with his own wrist.

He stood at the bar. "Kushe, Nene. Aw di bodi?" he said. Sandi was forever reminding him that it was impolite to get right to the point in a conversation. You had to take the time to talk to people, to ask how they were, how their families were.

"A wehl, aw you sehf?" said Nene, a solid, middle-aged woman with two gold front teeth and the rough charm that Richard associated with all publicans.

"Misehf a wehl," Richard said. "Aw di wok? Aw di fambul den?" he asked.

"Fine, fine, doctor."

"Nene, a dae drink one sta bia, tenki," Richard said. He reached into his pocket for his last note, and Nene gave him a dazzling grin as she placed a dripping Star beer on the counter. "Bohku tenki," he said. He loved Krio. It looked like nonsense written down, but the meaning unfolded as you said it out loud.

"So, Richard, you have joined the winning team," Turay said when Richard sat down. "I have been the only one supporting Manchester. Now we are two." He held Richard's arm in the air. Richard had never understood sports, and the racket coming out of the speakers meant little to him, but he liked watching the heated reactions of the policemen, who were cheering for Arsenal, and Turay, who was shouting at Manchester's players.

At halftime, Nene switched over to the BBC *World Service,* and Richard listened to the headlines, wondering if there would be anything about the war, but there wasn't. Back in Canada and even since they'd arrived in Sierra Leone, they hadn't heard much about the rebel incursion, which Richard understood to be a spillover from the civil war in neighbouring Liberia. From what Richard had gathered, the rebels had been capturing towns and terrorizing civilians near the Liberian border for a couple of years already. When twenty-something army captain Valentine Strasser became head of state after leading a military coup against the inept and unpopular government, he had promised to end the border war and return the country to multi-party democracy. In the year and a half since the coup, Strasser's forces had recovered rebel-controlled areas in the east and south, and although there were rumours about Strasser and his comrades illicitly mining and selling diamonds and the army looting property and torturing and summarily executing suspected rebels, it seemed as though people supported Strasser's leadership and the war was dying down.

Turay hissed at a girl passing by with a platter on her head. He ordered two buns filled with beans and caramelized onions, and gave one to Richard, who only then noticed how hungry he was. Leaning back in his chair with his cold beer and his sandwich, sweat running down his back and along his hairline, listening to his colleague's exchanges with the policemen, Richard felt perfectly content. He loved Sierra Leone. The people, the landscape, the language, the food. He even loved how difficult it was. He had always found a pious satisfaction in hardship, and he enjoyed how after starving and sweating all day a cold beer felt like a minor miracle. Making do with less made everything he did have better, and he suspected that it was making *him* better, too.

"Your son is very troublesome, Dr. Berringer," said one of the officers, and all of Richard's warm feelings disappeared.

"You don't have to tell me," he said, hoping the man would spare him an embarrassing story.

"Yesterday we were playing football at the police barracks, and he came on his bike and told us to scatter! I told him I would beat him if he did not stop interrupting our game, and he said, 'You can't beat me, I'm a big man!'" The police officer laughed, and his belly shook under his uniform.

"You have my permission to beat him any time you like," Richard said, and for a moment — before he internally reprimanded himself for having such a callous thought — it occurred to him that if the war got any worse he would have a good excuse to send Ann and Torquil home, and then, finally, he could have a break from Tor's antics, Ann's misery.

He would never have guessed that he would one day look back fondly on the period when Ann was renovating the house in Nova Scotia, when her persistent unhappiness was at least occasionally interspersed with periods of extreme excitement verging on mania in which she would keep him up at night talking about her plans. She drew designs on napkins, on letters clearly addressed to him, on receipts stashed in the middle console of the station wagon. No scrap of garbage could be thrown away before being checked for sketches, notes, dimensions. There would be a room for everything. The meditation room, the exercise room, the library, the games room, the music room. Once, when in an argument he had complained that there was no room for anyone else's emotions in their house, she'd laughed and said they could add one.

Richard never questioned how much money she spent on the house, because he knew she wouldn't be happy if she didn't have the biggest and best house in town, and he had to do whatever it took to make her happy, because otherwise his life was unbearable. He had never been foolish enough to think it would satisfy her permanently, but for a while it kept her mind off other things, even if she did complain constantly, and even if he came home from long, exhausting days to discover that his work was only beginning. But at least they had been working toward something. The house had represented a possible life, anyway. And there was a grandeur in what she had tried to do that he had admired, a vision he'd thought he could buy into. But when they finally did move in, she managed to be happy for about two weeks before she decided that the walls were killing her, and that was the beginning of the end. Then she found out about his affair, and that *was* the end.

In retrospect, he saw the house as a catalyst for an almost comically rendered chain of events. Because of the house, they couldn't afford the bill for the office expenses. Because they couldn't afford the bill, Ann forced Richard to confront Don. Because Richard confronted Don, Don began a program of covertly punishing Richard, giving him the worst patients and turning the office staff against him. Because of these covert punishments, Richard became suspicious and resentful of Don and the staff, and so when Torquil pulled his idiotic prank at Richard's office, Richard blamed it on them, making a fool of himself and destroying what little credibility he'd had left after the rumour mill got hold of the fact that he'd had an affair and his wife had lost her mind.

Still, despite all of this, Richard did feel proud that he had clung to the apparent idiocy of idealism by coming to Sierra Leone. A miserable series of events had allowed him to finally do what he had wanted to do all along. That everyone back in Nova Scotia thought he had left in disgrace only made his real reasons for leaving feel more honourable. He could have stayed and weathered the gossip until people got bored with it, could have let Ann leave him so that he might once and for all be free of the insane stress of living with her and Tor. Once his contract with Don had expired, he could have started his own practice and put Don out of business or moved somewhere else and started over. He could have done any number of other, easier things, but he hadn't, because unlike so many people he came across, he took his duties seriously, and he wasn't yet corrupt enough to give them up for the sake of his own comfort and happiness. He believed that you had to try to do good in the world, even if you suffered, even if you failed, because that was the only thing that gave life any meaning at all.

CHAPTER 3

"NO, YOU'RE TONI, I'M JED." Tor wiped his Swiss Army knife on his royal blue school shorts. "I'll lead first squad, which is me, Matty, and Tanner. We'll go upriver and wait for the wind, then we'll light fires to make a smokescreen. Robert and Danny will be second squad. They'll do covering fire from that ridge. You and Erica will stay here with a shit-load of grenades and wait for my signal. When I give the signal, you will roll burning barrels of oil toward the target to start the attack."

Kelfala licked juice from his wrist. "I am Robert?"

"No, you're Toni. Toni, Toni, Toni."

"Toni," Kelfala said. He took a bite of the mango that was dripping juice down his arm.

The two boys were crouching on a ridge near where the cashew plantation met the main road. Through the trees, they could see the bridge checkpoint — a piece of rope strung between two wooden tripods and manned by a group of young men in mismatched fatigues.

"We'll charge from across the river," Tor said, jabbing the middle and index fingers of his right hand toward the water. "You'll throw grenades, and second squad will lay covering fire from that ridge until we secure the perimeter."

The bridge-checkpoint boys were playing "Bam Bam" by Toots and the Maytals on repeat, as always. Tor could hear the tinny beats from their ghetto blaster from his bedroom, and falling asleep every night listening to the same song over and over had fuelled the kind of fantasy he was explaining to Kelfala now. "We should also have a sniper in that big tree there, if possible," he said. "Maybe Aardvark."

There was no Tanner. No Matty, no Danny, no Erica, no Robert, no Aardvark. It was just Tor and Kelfala watching the bridge-checkpoint boys from the cashew plantation that extended from the Foundation House most of the way to the school.

When Tor had started school two weeks earlier, he had ridden his bike along the main roads, but now Richard was taking the bike to the hospital because the truck was broken again, so Tor was forced to walk. On his bike, he could speed the whole way shouting, "Scatter! Scatter!" and usually he made it to school without anyone heckling him or trying to pick a fight. On foot, though, he would have been an easy target for bigger boys, so he chose, instead, to take the long way through the plantation, and Kelfala had invited himself along.

The first two months the Berringers were in Sierra Leone, there was a teacher's strike, so Tor had stayed at home with his mother, but now that the strike was over Ann said he had to go to school every day, no matter how much he complained. He hated school anyway, but it was especially hard to leave his mother when she was sick, because he wanted to take care of her. Actually, what he really wanted was to play Gwendolyn and Ernest with her, like they used to.

The last time they had been Gwendolyn and Ernest was after they moved into the new house in Nova Scotia. Richard had given Ann a box of chocolates, which Tor regifted to her as Ernest during a chess game on a day when she had allowed him to stay home from school.

"Please accept these as a sign of my never-ending love," Tor said in his shaky old man voice, his hair smoothed over his forehead with spit.

"Oh, Ernest," Ann said. "How thoughtful of you, but... how did you ever pay for them?"

"I sold my stamp collection. But never mind that. Nothing is too good for the most beautiful woman in the world." He opened the box and took out the description card. "You may choose your preferred delicacy from this legend, my dearest darling."

Ann took the card. "Why Ernest, they all look equally..." she picked out a heart-shaped one, took a bite and spat it into her empty teacup "...delightful," she said, and Tor fell on his back laughing.

"Oh marry me, Gwendolyn, please!" he said, grasping her hand.

"No, no, I can't. I mustn't," Ann said. "I am much too young to be marrying an old fellow like you."

"But if you loved me, you would agree to be with me forever," Ernest said. "What are you afraid of, my dear, dear Gwendolyn?"

"What if I love you too much and you leave me?"

Tor was sucking on a maraschino cherry chocolate. "I have to shpit," he said, and she handed him her cup.

For the rest of the afternoon, Ernest tried to convince Gwendolyn to marry him and Gwendolyn fished for compliments. Meanwhile Ann beat Tor ten times at chess and they both kept trying the chocolates and spitting them out.

That was a good memory. Not only because it was one of the few times in the past year that he'd seen her laugh, but because at that time it had seemed as though she was finally going to divorce Richard, and that had made everything seem possible and good.

"When it's over, first squad takes the checkpoint, second squad creates a perimeter, and you guys watch the road. Got it? Wolverines." Tor held out his fist, and Kelfala pressed his own fist against it like Tor had taught him.

"Wolverines," Kelfala said.

Tor closed his Swiss Army knife, took out the crumpled pack of 555s he kept in the breast pocket of his school shirt, and lit one.

"My uncle know how to get gun," Kelfala said.

"It's not real, you idiot," Tor said. He wondered if Kelfala was serious about the gun. Tor had never held a real gun, and he'd had to hide every BB gun and shooting game he'd ever had, because his mother was such a weirdo about violence. Whenever his friends gave him gun-related toys for his birthday, Ann forced him to give them back. "Tell him we don't have violent toys in this house," she said. His friends didn't mind, of course. They got to keep the toys themselves.

Tor had tried so many times to explain to her that it wasn't normal to not be allowed to watch wrestling or play Duck Hunt, but she wouldn't budge. He wasn't even allowed to have a water gun. In a pathetic attempt to make up for this, Ann once bought him this plastic elephant that sprayed water out of its trunk. "Real badass, mom," Tor said when she showed him how it worked, and he felt sad that she never got him things he liked, not because he had to do without them — after all, he'd stolen enough money from his dad's briefcase to buy all the water guns he wanted — but because it showed that she cared more about her principles than she cared about his happiness.

THEY HEARD WHISTLING behind them. Tor took Kelfala's arm and they both crouched down. Through the trees they could see a dishevelled man carrying an oar and marching toward the main road. Tor had seen the man before, coming and going in a wooden boat, which he must have tied up out of sight, because he always swam ashore with his oar and came out of the water near where people washed their clothes. The people around the river made hooting noises and shouted at him. They even called him *oporto*, which made no sense, because he was black.

"Crazy man," Kelfala said.

"Shut up," Tor said, but it seemed like the man hadn't heard.

"But he is crazy man," Kelfala said.

"Shut *up*, you idiot." Kelfala was so annoying. He was always doing stupid things to impress Tor, he talked constantly about how he was going to be a US Marine when he grew up, and he kept trying to teach Tor to fight, but whenever Tor went along with it, Kelfala ended up taking it too far and hurting him.

Tor knew plenty of kids like Kelfala back at home, but the difference was that they were all girls. The only exception was Aaron Oikle, and he was the biggest loser in the whole school. He told lies all the time, he would do anything to make friends, and he didn't care how mean people were to him as long as he could hang out with them. But now Tor was the one who was desperate to hang out with someone normal, someone who wouldn't treat him like a zoo animal or ask him for his watch or try to fight him.

He desperately missed having things to do other than hanging out with Kelfala and things to eat other than sweetened condensed milk. He missed feeling clean after a hot shower instead of being always covered in dirt and open sores. He missed sleeping through the night without worrying about being attacked by biting ants or crawled on by cockroaches. He missed snow, trading wrestling cards with his buddies, playing street hockey until it got dark and his mom called him in for supper. He missed Lisa Formier, the prettiest girl in the world apart from his mother. Most of all he missed having a television, which was a guaranteed escape from any problem, even the problem of living in Sierra Leone.

Tor stood and stamped out his cigarette in the dirt. He looked at his watch. "Do you know what time it is?" he said. Kelfala shook his head.

"Assembly is in ten minutes."

Kelfala shrugged.

"Don't you care that Mr. Bangura's going to flog you?"

Kelfala laughed. "Mr. Bangura. He know how to flog!"

"I'd like to flog that bastard," Tor said. Since he'd started school, he had spent a lot of time imagining taking one of the teacher's canes, breaking it in half, and throwing it out the window.

"If you flog a teacher, you will not set foot in the school again," Kelfala said.

"Don't you ever want to fight back?"

"Your parents have been struggle to pay the money," Kelfala said.

"It's not that easy, so what they do now the teachers is to help the parents on how to educate you."

"Screw that," Tor said. "That jerk enjoys it." Tor knew this was true because he recognized the look on Bangura's face. It was the same look Richard had when he was searching for reasons to punish Tor, like he took pleasure in making people miserable just to prove that he was in control.

Richard's rules had nothing to do with fairness or sense, and this meant the threat of punishment wasn't really a deterrent to Tor any more, because he knew there was no way to avoid it. Richard insisted, for example, that Tor sleep facing the wall, but even as a small child Tor had known there was no good reason for it. For a while he did it anyway, because he thought if he was good his father would be nicer to him, but at some point he had realized that Richard was going to hate him no matter what he did, and after that he refused to back down again. Instead, he became determined to make things fair, no matter what it cost him, and as a result, he'd spent huge amounts of his childhood in his bedroom, but rather than seeing it as a punishment, he went to sleep early so he could be up at night and have the house to himself to watch R-rated movies, eat junk food, and come up with creative ways to get even with Richard.

"REMEMBER, YOU AMBUSH, take out one target, and retreat," Tor said as he and Kelfala continued to walk toward the main road.

"That's right," Kelfala said. "One target only."

"One at a time. You hit their supply lines, take out transportation, communication, leadership. It's strategic. The element of surprise is always the most important thing."

In Nova Scotia, in winter, Tor and his friends would wear all white clothing and arm themselves with Swiss Army knives and BB guns to go on Wolverines missions at the golf course. They pretended that Russians had invaded the town and the Wolverines were the only hope for the citizens, who had all been rounded up into camps. They would plan and execute raids on the golf course club-house, which was the Russian base, trying to get as close as they could without being seen by any of the diners inside.

Sometimes they got caught, and the security guard would threaten to talk to their parents. Once they found a dead squirrel and Trevor Pothier tasted some of its blood like the kid from *Red Dawn* does when he kills the deer. Most of the time they hung out in a fort they made in the woods eating junk food, looking at pornos, arguing about hockey, maybe sharing a beer that one of them had stolen from his dad.

They also spent a lot of their time in the fort arguing about who would be Jed, the leader, Matty, his brother, and Tanner, the heroic air force colonel. Tor was always Jed, and his best friend, Andrew, was always either Matty or Tanner. It didn't seem right to let Kelfala be either Matty or Tanner, so when they started to play Wolverines together in the cashew field, Tor told Kelfala his character was named Toni, and he didn't mention that Toni was a girl.

It was typical of how everything sucked in Sierra Leone that Tor had to play Wolverines with a kid he didn't even like who was playing a girl from a movie he had never seen. The only good part, which never happened in Nova Scotia, was when Alpha jets flew overhead on their way to Liberia, and Tor screamed, "Avenge me!" at them, pretending they were fighting the same war.

After Richard and Ann decided they were going to Africa instead of getting a divorce, Richard kept telling Tor that there was nothing good in Sierra Leone. "They don't have Coca-Cola," Richard told him. "They don't have brand-name clothing. They don't have video games." Tor got the point Richard was trying to make — he got it without ever going to Africa. He was lucky. He had lots and other people had nothing. What he didn't understand was how exactly it would help those have-nothing people for him to go and have nothing too.

It had turned out that Richard was totally wrong about the Coca-Cola and brand-name clothing. When they arrived in Freetown and Tor saw a baggage handler at the airport wearing a Bugle Boy T-shirt and a gold watch, he felt some hope that Richard was just being a prick, as usual, and he would, in fact, be able to watch the VHS copies of *Red Dawn* and *First Blood* that were taking up precious space in his suitcase. It had turned out that Richard was only partly right — there was a TV at the church, but Pastor Mark kept it locked up and said it was only for watching movies about God, so it was useless to Tor.

IT HAD STARTED TO RAIN, so Tor and Kelfala were waiting it out under a tree to keep their uniforms from getting soaked.

"Let me show you how to choke person," Kelfala said. He held his hands up toward Tor's throat.

"No!" Tor pushed Kelfala's hands away.

"I am writing a new rap song," Kelfala shouted.

"Okay, fine, what is it," Tor said.

Kelfala always claimed to have written his songs himself, but it was obvious when he had, because the ones he wrote never made any sense. He insisted that he had been to America, too, but Tor didn't believe it. He would say the names of things he had heard of and expect Tor to want to be his friend because he had said Busta Rhymes or "Ice Ice Baby" as if it was some secret password. When Tor quizzed him about his time in America, the only thing Kelfala had been able to come up with was that he went to New York, ate a hamburger and wore blue jeans. He didn't even know what a billboard was.

"We will sing it together," Kelfala said.

"I don't know the words."

"No, no. I will say something, and you will say goat."

"Like the animal?"

"No."

"Goat?"

"Yes."

Tor sighed. "Okay."

Kelfala closed his eyes and brought his cupped hands to his mouth to lay down a beat before starting. "I wanna tell you something."

"Goat," Tor said.

"It really make me mad."

"Goat?"

"My mamma beat me tonight a."

"Goat."

"My mamma curse me tonight a."

"Goat."

"Stop mommyyyyyyy!"

"Goat."

"Please stop mommyyyyy!"

"Goat."

"You really make a me sad a."

"Goat."

"You really make a me mad a."

"Goat."

"Whadabadaba whatsup whatsup."

"Goat."

"Whadabadaba whatsup whatsup."

"Goat."

"Goat." Kelfala said. He leaned back and crossed his arms over his chest.

"That's the stupidest thing I've ever heard," Tor said. He checked his watch again. "We're so late."

Tor held the waistband of his shorts to keep them from falling down as he ran, trying to jump over the biggest puddles. It had only been a month since the shorts had been made for him by the tailor, but already they were too big, and he had to tie his old belt in a knot to make them stay up.

When he and Kelfala got to the main road, their white socks were brown and their uniforms clung to their bodies. At the market, people who had pulled their goods in out of the rain were busy laying them out again. Immediately Tor heard the shouts of "*oporto, oporto*," but he refused to respond to anyone who called him that. As he walked down an aisle of fruit and vegetable stalls followed by some kids shouting "*oporto, oporto, oporto seke*," Tor thought he saw the driver's son, and his first impulse was to hide, but then he realized it was someone else.

Sometimes the driver's son rode in the back of the truck when the driver picked the Berringers up, and early on Tor had noticed that the tailgate the boy sat on was held closed with only a piece of elastic. When Tor told him not to sit there, the driver's son said, "Don't tell me what to do, little boy." Since then, whenever they were both in the back of the truck, Tor hoped the tailgate would open and the driver's son would fall out.

Recently, on the way to church, the driver's son had been sitting on the tailgate as usual, and Tor had been standing up holding onto the top of the cab. Tor horked and spat, meaning to spit off the side of the truck, but instead the spit landed in the driver's son's face. "I will beat you!" the boy said as he wiped the spit away, and Tor laughed because he knew the boy wouldn't do anything with the grown-ups there.

A few days later, the driver dropped Richard off after work, and while Richard and the driver were arguing about money for a repair on the truck, Jusuf and the driver's son talked in Krio. Tor understood more Krio than he liked to let on, and he caught enough to know that Jusuf and the driver's son were talking about him. When Jusuf laughed, Tor, feeling betrayed, asked what was going on.

"He say let you give him some sweeties," Jusuf said. Tor took a flaccid piece of Jenka gum out of his back pocket and held it toward the driver's son. When the boy reached out, Tor took the gum back, opened it, and put it in his own mouth.

"One day, little boy," the driver's son said, smiling.

"If you touch me, I'll smash your face in," Tor said. He stuck out his chest and chin to show that he wasn't afraid. The driver's son didn't say anything else, but Tor was sure that the thing between them wasn't over yet.

TOR THOUGHT ABOUT buying a can of sweetened condensed milk at the market, but he didn't really want any. It had become like medicine — simply a way to stay alive. He had made up his mind that he wasn't going to eat anything but sweetened condensed milk until his parents came to their senses and took him home, but Richard didn't seem to notice; and Ann just said he looked beautiful as he wasted away.

Not eating was only the latest in Tor's series of failed attempts to convince his mother to take him home. When Richard told him that if he didn't cover the cuts on his knees he'd get an infection and they'd have to go back to Nova Scotia, Tor had gone out of his way to make it happen, rubbing dirt in his wounds, but instead of a real infection all he got was shallow sores that constantly leaked clear liquid down his legs. He'd contemplated burning the hospital down, but that would only give Richard a reason to stay longer and rebuild it. He'd tossed around the idea of writing some fake letters that would get his mom to leave Richard or get Richard kicked out of his job or something, but his mother read all the letters that went out of the house, and anyway, he couldn't spell.

So now he was starving himself. He went to bed every night and woke up every morning with hunger pangs, he was constantly constipated, and none of his clothes fit him, but he was going to prove his point, no matter what it took. Occasionally his mother tried to get Jusuf to cook things she thought would appeal to him, but they were always disgusting versions of normal food, and the way she presented them to him like she was so proud of herself was typical of her complete ignorance about what he liked, which she had demonstrated to his despair every birthday and Christmas of his life.

"*Oporto,* gi me money," one of the vendor women shouted at him, and the women around her laughed.

"Eff off," he said, but that only made them laugh more.

"*Oporto,* you no dae bai mango? *Oporto,* what is your name?"

"My name is Ass Muncher," he said. "Asssss Munchah."

A tall man in a mesh muscle shirt came out of a stall nearby. "Hey, my *friend*," he said very slowly as he approached Tor and Kelfala. He was smiling in a weird way, fluttering his half-closed eyelids and holding out his hand, which Tor didn't take.

"This is my uncle," Kelfala said. Tor looked up at the man. Was this the uncle with the guns?

"Wetin na you nem?" the uncle slurred, and Tor realized he must be drunk.

"Torquil."

"Ah gladi fo mit you," the uncle said. "Usai you komot?"

"Canada," Tor said. He turned to Kelfala. "Come on, we're late."

"Canada!" the uncle shouted. He grabbed Tor's hand. "Toronto? Vancouver?"

"Yeah, sure," Tor said. He tried to take his hand back, but the uncle wasn't letting go.

The uncle spoke to Kelfala in Temne. "He says he sees you on your bike," Kelfala said. "He says let you give it to him."

The uncle laughed. "My friend, my *friend*," he said as he shook Tor's hand back and forth.

"We should go," Tor said. "We're late for school." He pulled his hand away, and this time the uncle let him go, instead taking Kelfala by the wrist and talking to him in Temne. Tor was thinking it was so gay how guys held each other's wrists in Sierra Leone until he realized that the uncle wasn't being affectionate.

"What's he saying?" Tor said.

"He says let me go to Guinea with him," Kelfala said.

"You have to go to school. Why does he want you to go to Guinea?"

"He goes to take some things in Guinea for bring to Freetown. He says let me go and help him."

"No!" Tor said to the uncle. He pulled on Kelfala's arm, but the uncle was holding Kelfala by his wrist. Tor pulled harder, and finally the uncle let go, shouting something in Temne that included the word *oporto* twice and made the people around him laugh.

"Yeah, screw you," Tor said over his shoulder.

When they got to school, the students were already singing the national anthem, and there was a line of kids waiting at the gate to hold out their hands for Mr. Bangura to inspect. Mr. Bangura started the morning with the gate open and gradually closed it so that the kids had less and less of a window to get past him when they arrived. Once the assembly started, he closed the gate to a crack, and anyone who wanted to get through had to submit to a fingernail check and a rap across the hands, or wherever else Mr. Bangura felt like hitting them.

When Tor told his mother about the kids being flogged at school, she got really mad like she used to in the old days, but she didn't do anything about it. He assumed this was because the teachers didn't flog him. There was no way she would have allowed that, no matter how sick she was. Mr. Robinson, the last teacher he'd had before they left home, had hit Tor's knuckles with a ruler once because Tor accidentally forgot to stop drumming on his desk, and when Tor told Ann she showed up the next day in the middle of class and told Mr. Robinson that the next time he touched her son he would be answering for his behaviour in court. From then on, Mr. Robinson had been more careful.

When the boys reached the front of the line, Kelfala held out his hands, but Tor pushed them down. "It's not his fault we're late," he said. "We had to stop because of the rain, and his uncle was trying to force him to work instead of going to school."

"Go to your class," Mr. Bangura said to Tor. He lifted his cane and raised his chin at Kelfala. Again, Kelfala held out his hands, and again Tor pushed them away before Mr. Bangura could hit them. Tor wasn't even sure why he was doing it. Kelfala didn't care, Mr. Bangura

59

didn't care, but Tor cared, not because he didn't want Mr. Bangura to hit Kelfala, but because it wasn't fair for Mr. Bangura to hit Kelfala for something that wasn't Kelfala's fault.

"It's not fair!" Tor said. He reached for the cane, and Mr. Bangura let him have it. Tor held one end of it in each hand, lifted his knee and brought the cane down over his leg, but it didn't break. Mr. Bangura tried to take it back, so Tor had to hop backwards to get away, and he almost fell over. When he had his balance, he cracked the cane over his leg again, and it broke a bit, but not the whole way through. On the third attempt it snapped in two, but without the satisfying sound he had imagined. He had tears in his eyes as he stared defiantly at Mr. Bangura and threw the two pieces of the cane onto the ground.

Mr. Bangura, who had watched with an amused look on his face as Tor essentially flogged himself, told Kelfala to get another cane. Tor wasn't sure what he had expected — to be hailed as a hero, to be beaten himself, to incite an uprising against the teachers — but he definitely hadn't expected what did happen, which was nothing. Kelfala got a new cane, Mr. Bangura used it to hit Kelfala's hands, and both boys were told to go to class. As they walked along the gravel courtyard, Kelfala took hold of Tor's wrist, and Tor let himself be held like that all the way to the classroom.

CHAPTER 4

FLANKED FROM BEHIND by the cashew field and losing ground to the river in front, the buildings of the Foundation House resembled a pack of animals who, finding themselves surrounded, had huddled together to die. The house itself was like a museum of bad ideas — imported materials not suited to the climate, an oppressive rabbit-warren layout, and no thought given to light or ventilation. In front of the house was the kitchen hut, a circular mud and thatched roof structure Jusuf used instead of the actual kitchen, which lacked both electricity and windows. Behind the house was an ancient latrine, and next to it a pile of things in various stages of decay. Deep tire ruts and a half-submerged badminton net hinted at the width of the original lawn, which had been shaved back to a narrow patch of grass by a receding mud embankment. Ragged mesh littered the water's edge, where people gathered to bathe, wash clothes, and fish. Further out, at the end of a long concrete jetty, was the octagonal dockhouse, which was meant to be a dramatic guest apartment, but which, like the rest of the property, had fallen to unromantic ruin.

Ann sat in a rusty chair under the broken satellite dish on the sunless side of the balcony that framed the dockhouse. She held Billy between her knees and tried not to gag as she rubbed Dettol onto the raw, open wound on his face.

Richard and Tor were gone for the day, and she had once again been left to suffer being nursed by Jusuf, whose modesty made everything an ordeal and left her feeling more alone than if he hadn't been there at all. She had spent the morning lying in bed trying to meditate but instead worrying about Tor and money and mould and imagining Richard rubbing oil on that filthy woman's belly. Richard complaining to that disgusting bitch about how controlling and crazy his wife was. Richard telling Ann she was the only person he'd ever loved and he would be the best husband in the world if she would forgive him only days after he took that cheap woman to some cheap hotel and had sex with her in a bubble bath while Ann sat at home oblivious, planning their future.

How could he have done it? If Maria had been attractive or brilliant Ann might have understood, but how could he subject them all to so much misery for that *nobody?* Ann knew she was recovering when she started to have these thoughts, but she also knew she would never really get better if she allowed herself to follow them, so she decided to do something about Billy's wound, which she swore she could smell from her bedroom.

Transitioning slowly from lying down to sitting up — how embarrassing to notice the open buttons on her nightgown, her breast exposed, and the ghostly shape of her body in sweat on the bed — to standing and finally dressing and brushing her hair, she had gone outside to find Billy licking his paws and rubbing them in the pus and blood seeping from his cheek. She swatted away the flies that had landed on his head, got her book and the first-aid kit, and took Billy down to the jetty so that she could sit on her chair on the dockhouse balcony while she cleaned his wound.

The dockhouse was where Richard spent most of his time when he was home. Ann couldn't go inside because of the air, but sometimes she sat on the balcony and read her book or meditated while he did whatever he was doing in there. She would have much preferred for them to spend the evenings together as a family playing games or reading, but there was no way to convince either Richard or Tor to do that.

In the beginning of their relationship, she had figured out pretty quickly that Richard's idea of spending time together meant either reading independently in the same room or watching the news next to each other on the couch in silence. Ann had tried to go along with it initially, but she found it almost impossible not to comment on the news or read him excellent passages from her books. She always ended up being hurt by him dismissing or ignoring her, so the next time she found something she wanted to share with him she would will herself to keep quiet, but each time she felt so certain he would appreciate the quote or comment or story, and surely that was what partnership was about — sharing the things that mattered to you — so she would say, "Can I tell you one thing?" and he would look up at her and sigh or hold up a finger and lean toward the television, or say, "mmhmmm," and keep staring at his newspaper until she was finished, when he would again say, "mmhmmm," and she was sure he hadn't heard her at all.

Still, at least in the past he had sat next to her and feigned interest, and at least in Nova Scotia she had Julia, who was always interested in talking about deeper things. But now she had no friends to talk to, Richard spent all his spare time in a room where he knew she couldn't go, and when she tried to get as close as her allergies allowed he didn't even acknowledge that she was there.

A group of children stopped to watch her torture Billy with the antiseptic, and when she finished and he ran away, she offered them some cotton balls and the bottle of Dettol to use on their own cuts and scrapes.

Richard said that Billy's wound should heal on its own if they kept it clean, but despite Ann's best efforts, it was only getting worse, and this was simply too much to bear on top of the mould and the pests, which were already totally unmanageable. She swore she could smell *everything*, and it was torture. The worst was the mould, which persisted despite regular bleach and boiling water interventions, but there was also the rat poop at the back of the cupboards, the burned plastic smell of the garbage pit, the chemical soap Jusuf used, the yeasty odours of sweat and tropical damp in all of her clothes, and on top of all this, the putrid and inescapable stench of Billy's wound.

Richard was the only one who didn't seem to mind. She should have guessed that he would turn out to be like Jim, her stepfather: kind to animals but cruel to humans. Even before Billy was wounded, Richard had shown the dog the kind of affection Ann could only dream he would extend to their son. He fed Billy from his plate, took him for long walks, and let him sleep at his feet while he worked in the dockhouse. Once she'd caught him cooing, "Kisses for daddy," as Billy licked his face. She found it hard not to take her resentment about this kind of thing out on the dog, and that Tor felt the same resentment and acted on it was, she felt, inevitable.

Billy's wound was the festering injury at the heart of their family life made visible. It was meant to teach Richard that ignoring deep wounds doesn't make them heal, to teach Tor that his actions had consequences. But Ann was the one who had to deal with it more than anyone else, and what could it possibly be teaching her? Or Billy? These were not rhetorical questions. She truly wanted to know. She demanded to know. Why was she sick? Why was she being forced to live in circumstances that made her more sick? Why was she going through all of this alone? And why, for that matter, had God chosen the moment when she was weaker than she had ever been to make her such a hideous wreck?

For a while after she first found out about the affair she'd looked better than she had in years. Her skin was luminous, even though she didn't bother with moisturizer or makeup any more. Her eyes were always shining and clear, despite the constant crying. Her hair was lustrous and soft, though she rarely washed or brushed it. She would sit in front of the mirror and cry, and nestled right next to her despair was the satisfaction of knowing that she was right, finally, and Richard loved her, had never loved her more than he did then, and she was still beautiful. She could still leave if she wanted to. It was a choice. But once that crazy first stage was over, it was as if she woke up one day a haggard old woman, and then she had lost her freedom to choose, because if she left him she would be no different than all the other tragic divorcees desperate to find a man and have another child before it was too late.

Now when she looked in the tiny, cracked mirror above the sink in the ensuite, she felt completely defeated. Things had gone too far, that was clear. Mostly she blamed Richard for this, but she also blamed her stepfather, who had forced her and her sister to work like fiends on his farm until their skin blistered and peeled off in strips. Seeing her uneven complexion made her actively hate Jim again, something she hadn't done for a long time. For years after she'd left home she'd refused to call him anything other than "that goddamned old hunchback," which hadn't helped her already strained relationship with her mother. When her mother died and Jim moved to the nursing home, Ann visited him sometimes and couldn't help taking advantage of his growing confusion. "What do you mean, it's nice to see me again? I've been here all day," she'd say just after she arrived. Or "I'm not Ann, I'm Dot. Don't you remember me?" When he was further gone, she'd made an Easter egg hunt in a potted fern and watched as he destroyed the plant and ate the eggs with the foil still on.

It wasn't until a few months before his death, during the frightening period after Tor's birth, that Ann made peace with her stepfather. She and Richard were living in Halifax then, and she was still struggling to come to terms with the idea that she might have agreed to live the rest of her life in Nova Scotia, the one place she had never intended to be but always kept ending up.

One afternoon she had talked herself into leaving Tor in order to fulfill a strangely urgent desire to be in a church again. It was the first time she'd even thought of going to church in years, and she later decided it was because Catholicism didn't seem so threatening compared to everything else that was going on in her life. She cried the whole way, imagining Tor's feelings of abandonment, and by the time she arrived at the church, the front of her blouse soaked with breast milk, she felt only depleted and annoyed at this interruption of her new calling, which felt so much more momentous than Catholicism did when she was a little fanatic.

She thought she would walk in, give a cursory confession, and sneak out. But as soon as she sat down and the organ began to play, she was filled with the same terror and shame that had defined her childhood. The potency of those emotions felt like a physical presence, like a huge hand pushing down on her head, forcing her knees to the prayer bench, where she stayed for what seemed like hours, asking for forgiveness and praying for Tor and Richard and herself.

When she had worn herself out with crying and imperfectly praying all the prayers she could think of, she had pulled herself together enough to make three resolutions, which were:

1. To go to church again;
2. To give her son the childhood she wished she'd had;
3. To pray for her stepfather at least once a week until he died. She didn't have to pray to like him — she simply had to go into the church and say, "God Bless Jim." At the time, she'd thought this would be the most difficult of all.

ONCE THE CHILDREN had returned the Dettol, they backed off to a safer distance and resumed their pretence of fear, the small ones coyly peeking at Ann from behind the bigger ones. This would have inspired an earlier Ann to thrust out her tongue and invent a terrifying dance to ridicule their belief that she was some sort of water devil, but instead she turned away from them and picked up the *Course in Miracles* book Julia McCann had given her as a parting gift.

Julia had introduced Ann to a lot of the authors she had been reading in recent years, authors who had made it possible for Ann to continue thinking of herself as a Catholic despite her anger and doubts about the Church. These authors helped Ann to see Catholicism from a new perspective and confirmed her inherent belief in a different kind of God — a God of love instead of wrath, who was in her and in everything, not in the clouds, judging. But now, after what she had been through, she didn't care any more about theories or ideas — she wanted to experience God in some manifest and undeniable way. She'd had enough of analyzing and debating the attributes of a being she feared might be the same vengeful bully who had terrorized her as a child. After all the years she had spent speaking to God and reading about him and worshipping him, she wanted to see his face.

Julia said that was what *A Course in Miracles* was about, helping people to experience God within themselves, and that the woman who wrote it was taking dictation directly from Jesus. Ann looked at the heavy book in her hands. It included a *Text,* a *Workbook for Students,* and a *Manual for Teachers.* Julia and Tony were working through the workbook together. Ann imagined them reading to each other, doing the exercises, discussing and sharing and healing and growing. She wished so much that it could be like that for her and Richard, and although she knew it was probably never going to happen, she hated to go ahead without him, because she didn't want to leave him behind.

She had already tried the first exercise in the workbook and didn't see the point of it at all, but she was prepared to try again. The idea was to look at things in your immediate vicinity and tell yourself they didn't mean anything. *This railing doesn't mean anything. Those cotton balls don't mean anything. That wedding ring doesn't mean anything.* Then you were supposed to look at things farther away and do the same. *The river doesn't mean anything. The bridge doesn't mean anything. Those children don't mean anything.* That was it. In her current state of mind Ann found it easy to convince herself that everything was meaningless, but how could that possibly be helpful?

She closed her eyes and tried to feel peaceful. She breathed in through her nose and out through her mouth. She recited her prayer word. *Ma-ra* in breath. *Na-tha* out breath. *Come, Lord.* Throbbing pressure in her head. *Let go of thoughts.* An itch on the back of her neck. *An insect there. A biting one. Ma-ra* in breath. *Don't fight it. Na-tha* out breath. She wasn't getting enough air. *A poisonous one.* Her tongue felt enormous. Her eyes were swollen and burning. *Tor was crying before he left for school. Ma-ra* in breath. *Na-tha* out breath. Maybe she was reacting to the air from the dockhouse. Maybe she shouldn't sit so close to the window. *Breathe normally. Breathe normally. Ma* in. *Ra* out. *Poor Tor. Na* in. *Tha* out. *Let go, let go.* She could feel her pulse behind her eyelids. *Let go, let go.*

It was like trying to hold back a river with a bucket. She gave up, opened her eyes and saw the meaningless river and trees. She thought, *God, please be with me.* She looked at her meaningless face in the dirty, broken, meaningless window. Her eyes were swollen. Her mouth felt inflamed, but she wouldn't know how to describe the feeling to Richard if he asked, which he wouldn't. She looked ugly and ancient. She thought, *Who would want to be with you?*

She tucked the book under her arm and went back to the house, where Jusuf was sweeping the corners of the living room with a grass broom. He was wearing a threadbare Dukakis Bentsen '88 T-shirt and the hot pink Vuarnet France running shorts Richard had given him. He kept raking his broom across the floor without looking up when she came into the room, and she felt annoyed when it occurred to her that he might be feeling awkward about their forced intimacy during her latest illness, which seemed, mercifully, to be over.

He was a nice guy, and it was a shame to have to fire him, but if she was going to be sick all the time she needed an employee who could come into her bedroom without looking like he was going to die of embarrassment. If he'd been good at other things she might have been able to justify keeping him, but he was a mediocre cook, and any cleaning he did, he managed to undo ten times over with his idiotic ideas. The most unforgivable example of this was when he scraped the mould off the walls, releasing the spores that now lived in her lungs and consumed her thoughts. But this was only one of many examples of his incompetence. A few days earlier she'd caught him feeding sugar water to the ants in the kitchen. When she'd confronted him, he'd said, "If we give them what they want, they will go away."

"Jusuf," she started. He stopped sweeping and looked up. "I need to talk to you. Could we have a seat here?"

She sat on the leather couch whose legs Billy had chewed to ribbons, and Jusuf balanced his broom carefully in the corner before sitting down next to her.

"It looks like we're going to have to let you go," she said.

He nodded and ran his tongue over his teeth inside his mouth. "Okay," he said.

She wasn't sure if he had understood. "We'll give you next month's pay, and I'll help you get good job."

"Thank you," he said. He shook his head, looking more perplexed than upset.

She wondered if Tor would mind, and realized that he might. But she couldn't keep Jusuf to be a companion for Tor. Tor needed to make friends his own age, and Jusuf needed to find work that was better suited to his skills. He was a big, strong man, and he seemed smart enough. She was doing him a favour. It was degrading for a man like him to be a servant.

"I'll ask Mrs. Bergman if her husband will give you fine, fine job," Ann said, thinking this was a brilliant idea before she remembered that the Bergmans were leaving.

"No problem," Jusuf said, and Ann slumped off to bed.

SHE WAS WOKEN from her nap by the smell of food cooking, and opened her eyes to the distressing sensation that the late afternoon was lapping around her, dragging her out into the riptide of yet another wasted day. Her bed was wet with sweat, and the sheets stuck to her thighs and torso. Her body felt painfully unbalanced, and she wondered if she had been too quick to decide she was getting better. She felt her head to see if she still had a fever, but it was so hot in the room that she couldn't tell what was normal.

Through the window, she could hear the chatter of the people in the river, the music from the bridge checkpoint, the cries of the shrill dive-bomber birds, who always seemed about to collide with one another. The teenagers, who used to keep their distance as long as the Berringers were home, had become bold, now venturing as far as halfway down the dockhouse jetty to jump off the rails in heart-stopping displays of adolescent stupidity. Ann found the sounds of their play the most distressing of all the disturbances of that hour — not their shouting and laughing, but the sound of splashing water, rich as cream but totally forbidden.

Over all of this late afternoon racket, Ann could hear Tor turning circles on the bike in the yard and other children shrieking with laughter and pain. She guessed that Tor had some kind of weapon he was using to hit anyone who tried to get on the bike or knock him over.

He'd been at her again with his case for home. "At home you would never have malaria," he said. Sometimes she thought they should go home, but what was waiting for them there? The stain of small-town scandal and a house that had tried — in some ways she felt was still trying — to kill her. But at least in Canada Tor would be happy, and at least she wouldn't be at risk of dying from some hideous tropical disease, and at least she could sort out the tax thing, which had been on her mind constantly since she got those letters. If they could sell the house and move somewhere else and have another child, maybe they could still start over before it was too late.

She'd tried to bring up the war as a reason to leave, but Richard just said that if she thought it was unsafe she and Tor should go, but he had promised to stay for six months. The truth was that Ann rarely heard anyone talking about the war. From what she had understood it was basically a border dispute, but they were as far away from the Liberian border as you could get and still be in the country, so it didn't affect them. The refugees they occasionally saw crossing the bridge on their way to Guinea were simply displaced by the fighting, like Joyce's family, and would be going back once it was over.

Ann heard the truck pull into the driveway and the door slam. "Richard," she called. She wanted him to lie down with her, and something about the soft light and the close, sleepy atmosphere in the room made it seem possible, as long as neither of them spoke.

Sometimes she felt she would be healthy if only he would hold her and tell her that everything was okay and he loved her, but he rarely even allowed himself to be hugged any more, and when he did, it was as if he was subjecting himself to some painful duty. With the exception of the brief period after she'd found out about his affair, he had always been that way. When she was pregnant with Tor and he'd kicked for the first time, she'd held Richard's hand to her belly, but after a few seconds he took his hand away and went back to what he had been doing. "I've felt lots of babies kick," was his reply when she told him how hurt she was that he couldn't be bothered to wait to feel the first movements of his first child.

He liked to keep her needing more than he could give. The only time he ever came to her on his own was when he wanted sex, and even that wasn't very often any more, although she wasn't sure if this was because he was giving up on her or because he was finally cluing in to how unpleasant sex had become for her since she got ill.

Most of the time she couldn't breathe properly, and sex, she now knew, was like a symphony of breathing whose various movements left her feeling like she was being suffocated. The fact that Richard saw her struggling and continued without even asking her if she was okay meant that either he didn't notice she couldn't breathe, didn't care she couldn't breathe, or didn't *believe* she couldn't breathe. She wasn't sure which was worst, but, for reasons that had to do more with her general aversion to speaking about sex than the satisfaction of being right and saying nothing, she would never tell him how much it hurt her.

She was about to call for him again when he marched into the room, heading straight for the ensuite. He was taking off his watch and unbuttoning his work shirt.

"What time is it?" she said, and he spooked before continuing his urgent undressing. She considered holding her arms out toward him, but she couldn't bear to be refused. If only he would come and sit next to her on his own, notice that she was suffering. *Desperate.* A humiliating high school word for girls who liked boys more than boys liked them.

"Why are you still in bed?"

She cleared her sinuses once, timidly, then a second time, more loudly, but the dense, disgusting mass in her nose was unmoved. "I'm not still in bed," she said. "I was up most of the day. I've had a nap."

She tried to clear her sinuses again. She knew that Richard hated the sound of it. She hated it, too. Like a choked engine failing over and over.

"The Sandis will be here in half an hour."

"What? Why are they coming here?" He stopped in the middle of unbuttoning his shirt cuff and stared at her. "What?" she said.

"You invited them for dinner."

"No I didn't."

"Well I certainly didn't."

"That doesn't mean I did." As she said this, she vaguely remembered seeing Joyce Sandi and inviting her to something. "I think I'm still sick," she said. "Can you feel my forehead?" Richard took a deep breath and came over to the bedside. He held the backs of his fingers to her head.

"You feel fine," he said. "You need to get up."

"Is Jusuf cooking?"

"Who else would be cooking?"

"I was going to cook," she said. Outside, she could hear Tor singing one of his songs and hacking at the mango tree with the machete. "I fired Jusuf today, but I guess he didn't understand me."

"Are you insane? You can't fire him." It wasn't like Richard to interfere with household things, and he interacted with Jusuf so little that Ann wasn't even sure if he knew his name, so she was genuinely surprised by this reaction.

"Um, yes I can," she said.

"No you cannot."

"Yes I can."

"He was hired by the Foundation, Ann. He's worked here for years. He's an orphan for Christ's sake!"

"Well there are lots of orphans around, Richard. Am I meant to hire every orphan who shows up? Should I make it a requirement for his replacement?"

"He's not going to have a replacement."

How dare he stand over her and dictate how it was going to be, and how dare Jusuf stay and cook dinner after she had fired him?

"You don't get to decide that," she said. "He works for me, not you. I'm the one who's here with him all day, and he's totally useless."

"Keep your voice down," Richard whispered. He sat on the bed beside her. "Would you shut up!" he said, and it took Ann a second to realize that he was talking to Tor, who was outside their window now, still singing. This was Tor's cue to sing louder, hanging on the bars of their window and howling, "...I see the rebels are fi-igh-ting, oh yeah. A wa-a-a-ar against the go-vern-ment. Fighting, fighting!"

"Get up, Ann," Richard said.

"Not until you tell Jusuf he's fired."

"We can discuss this later," he said. "Now get up and get dressed. They're going to be here any minute."

"No."

"And who do you think is going to finish making dinner if Jusuf's fired?"

"After tonight he's fired then," she said.

"You cannot dictate who we hire here. The Foundation...."

"Of course, of course," she said. "The *Foundation*. The *doctors* from *England* made *arrangements* for us, so we should do what they say, never mind what we actually want." Secretly, she wanted a woman. A big, fat African mamma type who would cook rich food and comfort her when she cried, not sinewy, diffident Jusuf, who stayed out of her way as much as possible.

Richard pointed his finger as if to deliver some lecture, then turned it into a fist and held it under his nose. "I have had a difficult day, and all I'm asking you to do is get up and be ready for the guests that *you* invited. You are going to get out of this bed right now and put some clothes on. End of discussion."

"I'm sick," she said. He tried to leave, and she held his arm. "I can't cope all by myself." She knew he hated her grabbing at him, but it held him somehow. He breathed deeply, deliberately. She wondered if he was counting in his head like the therapist had taught him.

"Listen," he said. "What if we keep Jusuf to do the cooking and cleaning, and we can hire Aminata from the church to come in when you need extra help."

"Who?"

"Aminata, the girl who sits up front. She plays the tambourine."

"I have no idea who you're talking about."

"The one who sits at the front and plays with the choir. She lives at Maggie's...."

"That polio kid?"

"That's not how I would describe her."

"Oh that's great. How is she supposed to help me? She's handicapped."

"She's a lovely girl. She would be good company."

"Is that what you think this is about? Someone to keep me company? I haven't even been able to get out of bed half the time we've been here. Can't you see that I'm...." She didn't want to cry, but she couldn't help it. Richard sat on the edge of the bed looking at the floor while Ann curled her body into a fetal position and sobbed, telling herself that she was so alone.

Once she started crying about something, it wasn't long before she was crying about everything. She could tell he was thinking, *shit, when will this be over?* But she wished he could understand that what she found most unforgivable wasn't what he had done in the past, but what he didn't do now. He didn't comfort her when she cried. He didn't let her talk about her feelings. "Here we go again," he would say if she brought up anything that had happened. "Ancient history. That's your favourite topic, right?"

Of course he had put in his time in the beginning — he was penitent and took her to the Digby Pines for a romantic weekend. He went to Marriage Encounter with her. He sat through her hateful tirades at the marriage counsellor's office and even in public. When she said, "How could you put your penis in that disgusting woman who smells of urine?" he said, "What I did was wrong, and I don't expect you to forgive me." When she said, "I hate you, you miserable bastard," he said, "You're the only person I've ever loved." When she said, "I can't stand the sight of your stupid lying face any more," he said, "I feel so much better about myself when I think of myself as a husband and father. I'm so proud of you and Tor."

He said all the right things, but of course he was lying, because that was how he had learned to survive. Still, she had been forced to believe him, because she was running out of coping skills, she couldn't manage on her own, and despite all the pain, he was finally giving her what she had always wanted. But as soon as he caught wind of her surrender, he decided that her time was up. He had said sorry, he had admitted he was wrong, he had gone to therapy (at least until she quit — conveniently for him — after the therapist suggested that she had been molested by her father), he had gone to confession, he had kissed her and passed the peace in church every week as if he gave a damn about her peace. It was over.

What he didn't get was that it wasn't just about him. His betrayal was only the culmination of all the betrayals of her life, and when she'd found out about it, a fountain had started in her that she couldn't turn off. She would go to the supermarket and wander around crying, grasping a can of beans and desperately wishing for a mother to love her. She would go for jogs on the old railroad tracks and cry the whole time, crouching in the bushes to hide when four-wheelers zoomed past.

Life with him had never been what she imagined, was always a compromise, but the potential for perfection had been enough to sustain her until she found out he'd had sex with that scumbag. After that, everything was permanently polluted. It could never be like it was meant to be. It could never, ever be mended. That was what she told herself as she cried everywhere she went all day long, hoping to get it over with so she could go home and be a parent for Tor again, but when she got home she continued crying, because she really couldn't stop.

TOR STOOD IN THE doorway of the bedroom, still in his dirty school uniform. "See what you've done?" Richard said. "Get out of here and get dressed." Tor dodged Richard and ran to the far side of the bed.

"Leave him alone," Ann said, holding Tor to her chest. Richard stood up, grabbed Tor by the arm and yanked him to his feet. He leaned in close to Tor's face and said, "Get dressed *now*," then shoved Tor out the door and slammed it behind him.

Tor bashed the other side of the door with what sounded like a heavy metal object, and Ann had a second to be afraid of how Richard would react before he started his deep breathing again, signalling that he would save his punishments for later. He sat next to her. "Ann, I'm begging you. Get up and get dressed now. You invited these people, and they will be here any minute, and this man is my colleague, someone whose opinion matters to me. Please, please, please, get up!"

Ann stared at the hills and valleys in the sheet bunched up at the edge of the bed. She wondered if her blue dress would be dry enough to wear and if there was enough *poyo* left over from the last time they had guests. She could hear Tor outside attacking the mango tree with the machete and Jusuf gently imploring him to stop, telling him that the mangoes wanted to live. There had been no big blow up, no cathartic venting. She hadn't said what she wanted to say and it shouldn't be over yet, but searching for some last ember of wrath to hurl at Richard, she found there was nothing left.

CHAPTER 5

THE DINNER PARTY was a disaster. Ann insisted that Richard
clear the air by inviting Tor to play badminton with him before the
Sandis arrived, and Richard, grateful that she was up and getting
dressed, capitulated. He had assumed Tor would say no so they could
both get on with their evenings as far away from each other as possible, but Tor must have heard this hope in Richard's voice, because
instead he smiled and nodded, and then Richard knew he was in
for it.

As soon as they got outside, Tor started making those unbearable fart noises with his lips. When Richard asked him to stop, Tor
did it ten more times, as usual, but Richard kept his cool. Then Tor
intentionally spiked the birdie at Richard's face, but again, Richard
managed to control himself. "Let me show you how to serve properly," he said. He joined his son on the other side of the net and
tried to hold him from behind to show him the proper motions for
his arms, but the little jerk went limp and shouted, "Get away from
me, you homosexual pervert!" And that was as much as Richard
could take.

Of course, Ann hadn't seen any of this, but as soon as Richard
responded, just at the moment when he gave Tor a tiny tap on the
back of the head with his racket, she was suddenly there beside him,

and he had to submit to her lecture about his "abusive behaviour" with Tor watching because he was guilty, guilty, guilty and he would be punished in any way she pleased for as long as she wanted.

She was still shouting at him when the Sandis arrived, and instead of greeting them, she stormed upstairs and started performing a passive-aggressive show of setting the table and serving the food herself while Jusuf looked on.

After dinner, she verbally abused Joyce Sandi over an ill-conceived game of charades. "Come *on!*" she shrieked at Joyce, who was doing her best to stay out of range of Ann's flailing arms, and all Richard could do was watch helplessly until the timer ran out and then try to patch things up by saying, "Good try, Joyce. That was a hard one," which only made it worse because of course Ann had to say that it wasn't. Afterward, she announced that she was going to do the washing up herself, and Joyce offered to help her, so Richard mixed some weak gin and tonics and led Sandi to the dockhouse balcony, where they sat on the concrete ledge and dangled their legs over the side.

"I want to talk to you about something sort of sensitive," Richard said. Sandi watched the river with an unreadable expression on his face. "I was going through some papers that were left behind in the bookcase here, and I found a report about local traditional practices written by an English GP who was here for a while. Sarah Wraggett. Do you remember her?"

"Yes," Sandi said.

The report had confirmed Richard's notions about how barbaric the practice of circumcision was, but he knew he couldn't put it like that to Sandi. "Look, I know this is a touchy topic," he said. "And I'm sure that the *Bondo* society promotes bonding and solidarity between women and everything, and, I'm in…I know I'm in no place to criticize someone else's culture. But surely your professional, or surgical training must have convinced you that this practice of circumcision is…well, wrong…and that many girls…and women are being...mutilated and suffering...severe consequences...as a result of these traditional...practices...so, what I'm wondering is what can we do, or what can I do to help you to, um, educate people to stop this without...being, or, or making pejorative statements about their...customs?"

Sandi, who had continued to stare blankly out over the water while Richard spoke, leaned back, looked directly at Richard, held up his hand, and not angrily, not even sternly, but in a tone that offered no invitation for further discussion, said, "Don't go there."

Richard took a sip of his drink as he adjusted to the realization that the gulf between them was only widening the more he tried to bridge it. "I only wanted to hear your thoughts on it, as someone who is sort of...in both worlds," he said. A rat ran along the balcony behind them, and Richard, startled, made an unmanly noise which he tried to conceal with a deep cough. He turned to see where the rat had gone, but there was no sign of it.

Sandi sighed. "There are certain realities you have to consider before you just jump in and try to impose solutions from outside, Richard. You have to slow down and understand the culture you are...."

"This isn't about culture," Richard said. "This is a human rights issue. It's child abuse.... Look, Sandi, I can see that it's a complex issue, but I think we have a moral responsibility to address it. For example, we could do a community outreach program, like you did for the free vaccinations."

"Richard, this country has among the highest rates of infant and maternal mortality in the world, so we want to do everything we can to get women to trust us and come to the hospital, not drive them away by lecturing them about their customs. If we were going to address it, we would have to look at what people are already doing and see what is the best way to go forward, because there are a lot of complicated factors involved, including financial ones. We are already starting to work with the traditional birth attendants, because people trust them more than doctors, so we want to use them to refer patients and give them some training, and part of that will hopefully include getting them onboard to reduce the negative impacts of certain traditional practices, but it's not going to happen immediately, and to be totally honest, if it was, I wouldn't want you to be involved."

"Because I'm just another arrogant white man coming to tell Africans how to live? What about the fact that I'm a physician and it's my job to take an active interest in my patients' health? What about the fact that I'm a human being, and I don't want to stand aside when I know that young girls are being mutilated?"

"Tell me, Richard, did you have Tor circumcised?" Sandi said.

The idea that the existence of one culture's abusive practices was an argument for perpetuating another's enraged Richard. "We both know that it's not the same thing, but as a matter of fact in my practice I don't perform circumcisions unless it's medically necessary, so…."

Sandi cut Richard off. "Look, I know you see things that upset you, and I'm not saying you have to accept everything, but you have to try and understand where people are coming from before you start trying to change them. And you have to understand where *you* are coming from, too."

"So it is because I'm a foreigner," Richard said.

"No, it's because you don't listen! You are too forceful. The staff have a really hard time with that, too. You are making things very difficult for them, because you want to try everything immediately even when we tell you it's not the right time or it won't work. Richard, we need a new generator. We need an ambulance. We need more reliable supplies of essential drugs. We need all the resources we have just to continue with our day-to-day at the hospital. We need to focus."

"So shut up and write my proposals. That's all I'm good for, right?"

"You know, if you would stop defending yourself all the time you might realize that no one is attacking you," Sandi said. He looked at his watch. "We really should get going."

As they walked back to the house, Richard watched Sandi from behind. You had to wonder about someone who claimed to care about the people he served but was unwilling to stick his neck out for fear of upsetting the status quo. Or maybe he supported the status quo. It was impossible for Richard to find out, because he wasn't allowed to *go there*.

After the Sandis left, Richard called Billy and went back to the dockhouse. On his desk was *Andy Collins-Bridge's Guide to the Eradication of Household Pests* and the components of the new trap he was working on — a jerry can with the top cut off, a plank made from a Carnation milk tin that he had hammered into a long rectangle, hooks made from a scorched Spam can he'd found in the garbage pit, a baggie of groundnut paste, and a ramp made from the cover of a public health book someone had left on a shelf in the living room. He'd found Collins-Bridge's book on that shelf, too. The rats had been at the spine and back pages, and the pages that remained were heavily thumbed and underlined, as if the book itself were a record of a war of attrition between man and rodent.

Richard attached the ramp to the edge of the jerry can with the Spam hooks and opened Collins-Bridge's book to the page he had marked. *Rats have an extremely well-developed sense of smell, so they will be naturally attracted to pungent foods, such as strong cheese or cured meat.* Richard smeared some of the groundnut paste onto the end of the plank and attached the plank to the edge of the jerry can, bending the metal down to hold it in place under the Spam hooks. *Smelling food, the rat will climb to the top of the bucket and attempt to walk out onto the plank in pursuit of his next meal. No sooner does he place his weight on the plank then he will fall into the water, drowning himself.* "Yes, they do it all by themselves," Richard said to Collins-Bridge.

It annoyed him that the author referred to the rats as *he*. They were vermin. Sometimes Richard regretted that killing them was such a gruesome business, but they had to go. They ate holes in his

clothes, they shat all over the place, and they were an unneeded con-
tributor to Ann's mania. Collins-Bridge said that rats could enter a
house through a hole as small as a quarter, so there was no hope of
keeping them out, the Foundation House and the dockhouse both
being full of holes. When Richard consulted the section called "Rat
Behaviour" in Collins-Bridge's book, he had learned that the kind of
rats he was probably dealing with lived in polygynandrous groups
within shared burrows. This meant that if he found the burrow, he
might be able to get rid of all the rats at once. But after crouching on
the floors looking for greasy marks on the walls, and searching the
perimeter of the house for a covered hole with a well-worn track
leading into it, knowing that the burrow could be anywhere — in the
roof, in the floor, under the house or inside the walls — he had given
up any serious hope of finding it. Instead, he was killing the rats one
at a time, hoping at least to give them the strong message that they
would be better off moving somewhere else.

He'd wanted to buy a live trap, reasoning that he spent enough
time rummaging around in guts without having to clean up rat
entrails at the end of the day, but Jusuf said that none of the shops
sold them. He'd tried glue boards, but found the results too distressing. He'd tried poison, but he was always nervous that Billy would
get into it or eat a poisoned rat, not to mention the danger of having
rat corpses rotting behind the walls. The water trap would be a clean
solution that wouldn't pose any danger to Billy and might, with any
luck, work.

Admiring the finished trap, Richard chuckled, picturing Wilson
and Harris from *The Heart of the Matter* making a sport of crushing cockroaches with their slippers after mesmerizing them with
torches. He had just pulled back the carriage on his typewriter when
he looked out of the broken window to see Ann sitting on the balcony
in the darkness, swatting at herself.

All he asked for was some peace in the evening to work on his
rat traps and his funding proposals, but instead she wanted to read

at him from her self-help books and talk about her "symptoms" and how he could "heal" his relationship with Tor. If he didn't cooperate, she would find a way to pick a fight, usually involving abusive references to his affair and making him look like a monster because he refused to give in to her victim fantasies when she fell onto the floor crying, "I can't cope." At that point, of course, Torquil would appear to comfort her in the disturbingly intimate way he always did, and Richard would end up back in the dockhouse, more exasperated and more tired. Better to avoid the whole script and hope that if he ignored her, she would go away.

He adjusted his chair enough to remove her from his peripheral vision, wedging himself in between the pile of broken oars and other ancient boating paraphernalia that he'd shoved into a corner when he claimed the dockhouse as his office. Despite the clutter and musty air, Richard much preferred the dockhouse to the Foundation House, which was like a fortress that was easy to penetrate but difficult to escape. What few windows there were had heavy bars on them, but no screens, so insects and rodents could come in, but, if there was a fire, the Berringers would have no way out. Every entrance had two locking doors, one metal and one barred, but the air bricks on the outside made it easy to climb to the top balcony, from where you could walk down the stairs and through the unlocked door to the kitchen. Along one side of the house there was a narrow corridor to nowhere with a locking door at one end and air bricks on the outside, which blocked the only direct sunlight the house could have had. The effect of all of this was darkness, damp, and the inescapable sensation of being locked in.

Billy, lying at Richard's feet, groaned in his sleep. Richard picked him up to have a look at the laceration in his cheek and was surprised by how light he had become. His wound was infected and weeping, and his tongue was visible through the hole, which hadn't closed at all. It must have been preventing him from eating and drinking properly. "Poor you," Richard said, rubbing the dog's ears.

When Billy was first wounded and Ann brought him to the hospital, she'd made up a story about a kid from the river throwing stones at him, which she recanted a few days later after making Richard promise that he wouldn't give Tor a hard time about it, because Tor already felt "so bad." Richard had considered giving Billy a local anaesthetic and trying to repair the outside of his cheek with sutures, but he couldn't justify using the pharmacy's limited resources to treat an animal, so he cleaned the wound and left it to heal on its own, which he reasoned it would be likely to do, being in an area with a good blood supply. It clearly wasn't healing on its own, though, and now it was probably too late to do a delayed repair. He would have to think of another solution. But why did he have to take all the responsibility? Why hadn't anyone else noticed that Billy was losing weight?

He dared to peek out the window at Ann, despite the probability that she would try to hook him with one of her looks. That woman out there with the insane hair and red eyes was nothing like the person he had married. Before she got sick, she'd had the energy of ten people, although there was no way to predict how she would use it. She broke china, berated shopkeepers and waitresses, hit him and pulled out his hair, but she didn't sit around snivelling for his attention. She didn't make up sicknesses for sympathy. In some ways, he had respected that Ann, even if he was terrified of her. He'd admired her personal power, her willingness to say whatever came into her head, crazy as it often was.

Tor appeared next to Ann and stroked her hair. "Torquil, go to bed now," Richard said. He disliked his son's name and couldn't remember why he'd agreed to it, or even if he had.

Tor stared at Richard and puffed out his cheeks. He forced air out through his flaccid lips then pulled his lips in and made a smacking sound.

"Tor, can you *please* not make that noise."

"Sure thing, Dick."

"Don't you dare call me that."

"That's your name, isn't it?"

"To you, my name is Daddy."

"You seem more like a Dick to me."

I'll wipe that smile off your face, Richard thought. He went outside and grabbed Tor's upper arm. "Ow, you're hurting me," Tor said.

"You're hurting yourself."

"Let go of him," Ann said. It never failed.

Richard dragged Tor down the jetty by his arm. "This is my office!" he shouted. "This is the one place I have!"

When Richard let go, Tor turned around and said, "Goodnight, Dick," and Richard couldn't resist giving him a kick in the pants for that.

"You always do it, don't you?" Ann shouted at him from the balcony. Now she had him. "You're such a bully. Why can't you ask him politely if you want him to go?"

"Don't you get it? He engineered that whole scene. He has no respect."

"How do you expect him to respect you when you have absolutely zero respect for him?"

Richard went back into the dockhouse and slammed the door. He sat at his desk. "You should go and apologize to him," Ann said through the broken window. "That's a horrible, horrible way for a child to go to bed."

He couldn't believe how indoctrinated she was. Living with that kid was like living with a terrorist, but from day one, Ann had always taken his side. When Tor was a baby, his default behaviour was screaming, and Ann insisted on having him with her at all times, not caring if the presence of a shrieking infant might disturb other people. She was obsessed with the idea that he should never cry alone, so she spent hours every night singing and rocking him to sleep, and more often than not she fell asleep before he did, which meant that she and Richard had no time together. If Richard dared to move Tor to his crib before he got into bed with Ann, the moment he managed to fall asleep she would wake up in a panic and say, "Where's Tor?" and he'd tell her he couldn't understand why she'd spent a thousand dollars on a cot she never intended to use. Then she would go and check on Tor, and Tor would wake up and resume his screaming, and that was the end of Richard's sleep.

The exhaustion and frustration and the fact that Ann was allowing herself to be manipulated by a baby made Richard so angry there were times he imagined harming Tor. Sometimes he'd say things like, "I'm going to bite your head off if you don't shut up," in a soothing voice as he swaddled Tor tightly and turned on the singing mobile. Once Ann had walked in on him shaking Tor by the shoulders and telling him to shut the hell up, and she'd never let him forget it.

Sometimes, in his worst moments, Richard did wonder if there was something he had done to deserve a kid like Tor, but ultimately he knew that he wasn't to blame for Tor's behaviour, no matter how much Ann tried to convince him otherwise. He was a good person doing his best in a very difficult situation, and he put up with more than most people would have, much more than he would have ever thought was possible.

A large insect was caught in the flypaper that hung over the desk, and the yellow strip swung back and forth above Richard's head. He watched for a while as the insect flapped its wings in wild futility, and when it finally stopped, he poked at it with a pencil to start it up again, reasoning that the best thing was for it to wear itself out quickly.

Next to him was the public health text he had taken apart to make the ramp for his trap. He picked it up and leafed through the pages, sighing aloud to think of how much work he still had to do on his latest funding proposal, in which he had the tricky task of articulating the hospital's needs in a compelling way without making too many specific promises about how the money would be spent.

If people were going to give you money, they generally wanted you to cut up their meat for them, offer them something limited, specific, and measurable. This was why the ambulance and generator would be easy to drum up funds for, but "we need funding to continue to cover our normal operational costs, salaries for our staff, and maintenance of equipment and infrastructure" was harder to sell.

Richard was proud of the hospital's successes, but the problem was that it cost too much, and just to maintain it required enormous effort. The Foundation couldn't afford to hire a fundraiser, and volunteers were usually more trouble than they were worth, because they did things on their own terms and required constant expressions of appreciation just to stay interested. There were board members, a student organization at the medical school in London, some friends in England, Canada, and Freetown who took care of phone and mail campaigns and managed private and corporate donations, but most of the funding came from grants, which had been Ann and Richard's domain since the beginning.

Ann used to be quite good at writing grant proposals, and her fundraisers were almost the only occasions where Richard saw her acting in the warm, unpretentious way he had come to associate with Canadians in general and Nova Scotians in particular. When she first said she wanted to come to Sierra Leone, the idea had been that she would continue writing the proposals and take over writing the "on-the-ground" articles for the newsletter, a task that was normally performed by interns and other visiting volunteers. But she was too busy being ill to do anything she had promised to do, and the Foundation had decided not to send any more volunteers until the situation with the war stabilized, so all of these tasks fell to Richard. It wasn't the best use of his time, but Sandi was the only other person capable of doing it, and he and Richard had agreed that it was better for Sandi to be on call in the evenings instead, because he lived closer to the hospital. In any case, Richard did sort of enjoy the task, and it gave him a good excuse to stay in the dockhouse instead of dealing with Ann.

She seemed to be gone, so Richard stepped out onto the jetty to get some air and enjoy the view of the moonlit water reflecting the trees on the banks and, in the distance, the bridge, whose supports spanned the wide river in elegant arches. There were sounds from every direction — of night birds, music, dogs, crickets — and it seemed to Richard that in all of it there was some indescribable magic. He had never felt attached to any place before, but at that moment he felt something like a premonition of longing, knowing that whatever he loved about Sierra Leone he would continue to seek for the rest of his life.

He thought about the part in *The Heart of the Matter* when the main character, Scobie, is wondering why he loves Sierra Leone so much and decides it's because things are out in the open, and no one is pretending that the world is some paradise. *Here you could love human beings nearly as God loved them, knowing the worst.* Certainly the idea of transparency appealed to Richard, who had never been much good at guessing what was going on in other people's heads, but he wasn't sure he had found that in Sierra Leone. He couldn't understand what made people tick here any more than he could anywhere else, but the difference was that here no one expected him to. So perhaps what he truly loved about the place was not what it revealed about others, but what it allowed him to conceal in himself.

There was one bird in particular that made a lot of noise around the dockhouse at night, and listening to it, Richard realized he had no idea what it was called. Jusuf was sitting outside the kitchen hut smoking a cigarette, so Richard walked down the jetty to join him. "What do you call that bird?" Richard asked, holding his cupped hand to his ear.

"Bird," Jusuf said.

"But what's its name?"

"Jusuf," Jusuf said, touching his own chest.

"I know *your* name!" Richard said. "What lives in the water here, Jusuf?" he asked, deciding to give up on the bird. "Are there crocodiles?"

"No crocodiles."

"What then?"

"Only fish. And some people say there is a devil in here, but me I don't know devil."

"What kind of devil?"

"I don't know! I don't see! I only have my own eyes that God give me."

"Well what kind of devil do other people say it is?"

"The Chinese people that were making that bridge to Guinea, they were saying that we are having a devil there. At any time when they make, the devil come and destroy everything. So they contact the freemasons to catch him, and they did, and they carry him to China. Do you know who is a freemason?"

"It's an organization of men that does secret things. It's like a secret society."

"Yes!" Jusuf said.

"My father was one," Richard said. "I don't know what it is. Because it's a secret, so how can I know?"

Jusuf nodded. "It's a secret. You cannot know."

"So the freemasons took the devil to China?"

"So they are saying, those that have those eyes. As for me I never saw any devil here."

"Because it's in China, right? Why do people still think it's here if it's meant to be in China?"

"The problem is, they don't see it with their own eyes, so they don't sure it is gone, and sometime people still see her."

"Her?"

"This is a traditional belief. They say this devil live by the riverside. They say that when you saw him, he will give you luck. You will have money."

"Him or her?"

"A woman. Like Mrs. Berringer. She have black hair. She drown people in the river."

"Why do they go in the river if they think there's a devil in there? Aren't they afraid?"

"Yes."

"But people go in the water all the time. They don't look afraid."

"If you don't see devil, they won't harm you. They won't get any contact with you. They can only harm those God gave the eyes to see. We say those people have four eyes."

"How does someone get four eyes?"

"It is a gift to them by God."

"So that means it's good?"

"Yes."

"So it's good to see devils."

"It can bring benefits to you. According to what they are saying, the devils tend to greet them, ask them what do you want? So if you fail to do the arrangement and he or she is doing what you arranged together, well there lies the problem. Example: when the devil said, give me a white sheep, that means a child. When you refuse to give that, he will harm you."

"Why does the devil want children?"

"Because it is his own interest...."

"And those people who see devils, how do they know they are seeing devils and not other people?"

"Well, they are saying that devils are white in colour. So they are saying."

"So how do you know I'm not a devil?"

Jusuf laughed. "I don't see devil! I don't have this gift."

"But it sounds like a bad gift. More like a curse."

"The problem is when God give you the gift for you to see those devils, don't arrange anything to them. Even if you want to arrange something to them, arrange something that will give you benefits till God take your life again. Because people are arranging things that don't benefit them."

The pervasiveness of this kind of superstition baffled Richard, and frustrated him, too, because it was impossible to get a sense of what was normal and fine and what was dangerous or even deadly when people had such irrational and inconsistent beliefs. Turay had warned Richard that in Sierra Leone, if he told people he didn't believe in God, they might not even be willing to *eat* with him, but people seemed to have extreme tolerance for each other's religions and to mix their religions freely with traditional beliefs. Even quite educated people had spoken to Richard earnestly about things like river devils and witch guns. Lately there'd been a rumour about a bewitched girl who went around tormenting people at night, and Richard had overheard some of the nurses gossiping about it, saying the girl was trying to destroy people's businesses and kill her enemies in the spiritual realm. He was horrified to discover that nurses trained in medical science could actually believe in such things, but on the other hand, he saw that this tendency toward syncretism could be an advantage in cases where he hoped to change people's minds, because they were open to new ideas. And he was willing to be open-minded, too, to a degree. For example, he was open to the possibility that the herbalist's remedies might be somewhat effective, or at least have a placebo or psychotherapeutic effect. He was sure, at the very least, that some of them could be harmlessly combined with western medicine.

"Building Bridges," Richard said, holding out his hands in a visionary gesture.

"Sorry?" Jusuf said.

"Or Sharing Strengths. Something like that. Toward A Holistic Model of Healthcare in Sierra Leone." It would be great, and it would sound great, too. For the first time in a long time, Richard felt excited. He was going to write an excellent new proposal, and he was going to at least meet with the herbalist, despite Sandi's objections.

CHAPTER 6

"THAT'S DISGUSTING!" Ann screamed.

Tor was lying in bed feeling the sharp bones in his hips and thinking about the parmesan cheese Rita Bergman had given them, which his mother had promised to serve with spaghetti that evening. When he heard her voice from the living room, he froze.

"My God, it's everywhere!"

He assumed that she was talking about mould. Why couldn't she ever shut up about it? He didn't feel afraid of mould at all, but he tried to be understanding, because he knew it was scary for her. It started after they moved into the new house in Nova Scotia. She kept saying there was something in the walls and she had to find it. One day Tor was reading *Calvin and Hobbes* next to her on the couch in the music room when out of nowhere she told him to get her a hammer and started attacking the wall and shouting at him for not helping her. Once she'd taken half the wall down, she went totally berserk, puking and bawling and rolling around outside on the deck. She pulled on her hair and said that she had ruined the vapour barrier and she was going to live on the deck forever.

Not knowing what else to do, Tor went and got Maria, who was vacuuming in the basement. Maria called Tony McCann, and after that the Berringers went to stay at the McCann's summer house, and Ann was alright until they moved back into their house and she found out about Richard's affair. At first, it looked like she was going to divorce Richard, and Tor was surprised to find that he had mixed feelings about that. He had been wishing for them to split up for as long as he could remember, but now that she had started to say alarming things such as, "I would kill myself if it weren't for you," sometimes he wasn't sure that he wanted to be left alone with her.

She cried all the time, and he didn't want to go to school any more, because he was afraid she would kill herself. He would hear her crying and he would have knots in his stomach, and when he went to comfort her, she would say, "What am I going to do?" and he would say, "You have to leave him, mommy," and she would say, "I can't. The house...," and he would say, "It doesn't matter. We could live in an apartment," and she would say, "Yes, I'm going to leave him," and she would be purposeful for a while and wash the floors or cook a meal, but then he would come into the kitchen to find her crouched in a corner again, sobbing.

It was hard to live with, but he did love his mom so, so much, and he knew she was trying her best. He felt bad having bad thoughts about her, because she was the best mom in the world, and he was sympathizing with her a lot, because it wasn't her fault she was allergic to things, but he was also sympathizing with himself, because he wanted spaghetti with parmesan cheese.

"No! No! Don't touch it," Ann shrieked from the living room. Tor came out of his room and saw Billy lying next to the kitchen door wearing the cardboard cone Richard had made for him. When Billy saw Tor he ran away, and this gave Tor an overwhelming urge to chase him. It turned out that the black mould had returned in the corner by the front door, so Ann said no one was allowed in the living room any more, which meant they would have to enter the house through the back door.

Ann got into bed and cried into a sweater while Tor rubbed her back and tried to think of something helpful to say. "We could go home, mommy," he said. She ignored him. "I love you dear Gwendolyn. I love you my Gwynnie," he sang in Ernest's old man voice, to the tune of the happy birthday song. He thought this might make her smile, but instead it seemed to make her angry. She told him to go to school, and she went back into the living room to shout at Jusuf.

There was no water in any of the buckets, and Jusuf was too busy helping Ann clean up the mould to get more. Tor found some boiled water in a glass jug in the kitchen and used it to clean his face and hands and the cuts on his legs. When he put on his uniform it was damp, and there were new holes in the right leg of his shorts.

The night before, he'd moved his bed and set up a pulley system from the hook in the ceiling that held up his mosquito net. He put some bread on the floor, tied a rope around a cement brick he'd found by the old latrine behind the house, and stood on a chair to link the rope over the hook. Then he hoisted the brick up and waited for the rats. None came, and eventually he fell asleep, but of course when he woke up the bread was gone, he was covered in mosquito bites, and the rats had been at his uniform again.

Before he left for school, he reached into the hole in his mattress and took a 500 leone bill from his tin of leones, in case there were cookies at the junction. His collection of leones, which he used to buy cigarettes, sweetened condensed milk, and whatever candy was available, was kept in a separate tin from his Canadian dollars. He had almost eight hundred dollars in there, stolen from his father's briefcase over several years. He had found a guy at the junction who would exchange twenty dollar bills for leones, but so far there had been no point, because Ann gave him pocket money, and there was so little he wanted to buy, he had trouble spending even that.

When he was halfway down the big hill on his bike, his front wheel started to wobble, so he had to get off and walk.

Kelfala hadn't been at school for a few days, and this made Tor realize how much he'd come to rely on him as an ally. As soon as he got off the bike, some young men started walking next to him.

"*Oporto* seke," one of the men said.

"My name is not *oporto*," Tor said. He walked faster, but the men kept up.

"What is your name?"

Tor sighed. "Han Solo."

The men spoke to each other in Krio, saying that he was Dr. Berringer's son.

"A dae understant you," he said.

"You sabi how for tok Krio?" one of them said.

"Smohl smohl," Tor said.

"Hey, you dae tok Krio fine fine," one of the men said. The others laughed. Tor looked down at his shoe, which had started to come apart at the toe.

"Wetin make you no ride you bicycle?" one of the other men said.

"It's broken."

Tor got back on the bike and tried to see if he could make it down the hill, but the wheel was wobbling too much, so he had to keep walking.

By the time he got to school he was late for Mr. Bangura's class, which made him feel bad because it wasn't fair that he didn't get flogged for being late like everyone else.

"How many times does Caesar refuse to be crowned?" Mr. Bangura was brandishing his cane and pacing the rows of children. "How many times does Caesar refuse to be *crowned?*" He stopped in front of the desk of the girl next to Tor.

Nobody in the class had read the play, Tor was sure about that, so the whole lesson was just an excuse for Mr. Bangura to flog them. When Tor told Kelfala that no one in the rest of the world read Shakespeare, Kelfala had laughed and said, "This is Africa, man. We have to learn to suffer."

The girl put her hands on her desk and winced. "Two times, sir?" she said. Tor had looked away, so it wasn't until he heard the cane snap across the girl's fingers that he knew the answer was wrong. She shook her hands and cried, "Why!" and the other kids laughed at her until Mr. Bangura held his cane in the air again, reminding them that the question still hadn't been answered.

Tor spent the rest of Mr. Bangura's class making a list entitled "Whites in Our Town," which included his family, Miss Maggie, the Bergmans, and the Lebanese people who had a shop at the junction. There had also been some people from the Foundation at the beginning, he remembered, so he wrote "Foundation people," and once he had seen a white man driving a red van through the junction, so he wrote "Man in red van."

At lunchtime, Tor bought a piece of dry bread and sat under a tree at the edge of the schoolyard. His hands were covered in chalk from Mr. Best's class, where everyone and everything was always covered in chalk because Mr. Best hit the kids on the head with shammies instead of flogging them with a cane. Tor clapped a few times to try to clean the chalk off before eating his bread, but his hands were so dirty anyway that it made no difference. He examined the rest of his body. His white school shirt was filthy. His arm was bruised from Richard squeezing it. His shorts were way too big and full of holes. His legs were ugly and bony and leaking.

He took out his Walkman, which he kept in his bookbag along with his smokes and matches, his Swiss Army knife, and a razor blade. He slipped his headphones out of the bag and felt around for the play button on his Walkman. Ants crawled on his arms and legs as he ate his bread, listened to Guns N' Roses, and thought about how much he hated Africa. It was so weird and poor and *boring* in Africa. There was nothing to do, nothing to eat, and everyone and everything was always trying to mess with him. Like the rats waiting for him to go to sleep so that they could come out and wreck his stuff. He had a firecracker hidden at the bottom of his suitcase, and he wondered if it would be possible to somehow catch one of the rats, strap the firecracker to its body, light the fuse, and let it run back to its burrow, but so far he hadn't had any luck catching one, dead or alive, and he was starting to think that it might be time to give up trying.

Until his last birthday, when he'd found out that instead of splitting up, his parents were moving to Sierra Leone and forcing him to go with them, Tor had been a pathological optimist. He always believed things would go his way, and if they didn't, they would next time. He would get a better teacher next year, Lisa Formier would be his girlfriend, his mother would divorce Richard, he would become the best player on his hockey team, he would beat anyone who tried to fight him, he would get all the stuff he wanted, eventually.

This optimism meant he had always been a sucker for the idea of things — a plan lovingly described was almost as satisfying as a plan carried out — and this made it possible for him to reset his positive outlook every year about three days after Christmas, when he started planning how it would be different next year.

Every year he told his mother what he wanted, and every year she screwed it up. He knew she was capable of following traditions — after all, they never failed to go to mass on Christmas Eve, and Tor always went along on her account even though he thought it was total horseshit — but she never seemed to get around to doing the important things, like putting up Christmas lights or leaving cookies and milk for Santa or making fruitcake and eggnog (she said this was because none of them liked fruitcake or eggnog, and they always went to waste, to which Tor replied, "But mom, it's *traditional!*").

He would have liked to believe that his mother's failure to make these holidays great was something solvable, something that was getting better with time, but in his heart he knew that she simply didn't care that much about the things that were important to him.

On the final Thanksgiving before they left home, he'd been trying to get her to commit to coming to the Thanksgiving celebration at his school, and she wouldn't even look up from the piece of paper she was reading. He'd been telling her how the teacher was going to dress up as a turkey and all the mothers were invited to come and eat pumpkin pie, and when he came around to asking if she would come, she'd said, "I'd love to, deductible," which was typical of her. She never gave her full attention to anything that he cared about. She was always scattered and frazzled, and he knew it was because she was busy and Richard was a jerk, but he wished she could see how much better things could be if you had a few good things that would always be the same, year after year. Most of all, in those days, he wished that the house would be finished and she would lose her stupid fake accent and finally embrace being from Canada, the greatest place on earth.

It was only recently that he'd realized his mother was Canadian, because she was always pretending to be English, and when he figured out that she actually grew up in Nova Scotia, he'd felt a new sense of hope that they could be normal. He became determined to bring out the Canadian in her, get her to drop all the stuck-up English crap and reveal the pumpkin pie-making, skate-tying, bleacher-cheering, Christmas-, Easter-, Thanksgiving-, and Halloween-celebrating person he knew she was underneath. He had given up on having a father, but he needed his mother to get with the program, especially on the holidays, because he couldn't rely on his friends' moms for that. He needed his own mom to do it, and to do it right, and he believed that if he kept at it, eventually she would. Every year he was disappointed, but every year he made up his mind that next year would be different. His mother knew this—he knew she knew it—and that made it all the more unforgivable that of all the days she could have chosen to deliver the news that they were going to Sierra Leone, she chose to tell him on his birthday in the year when his hope needed restoration more than ever.

TOR WAS WATCHING the kids in the schoolyard and whispering along with the rant from "Get in the Ring" when someone pulled his headphones out of his ears. He turned to see Isatu from his math class standing behind him with some of her friends.

"What the hell is your problem?" he said. He couldn't stand her. She was so full of herself because she'd won some debating competition, and she always wore the full dress uniform with her medal pinned to the pocket.

"Let me listen," Isatu said. She tried to take the headphones from around his neck, and Tor pushed her away. "Look at Esther," she said. She lifted her chin in the direction of one of the girls standing behind her.

"Mess off," Tor said.

Isatu pushed Esther toward Tor. Esther was giggling, and Tor felt a rush of excitement as the other girls pulled up Esther's skirt to reveal an ugly scar on her upper thigh made using resin from the shell of a cashew nut. Tor looked away.

"No, look am," Isatu said. "Look what is written there. It says, *I Love Takwill.*" The girls laughed and held each other's arms.

"First of all, my name isn't *Takwill,* and second of all, you're an idiot," he said. "And so are you an idiot," he said to Esther. He got up and walked away, leaving his bread on the ground and the girls cackling behind him.

He spent his last two classes composing a second draft of a letter to Richard's mother, who he barely knew. He didn't want to, but Ann had threatened to take away his bike privileges if he didn't write to his grandmother and the McCanns, and now that the bike needed fixing, she might try to use that as leverage.

Every letter Tor wrote went through at least two drafts because of his mother's censorship. In the first version of the current letter to his grandmother, he had written:

Yo Grandma,

Thanks for the money for Xmas and Easter and for my last birthday. I was forsed to use it to help pay for all the stuff I broke at the McCanns house, but it was a nice thot anyway. As you know, we live in Sierra Leone now. Well I say "live," but it's not really like living. Our house is like Alcatraz. We have bars all over our windows and we live close to army head corders so were not allowed to go out of our jail after 10pm or we'll get shot. We live by the river but we can't swim in there becose we can get a worm that makes you go blind. Nobody has alarm clocks so they use roosters starting at four o'clock and then the preying at the mosk that sounds like alien overlords and it lasts way longer than you coud ever imagin, and then it stops and starts agan somewere else! you feel like taking your dirty underware and shoving it down there necks. Then the idiots at the bridge checkpoint start playing this one song and they play it all day long!

My infecions are getting wors. I've had 7 infecions in my life five have been here 2 at home. Dick says if I don't keep them clean I might get a blood infecion that can kill you, so I'll probably die from them. I hate church I hate school I hate having no food boiled water that tastes like smoke no tv no nintendo cold showers hot wether no electrcity insted of rattling of another billion things why don't I say it all in one I hate sierra leone!!! Rite now I'd normally be watching top cops with two grilled cheese sanwiches and a choclate milk but insted I'm writing this stupid letter.

I wish we coud go back to Nova Scotia and live in our house, and I wish my mom woud be happy. Mostly I wish I had a father who was nice but I got a jerk. Anyway, thanks for the money. And actully, can you please stop sending me money from now on becose I have to write a letter evry time and its not worth it for five bucks.

Yours truly,
Torquil Berringer

ps I know I can't spell. If only I was as smart as you.

Tor knew as he was writing the letter that his mother would throw it away, but on principle he felt he had to write the truth, at least the first time, even if it did mean twice as much work. For the second draft, he wrote directly on a blue airmail envelope, and this time he gave his mother what she wanted — a nice lie.

Dear Grandma,

How are you? I'm fine. I love our new house and I am having a great time with my family in Sierra Leone!!! Mom makes spaghetti with palms and cheese for dinner evry night. Me and my dad have hour-long talks each and evry day and my mom helps me get reddy for school and she lafs all the time! I am getting great marks in school, and I woud honestly say that my relashionship with my dear, dear parents is better then it has ever been. With the money that you were generis enugh to sent me, I bought a boxing bag. I wasn't alowed to bring it to Africa, but that's okay becose since I'm so happy at home and school I have no agreshion to get out on it. Thank you so very much, and God bless you!

Yours truly,
Torquil Berringer

BY THE END OF THE DAY, Tor was so exhausted from heat and hunger he wasn't sure if he could make it home. His shoe — some plastic piece of crap his mother had bought in Freetown — was falling apart, and the toe flapped open with every step he took. Clear liquid from the wounds on his legs made tracks through the fine red dirt that coated his body. He was pushing the bike slowly up the steep hill when he passed a girl with a jug of water on her head who was letting some of the other kids have a drink. He was tempted to have some too, but he couldn't afford to get sick. Things were bad enough as they were. He asked the girl to pour some water over his head, and she did, standing on her tiptoes.

Some kids started shouting *oporto* and laughing at him. "I am not *oporto!*" he said. "My name is *Torquil.*" He knew they were just trying to piss him off, and he didn't want them to see that it was working, but he couldn't help it.

One of the kids stood in front of Tor and stared him down. "*Oporto,*" he mouthed.

"Call me that again and I'll beat your face," Tor said.

"*Oporto, ça va bien?*" said a little girl next to him. He spat on the ground and kept walking, and the kids followed him, singing *oporto, oporto, oporto, oporto, seke.* At the corner by the army barracks, he heard a vehicle behind him. He turned to see the hospital truck, and he was so exhausted that he dropped the bike and waited for the driver to stop and pick him up. The driver didn't stop, though, and as the truck passed, Tor felt something burning the back of his head. He fell to his knees and clasped his hand to his skull. By the time he looked up, the truck was going around the corner, but through his tears he thought he could see the driver's son on the tailgate, and it looked like he was laughing.

Tor took his hand away from the back of his head and checked his fingers. He wasn't bleeding, but he could feel a lump starting to form already. That fucker must have thrown a stone at him. He punched the ground and cried out from the pain. The other kids laughed, and he wanted to fight them so badly, but he knew that it would only make things worse, so he got up and kept walking.

"*Oporto,* gi me you bike," some kid said.

"You want my bike?" Tor screamed. "Come and get it if you want it. Come and get it!" The kid backed away.

Walking home in a blind rage, Tor wondered if it had been Richard who threw the rock. When Tor was little, every time he agreed to do something "fun" with Richard he ended up getting hurt — being half-drowned during a "game" in the pool or nearly blinded by a snowball filled with ice. The last time he'd gone with his dad on one of these bonding trips Ann liked to arrange was after he'd found out about the affair but before Ann did. They were canoeing, and Richard was at him the whole time, telling him no one could stand him. When Richard said, "Even your mother's sick to death of you," Tor decided he'd had enough and did the only thing that made sense to him at the time, which was to tip the canoe over.

"You're going to be so sorry!" Richard was doggie paddling

behind Tor, towing the sinking canoe, and Tor was too scared to laugh about how funny his father looked, his red face bobbing above the water. Once Tor got to the riverbank, he took off his shoes and ran all the way home barefoot. He hid in the bathroom closet, shivering, until his father went to the hospital, and to his great surprise, Richard never mentioned it again.

After that, Tor decided it was much easier to act like he was going along with whatever moronic plan his mother came up with and ditch Richard as soon as they were out of her sight. Richard expected this, and he tried to stop Tor from getting away, not because he wanted to spend time with him, but because he wanted to control him. The element of cat and mouse that this created made these trips sort of fun for Tor, and as long as he got away, he was home free, since Richard never told Ann.

WHEN TOR GOT HOME, the truck was outside, and there were some kids in the garbage pit. "Get off our property," Tor shouted. They didn't move. "Get off our property or I will chop you up into pieces!" He ran toward them, and they clambered out of the pit.

Richard was on the back steps talking to the driver, but the driver's son was nowhere around.

"I'm sorry, John, but you'll have to make do until it stops altogether," Richard said.

"Why didn't you pick me up?" Tor said. He was afraid he might start to cry again.

"Don't interrupt," Richard said.

"No. I want to know why you drove by and didn't pick me up." The dog was underfoot, and Tor wanted to kick it down the steps.

"I thought you could use a walk."

Tor pointed at the driver. "His shit-eating son threw a rock at my head!"

Richard smacked Tor's face, and Tor put his arms around his head and screamed, "That's where the rock hit me!" even though it wasn't.

Billy was barking at Tor from behind Richard's legs. Richard looked down at the dog. "That serves you right," he said to Tor.

"I hate you!" Tor shouted at Billy. He ran to his room, fell on his bed, bit down into his pillow and cried. After a few minutes, Ann came in, and she looked like she had also been crying. He held out his arms to her.

"What's happened, my baby?" she said. "What's wrong?"

"Everything." He cried into her flannel nightgown, which was damp with her sweat.

"Good grief!" she said when she felt the lump on his head. "What happened to you?"

"Mommy, please, please, please can we go home," he sobbed. "Please. I hate it here."

"Shhhh," she said. "It's just a few more months." She rocked him gently and stroked his head. It hurt, but he let her continue while he thought about how he was going to make Richard and the driver's son pay. Maybe he would do something to the truck. Maybe disconnect the brakes. But how? He used to be so good at coming up with plans for revenge. He hid crushed up sleeping pills and laxatives in Richard's food. He replaced the cash in Richard's wallet with Canadian Tire money and imagined him pulling out the useless five and ten cent bills at a restaurant. On a camping trip, he tied together the zippers on the tent, screamed, "Fire!" and watched from a safe distance as Richard shouted at him through the little window flaps. But lately he found it almost impossible to come up with any good ways to get back at Richard, and it made him wonder if he was brain damaged from starvation.

Ann brought him some food in his room. "Please eat, darling," she said, holding out a plate of potato leaves and rice.

"Get that away from me. It stinks," Tor said.

"I'll leave it here, in case you change your mind." She set the plate by his bed and closed the door behind her. The smell was disgusting, so Tor picked up the plate and took it outside.

He found Jusuf on the back steps. Two girls had wandered up from the river with buckets of clothing on their heads. One of them was wearing a wet T-shirt, and while she and her friend talked to Jusuf, Tor snuck glances at her small, hard nipples and imagined what it would be like to touch them.

There were always lots of topless girls around the river, and by then Tor had seen every kind of boob there was, but somehow it was more exciting to see them through wet fabric. He had managed to save two pornos from the stash his mother had set fire to in one of her shame ceremonies, and even though he had seen all of the girls in there hundreds of times, they were still more interesting to him than any of the real naked girls by the river. Sometimes before he went to sleep he would prop his lantern at the edge of his bed and bring out the weathered and torn magazines. "Look at you with your big boobs," he said to the pictures. "Wow, those are big ones." Those girls were always waiting for him, and they could never get ugly or put their clothes back on.

Tor checked to make sure his parents weren't around before taking out two cigarettes and handing one to Jusuf. "Did you knock down that wasps' nest?" he said. Jusuf had promised not to knock down any nests if Tor wasn't there, but the one on the back of the house was gone.

"They are attacking me." Jusuf pointed to some welts on his legs. "I ask them to shift houses." He stood up and put his cigarette in his pocket. "I dae go," he said. Tor was going to offer him the bike, because it was too late for him to walk all the way home, but then he remembered about the wheel.

Billy was jumping up on Jusuf's legs. "Here, Billy," Tor said, putting his plate of food at the bottom of the steps. Richard had said that no one should feed Billy any more because Richard was feeding him through a tube he had stuck into the hole in Billy's face, but Billy was obviously starving.

"Bye bye, troublesome," Jusuf said. Tor waved and watched him until he was out of sight. "Bam Bam" was playing at the checkpoint, and Tor sang along without meaning to, imagining his father, the driver, and the driver's son realizing halfway down the big hill that the truck's brakes weren't working. They wouldn't die — that was too much — but the truck would be broken forever, and every day Tor would pass Richard walking home and overtake him on the bike and say, "You looked like you could use a walk."

He knew it was illogical. If he did wreck the truck, he would only be hurting himself, because Richard would have to take the bike to work and Tor would have to walk every day. There was no way to win, and whatever he did to try to make things better only made them worse.

Billy was hunched over the empty plate making hacking noises. Tor reached down to pat him on the back, and Billy coughed up a long piece of potato leaf. When Tor tried to pick him up, Billy yelped and snapped at him, so Tor put him back down and let him run away to the dockhouse, to Richard.

THE MAIN REASON Ann wanted Tor and Richard to go on a hike was that they needed to work on their relationship. Begging Richard to be kind to Tor would do no good as long as Richard had no basis of positive regard for him. Ann needed Richard to see how extraordinary and sensitive Tor was, and the only way that was going to happen was for them to spend time together without her, because when she was around they just tried to get her to take sides.

The other reason she wanted them to go out for a while was that she needed some time to compose a response to the tax letter. She didn't want to mention it to Richard, because she knew he would overreact and start accusing her of things. He always thought she was at fault, no matter what the situation, but she knew she hadn't done anything wrong. Not like Don and Pat. They were the ones who should have been audited. Ann knew for a fact that Pat billed the provincial government for more expensive procedures than Don had performed and Don pocketed the cash people paid him for insurance medicals. Ann hadn't done anything like that. She'd simply given the accountant a list of all of their expenses and told him to make as much as he could tax deductible. If he chose to include their personal vehicle or dinners out or office space in both of their homes, that was his business. He was the professional.

It was true that she hadn't paid the taxes before they left — she wondered now if that was the reason for the audit — but it was Richard's fault, because he had insisted on allowing Don to steal from them with that ludicrous bill he issued at the end of Richard's first year as a supposed full partner in the practice. She had put aside money to pay the taxes, but after Richard had paid Don, there wasn't enough left for the last installment, so she'd decided the best thing was to ignore it until they had the money, because the late penalty would be less than the cost of taking out another loan.

She couldn't tell Richard this, though. He didn't know anything about managing finances, because Joan had done it for him before Ann took over. He was like a child in that way. And it was because of his ignorance about money that they were in this situation in the first place. If he had involved her in his contract negotiations with Don, none of this would be happening. She would have seen through Don's smooth talking and recognized that he was always going to take advantage of Richard, because that was how he operated. It was too late to do anything about it now, though, so the best thing was for her to keep the audit to herself.

Since she was feeling relatively okay, she thought that before she tackled the letter she might try to meditate or read, but as soon as she sat down on the front steps with a cup of tea and her book, Maggie showed up with Aminata.

Ann tried to remember the arrangement she'd made with Maggie. She was sure she'd said it would just be for one afternoon, just to try it, and she was sure she wouldn't have agreed for it to be a weekend, because she liked to have time for Richard and Tor when they were home. Maybe Maggie had misunderstood, or maybe she was going to pretend she'd misunderstood because it suited her better that way. In any case, there they were, and Ann couldn't hide, because they had already seen her.

Richard had dug in his heels about firing Jusuf, and since there was no money to hire a second person, he had convinced Ann to try having Aminata come and help around the house. Ann didn't really know who Aminata was at that point, but she'd looked out for her at church that Sunday. There was no Catholic church in town, so Ann and Richard had to go to Maggie's church, which was hard for Ann, who found all the holy roller stuff undignified and couldn't stand being shouted at and called a sinner. In the Catholic church, Ann found it relatively easy to take what worked for her and ignore the rest, but at Maggie's church, the parts that didn't work for her were very hard to ignore. The pastor was a Beninese man named Mark, who, along with his wife, Emily, helped Maggie run the orphanage. Something about Mark reminded Ann of Mr. Carter, her tyrannical grade twelve English teacher, and she never listened to his sermons, which were always about Satan and hellfire. Sometimes he just shouted one word, like, "Fire! Fire! Fire!" and she had to put her hands over her ears or go outside. She did find the music moving, though. She had always had a voice in her that said *Sing! Rejoice!* and the music they sang in that church touched her much more than the staid hymns she was used to.

The choir was made up of kids from the orphanage, including Pastor Mark and Emily's daughter, Marian, and their son, Daniel, who endeared himself to Ann with his fidgeting and face-pulling during the service. The kids were useless singers and musicians, but Aminata had real presence. She kept her eyes closed most of the time and somehow managed to keep the rhythm with her tambourine while leaning her armpits on her crutches and occasionally raising her hands and singing to the roof of the church. She seemed to be so full of devotion, and it was adorable, but also sad. It was a kind of violence against innocence, Ann thought, to initiate children so young into the cold, adult world of judgment and guilt, but it was also touching to see in children like Aminata how that pure goodness still shone through, at least for a while.

WHEN AMINATA ARRIVED at the Berringers' house for the first time, she was wearing a shiny golden dress, which she flattened carefully with both hands after getting out of the truck. Maggie had told Ann that Aminata was thirteen, like Tor, but she didn't look older than nine or ten. Her hair was done in a wave of braids that curved to one side of her head, and she had a long, serious face with wide eyes and a pretty mouth. Her left leg was noticeably deformed and withered, and her foot dragged on the ground as she walked toward Ann on her crutches.

"You have everything?" said Maggie. She was wearing her denim dress, which had a crudely sewn up hole in the collar.

"Yes, ma," Aminata said. Ann wondered if the girl would be capable of reading to her, and she thought that might be nicer than writing the letter, which she could put off until tomorrow anyway.

"Now you be a good girl," Maggie said. "Do what Miss Ann tells you."

"Yes, ma," the girl said again.

Ann put her arm around Aminata's shoulders. She smelled of fresh sweat and carbolic soap. "Aminata's very welcome," Ann said. "I know you're overrun at your house." It was important that Maggie not think she was doing the Berringers a favour, because then she would want something in return.

"Okay, bye," Maggie said. "I'll be back for her by seven."

Once Ann and Aminata were alone, the girl went mute, giving only one- or two-word answers to Ann's questions.

"Can you read, sweetie?" Ann asked.

"Yes, ma."

"Okay, I don't want you to say that any more," Ann said.

"Yes, ma."

"Why don't we read together?" Ann went inside and brought out *Diana: Her True Story,* which she had already read twice.

Aminata looked at the cover. "Fine," she said, touching the photo of Diana in a white, one-shouldered gown. "Who is it?"

"She's a princess," Ann said.

Ann and Aminata sat on the front steps, and Aminata tried to read the book, but she was excruciatingly slow and couldn't pronounce half the words. After a page, she slumped forward. "Where did you get this dress?" Ann said, taking the slippery, synthetic fabric between her fingers.

Aminata brightened. "I get it from Miss Maggie. All of the other childrens want this clothes, but me I get it."

Ann still had to clean Billy's wound and give him water through the tube before starting on the brunch she had planned to surprise Tor and Richard with when they came back. Aminata held the dog while Ann dabbed the hole in his face with Dettol, working around the tube Richard had inserted down his throat and into his stomach through his cheek. Then she found the port, which was taped to Billy's neck, and gave him water through a syringe as Richard had instructed her to do. When she'd finished, she suggested to Aminata that they cook the meal together. Aminata took a minute to get her crutches and stand up, but she seemed to have adjusted to her disability well, because she was surprisingly quick and never once asked for help.

In the kitchen, Aminata stood behind Ann as Ann bent over to look through the cupboards. There were beans and bread, but the thought of all that brown food was not appealing. There was the spaghetti and parmesan cheese, but Ann was saving that for a really special occasion. In the second cupboard, she found two yams and a can of Spam.

"Hey!" she said. "Bacon and chips. Tor will like that for a treat."

"You don't have to cook, because you don't well," Aminata said.

"Because you're *not* well," Ann said. "We'll do it together."

Aminata sat on a stool in the kitchen hut to peel and chop the yams while Ann knelt on the ground, sliced the Spam into thin strips and fried it until it was crispy. Billy hung around whining, and Ann threw him a piece of Spam before she remembered she wasn't supposed to be feeding him, because Richard said that if he ate food any other way than through the tube it would come out of the wound and stop it from healing.

She felt so happy imagining Tor coming home to food he liked. He had always been extremely fussy, and Ann had thought that Sierra Leone might be an opportunity for him to develop a more sophisticated palate, because the food was delicious and almost none of the bland, unhealthy junk that he ate at home was available. But he had flatly refused to even try the local food, and instead he lived on sugar and the occasional piece of bread. Richard said that he wouldn't starve himself, though, so Ann left him alone initially, expecting him to come around, but it was looking as if Tor was going to be as stubborn about this as he was about everything, and of course Richard would be equally stubborn, so they were at an impasse, with Tor becoming startlingly thin and Richard pretending not to notice.

Ann transferred the Spam to a bowl, poured more oil into the hot pan, and added the yams. In the kitchen, she found two mangoes, an overripe banana and a plantain in a bag Jusuf had hung from the wall. She used the mangoes and banana to make a fruit salad and had Aminata slice the plantain lengthwise and fry it in the same oil as the yams.

Ann was setting the table on the top balcony when Tor and Richard got back. Tor ran up the stairs and fell down on the tiles, panting.

"How was it?" Ann asked when Richard, also out of breath, stepped onto the balcony.

"Great," Tor wheezed. "We saw monkeys." Ann was thrilled. She hugged Richard. At that moment, she felt there was nothing he or Tor could do to stop her loving them. Her love for them was invincible, and she wondered if they appreciated the safety of that kind of love, which she hadn't felt herself since her father died.

Tor helped her to finish setting the table while Richard sat on the top balcony feeding Billy milk through the tube and telling Aminata about the Black Loyalists who left Nova Scotia to settle in Sierra Leone in the late eighteenth century. When he got to the story about the Nova Scotians holding a Thanksgiving service under the Cotton Tree after they arrived, Aminata, who was clearly not following him, said, "I love Miss Maggie, because we two of us we are praying to God. Some they don't pray. We, we are praying. I am God's daughter. I love Jesus, because He is my father."

"Mommy, did I tell you about the monkeys?"

"Don't interrupt," Richard said, which was absurd, because Ann and Tor weren't part of Richard's conversation with Aminata.

"I'm talking to mom."

"So is Aminata."

"They were on someone's porch, and they had their legs tied with rope," Tor said. "For soup."

"Oh hush up, Tor," Richard said. He pulled Billy onto his lap to get better access to his feeding tube, and Ann almost vomited when she saw the warm milk and pus oozing from the wound.

"Do you remember what the Loyalists did under the Cotton Tree?" Richard said. Aminata shook her head. "They had a th... a than...a thanksg..." Richard said.

"I don't know it!" Aminata said loudly. She seemed to internally correct herself before demurely shaking her head and saying, "I don't remember again."

"I saw a snake, too," Tor said. "And I found a perfect mango for you but I lost it on my way home."

Ann asked Tor to go and get water and glasses, but he wouldn't leave her side, so she went with him and coached him on his manners, which she knew were important to Richard, and suggested that at lunch they play their game of pretending they were dining with the Queen.

Once they were all at the table, Ann looked around and felt so proud. Sure it was canned meat and greasy yams, but for once they were all at the same table and it wasn't too hot and she wasn't feeling particularly ill and Tor looked willing to eat what was in front of him.

It was perfect, and the perfection made her nervous, because it was so fragile, but she could still stand back from it enough to enjoy it, which was good, because it didn't last even five minutes.

First Tor started rapping, and as usual he had to keep going for a few seconds after being told to stop, which always made Richard react badly.

"I said shut *up*." Richard hit the table with his fist. Tor did two more beats.

"Remember, the Queen," Ann said. Tor sat up straight, pulled his lips in, narrowed his eyes and looked down his nose at everyone at the table. "Mahhhvelous, mahhvelous," he said. He made a big show of picking up his knife and fork, and Ann realized it had been a mistake to suggest the Queen thing.

"Get your elbows off the table." Richard shoved Tor's elbow.

"Ow!" Tor said. He dabbed his gums and looked at his finger. "I'm bleeding!"

Aminata had stopped eating.

"Let me have a look," Ann said. Tor opened his mouth, and Ann held him under his chin. There was some blood in his teeth.

"You let him lie all over the table to eat," Richard said.

"Nobody said you have to look at me," Tor said. Ann wanted to scream at them both, but at the same time she felt sorry for them, because they couldn't help themselves, and she reminded herself that as long as they were fighting, it meant they all still cared.

"I can't digest my food with you sitting there like some wild animal with your mouth wide open," Richard said. "And in case you haven't noticed, we have a guest. You should be able to eat like a human being for her sake, if not mine."

"I was taking tiny bites like mom," Tor said.

"Can't we just once have a nice lunch together?" Ann said. "Can't you ever think about anyone but your own selves?"

Richard got up to leave. "Good riddance," Tor said under his breath.

Richard took Tor by his chin and the back of his neck. Tor held onto Richard's wrist, and Richard shook Tor's face and said, "You are going to learn some respect."

"Stop it!" Ann said, trying to pull Richard's hands off Tor.

"You think you're so smart," Richard said. "But you are going to learn that you are a child, and you have to respect adults. Now get to your room." He pushed Tor away, and Tor, who was crying now, spat blood at his feet. Ann stood between them, even though it was the last place she wanted to be, and told Tor to go.

"But he..." Tor said.

"Go to your room," she said.

Tor crossed his arms. "No, I will not go, because it's not fair!"

She would not get angry. She would not let them make her do something she would regret. "Tor, please go now and we can talk about this later," she said. Richard stood behind her, and she knew that he had positioned himself there as a way of showing Tor that his parents were united against him. He couldn't support her when she needed him, but as soon as he saw an opportunity to use her to win a battle with Tor, he was right behind her.

"Go!" she said to Tor.

"He cuts my mouth and I have to go to my room? Why don't you send him to his room?"

"Just go!' she said, but Tor didn't move, and finally she'd had enough, and she lost control and hit him.

Tor laughed. "Is that all?" he said. She already hated herself for what she had done.

Richard, who had been standing by and watching her lose her cool instead of trying to help her to calm down like he should have, said, "That's it." He twisted Tor's arm behind Tor's back and pushed him toward the concrete steps. For a second it looked like Tor would fall down the stairs, and Ann screamed and reached out her hand, but Tor caught himself on the banister and walked away without looking back.

"Why, why, why do you have to do it?" Ann said when Richard sat back down at the table. She was crouched on the floor, her back to the railing.

"I don't know about you, Ann, but I am not going to let that child ruin this meal that you and Aminata have worked so hard to make." He didn't deserve to eat a nice meal. Neither did she. But he was already eating, as if nothing had happened. Ann would have preferred to talk to him without Aminata there, but if she tried to change locations, he would go to the dockhouse, and Aminata seemed to be sort of in her own world anyway.

"Why can't you ever let things be nice?" she said. "Why can't you just leave him alone?"

"You are completely blind," he said. He picked up his plate and walked away, and she followed him downstairs. She expected him to go to the dockhouse, but instead he went into the living room. "Don't go in there!" she said, hovering in the doorway. He sat on the sofa with his food on his lap. "Richard, you know this room is full of mould." He picked up his book.

"Richard!"

"Oh, give over," he said.

He expected her to lose her cool. He relied on it. He knew all the right buttons to push so that she would go mental and he would never have to look at the root of the problem because all the focus would have shifted to her outburst. "You can't keep doing this," she said. He ignored her. She turned her face into the hallway and breathed in. Already she could feel tightness in her throat, stinging in her nostrils.

"Richard, please don't ignore me," she said. He turned his back to her. "Richard, please," she said, knowing she had reached the end of her patience, knowing he knew it, too. He turned a page in his book. She took one more breath in the hall, came into the room, snatched the book out of his hands and ripped it in half. She was surprised by how easily it came apart. He was nodding slowly as if to say *this is what you can expect from a lunatic*. She threw the two halves of the book at him. One hit him in the face, and he flinched but didn't move. The other landed in his food.

"You're totally insane," he said, and she would have called him by his father's name then if she hadn't promised not to in Marriage Encounter.

"Why do you have to be so cruel?" she said, still holding her breath.

He held up his hand. "We'll talk when you're in a rational frame of mind."

She pulled her T-shirt up over her face and breathed in. "Can't you see that he wants you to love him?" she said through the shirt. She hated Richard seeing her stretch marks, especially when they were arguing.

"Come on. Get real. Get *real,* Ann. That kid has you wrapped around his little finger. He wanted us to have this argument. He's playing you and you don't even see it."

"I thought you had a lovely time together today. Why can't you make any eff...."

"Yes, we had a *lovely* time, Ann. He ran away from me as soon as we were out of your sight, taking all the food with him, by the way, and I didn't see him again until I came back from my walk and he scared the living daylights out of me by jumping out of a tree!"

She thought, *How could you have sex with that whore, you son of a bitch?* She said, "You know, it's not the abuse that will make him hate you in the long term, it's the lack of love."

"Abuse! You say I'm abusing him if I tell him he can't have something he wants. Any punishment is abuse. Any response to your son's psychopathic behavior is abuse."

"No, I am talking about the fact that you hit him and kick him and criticize him all the time. That's what I mean when I say abuse, to be specific. Aminata and I spent all day cooking. Why couldn't you let us have one meal without this...." She knew it was hypocritical, but she also knew he would never point out her hypocrisy, because

121

he would criticize her for everything else, but he would never criticize her for hitting their son.

"It's him!" he said. "He loves doing this to me. And you play right into his hands because you can't see it and you never ever *ever* take my side." He picked up the back half of his book, which was soaking up grease on his plate.

"That's not fair," Ann said. "Richard, put down your book." He flipped through the pages, trying to find his place. Ann took a glass from the table next to him, and he looked up in time to cover his ears before it hit the wall. "Why don't you get it?" she screamed, letting the T-shirt fall from her face. She didn't care any more. She fell to her knees and cried, and he ignored her.

The dog came into the room, and Richard had to put it outside so it wouldn't step in the glass. When he came back in, he stood next to the shards.

"You broke some glass here," he said.

"I don't care," she said, hating herself.

"It's all over the floor."

"I said I don't effing care." He went away, and when he came back with a broom and started sweeping up the glass, her remorse came, and she took the broom and dustpan from him and said she was sorry and she would clean it up. After she'd finished, she went to Tor's room to tell him how upset she was with him, but she was feeling tired and guilty and she couldn't breathe and her eyes were burning, so when he said, "No mommy. You're not upset with me. You're happy with me and you love me," she was defenceless. She let him come and sit at the table. He ate both his own lunch and hers, and everything looked perfectly normal by the time Maggie came to get Aminata.

CHAPTER 8

IT WAS THE HOTTEST DAY they'd had yet, and of course John had failed to show up with the truck, so it looked as though they would have to walk to the Bergmans' going-away party, and Richard would have to carry Billy, who couldn't be left alone all day and wasn't strong enough to walk in the heat. Torquil said he was going to take the bike, but Richard vetoed that. He didn't want Tor to come at all, actually, and he'd tried to tell Ann that he didn't think the party was for children, but that had never deterred her or Tor before.

Tor got on the bike and tried to pedal away, so Richard grabbed his T-shirt to stop him, and Tor lost his balance and fell on the ground. When Richard tried to help him up, Tor shrieked, "Why! Why!" which he seemed to think was very funny, but as soon as he saw Maggie's truck coming down the driveway, he started crying, as if Richard was really hurting him. Richard told him to go to his room, but instead of going back inside, Tor ran into the cashew field, and Richard couldn't go after him because Maggie and Aminata were there.

Aminata had been spending more and more time with Ann. Maggie or Mark would drop her off after her classes (which Richard assumed involved a lot of Bible study and not much else), and she would stay all evening, sometimes reading while Ann lay in the hammock, sometimes doing simple chores. Her cooking was better than Jusuf's, and with her to keep Ann busy, Richard was making good progress on his new proposal. She was also bubbly and warm, and after years of coming home to nothing but complaints, it was nice to be greeted by one of her enthusiastic smiles. So he was happy to have her around, but he couldn't help being a bit disturbed by the instant intimacy that seemed to have developed between her and Ann, who had a history of collecting and dropping people as it suited her.

Aminata opened her door, and Richard was about to go and help her down from the truck, but she seemed to have it figured out, so he left her to it. "Wait, Maggie." Ann came outside in a wrinkled white dress, her hair all on end. "Can you drive us to the Bergmans'?"

Maggie sighed. "You'd have to be ready to go right now. I gotta be back home in twenty minutes."

"That's fine, Maggie. We can walk," Richard said.

"No we can't," Ann said. "It's boiling hot, and there's no way Aminata can walk there."

"Oh, are you coming with us Aminata?" Richard said.

"Of course she is," Ann said. "Why do you think she's here?" Richard wanted to say that he had been asking himself the same question. "Anyway, we won't be a minute, Maggie," Ann said. "Let me find Tor and my hat."

Aminata climbed back into the truck next to Maggie, and Richard called Billy and held him on his lap in the truck bed. Fifteen minutes later, Ann returned wearing a huge sun hat and a preposterous pair of white gloves. It took a further ten minutes of looking for Tor and bemoaning the fact that they could never do things as a family before she gave up and agreed to go without him.

"I'll bring you back some sausages, sweetheart!" she shouted to the trees.

Watching Ann preen in the side mirror of Maggie's truck, it occurred to Richard that her outfit was exactly her idea of what the person she *wanted* to be would wear. This was the way she was — more like a character in a story about herself than a real person. On her birth certificate she was Theresa Ann Mason, but some time after moving to England at seventeen to avoid cucumber-picking season, and after completely misunderstanding *Gone With the Wind,* she had unofficially changed her name to Scarlett. When she came back to Nova Scotia, she switched to her middle name, which — along with an unidentifiable mixture of Canadian and English accents and a ludicrously revamped life story that completely omitted the detail of her first marriage — she probably thought better suited to her new incarnation as a cosmopolitan sophisticate deigning to make a home in small-town Nova Scotia.

She never spoke to her old friends. She avoided questions about where she had gone to school. The only thing she kept from her former life, and brought up at every opportunity, was the English war-hero father who died when she was twelve. His great aunt had married into the British peerage, or so Ann claimed, but Richard knew that her ideas about good taste and decorum were not based on any lived experience but had sprouted full-blown from the sheer ardour of her aspiration. She was filled with such maxims as, *Posh cars are for the nouveau riche* and *It's rude to arrive on time to a party,* which seemed to impress her more abject Canadian friends.

When they arrived at Rita and Johannes Bergman's house, the Sandis were already there — without their children — and a man Richard hadn't seen before was sitting at the table with Johannes. Rita introduced Richard and Ann to the man, a South African pilot named James, and Ann guffawed when Rita called Richard Dr. Berringer. Sandi greeted Richard with a curt nod, and Richard wondered if there was some underlying hostility in it, but he told himself he was just being paranoid. Johannes, who was already drunk, didn't even offer either of the Berringers a chair at the table where he and the pilot were working their way through a platter of shrimp as if they were peanuts.

Richard had never got a straight answer from Johannes about what he did for a living, but he assumed there was something shady about it. Johannes and Rita struck him as the kind of people who came to Africa so they could get away with things they could never get away with at home, and he was embarrassed to be associated with them, never mind going to their gated compound to play croquet, of all things, but they were good at entertaining and they had a knack for making the most of the available resources. In short, they weren't the best people, but they did have the best food, and while he wouldn't miss them, he would miss coming to their house once a fortnight to eat well and enjoy their air conditioning.

Richard found Billy a quiet corner and gave him some water through his tube. His wound wasn't looking any better, but Richard still hoped that without the irritation of food and dirt and with the benefit of regular nutrition and daily cleaning, it would heal.

When Richard came back to the table, Ann was by the buffet, and he squirmed at the sight of her greedily balancing piles of food on one of the dainty plates Rita had set out.

"My father was a pilot," Ann said to the pilot as she stole Johannes' chair.

"How is your family?" Rita asked Joyce Sandi.

"He was in the RAF," Ann continued. "He shot down six German planes in the Battle of Britain and Winston Churchill shook his hand." Richard, who had heard the story a thousand times, helped himself to a few of the remaining shrimp.

"It's difficult, because people here are suspicious of Liberians," Joyce said. "Everyone is saying, 'Watch your neighbour,' because they are afraid of rebel spies. I tell them, 'Remember if Sierra Leone falls, you too could be a refugee.'"

"I thought you were from Canada," Johannes said.

"My mother is," Ann said, slurping plum sauce from the side of her hand.

Richard sat next to Joyce and arranged a napkin on his lap.

"I still don't understand what the rebels want," he said. "If they wanted the government overthrown, Strasser has already done that, and it seems like it was pretty easy, too. So why are they raping and murdering their own people?"

"Money!" the pilot said. "As long as this country is in chaos, they can keep mining diamonds."

"But you grew up in England?" Johannes said to Ann.

"You know many of them are forced," Joyce said. "And there are so many young people with nothing to do, no jobs, no education, no opportunity, fed up with the rotten government. So they are ripe to be used by the architects of this madness."

"My father was a war groom," Ann said. Richard saw her eyeing his shrimp, so he quickly ate two of them. "He married my mother while he was in Canada training with the air force. Mostly it happened the other way around."

"On the radio they said that the army has pushed them back to the border," Richard said.

"The army is full of rebels," the pilot said.

Richard said, "But it *is* dying down, isn't it?" at the same moment as Johannes said, "And I take it he didn't like Canada much?" The group's conversations, having converged, would now follow from whichever question was answered first.

"What do you mean?" Ann said. She was wiping the sauce off her plate with her fingers and licking them clean. Watching her, Richard thought how much her table manners gave her away. She was always wolfing food down as if it was going to be taken away and then succumbing to fits of belches, which she tried to pass off as hiccups if he confronted her.

"You moved back to England, I assume." Johannes said.

"He died," Ann said.

"So you moved back to England after he died?"

"A bit later." Ann reached past the pilot, took the last shrimp from Richard's plate and ate it before he had a chance to react.

"So you didn't grow up there."

"Yes, I moved there as a teenager," she said, trying for dignified closure, but concluding instead with a gut-pit belch.

"But you're from Canada." Richard was about to try and redirect the conversation when the pilot clapped his hands, making Ann jump. "I say," he said with pinched nostrils. "Anyone keen on croquet?"

"Splen*did*," Sandi said.

While Johannes collected the mallets and balls, Rita began the game by passing around a hat with numbers in it, asking each person to pick one and team up with the person with the matching number.

"No, that's a silly way to decide," Ann said. She moved toward Richard, who had just bitten into a cracker with some miraculous white goo on it, and he almost spat it out in his haste to stop her from announcing the teams herself.

"Why don't you pair up with Aminata," he said, bits of cracker flying, "and I'll be with…." He looked wildly around the circle, and his gaze landed on the pilot.

"James," the pilot said. Already Richard was longing for the comfort of the dockhouse, his rat traps.

"No, I want to be on your team," Ann said. "James can be with Aminata."

Richard looked at Aminata sitting in the corner stroking Billy, the condensation from her Fanta dripping down her arm.

"James might want to pick his own teammate," Richard said.

"He doesn't mind," Ann said.

"Maybe we should do boys against girls," Rita offered.

"That's alright," James said. He looked at Aminata. "I've got a feeling that one's a crack croquet player."

"See?" Ann said, and instead of slapping her, as he would have liked to, Richard chose a yellow mallet from the case that Johannes was holding in front of him.

For the next twenty minutes the players tried to agree on a set of rules but managed only to state the differences in their various ways of playing, Sandi arguing for the figure of eight course and Richard for the single winding line he remembered having great fun with as a child. Richard only agreed to Sandi's boring setup when the pilot said, "Either fight it out or flip a coin, girls."

The Sandis worked well together and quickly took the lead because of Osman's insistence on rules Richard had never even heard of, but which always seemed to work against him. Johannes was drunk and obnoxious. He kept calling Rita "my gorgeous wife" or "my brilliant wife," and she looked mortified but followed him dutifully around the course. The pilot carried a chair for Aminata to sit on, and he didn't seem to care at all about winning, while Richard and Ann were stuck in last place thanks to Ann's absolute refusal to stop and think before she took a shot.

There seemed to be an unspoken rule that no one would shoot the women's balls "out into the nether," as Rita called it, although the men shot each others' balls off the course at every opportunity. Richard told himself not to take it personally, but when Johannes gave Sandi a conspiratorial look after he shot Richard's ball all the way to the fence at the far end of the Bergmans' property, Richard was sure he was being ganged up on.

Near the end of the first half of the course, Rita nudged her ball with her foot as she took her position. She looked around to see if anyone had noticed, but Johannes and Ann were refilling their drinks, the Sandis were planning their next shots, and Aminata and the pilot weren't paying attention to the game at all. When Rita caught Richard's eye, she shrugged, as if to say that it was just a game anyway, and Richard said nothing, because he was sure that she was only doing it because she didn't want to disappoint her husband. When she did it again on her next turn, Ann saw it too.

"Let it go," Richard said.

"But she's cheating!"

"Who cares?" Richard hated playing games with Ann. For her, life was one big competition, and whenever she started to lose, she

129

first tried to change the rules and then outright defied them. If all else failed, she huffed off in a sulk, which she tried to pass off as a protest against the great injustice of it all.

It was Richard's turn next. There was a clump of grass directly in his ball's path, so he leaned down to pull it out.

"No grooming the course after the game has begun," Sandi said. Richard laughed stiffly and pulled on the grass. "You're not allowed to groom the course," Sandi said. Richard was blinded by the sun behind Sandi's head when he looked up.

"Are you serious?"

"I think he's serious," the pilot said. "No grass removals."

"No one else has had that advantage," Sandi said.

"Quite right, quite right," the pilot said.

"No one else has made this exact shot," Richard said.

"We've all had to make adjustments," Sandi said.

"Aminata's been playing the whole game with her footicap," the pilot said.

"You'll have to go around it," Sandi said, and Richard decided to let him have his way, since he and Ann were going to lose the game anyway.

"There you are, darling one!" Johannes shouted. "Well done! Did you see what my brilliant wife did, everyone?" Rita was standing with her back to the group, legs spread, at the far end of the course. Having made what Richard was certain was an impossible shot, she was aiming for the next hoop, which he was glad to see her miss. "Oh well, darling one," Johannes said. He draped a muscular arm over his wife's freckled shoulders.

Ann, whose turn came after Aminata's, started to "save time," as she put it, by preparing and sometimes even taking her shots while the pilot was helping Aminata to get set up. Ann got more and more brazen with each turn, sometimes actually picking up her own ball and moving it closer to the hoop. When she kicked Joyce Sandi's ball out of her way, Osman, who had finished the hoops and returned to the middle of the course to help Joyce get through, called her out.

"I saw that," he said. Ann pretended not to have heard him. "I said I saw that," Osman said again. Ann took her shot, but it ricocheted off the hoop. She threw her mallet at the ground and made a growling noise.

"You kicked Joyce's ball," Sandi said.

"Rubbish," Ann said, her face reddening. Richard knew this would end badly. Ann was not accustomed to being challenged, especially by men, who were supposed to find her irresistibly attractive despite the fact that she didn't even bother to brush her hair any more.

"I saw it too," Johannes said.

"What absolute rubbish."

"It's not rubbish, you were cheating."

"Why don't you ask your *darling wife* about cheating?" Ann said, turning on Johannes.

"Sweetheart?" Richard took Ann's arm.

"It doesn't matter!" Rita said.

"They should have to go back a hoop," Osman said.

"Come on, go back one," Richard said to Ann, although he knew it was hopeless. "We'll make it up later."

Just then Tor arrived on the bike. He gave a thumbs up and shouted "One love," to the party, rode right up to the buffet and let the bike fall on the bushes by the fence.

Richard dropped his mallet and left Ann arguing with the other players while he went to sort out her son, who was shoving cake into his mouth with both hands. Seeing Richard coming toward him, Tor started stuffing food into his pockets. His hands were black with dirt and his knees were leaking fluid. Richard almost didn't want to touch him, he was so revolting. When he grabbed Tor's arm, Tor yelped and some cake fell out of his mouth. "You'd better watch out when we get home," Richard said. "Now get that food out of your face and go and greet the Bergmans."

"Richard, leave him alone." Ann came running across the lawn.

"You're disgusting," Richard said, and before Tor had a chance to respond with one of his idiotic noises, Richard turned and walked past Ann and back into the game.

The pilot had managed to help Aminata get her ball to the end of the first lap, and now that they were both on their way back, he went through all but one hoop in one turn and shot three balls (Ann's, Richard's, and finally Sandi's) off course on the way. "You live by the sword, you die by the sword!" he bellowed as he shot their balls one by one under the deck, into a bush, and to the end of the driveway.

When Richard went to retrieve his ball, he managed to make an excellent shot, but whatever redeeming glory he might have gained from this was lost when Tor, his mouth still full of food, shouted, "Nice shot, Dick," and Richard looked up to see Johannes, Osman and the pilot smirking.

On Ann's next turn, she tried to get back at the pilot by shooting Aminata's ball off the course, but instead she hit herself in the foot with her mallet and cried when the others laughed at her. In the end, Aminata and the pilot beat them all, and Richard was so glad it was over he didn't care that he and Ann had come last.

As soon as the game was put away, Richard walked home alone, saying he had to finish some work before it got dark. He hugged Rita and wished her well, shook Johannes and Joyce's hands and nodded at the pilot, but he didn't bother to say goodbye to Sandi.

THE NEXT MORNING, a woman came into Richard's office with her two young daughters, one of whom had a fever. It was an unusually quiet morning, so Richard pulled Martha aside and asked if she thought it would be a good idea to try talking to the mother about circumcision. Sandi might be against a larger-scale sensitization program, but Richard thought that if he spoke to individual girls and women on a case-by-case basis, he might have time to change some people's minds before the big initiation ceremony that Martha said would take place after the harvest.

"You can do it, but you should be careful," Martha said. "The secret societies can become hostile if you disturb them in their business, and you do not want to face their wrath."

"All I'm doing is offering medical advice to people who come to see me. That's my job, isn't it?"

"You must be very sensitive," she said. "People have strong feelings about that. For example, you can begin by talking about the positive aspects of the culture, so they will be more open."

"Will you help me?" he said.

"It is too dangerous for me in my position," she said. "There are even stories about women being forcibly initiated if they say something against it in a case like mine. I want to help, but not openly."

This was disappointing. Richard had hoped Martha could lend some legitimacy to his efforts by being an example of a strong, intelligent, successful woman who hadn't been circumcised, but he understood her reasoning. It meant he would have to find another nurse to translate for him, though, and that wouldn't be easy, since he suspected that Martha was the only one who didn't give Sandi reports on him.

"Actually I don't want to be open about it either," he said. "It's not that I'm hiding anything, but what happens in my office is between me and my patients."

"I understand," she said. He didn't know what he would do without her. She was his only ally, the only one who made him feel he was doing something worthwhile. It occurred to him then that it wasn't right, the way he thought about her when he was alone, always in scenarios of conquest, without respect, and he resolved to imagine her from then on in loving ways or — better, but unlikely — not at all.

He was writing a prescription for the child and trying to decide which nurse he could ask to translate for him when the answer, in the form of a shy young orderly named Musa, passed by his window. Musa had translated for Richard once or twice before, and while Richard guessed that having a male translator was probably unorthodox under the circumstances, he reasoned that since he was breaking a taboo by bringing up the subject in the first place, he might as well do it with the help of someone who was unlikely to kick up a fuss.

He leaned out of his window. "Musa, can you come and help me for five minutes?" he said. Musa hesitated. "Or if you're...."

"No problem," Musa said.

Richard gave each of the little girls a wooden spinning top from his desk drawer and asked Martha to take them into the corridor, leaving him alone with Musa and the mother.

"I want to ask mum if she has already taken her daughters to the *Bondo* bush," Richard said.

Musa looked extremely uncomfortable, but he asked the question. "She says no," Musa said.

"Ask her if she is planning to," Richard said.

"She says it is women's business," Musa said. Richard was taken aback, but he continued.

"Okay, please tell her that I respect her customs, and I know that *Bondo* is important for women here, but what I want to tell her is that the particular practice of cutting is very wrong and dangerous. I understand people do it because they love their daughters and want what's best for them, but it is a violation of their daughters' rights." Musa translated, and the woman watched Richard with an expression Richard didn't know how to read. When Musa had finished, the woman responded.

"She says it is our own tradition," Musa said.

"Does she know how dangerous it is and how damaging it could be to her daughters' health and well-being?"

The woman didn't seem angry, but she spoke with the stern imperiousness of every scary feminist Richard had ever met. "She says thank you, but she will decide what is best for her daughters."

"No," Richard said. "She has no right to impose this on them.

We all make choices for our children, but paying someone to perform dangerous, medically unnecessary surgery on her daughters in unsanitary conditions without anaesthetic is not something she should be allowed to *choose*."

The woman responded, and Musa hesitated before translating. "Anyway, she says it is her own tradition, and she does not want to discuss with you about it more."

Richard wasn't used to being spoken to like this by patients, in Nova Scotia or in Sierra Leone. He knew he was right, but he was cowed by the woman's manner. He was about to continue when the woman stood up and left, thanking him on her way out, and he felt strangely guilty, and also angry about his guilt.

At lunchtime, the encounter was still bothering him, so he went to Nene's, hoping she would reassure him that he wasn't such a heavy-handed jerk after all. He sat on a stool and drank a Fanta while she entered calculations into a book on the counter. "Can I ask you a question?" he said.

Nene held up a finger while she finished working something out on her calculator. When she had written down the sum, she looked up at him.

"Sandi's always telling me I don't understand the culture here," he said. "I want to know if you can help me."

"What you want to know?" she said.

"Well, about the secret societies, for example. Some people have told me it's dangerous to even *say* anything negative about their traditions."

"Of course nobody like to be criticize," Nene said. "But they will probably say that you don't know them so that's why you criticize."

"But how can I ever know about their practices if I'm not allowed to talk about them?"

"Unless you are part of that society, you should not know," Nene said. "That is why you must be careful if you are walking in the bush, because if you enter their place, they will not like it."

"And how will they know if I've entered their place?"

"They will know, but you, you might not know."

"And what will they do to me?" Richard asked.

"They can deal with you very seriously," Nene said. "If I am in your position, I would not interfere with them at all." She turned back to her work, and Richard continued to sip his Fanta in silence.

He still found it hard to believe that a woman like Nene could be stuck in such a backward mindset of superstitious fear. That kind of fear was like an insidious sickness, preventing ordinary people from developing their vision and capacity because they lacked the courage to overstep the invisible boundaries they were raised to believe in, and preventing extraordinary people from transforming their vision and capacity into action because they were afraid of being punished. His problem, he realized, was the opposite. He couldn't help trying to change things. He felt compelled. Like the people Jusuf talked about who had eyes to see devils, Richard was also gifted with the curse of sight.

CHAPTER 9

WHEN TOR GOT HOME from school, Ann was in the hammock and Aminata was sitting on a chair next to her reading a book out loud.

"Mommy, do you want to play checkers with me?" he said. He wished Aminata would go away so he could have some time alone with his mother.

"I can play!" Aminata said.

"I'm talking to my mother," Tor said. Ann moaned and said something about her head, and Tor, who was used to such disappointments, simply gave her a kiss, got on the bike and went to the junction.

When he passed Kelfala's house on the way, Kelfala's mother and sisters were outside cooking. Tor stopped. "Is Kelfala here?" he asked.

"Wetin?" the woman said, not stopping her work.

"Kelfala dae na os?"

"Hey, my friend." Kelfala came out of the pink concrete house, followed by his uncle. "Welcome."

"*Oporto,* borrow me you bike for go na junction," the uncle said. Normally Tor would have told the uncle to fuck off, but he got the feeling that he should be careful. "Ten minutes only," the uncle said, and he seemed sober, so Tor got off and gave him the bike, looking directly at him to show that he wasn't afraid.

"Why don't you ever go to school any more, man?" Tor asked when the uncle was gone.

"I am working for my uncle," Kelfala said.

"Why the hell would you work for him?"

"He is my uncle."

"That's bullshit," Tor said. He couldn't believe he had handed over the bike. Richard was going to kill him.

"Una it don ready," one of the girls called.

"Come," Kelfala said.

"I'm not hungry," Tor said, but he still washed his hands and sat down with Kelfala's family.

"You no dae lek rehs?" Kelfala's mother said. She put a ball of rice and sauce into her mouth dramatically, to show Tor how good it was.

"No, tenki," Tor said.

"A lek rehs tomohs!" she said, and she and the girls laughed.

"My uncle he say he can get television, and if you can pay for VCR, he will bring it."

"Yeah, right," Tor said. "Really?"

"Yes."

"How much is it?"

"I don't know. Unless you ask him."

The uncle didn't come back for over an hour, and when he finally did return, Tor was so relieved he couldn't even be angry. He took the bike and went to the junction without a word to the uncle or Kelfala.

At the junction, he bought sweetened condensed milk and a packet of cookies, which were soft and stale. When he was on his way back home, Kelfala's uncle stopped him on the road near Kelfala's house.

"Give me again the bike," he said.

Kelfala came outside. "Don't give it to him," he said. "He wants to take it to Cameroon." The uncle picked up a stick, chased Kelfala to the front door and hit him on the head, then went back inside. Kelfala was crying, so Tor doubled him back to the Foundation

House. When they got there, they found Ann still on the top balcony with Aminata. Ann asked Tor to get her some juice and to keep the noise down, because of her headache. He leaned over the hammock, kissed her on the lips, and led Kelfala outside to the dockhouse.

He had been keeping an eye on the dockhouse ever since it became Richard's hangout. He snooped around in there when Richard was out, hoping to find something incriminating so that he could finally be free of that jerk forever. If he did find something — a letter from another woman, for example — he wouldn't hesitate to show his mother this time.

He didn't entirely blame himself for not telling Ann right away when he found out about Richard's affair. It happened around the time they moved into the new house, just after Andrew's dad had invited Tor to go on a sailing trip to Grand Manan with him and Andrew in the summer. Tor had spent what even he knew was an unhealthy amount of time thinking about the trip, spinning such elaborate fantasies that he was bound to be disappointed, even if he did get to go. Still, he let himself enjoy his daydreams and decided that knowing they would never come true must be some mysterious part of growing up.

He was stealing money from Richard's briefcase more often than usual so he'd have plenty of spending money for the trip, and he thought of this as payment for having to live with Richard. The briefcase was full of cash, ten and twenty dollar bills mostly. Tor took small amounts each time, so Richard wouldn't notice. Some of it he saved, some of it he used it to buy pellets for his BB gun or music or hockey gear or to treat his friends to movies at the theatre, meals at the diner, and Golden Axe benders at the arcade.

Sometimes Richard left his key ring in the briefcase, so once when Tor was sure Richard wouldn't be coming home any time soon he had all of the keys copied at Jim's General, which was the only place he could go any more, since every other store in town had agreed to phone Richard if Tor tried to break large bills or rent R-rated movies. He wasn't sure what the keys opened or how he would use them when he found out, but having them was like having a secret entrance into Richard's world — now he just had to figure out where it led.

One afternoon, Tor went into Richard's study to take some money from the briefcase, and there among the bills he found a letter from Maria that gave everything away. At first, he was excited, and he sat at the kitchen table for hours waiting for his mother to come home so he could show it to her. But Richard came home first, and for once he acted like a normal person and even asked Tor if he wanted to order pizza and rent a movie, because Ann wouldn't be back until late. The movie was boring and they only got one large pizza and no pop or candy, but Tor could see that Richard was trying to be nice, which was confusing.

He lay awake in bed until 2 a.m. waiting for his mother to come home, and when she did she let him have a drink in a fancy glass in the hot tub with her, and it was so nice that he didn't want to ruin it, so he decided to wait until the next day to tell her. But the next day she took down the wall with the hammer, and he thought it might not be the best timing, and after that things got worse and worse, and he hated himself for participating in his father's lie, but he had no choice.

When they got back from staying at the McCann's cottage, Tor tried to find ways to punish Maria. He peed on the bathroom floor so she would have to clean it up. He put insects in her purse. Once he wiped his butt with her sweater. When Ann finally found out about the affair on her own, Tor regretted not saying something sooner, because somehow Richard managed to spin it so that Ann had to feel sorry for him. He pretended to be so nice and great all of a sudden. Tor thought Ann would see right through it, but it worked. Richard won. He won so much that Ann once told Tor she couldn't wait until he left home so she and Richard could have a peaceful life. He won so much that they all had to go to Africa so they could save their marriage, and they had to tell him about this stupid plan on his birthday, destroying what was supposed to be the second-best day of a kid's year even more than they usually did, because that was what happened when his parents worked together on something.

THE DOCKHOUSE STANK of pee and mould, and there was a pile of old jerry cans and garbage in the corner. Kelfala poked his head in the window and watched as Tor leafed through blank pages and boring business letters before finding a neat stack of papers on a bench next to the garbage can. After skimming through a few lines, Tor shoved all the pages into the waistband of his shorts. He also found a letter crumpled up in the garbage can, which he put in his back pocket to read later.

As the boys walked back to the house, Tor noticed some children picking through the garbage pit for tin and wire to make their toy cars.

"Get off our property!" Tor shouted. The kids ignored him. Kelfala spoke to them in Temne, but they didn't respond.

"Get out of this place or my father will beat you," Tor said. He ran to the kitchen hut and started to pull handfuls of straw out of the roof. Kelfala helped him to collect the straw and throw it into the garbage pit. The kids stayed in the pit while Tor got a box of matches and found the can of kerosene that Jusuf used for the lamps. When he started to pour the kerosene on the straw in the pit, the kids scrambled out, trying to hold on to the cans they'd collected, but abandoning them when Tor lit a match. The kids watched from behind the kitchen hut as Tor threw the burning match onto the straw, and he and Kelfala laughed and danced around the garbage while it burned. When the fire went out, the boys used machetes to hack at dead cashew trees in the field shouting, "Death to all dead trees!"

Back in Nova Scotia, Ann and Julia McCann had brought Tor and the McCann girls to the riverbank one night to beat up trees with bats made of tightly rolled-up newspapers. Tor enjoyed this because Danya McCann was wearing a low-cut top, and every time she hit a tree her boobs jiggled. But the evening only became truly memorable when Julia started crying and screaming, "Fuck you, Tony!" as she beat a tree with her pathetic newspaper bat.

The McCann girls sat on a tree trunk looking embarrassed, but Tor joined Julia, screaming, "Fuck you, Tony" along with her and smashing his own bat against her tree. He had never liked her better, and although she never mentioned it again, he felt that she had appreciated his support, and that maybe in some small way it made up for what happened to her cottage when he was staying there.

After they had hacked at the trees for a while, Tor and Kelfala searched behind the house for wasps' nests. When they didn't find any, they sat on the back steps to smoke. Tor was lighting Kelfala's cigarette for him when he saw a flash of Billy's fur and heard a squealing noise as Billy pounced on something at the base of the pile of garbage by the latrine. The dog shook his head with his face tilted upwards to keep his cone from dragging on the ground. There was a rat in his mouth. Tor stood and shrieked, "Yeah!" Billy lowered his head and dropped the rat for a second, but it was still moving, so he bit down into it a few times, picked it up and shook it again. When he dropped it the second time, it convulsed on its back and then lay still.

"Did you see that?" Tor said. "Oh my God, did you see that?" Kelfala was leaning back on the steps, smoking. Billy was sniffing around at the base of the pile, and Tor went over and tried to pet him. "Good *boy*, Billy," he said. The dog slunk away and moved some leaves with his nose, revealing a hole in the ground. Tor crouched down beside him. "This must be where they live!" he said. Billy had started to dig, but his cone stopped him. He was whining and breathing heavily, and it was so exciting, but Tor was also worried that Billy would get his wound full of dirt and garbage, and he didn't want to get blamed for Billy ruining his cone or the tube thing, so he was sort of relieved when Billy gave up and lay down, immediately transforming from a vicious rat killer back into the slow, miserable animal he usually was.

Tor ran upstairs to the top balcony. "Mommy, guess what Billy did!" he said.

"Where's my juice?" she moaned from her hammock. "I'm *dying* of thirst."

"Sorry mommy, I forgot. I'll get you some now."

"Aminata already checked. She couldn't find any." Aminata smiled at Tor, and he felt like punching her even though he was grateful that she was taking care of his mom.

"Let me go and look," Tor said. He had a Fanta under his bed, but when he came back with it, Ann said it was warm and she didn't want it and told him to give it to Aminata. "That's my last one, just so you know," he told Aminata.

"Thank you," she said.

Tor heard hooting noises and shouts of *oporto, oporto*. He looked over the balcony railing to see the crazy man wading out of the water with his oar, a group of kids trailing him. Tor walked around the balcony, tracking the man below. At first he seemed not to notice the people shouting at him, but when he got close to the cashew trees he bent down, picked up a stone and threw it at one of the kids. The stone hit the kid in the shoulder, and the kid shouted "Why!" as the man disappeared among the trees.

From that side of the balcony, Tor could see Billy nosing around the garbage pile again. He had left the rat alone once it was dead, so Tor hadn't bothered to take it away, but now he wondered if Billy might try to eat it, and if that would be bad for him. Andrew's dog, Maisie, ate rats, and Andrew told Tor that on the farm they attached one end of a length of hose to the exhaust on their four-wheeler and stuck the other end in rat holes to smoke them out so Maisie could catch them. Maybe Tor and Billy could do the same. It would be just as exciting as the firecracker idea, and it would also be easier and much more likely to work. He'd have to borrow a car though. Kelfala's uncle might be able to help with that, but Tor didn't really want to have anything to do with him.

Kelfala was still on the steps, smoking. Tor sat with him for a while and listened to him talk about his problems with his uncle, and afterward they went inside and drank smoky water, and Tor showed Kelfala the cover of *First Blood*.

"Yes," Kelfala said, pointing at Sylvester Stallone. "I remember this man."

"No you don't," Tor said.

"Yes, but I have see this film. This is fine film."

"Yeah, in America, right?"

Kelfala turned the movie on its side and read the label. "What is Video Plus?"

"It's the name of the store where I rented it." Tor had a bad habit of returning movies late or not at all, but he'd managed to get his accounts in Halifax cleared by calling the stores and telling them that Tor Berringer was his brother and he had died in a car accident. "Your phone calls are *killing* my mother!" he told them, and they apologized and sent him free rentals in the mail.

"Let me show you how to blind person," Kelfala said. He brought the middle and index fingers of his left hand toward Tor's face.

Tor pushed his hands away. "No, man. I told you, I don't like to fight." If Kelfala had been smaller than him, Tor would have taken great pleasure in pummelling him, but as it was, Tor didn't stand a chance.

"Will you like to hear a new song I have written?" Kelfala said.

Tor said no, but then he felt bad, so he let Kelfala sing him the song and said that it was cool, to be nice. Kelfala went for a swim before going home. Billy put his feet in the water and drank some, and Tor knew he should stop him because the water would get in his wound or ruin his cone, but he didn't want to bother him. He wished he could swim too. Sometimes he thought Richard had made up the thing about the worms in the water, because no one else ever seemed worried about getting sick or blind after swimming in there. But he couldn't risk being any more uncomfortable than he already was, so he sat on the bank, smoked a cigarette, burned the pages of his father's funding proposal and thought about how when he grew up he was going to marry Lisa Formier and live way up in the Yukon and have a snowmobile and a big house and a four-wheel drive truck and lots of dogs. He also thought about Grand Manan, and Andrew, and how messed up everything was, and how much he was missing out on.

CHAPTER 10

Dear Mr. Corbett,

*Thank you very much for your letters. My husband Dr. Berringer and
I are currently in Africa, doing humanitarian work in a small village
in Sierra Leone. We have arranged to have our mail forwarded to us
on a monthly basis, and the postal service is very slow here, so I only
received your letters recently, when I made a rare trip to the capital city
of Freetown. I'm afraid that the period in which you required a response
from us has elapsed, and I offer you my sincere apologies for this.*

*As you might imagine, it is extremely difficult for us to maintain any
kind of reliable contact with the outside world from the remote village
where we are living, so it would obviously be all but impossible for us to
fulfill the requirements of our audit. However, when we return to Canada,
we will be more than happy to supply all of the requested records.*

*I can assure you that everything is in order, as I am certain that you
yourself will be satisfied when we provide you with the records.*

Thank you for your understanding, and please do have a wonderful day.

Sincerely,
Dr. & Mrs. Richard and Ann Berringer

ANN DATED THE LETTER earlier than it was, to emphasize how long it took for mail to travel between Sierra Leone and Canada. She felt such a sense of accomplishment when she licked the envelope and put it in the pile to be mailed that when Maggie arrived with Aminata, Ann invited Maggie in for tea. Maggie moved toward the front door, but Ann asked her come around to the back entrance instead. "Why don't y'all use the front?" she said.

"I don't like the living room," Ann said.

"Why not?"

Ann hedged. She didn't want to set herself up to be branded a hypochondriac, but she didn't like to lie.

"I just don't like how it feels in there."

"You mind if I have a look?" Maggie said.

"Okay, but if you're planning to tell me it's all in my head, please don't bother."

Aminata made her way up to the top balcony while Ann went into the kitchen and Maggie checked out the living room. Jusuf was at a wedding, and Ann realized she should have thought more carefully before inviting Maggie in, because they didn't have any food. She searched through the cupboards, most of which were empty save for spiders and geckos that shot into the corners when she flung the doors open.

She heard Maggie shuffling around in the living room and felt more and more annoyed. When she'd first made the connection between her sudden health problems and the strange smell in the house in Nova Scotia, she'd brought various people in to investigate, and they'd all had the same condescending attitude, saying there were bound to be some funny smells in an old house, but it was nothing to worry about. She'd hired an expert to test for mould, but he said he couldn't find anything out of the ordinary. She had wanted to hit him and break his instruments, but instead she asked him to check again, and still he found nothing.

When she began her own investigations and started to suspect that the smell was coming from the built-in cupboards in the music room, she told Tor and Richard that the room was off limits, and Richard said she could do what she wanted, but he wasn't prepared to write off entire rooms. It didn't help that after she stopped going in that room she could smell the cupboards even more than before, so Richard felt he had proof that it had all been in her head. She would shake him awake in the middle of the night, panic-stricken, and tell him she could smell the cupboards. He would say he couldn't smell anything and tell her to go back to sleep, and she would despair, because if the smell wasn't coming from the cupboards, she had no idea where it was coming from.

Every time she smelled it, half of her brain told her that she would die if she didn't find and get rid of whatever it was, and the other half told her that she would die if she didn't stay as far away from it as possible. Since she could do neither, and since her husband wouldn't even consider the possibility that her problem was real — since he reminded her that this was what she had wanted and they had spent every last penny they had on it — she was trapped.

One day she was lying on the couch dwelling on her bitter certainty that there must be something Richard could do to help her, if only he cared enough, when she thought how peaceful it must be to die. Tor had skipped school and was sitting by her feet reading a book, and when she thought of how easily she had accepted her own death, she felt so, so guilty. Without her, he would be left alone with a parent who hated him, like she had been. How could she be so selfish?

"Get me a hammer," she said.

"What?" he said.

She sat up. "I need a hammer. I'm going to find out where it's coming from."

"Let's wait until dad gets home."

"No, get me a hammer now."

In the music room, Ann put her nose close to the wall and held her hands to the floral Laura Ashley wallpaper that she had driven all the way to Montreal to buy. Her sense of smell was already warped by her sensitivities, so she was mostly going by instinct. She moved up and down the wall, crouching and standing, taking a step to the left and crouching and standing again, covering the whole surface. When she got to the corner where the cupboards were, she leapt backward. Something about that spot radiated vile, dangerous energy, and even though she couldn't exactly smell it, she knew that this was it, whatever *it* was.

"The hammer!" she shrieked at Tor.

She used the back of the hammer to rip off the wainscoting and the front to smash through the wall. Her memory of what happened after that was hazy. She remembered crying and throwing up, and she remembered being on the porch and telling Tor she was going to stay there forever.

Tor called Tony McCann, who brought Ann to his house, offered her some nasal spray that he found in Julia's bedside cabinet, and told her about farmers on the prairies who were exposed to mould from grain elevators, and how the mould grew in their lungs and burst out through their chests.

He arranged for the wall to be investigated by another mould expert he knew of, and he suggested that the Berringers stay at his family's cottage until the problem was resolved. This ended up being very hard on the Berringers' relationship with the McCanns, especially Julia, who blamed Tor for every single thing that was out of place when they left, but at the time it was an absolute godsend for Ann.

In the end, the problem turned out to be black mould resulting from water damage which could have happened a century earlier, and since no one could give Ann a straight answer about whether tearing down the wall would spread spores all over the house, she opted to have the whole music room sealed off with plastic indefinitely. This meant accepting that they would always have to go through the kitchen to get from the downstairs landing to the conservatory, but suddenly the open layout Ann had so carefully designed didn't seem important any more.

A month later, she started to react to the mould again. By then

Richard had pulled down the plastic seal around the music room in an act of defiance that Ann hadn't protested against because she didn't have the resources to make a fuss about anything any more. Deep in the throes of her breakdown, she'd surrendered, deciding to let the mould have the house, where it had probably been thriving for generations before being moved to a river lot and tastefully wallpapered over by her.

She went upstairs and crawled under the covers, fully prepared to stay there until she died. When Richard got home, he was so disturbed by the state he found her in that he asked Don to come and look at her, and she was too weak to feel vindicated when Don told Richard she should have been prescribed antihistamines and a puffer at the first signs of an allergic reaction. Richard actually said sorry to her once Don was gone. He was saying sorry a lot in those days, after years of saying it exactly never, and she was amazed how little difference it made.

In the end, the puffer didn't make much difference either, and Richard obviously hadn't learned anything, because when they arrived in Sierra Leone and she almost immediately started to react to the Foundation House, he picked up right where he had left off. He told her it was in her head, and once again she was left to cry herself to sleep and have horrific nightmares about tenacious spores living in her lungs and erupting out of her chest and finally engulfing her whole body like the weeds that had probably taken over the gardens of her beloved home.

Ann pictured the place empty and covered in snow, the driveway unploughed, the hedges bare. Abandoned. What if her letter didn't work? What if this Corbett guy kept hounding her? She would have to try and explain herself to him, and like Richard, he would never understand. But they could always go to England. They always had that option. And that meant that no matter what happened, it would be okay, even if they had to sell the house for nothing to some person who had no idea what it was worth. What it had cost her.

HAVING SEARCHED THE whole kitchen, the only thing Ann could find to eat was a dusty packet of biscuits. She was about to give up when she remembered that she had a few Belgian chocolates from the Bergmans hidden in a drawer in her bedroom. She decided to offer them to Maggie and Aminata if Maggie didn't make fun of her about the living room.

"I can see why you don't like it in there," Maggie said when Ann got up to the top balcony. Ann breathed in as deeply as she could, and her nostrils burned. She exhaled and took another shallow breath in, trying to clear her sinuses, but it didn't work. *Great,* she thought, and she couldn't help resenting Aminata and especially Maggie for probably ruining her day by making her breathe that nasty cupboard air.

"Why," Ann said. She put the tray on the table and poured water into three glasses.

"Well, you know what those masks on the walls are?"

Ann shrugged. "Someone from the Foundation must have put them there."

"Those are devil masks."

"So?"

"You said you don't like to be in that room, and I'm saying I think that's why."

"So what's wrong with the masks?" Ann said, still not sure if Maggie was serious.

"People are always coming to Africa and buying stuff like that thinking it's some nice decoration, but it's not a decoration. It's very dark, and it's very, very dangerous."

"I don't believe in that," Ann said.

"What? Satan? Well, I can assure you that Satan exists, and not believing in him is exactly what he wants you to do."

"I don't believe that the devil is a real being," Ann said. "It's like a metaphor for the...shadow side of human beings, something that's...moving away from God instead of...towards God, which is another name for love."

"You can believe that if you want, darlin', but that's not what the Bible says and the Bible is the truth. God says there is a spirit realm and it is evident wherever we are, and we can be fearful of it, but with God you can have confidence in the midst of chaos, because God has the answer for everything. Like those Islamists saying if you don't pray five times a day you're going to go to hell and, I think it's Buddha, where the kamikazes were told that you will make it to the highest place in heaven if you put a bomb in your plane and you crash the plane into something. It's a lie. And all of those things are causing people to be robbed of the victory that Jesus paid the price for all of us to have. That's why I came here to tell people the good news. God is God, God is truth, God is real! If you believe in Him you don't have to live in these circumstances."

"Would you like a chocolate?" Ann took the heat-warped chocolates out of the pocket of her dress.

"I haven't had a real chocolate in years," Maggie said.

"These are Belgian, from Rita Bergman." Ann brushed some lint off one of them before giving it to Maggie.

"Here, sweetie," Ann said. She passed Aminata the other chocolate.

"Thank you, ma," Aminata said.

Maggie had her eyes closed, and she was moving her jaw in slow circles and making groaning noises. She looked at Ann and beamed. "God is so good," she said. She leaned forward. "Look, it's simple, sugar. There is a spirit world of darkness and there is a spirit world of light. Satan is the head of the spirit world of darkness and he has a *lot* of followers. He took a third of God's angels, and that's many million billion zillion. They are actively working in and through people to destroy lives, and the only way to combat that world of darkness is spiritual warfare. You can't pretend it's not there. You have to face it and destroy it."

"So you're saying that the masks carried evil spirits into our house?"

"You've been sick for a while now, right?" Maggie said.

"I'm allergic to mould."

"When did you first get sick?"

"It's been going on for a long time. It started in Canada, and we found out it was because of mould in the walls, and now we're living with mould again. This place is so damp, it's awful. I can't breathe here."

Maggie made a sympathetic face, as if she knew exactly what Ann meant, and Ann began to cry. "It's so hard," she said, tears falling into her lap. "No one believes me, and it's hard not to feel totally alone. I feel like I'm being attacked when it happens, you know?" She didn't want to be crying in front of Maggie like that, but it was so unusual for someone to ask about her illness.

"Shhhh," Maggie said. She rubbed Ann's back tenderly, and Ann cried harder, because it was so long since anyone but Tor had done that. "Hey, oh sweetie, there's no need to cry, because Jesus has the answer. He says, 'For I know the plans I have for you, plans to prosper you and not to harm you, plans to give you hope and a future.'"

Ann wished she could believe that it was so simple. Imagine, she thought, believing the world was like that. Every bad thing that happened was the devil and every good thing was God and all you had to do was be on God's team and you would be safe. If you believed that, you would never have to feel forsaken. You would never have to feel alone.

"Shoot, I have to go," Maggie said. "I'll be back in a few hours." Ann wished Maggie would stay and talk to her more, or at least rub her back again, but Maggie was already on her way down the stairs.

Ann asked Aminata to fetch the big blue *A Course in Miracles* book.

"Where is it, ma?" Aminata said.

"I think I left it on the front steps," Ann said.

It was hard for Aminata to navigate the stairs, especially going down, but Ann felt that it was important not to treat her like she was made of glass. This meant waiting around for her to do things, though, and Ann was almost ready to give up and get the book herself when she finally heard Aminata's crutches on the stairs.

She had Aminata read the instructions for the first exercise, and they tried it a few times, but Aminata was incapable of coming up with any sentences of her own. "Now *you* say something," Ann said, and Aminata repeated what Ann had already said. "No, think of your *own* thing," Ann said, and Aminata shrugged and looked like she was going to cry. Ann realized she was probably wasting her time, and somehow hearing the girl parrot her sentences — *This book doesn't mean anything. This table doesn't mean anything. Those crutches don't mean anything* — made the exercise feel even more pointless than it had when she'd done it on her own.

"Mom, what you weared when you marrying Dr. Berringer?" Aminata asked. Ann wasn't sure about Aminata calling her mom, but it seemed cruel to ask her to stop.

"I have to do the ironing, sweetie," Ann said. "I'll bring everything we need up here, and you can heat up the iron while I go and get the washing, okay?"

Jusuf insisted on ironing everything they owned because he said it was the only way to destroy the insect eggs that would otherwise hatch in their beds and on their bodies. He'd hung up the clothes before he left that morning, but he'd still have to make supper when he got back, so Ann needed Aminata to help her get started on the ironing, because she had no idea how to use the charcoal iron herself.

"You weared white clothes when you marrying Dr. Berringer?" Aminata said when Ann came upstairs with the clean laundry. Ann considered telling her about the dress she wore for her first marriage, to John, but Tor still didn't know she'd been married before, and who knew what Aminata might blurt out.

"When I *married* Richard, I wore a cream silk dress with a round neck and pintucks down the front."

Aminata closed her eyes, and Ann thought she must be imagining what Ann had looked like in her dress.

"And I had lily of the valley in my hair," Ann said. She sat next to Aminata.

"What is it?" Aminata said, opening her eyes.

"It's a tiny white flower."

"And Dr. Berringer? What he wore?" Aminata stirred the coals in the iron. Ann frowned. She couldn't remember what he had worn to their wedding. Something plain. A brown suit, probably. Or no, it had been a black suit with a thin tie. Or was it a brown suit? It must have been John who wore the black suit. That was just like him, trying to be a beatnik.

Ann had cried all morning on the day of her wedding to Richard. After divorcing John, she had promised herself that her next wedding would be what she had dreamed of as a child, but somehow she found herself, yet again, settling for less. She had never met anyone so principled and idealistic as Richard, and she fell in love with that, but the truth, which she didn't admit to herself until the morning of their wedding, was that she didn't know him at all. She was terrified that she was doing something crazy and wrong, but then his mother, who had come over from England, showed her some photographs of him as a little boy, and Ann couldn't help but love him after seeing him like that.

When Richard was too awful to bear, Ann thought of the picture his mother had shown her of him as a child trying to run away on his neighbour's tricycle because he'd seen his mother's list of his punishable offences for the day and didn't want to be there when his father got home. Ann did this with Tor, as well, when she felt like he was too impossible, reminding herself that despite his tough exterior, he was still her little boy. They were both the same, Tor and Richard, if only they could see it. They made the same plaintive noises in their sleep, as if they were finally communicating across the chasm of misunderstanding that separated them in their waking lives, and Ann wished that she could make them see how alike they were, so that they could forgive and help each other instead of fighting.

She had a theory that people were like wind-up toys that got four windings. The first was when you were born, which was why the first months and even minutes of your life were so incredibly fragile. The second was in your adolescence, and generally determined the kind of person you became and the direction you took. The third, which usually happened in your late twenties, was the sudden solidification of everything in yourself and your life that had once seemed temporary and fluid. And the fourth, which happened sometime in your early forties, either confirmed everything you had been doing until then or, more likely, blew you apart entirely and left you to spend the rest of your life trying to put the pieces back together. That was why those pivotal moments were so perilous. Everything was so tightly wound that if something went wrong the whole rest of your life could go spinning off on some awful trajectory. The problem in their family, she had come to understand, was that they were all being wound up at the same time, so anything could happen.

WHEN SHE'D RECEIVED a letter from an anonymous hospital employee saying that Richard was having an affair with Maria, the reason Ann didn't believe it was not, as she would later claim, because she thought he was too honourable to do such a thing, but because Maria was a bedraggled ratbag with a houseful of kids that smelled like piss.

"Do you think it might be true?" Tony said when she called him.

"Of course it's not true," she said. "It's Don. He's trying to destroy Richard."

When Tony came over two weeks later and said that Maria had confessed to Julia about the affair, Ann still didn't believe it.

After Tony left, Ann called Maria and asked if she could come and talk to her. She found it odd when Maria didn't ask why, and she realized that part of her wanted it to be true, because it would explain so much.

When she arrived at Maria's house, Maria had set out a bottle of rum, a bottle of Diet Coke and two plastic cups on the table.

"Where are the children?" Ann asked.

Maria said they were in bed, but Ann could hear them fighting upstairs.

"Tony says you're having an affair with Richard. Is that true?" Ann hadn't planned to say it so directly. She had wanted to give both of them a way out, if that was possible.

"Yes," Maria said. She poured Ann a rum and Diet Coke, and Ann sipped it while she listened to Maria talk about how it had started, how she hadn't meant for it to happen, how much she loved Richard.

"Did he tell you he loved you?" Ann asked.

"He told me I was special. I'd say, 'Do you love me?' and he'd say, 'You're special.'"

Yeah, Ann thought. *Like mentally handicapped.*

"I told him I felt sorry for him because you were so mean and crazy, but...do you remember when you helped me do Jenna's room?"

Ann nodded. She'd hated to imagine a new person starting out life in one of the dark, depressing rooms of Maria's house, so she'd spent a weekend helping Maria to prepare a nursery — scrubbing every surface, painting the walls yellow, sewing new blinds.

"I felt so bad, because I saw you were a good person, and I felt so bad about what I was doing, but I couldn't stop. I was in love with him. You know, he told me he liked it that I was pregnant." Here Maria stopped to cry, and Ann thought it would make sense to join her, because nothing could have hurt her more than what Maria had said, but instead she put a hand on Maria's shoulder. She felt sorry for Maria, and she didn't know what was wrong with her to make her feel that way. She also felt a bit drunk, because she'd already finished two strong rum and Cokes.

She should have left, but she realized that too late. Maria was telling her things she should never have heard and could never forget. Ann could see even then that this was Maria's way of punishing Richard for not loving her. By poisoning Ann with every detail, Maria could make Ann punish Richard for her. But the part of Ann that was drunk and the part of her that felt sorry for Maria and the part of her that wanted to cauterize any love for her husband that might survive this experience made her stay and hear about how Richard loved Maria's children and how he bought presents for them and bought Maria oils to rub on her pregnant belly.

As Maria spoke, Ann felt the place that Richard had inhabited in her heart collapsing. Her dreams, her man, they were vanishing, and in their place she erected a cheap hotel where a stranger rubbed oil on this woman's pregnant belly while she, Ann, stood alone in the cold and wept.

By the time she left Maria's house, it was 4 a.m. Driving home drunk and numb she remembered when John took her to see *Gone With the Wind* in London and she'd decided she would prefer to die right there in the theatre than to return to the dreary disappointments of real life. She had wanted so much to be in Dixieland with Scarlett O'Hara — to *be* Scarlett O'Hara — but as Vivien Leigh was shouting to the sunset, the lights came up for intermission and Ann was jarred out of the sublime pain that the movie was inflicting on her. "Do you want an ice cream?" John asked. When he saw that her hands were over her ears and her eyes were shut, he tried to pry her fingers back so that he could shout into her ear again about the ice cream, and she felt utterly hopeless about how pitiful she had allowed her life to become.

She and Richard had planned a weekend trip, and they were meant to be leaving in the morning. She found him sleeping, the reading light still on, a book splayed across his chest.

"I've been talking to Maria," she said. She sat next to him on the bed. He didn't wake up, so she held her hand in front of his face and moved it closer and closer until he opened his eyes and cowered away from her.

"What the hell are you doing?" he said.

"I said, I've been talking to Maria." He didn't react. "So that's nice. You're completely deceitful. Thanks." She cried for a long time and he pretended to go back to sleep, or maybe he was pretending he had never been awake. That was his way of coping — he went to sleep. Sometimes it made her so angry that she kicked him out of the bed onto the floor, but that morning she lay there in agony and did nothing.

"Mom," Aminata said. She was sitting next to Ann now, her arm on Ann's shoulder. "Mom. You don't have to cry, or me too I will cry."

Ann looked at the girl. *Poor thing,* she thought. *She's all alone. We're both so alone.* She allowed herself to sob while Aminata stroked her back and the charcoal burned away in the iron.

CHAPTER 11

RICHARD OPENED HIS EYES to see his wife's feet in his face. She was lying the wrong way in the bed, panting and moaning in her sleep.

"Wake up," he said. Her face was twitching and her hands, which she held in fists near her nose, made spastic movements, as if she was fighting some tiny creature. He shook her leg. "Ann, wake up." She took a long, shuddering breath as she came out of sleep and sat straight up in the bed, looking at him with confused contempt, as if he were the one sleeping the wrong way around.

"I had the most horrible dream," she said. He took this as his cue to get up. He hated hearing about her dreams. "It was about George," she said. Richard went to the bathroom and poured water over his toothbrush.

"George?"

"He was holding me by the throat, telling me to be quiet. He told me he would kill me if I didn't shut up."

"George who?" he said.

"You know, that thing you got in India."

Richard couldn't help laughing. As a student, he had gone to India for a holiday with Joan, and while he was there he bought a human skeleton in a marketplace to help him with anatomy. He named it George and kept it in the sitting room of their flat in London dressed in a top hat and boa, but after he married Ann, she made him keep it in his study.

"Ah, so George finally has his say," he said.

"Don't laugh at me," she said. "Ugh, this thing reeks!"

Richard peeked out at her from the bathroom. She was lying down again, the side of her face on the bare mattress where the sheet had peeled back in the night. "He wasn't a skeleton in my dream, he was this skinny Indian man wearing one of those diaper things like Ghandi."

"You're serious?"

"Leave me alone," she said, and she turned to face the other way.

IN THE DOCKHOUSE, Richard found a dead rat in his water trap and the wastepaper basket under his desk knocked over. He looked through the crumpled pages to see if anything was missing. There were some aborted funding proposals. A letter to the Foundation that had struck too critical and negative a tone. Some pages from the proposal that had gone missing a few days earlier.

When he'd discovered that the proposal was gone, his first reaction had been to blame the rats, but it was highly unlikely that they would have taken thirty pages at once. His next thought was Tor, and although destroying a proposal to help the poor seemed too diabolical even for his son, after what Tor had done to his offices in Nova Scotia, Richard knew he was capable of anything.

He'd shouted at Ann, who was actually the one person he didn't think was responsible, and afterward he'd felt oddly relieved, because he wasn't so sure the partnership with the herbalist was going to be worth the conflict it would cause between him and Sandi, and if the proposal was gone, maybe it was for the best.

He locked the dockhouse on his way out, although it was pointless because of the broken window. He waited on the steps of the house for a while, and when the truck didn't come, he picked up the dog and started to walk. He had begun to take Billy to work every day in order to keep his wound clean and give him milk and water regularly. Billy was too lethargic to enjoy being outside anyway, so Richard didn't feel guilty about keeping him closed up in a supply closet at the hospital, where he was at least safe and cool.

During Richard's morning clinic, a couple brought in their son, who had been bitten by a snake. The child had already been treated by a witch doctor, and he was in very bad shape. Martha told Richard that people were saying the witch girl he'd heard the nurses gossiping about had transformed into a snake and bitten the child in his sleep. When the boy died, Martha stayed with the mother while Musa and Richard tried to convince the father that there was nothing supernatural involved in his son's death.

Richard had taken to asking for Musa as a translator when he had to have difficult conversations with patients who didn't speak English. Musa seemed to have a gift for consoling people and smoothing over tense situations, and Richard appreciated his gentle, unassuming manner, although sometimes he thought that the job must be a kind of torture for someone so sensitive. Musa had to deal with the same things Richard did, but unlike Richard, he had no power to influence the outcomes. He was just the messenger.

Sometimes Musa's translations seemed significantly longer than what Richard had said. "It's important not to embellish, Musa," Richard said when he first noticed this. "People need to know exactly what I'm telling them."

"In Africa you can't tell someone they are going to die like that," Musa said. "You might as well kill them yourself. You can't know if they will die. Only God knows."

"So what do you tell them?" Richard said.

"If I am telling them something very difficult, I have to know them first, and I have to ask them questions, to prepare them. In other situations I make jokes. It gives people confidence in us."

"It can't be easy, Musa. You do a fine job."

"When I go home, sometimes I can't sleep," Musa said. "Deep

down within myself I am crying. But I wiped it out of my mind the next day. I said this is my job. I have to do my job."

"Well, keep up the good work," Richard said. He patted Musa on the back. "You never know where it will lead."

Musa smiled. "God is taking me somewhere. He is preparing me for my future. That is my idea. And because of this job I have so much compassion in my heart for humanity, so maybe that is why God is allowing me to go through these things."

WHILE RICHARD WAS doing his rounds, he had a visit from a former patient, who gave him a package wrapped in white plastic. Inside was a traditional men's suit of tapered trousers, a long tunic and a small round hat made of the same waxy green tie-dyed fabric as the rest of the outfit. People often brought him fruits and vegetables and sometimes even chickens, which was fine, but he resented being given more extravagant gifts. He found it difficult to deal with emotions anyway, but being forced to express false gratitude for things he didn't want while at the same time feeling beholden to someone and also genuinely touched was a real challenge for him.

"Bohku, bohku tenki," he said, holding the suit up to admire it. "Dis na very fine." He touched the elaborate white embroidery around the neck.

The man wanted Richard to try the suit on right away to see if it fit or if he should take it back to his tailor, and Richard felt he couldn't say no. He went into his office to change, and he had just come out wearing the suit when Martha appeared in the hall.

"Eeh fine and fit you oh!" the man said.

Martha was wearing her street clothes — a pink and orange skirt and a pink top that showed off her collar bone and shoulders. Her hair was tied back with a scarf. "Excuse me, Doctor Berringer. I've spoken with that traditional healer, and he's agreed to meet with us," she said.

Although he'd more or less decided not to bother with the partnership, he didn't want to say no to Martha after she'd gone to the

164

trouble to arrange the meeting. He also didn't want to miss an opportunity to be alone with her away from the hospital. "When?" he said.

"For example now," Martha said. "Can you?"

Just then, Sandi showed up, and he smiled when he saw Richard's outfit. "Where are you off to?" he said.

Richard hesitated. "Martha and I are going to meet the herbalist," he said.

"You know he's going to want money, right?" Sandi said.

"I know you aren't keen...." Richard wished he wasn't wearing the suit for this conversation. He took off the hat.

"I can't force you to listen to me," Sandi said. "But you shouldn't be taking the nurses away from their work."

"This is part of her work," Richard said. Martha took a step forward so that she was standing next to Richard, and Sandi gave them both a stiff smile and walked away.

Martha waited for Richard by his office door while he changed into his own clothes. As they walked to the herbalist's house, Richard imagined what it would be like to be married to someone like her. Having children with her would be very different than having children with Ann. It might even be enjoyable.

She stopped outside a cream cinder-block house surrounded by trees. In front of the house, a handsome, white-haired old man was sitting on a bench in the shade next to a middle-aged man and a teenaged boy. Nearby, a woman stirred a pot over an open fire.

The old man stood and greeted Richard and Martha warmly. "Is this him?" Richard said as he shook the man's hand. Martha nodded, and Richard noticed that she seemed timid in the herbalist's presence.

Richard asked the herbalist questions about his practice, and Martha translated. The man claimed to have over a hundred patients a week, and Richard began to feel excited about the partnership again, imagining all those people who could be coming to the hospital instead of wasting their money on herbs.

"And how does he diagnose his patients?" Richard asked, directing the question to Martha but looking at the herbalist.

"He says he has demons who work with him to help him with that," Martha said.

"Demons?" Richard said.

"He says he prays and calls the demons to him in a special ceremony. If necessary he ties the patient to a stick first. He says the demons come to him in the form of humans. Black men and white men. And they have their leaders."

"I don't get it. Are the demons good, or are they what he's trying to get rid of?"

"He says the demons in his patients are bad demons. They think that God loves humans more than them, so that's why they throw a disease at you or open your eyes so you can see them. But good demons like his will help people to see what is wrong and how to heal it."

"Okay," Richard said. "So the demons tell him which herbs to give his patients?"

"Yes," Martha said. "They show him where to find the herbs. But it's not always herbs he uses. Sometimes he uses other kinds of treatments, depending on what they tell him."

"For example?"

"For example sacrificing a sheep or a goat. He says that if an illness is very bad then it can take months to cure and it needs different kinds of treatments, but some can be cured in a day."

"Right," Richard said. "And so, what, these demons are just with him all the time?"

"Sometimes they come when they feel like coming and sometimes he asks them," Martha said. "Sometimes he's afraid of them, but he never regrets seeing them because they help him to get his daily bread."

"And ask him what he thinks about what I do as a doctor," Richard said.

"He says there are some ailments where you can do better than him, but anything with demons he is better for that. So any kind of mental illness, also epilepsy, that's definitely demons. He says witches can cause something like swelling of the stomach, because the witches give food in the dreams. Anemia is also caused by witches, because they are sucking your blood. So he says anything like that he can do it better than you because he's definitely giving people something that can cure them."

"Okay, can he give me an example of how he would treat something specific? Epilepsy, for instance."

The herbalist turned serious when Martha asked him this. "He says he could teach you many things," Martha said. "He says he has been doing this for over thirty years, so you would be getting a great benefit if he teaches you about his practices."

"Tell him I would like to teach him about our practices at the hospital, too."

"I think he means to say that you should pay him if you want to learn more about what he does," Martha said.

"I know."

Two little children, a boy and a girl, came out from behind the house. When the girl saw Richard, she screamed and turned back. Her brother, saying something about *oporto* and laughing, picked her up and carried her toward Richard as she cried and tried to get away.

Richard was used to this sort of thing, and he knew how to play along, but sometimes it still stung to be reminded that he would always be an alien in Sierra Leone. He knelt and smiled at the child, but when her brother tried to force her hand toward Richard, she reacted as if Richard's skin was an open flame and her brother had gone mad and was trying to burn her. She screamed and fought until she was released and ran to the woman behind the fire. As a joke, Richard made a scary face at the little boy, but he took it the wrong way and also ran off in fright.

Martha and the herbalist were laughing as Richard stood and brushed off the knees of his trousers. "Are there any patients here that I can meet?" he said.

Martha asked the herbalist, and when he answered she turned to the teenaged boy sitting on the bench next to him. "For example this boy," she said. "He doesn't speak, but the man is his father, so we can talk to him."

Richard and Martha moved closer to the man, and Richard knelt down. "Can you tell me about your son?" he said.

"He says that the boy's problem started when he was eight years old," Martha said. "He went to school. He can read and write. He is a very clever boy. But one day he suddenly started speaking complete nonsense. He was seeing people in the air coming after him, telling him to do things and wanting to kill him. At some point he stopped speaking, and later he became violent. They were afraid of him and they had to chain him. They have been here for two months having treatment and now the boy is much better. They are very pleased. He doesn't make palaver. He can wash himself and go to the toilet by himself. He sleeps at night. Maybe next year he will be back in school."

Richard suddenly felt incredibly tired and not at all interested. He thanked the man and shook his hand, shook hands with the herbalist, and said goodbye. When he started to walk back in the direction of the path they had taken to get there, Martha stopped him.

"Let's go this way," she said. She pointed toward the road.

"Why?"

"Now the snakes are warming themselves in the sun."

Richard rolled his eyes. "They weren't doing that ten minutes ago?"

Martha walked toward the road, and Richard was about to continue on his own, but after looking at the grass waving over the thin dirt path, he turned and followed her.

Now that he'd met with the herbalist and heard about his demons, Richard no longer had any hope that the man could offer the hospital anything useful apart from patient referrals. Although that was all

Richard actually wanted from him, it didn't sound like he was going to do it for free, and to pay for it felt wrong. In any case, Richard simply couldn't afford to keep shelling out cash. It would probably be useless to tell the herbalist this, since the herbalist would never believe that Richard didn't have money to throw away, being both an *oporto* and a doctor. What Richard would have liked to say — what he had explained to more than one of the nurses in moments of desperation — was that he was actually poorer than any of them. At least they owned whatever they had in their pockets, but thanks to Ann's never-ending renovations, he was deeply in the hole, probably deeper than he even knew, and he didn't dare to think how long it would take him to get out.

The spring before they moved into the new house had marked the beginning of their financial problems, or at least the beginning of Richard's awareness of them. He'd come home for lunch and walked straight into an ambush. The living room was strewn with paper clips and highlighters and hundreds of slips of paper among the half-packed boxes, and Ann looked like a mad genius sitting in the middle of it all with the oversized antiques looming above her. When she saw him, she picked up a piece of paper and shook it in his direction.

"What is this?" she said.

Richard froze under the doorframe.

"We are not paying this, Dick. We *can't* pay this. We barely have enough to pay our taxes."

He looked at the paper and tried to hide his own shock. "But I make far more than I was making last year," he said.

"You have no idea, do you? And I can't even tell you because I don't want to burden you, so I have to deal with it all myself. I've had to run two households, I have to pay builders, I have to buy materials," she was counting on her hands, but everything she counted got two fingers. "I have to pay contractors, I have to be at the new house all day long running things, trying to move us in while it's still being renovated, and I have no one to help me when things go wrong."

Richard was holding his hands to his temples. "I don't want to know about it. Please, please, please. I can't take this on as well."

"I have never asked for your help, but you won't even listen to me."

"I am working every day for you, and all you have to do is decorate a house. It's not exactly the most onerous task in the world, Ann."

"Decorating?" she said. "How can you be so mean?"

"So what, you want me to help you with the house on top of everything? What do you want me to do?"

He started to put his coat back on and the waterworks began. How could anyone cry so much? "I can't do this all on my own," she wailed.

"There's nothing I can do about it," he said. "This is what we agreed to. The contract is only for one year. There are only a few months left."

"This is what *you* agreed to. I was never asked."

This had been a theme in their relationship since the beginning. They would have an intelligent, adult discussion, reach a decision together, and as soon as some part of it didn't work out, she would say she had never agreed to it in the first place.

They had both agreed to stay in Nova Scotia, although she seemed to have forgotten that. They'd spent several years in rural Cape Breton, which Richard loved, but Ann complained that the place was too remote and the school wasn't good enough for Tor. Richard started to look for a different job, and when Don contacted him, it sounded ideal. Don ran an established clinic in a town two hours from Halifax that was known for the quality of its schools, and he said he was planning to retire in a year or two, at which point Richard could take over.

When they went for a tour of the town, Ann was charmed by Tony McCann, the hospital administrator, who fawned over her openly in front of his wife. Later, Richard arranged to do a locum so Ann would have a chance to try the place out before they made a commitment. Don and everyone else treated her like royalty, she found the house she wanted to buy, and she seemed perfectly happy with the idea of living there, but as soon as they moved in, she started to find problems. Soon everything was wrong, and it was all Richard's fault. This was also becoming a theme.

He couldn't believe he'd got himself wedged between those two — a hysteric and a con man. As soon as the house was bought and the renovations begun, Don announced he wasn't going to retire so soon after all, and so began his program of exploiting Richard, this bill being only the latest example. Richard hadn't wanted to be Don's partner, but after years of Don putting off retirement and Ann spending every penny Richard made, when Don offered Richard a guaranteed higher salary and the promise of a gradual shift in ownership, it had seemed like the only option, and Ann had agreed.

"I don't know what to tell you, Ann," Richard said. "I have never tried to limit you, even though I know you have been grossly overspending on the house and it's taken ten times as long as anyone could have possibly imagined, but you knew there was a bill coming for the expenses. How could you not plan ahead for that?"

"Yes, expenses, like paper and insurance, not half the property taxes for their building. Not rent for your parking space! I would never have agreed to that. We've already been paying their ridiculously inflated rent because they own the building. Don't you see that? They can charge whatever they want." She was shaking the bill at him again.

"Okay, great, so I'm a total moron. I blindly trusted Don, who is, of course, a criminal. Actually I think we should call the police. Yes, I think the police would love to know about this. Or maybe we can put this down to us being a bit naïve about how much it costs to run a practice. Don put his own income on the line for me by guaranteeing my salary this year. In three months, I will renegotiate my contract so that I'm fee-for-service, and we can renegotiate the expenses then, too. We just have to curtail our spending until then."

Ann looked miserable, but all the wildness was gone. "Why the hell didn't you ask to look at the books, to find out what the expenses were?"

"I just never imagined it could be so much." The truth, although Richard hated admitting it to himself and would never admit it to Ann, was that he was pretty sure Don had intentionally glossed over the details of the expenses, and he saw now that it would have been wise to include Ann in his negotiations, but at the time he couldn't stomach having her and Don haggling over his work, his time, his *life*, as though like he was a piece of property they were fighting over.

"We shouldn't have to pay it this year," she said. "We can't." He considered telling her about the cash Pat gave him for his insurance medicals, which he'd been saving in a briefcase in his study. But with the amount of money that he made, he was certain she must be exaggerating their lack of funds, and since she never brought it up again after he went ahead and paid the bill on his own, he assumed that his hunch had been correct — she had been trying to prove a point, and she didn't care if it made Richard's relationship with Don even more difficult than it already was.

There had been so many times in his life when Richard had looked around and thought, *what the hell am I doing here?* It all seemed so embarrassingly random. Coincidences, happenstance — these things had given his life its whole shape. Wearing black to a party had been all it took for him to find himself married to a woman he was afraid of and living a life he would never have chosen. Being so small in elementary school that he'd had to say he wanted to be a doctor to impress people had determined his vocation. Reading silly books about explorers in Africa had inspired the outdated notions of heroism and derring-do that had shaped the direction of his career. In university, he had looked out the windows of the science labs and seen the students demonstrating against the war in Vietnam, and he thought how boring and predictable they were. He was going to have a great life, which meant great works and great adventures, and it seemed obvious to him that this ambition could only be satisfied in Africa, the original theatre of life and death.

When Richard told the scrawny young African who sat next to him in one of his classes that he planned to spend his career serving the poor in Africa, he'd actually expected Sandi to be impressed. "If you're into poverty, man, come to Sierra Leone," Sandi said, and that offhand remark was all it took.

When he told Joan that he and Sandi were going to team up to start a hospital in Sierra Leone after they finished school, she immediately started involving herself, looking into sources of funding and writing to friends who might be able to help. It had disturbed Richard to have her making such claims on his future, because he had never given her any reason to believe their relationship was permanent. It was just another one of those things that had happened to him. One of his flatmates moved out, and they needed to get a replacement in a hurry. None of them wanted a woman, because they didn't want dripping underwear hanging in the bathroom or the complication of an in-house relationship. But when Joan showed up — a frumpy Canadian, ten years older than the eldest of them — it had seemed like a safe bet.

Things were fine at first. She kept the house clean and cooked most of the meals and even did Richard's laundry. But then he made the mistake of sleeping with her, and after that he kept things going out of convenience and misplaced kindness. This was his pattern with women. The moment he began to feel something beyond friendly attraction for a girl, she would start to expect things of him, and a paralyzing sense of duty would crush anything that might have grown into what people called love. Duty was the antidote to love, he had learned. And it was that same sense of duty that made him string those girls along until they finally tired of his coldness and inconsistency and dumped him, usually in a harshly worded letter.

His correspondence with every woman he'd ever dated told the same story, with different details and different names signed under salutations that changed over time from things like *Sincerely* and *Yours* to *Love* and *All my love* to *Patiently waiting* and *(Hopefully) yours* to *Fuck you, pal,* etc. The *Fuck you* letters were typically followed by something along the lines of *I'm sorry, but it's so rotten of you not to answer me, Dick,* and forwarded, ostensibly as a way of ensuring their delivery, but obviously as a form of appeal as well, to Joan, who kept up correspondence with several of Richard's former girlfriends, even after he'd started sleeping with her.

One night, after a particularly difficult exam, he and Joan had smoked a joint together after having sex in the freezing backseat of her car, and she'd asked him what he thought he'd inherited from his parents. Usually he didn't like how philosophical she got when she smoked, but he was feeling relaxed, so he impulsively told her about how he'd had his first physical examination the winter before he started medical school, and when he was called back to the doctor's office, the doctor had showed him his chest x-ray and said, "What's wrong with this?" and he said, "Well, doctor, I haven't seen many chest x-rays before, but I think you've got it backwards," and the doctor said, "It's not the x-ray that's backwards. It's you."

He had situs inversus, a congenital condition that meant that some of his internal organs were on the wrong side.

Joan started to giggle, then laughed out loud. "Now I'll have something to tell those girls when they come crying to me," she said. "I'll say that your heart's *literally* in the wrong place!"

He laughed half-heartedly at her joke, but he didn't find it funny at all. He gently pushed her away, and they both sat up.

"This girl in my class says she thinks we choose our families before we're born," Joan said, taking the joint from between his fingers.

"What?" he said.

"Like we can see down to earth and choose."

Because he was high, Richard tried to imagine this. Little fetus him peering in the window of his parents' apartment above the bakery, sizing them up. There was his mother, young and unharried, sewing and tapping her foot to a song on the radio. There was his father reading a newspaper, with no one to keep in line apart from the pretty girl sitting across from him doing her best impression of mature domesticity, and all of this would have been infused with the smell of fresh bread rising from below. Imagining this scene, Richard could see how his fetal self might have made such a fatal mistake. How could he have known that once they got started they would go on having babies until there was nothing left of his mother that resembled that pretty almost-child he saw through the window above the bakery in his dope-addled brain?

He pictured his mother's latter self, such a cliché of joyless, self-sacrificing motherhood, and wondered how it would have been if he was the only child in that house, as he no doubt would have been if he'd had any say. What if he had smothered his younger brother in his crib, as he had allegedly tried to do more than once, and his parents' horror at their neglect (for they would see that this had caused the desperate act) would make them think twice about having more children, or at least more than seemed physically possible, let alone desirable for people with so few resources.

He felt angrier and angrier thinking of all those unnecessary, congenitally defective children in such a world of need, his poor mother washing nappies by hand in cold water while his father sat on his stool at the pub. Surely his mother hadn't chosen to marry that chinless, sadistic, belt-cracking old bastard. Or if she had chosen him, what were her other options? How could people choose their parents if they couldn't even choose who they married?

He looked at Joan's face, rubbed raw by his two-day beard. She probably imagined she had set in motion a train of thought that would lead to his disclosing some secret part of himself that no one else could access. He reached for her breast, but stopped when he saw a look of pity in her expression. He felt wetness around his nose and cheeks, and to his horror, he realized that he had been crying.

As quickly as his intoxication would allow, he got out of the car and went around to the front seat.

"Are you okay?" Joan asked from the back.

"It's these drugs," he said as he clumsily inserted the key into the ignition and started the engine.

"You were thinking about what I said, weren't you?"

It was appalling. He felt pathetic and exposed. But turning to Joan with a smile he hoped would convey cool indifference he said, "Nope."

CHAPTER 12

KELFALA SAID THAT HIS UNCLE had bought a good television, so if Tor would pay for a VCR they could watch movies.

"How can we watch them without electricity?" Tor asked.

"He say he can borrow a generator if you pay the fuel."

"So we would have to do it at your house?"

Kelfala shrugged.

Tor didn't want to deal with the uncle, but he did want to watch movies, so he stopped at Kelfala's house on the way home from school the next day. The uncle was sitting on the steps.

"*Oporto,*" he said. "Aw di bodi?" He held out his hand and Tor slapped it.

"Kelfala said you have a TV," Tor said.

"You want buy VCR?" the uncle said.

"Depends. How much does it cost?"

"One hundred thousand leones."

"What about in dollars?" Tor asked.

"American?"

"Canadian."

The uncle thought it over. "Two hundred dollars."

"For what?"

"For VCR."

"What kind?"

"Us one you want? Sony? RCA?"

"Sony," Tor said. "But I don't have two hundred dollars." He wanted to see if the uncle was trying to rip him off or not, and he also didn't want to spend that much money on a VCR, although he would if he was sure it would work.

"Okay," the uncle said. "I make you offer. I go pay half, ehn you go pay half. Den we go do business."

"What kind of business?" Tor asked.

"Na cinema, people go kam pay we, ehn we go share di money."

"Fifty fifty?"

"No oh, bikohs na me dae provide di os, di generator ehn di television ehn you nar only half di capital for VCR you provide."

"Yeah, but I'm going to be providing the movies, too."

"Ohmos film you get?"

"Two, but I can get more."

The uncle rubbed his eyes and yawned. "Film na easy for get. You go get ten per cent profit."

"Make it thirty and you have a deal."

"Twenty," the uncle said.

"Agreed," Tor said. They shook hands, and Tor promised to bring the cash the next day.

When Tor got home, Ann was giving Aminata math problems on the top balcony. He stood at the bottom of the stairs and listened.

"Good!" Ann said. "Brilliant girl. Would you like another one?" She was using the same voice that she used to use with him when she helped him with his homework.

"Yes, mom," Aminata said.

Tor was glad that his mother was getting out of the hammock more lately and that she had Aminata to help her, but Aminata was unbelievably annoying. At first she had been shy, but now that she was comfortable, she never shut up. Ann used to laugh at Tor's impressions of the kids from Miss Maggie's home, how they banged their drums and shook their tambourines, but now he wasn't even allowed to point out any of the stupid things Aminata did or said, or his mother would get angry.

"This is a hard one, but I know you can do it," Ann said. "You write it down yourself. Two hundred and fifty divided by seven. No, divided by isn't like that, remember? Good. Good! Okay, don't forget the remainder. Good. Are you sure about that part?"

"No, no," Aminata said. "Like this!"

"Good. And the last one? Good! You got it! Good girl."

"Another one, mom?"

"She's not your mom," Tor said. He stepped onto the balcony, and Ann and Aminata turned toward him. "Why do you let her call you that? It's weird."

"Why don't you sit with us and write your letters?" Ann said. "The post is going out tomorrow."

"I don't want to write letters."

"Well, you don't have a choice. At the very least you have to write to the McCanns. Daddy thinks you did it months ago."

"I don't want to write letters!" Tor said, but then he thought about Mrs. McCann and how they had beat up the trees together. "Can I use Dick's typewriter?"

"He doesn't like you going in there," Ann said.

"He'll never know. Plus it will be easier to read."

"Alright," Ann said. "But don't touch anything, and if you hear the truck, for heaven's sake get out of there."

The dockhouse was locked, so Tor had to go in through the window. Inside, he found a rat drowning in one of the jerry cans in the corner. On the side of the jerry can was a ramp, which the rat must have climbed to get in, and there was a collapsed piece of tin, like a diving board, in the water with the rat.

It was exciting to watch the rat trying to swim, but also sad. When they were running around making his life miserable they were easy to hate, but seeing one trapped and about to die made Tor feel sorry for it, but not sorry enough to help. As he watched the rat claw hopelessly at the side of the bucket, he had similarly conflicted feelings about the trap's creator. It was somehow touching to imagine Richard out in the dockhouse alone, cutting and gluing and hammering this thing together out of garbage, and it was impressive that the trap had worked.

Suddenly Tor realized that he had what he'd wanted — a live rat in a trap — and if he could keep the rat from dying without letting it out of the bucket, he would be able to try his firecracker idea. But he didn't want to do that any more. Now that it was just him and the rat, there was something weirdly intimate about it, and anyway, he knew the firecracker thing wouldn't work. It was just another one of his stupid ideas that he would end up regretting for some reason that he was incapable of foreseeing. He had given up on the plan to smoke them out, too, because Richard had started taking Billy to work with him, and there was no point in smoking the rats out without Billy there to kill them. But watching the rat drowning in Richard's trap, Tor wondered if maybe he should tell Richard about the burrow, if they might be able to smoke the rats out together.

He pictured the scene: Richard sitting in the truck ready to rev the engine, Tor holding the end of the hose inside the hole at the entrance to the burrow, Billy sniffing the ground and whining while he waited to pounce on the rats as they came out. "Ready, Tor?" Richard would say, and Tor would say, "Give 'er, dad," and the smoke would pour down the hose and into the hole and the rats would come out and Billy would catch them and shake them to death.

The rat had stopped moving, so Tor pushed the jerry can to the corner of the room with his foot. He sat in Richard's chair, interlaced his fingers and cracked his knuckles before feeding a fresh sheet of paper into the typewriter. *Dear Mrs. McCann,* he began.

I am sorry that your house was treated so unfortunatly by me. You were rite that I shoud have more respect for other peoples property, espeshally when they are kind enuf to be hospitible to us when we coudn't stay at our own house. You had evry rite to be angry when you found your house vandulised, even if it was axidental.

What he wanted to say was that it wasn't his fault, because the McCann's cottage was a piece of crap. All of the stuff in it was garbage they didn't want in their real house, and if you touched anything it would break. Every time Tor moved in that place, something shattered, and then he — or he and his mom — would have to try and hide the evidence. Still, he liked Mrs. McCann, and he didn't mind apologizing to her if it would make her feel better. His mom called that being the bigger person.

I can understand how you woud be mad when Lisa coudn't watch a movie on her birthday because we forgot to tell you the VCR ate the tape. Also that the rocking horse had a lose head not because of the cost because of the sentimentle valew. I didn't mean to spill ink on the carpet, it just fell on there. I thout the doll in the living room was a cheap peice of plastic or I woud have never tuched it.

I did not mean to brake threw the front window, I was just giving it a push because I was frustraded when I got locked out. I didn't mean to brake the prepeler on the boat, it was just that I went over some rocks by axident. I knew you woud be very upset if you found out, so I thout it woud be better if you thout it had been stolen. As for the flowers, I can only say that I don't know what came over me.

I am sorry and this was a costly lesson because I had to pay for it with my own little allowence. I didnt know I broke the basment door but I am a bit energetic and careless somtimes so I know I coud have done it. I'm sorry you put so much in to it and we, presumibly me, broke it. Please forgive me.

Yours truly,
Torquil Berringer

TOR HEARD THE TRUCK coming down the driveway. He pulled the page out of the typewriter, folded it into a rectangle, put it in his back pocket and climbed out of the window, but he was too late. Richard saw him coming down the jetty. In part to distract Richard from this, and in part because his vision was still fresh enough to seem possible, Tor shouted, "Dick, dad, I found the rat's burrow! I'll show you where it is!"

Tor kept talking while Richard carried Billy into the house, and he was surprised when Richard came back outside and followed him to the latrine without saying anything. "I saw a rat come out of it when I was looking for wasps' nests, and Billy actually killed it himself, he like shook it to death, and I know you've been trying to get rid of them, so I can show you where they are now, and I was thinking...."

"Hey, breathe," Richard said.

When Tor moved some leaves to reveal the entrance to the burrow, Richard smiled. He started to walk around the pile, moving leaves and garbage out of the way. "What are you doing?" Tor said.

"There should be..." Richard said. Tor watched his father search around the pile until he found another hole just like the first one. He crouched down, and Tor crouched next to him. Their faces were inches from each other, and Tor could smell Richard's sour breath when he said, "Clever little devils."

"Now I get it," Tor said. "There are *two* holes."

"Front door and back door," Richard said.

"What Andrew's dad does on the farm is he puts a hose on the tailpipe of his four-wheeler and smokes them out and gets their dog Maisie to kill them...and I was thinking we could get Billy to kill them when they come out too because he knows how to do that. He did it, did I tell you? He killed a rat himself, and...well we can figure out the details later, but...." Richard obviously wasn't listening. "Or maybe you have your own ideas. But don't do anything without me, okay?"

"What were you doing in the dockhouse?" Richard said. His breath was disgusting.

"I was looking for you. I wanted to tell you about the rats." Richard raised his eyebrows and curled down the sides of his lips as if to say, *yeah, right*. He stood up, and as Tor watched him walk back the dockhouse, probably to see if anything was missing, he was sure it had been a mistake to tell him about the burrow.

Tor went up to the top balcony to show his mother his letter. She was sitting at the table cleaning Billy's wound and Aminata was working on another math problem. Richard had decided that Billy shouldn't be allowed outside any more because he kept getting dirt and bacteria in his wound, so when he wasn't at the hospital with Richard, he was kept inside the dockhouse and the main house, and Tor wondered if it might drive him crazy. He wondered if dogs could go crazy. He heard the people shouting *oporto* and hooting at the oar man, who was paddling across toward their side of the river. "That's right!" the man shouted. "I went to America in a peanut shell to destroy my brother's future!"

"Okay, now go and do your schoolwork," Ann said. She gave him the letter. He had expected her to tell him to write a second draft.

"Can't I do it here?" Usually she let him sit next to her, in case he needed help.

"No, you'll disturb us with your noises," she said. He felt like crying. She hadn't even looked at him.

"I see how it is," he said. He started to beat box. "You guys have a lot of work to do," he rapped, jogging around the balcony. Ann ignored him, so he leaned in close to her face and sang, "I see the rebels are fi-igh-ting, oh yeah. A wa-a-a-ar against the government...."

"Let's go downstairs, Aminata," Ann said. She stood up, collected the books, and started to walk toward the stairs.

"You know," Tor said to Aminata, "she used to make fun of you. She used to laugh at how you bang your stupid tambourine in church."

"Shut up," Aminata said. She lifted one of her crutches and tapped Tor on the back of his legs. He turned around, took her crutch from her and threw it over the balcony.

Now Ann was hitting him, and he laughed so that she would know he didn't care. When she stopped, he said, "You think that hurt?" and ran downstairs, ignoring Ann when she tried to call him back.

He found his slingshot in his bedroom and went out the back door into the cashew field, where he punched a tree hard three times. When he looked at his knuckles, they were bleeding, but he didn't cry. He ran through the field toward the checkpoint. It had started to rain. The water streaming down his face and the sound of the rain in the trees made him feel like he was in a movie, and he pretended he was Jed from *Red Dawn* and he was going to take out an enemy base single-handedly.

He could hear the Toots and the Maytals song playing at the checkpoint. When he was closer to the ridge he got on his hands and knees, then his stomach. As he crawled forward on the ground like a soldier, he collected rocks and put them in his pockets. When he reached the ridge, he peered over enough that he could see the boys sitting in the hut out of the rain.

A lorry stopped at the checkpoint. Some people were riding on the back of it, and when one of them got off and started shaking hands with the soldiers, Tor realized it was the driver's son. "You fucker," he said to himself. Another lorry pulled up, and the first one left, but the driver's son stayed at the checkpoint. Tor reached into his pocket and pulled out a rock. He put the rock in the slingshot and aimed at the driver's son's head. The lorry started to pull away. Tor pulled the rubber band back further. He was about to let go when he was grabbed from behind and dragged away from the ridge by the collar of his shirt.

"Let me *go!*" he shouted.

"Are you stupid?" the crazy man said.

"Let me go!" Tor tried to pry the man's hands off his collar.

The man let go and shook a finger in Tor's face. "Those people are trying to pass over into Guinea, and if you make problems with those boys, you make problems for those people."

"I don't care," Tor said.

"They could have shot you. Do you care about that?"

"I could shoot them."

"They have real guns, you fool," the man said.

"It's none of your business, you psycho," Tor said. The man turned and walked away. "And don't call me a fool," Tor said, but the man ignored him.

CHAPTER 13

ANN HAD BEEN LYING in the hammock all morning worrying about the taxes, thinking about her house, and trying to conjure some plausible hopes for the future. Sometimes the longing she felt for her house was not unlike the longing for a lover. She yearned for it. To walk through its rooms, to stand in its doorways, to touch its surfaces, to look out of its windows. The place was full of treasures. She'd ripped up the carpet to find perfect hardwood and stripped the vinyl siding to reveal cedar shingles. In the basement she'd found wide maple casings, corner mouldings, and baseboards thrown in a pile, and in the attic she'd discovered four stained-glass windows and three boxes full of gorgeous sconces, glass doorknobs and original light fixtures that had been replaced downstairs with tacky hardware-store versions.

When she'd started working on the house, she had thought it would be simple. She would create a beautiful home while Richard lived out his big-fish-in-a-small-pond fantasy, and once he got bored with that, as she knew he would, they could move to England. But she had underestimated how much a house could mean to a person. Every time she changed something, she became more invested, and the more invested she became, the more things needed to be changed. In the meantime, she made every detail of that property a reflection of an ideal she had pursued her whole life — how could she just walk away?

When she heard a vehicle coming up the driveway, she assumed it was Maggie dropping Aminata off. She sat up to look over the railing, but instead of Maggie's truck there was a Land Rover, and she could see a white man's arms behind the wheel. She rushed down to her bedroom, where she was dismayed by her reflection in the mirror over the sink. Her eyes were puffy, her hair was dry and wild, her skin blotchy and red. She pulled a brush through her hair, put on a swipe of lipstick and wiped it off so it wouldn't look as if she'd just applied it, dabbed some powder on her nose from the compact that she'd dropped and broken, so that she had to mash the powder brush into the bits of crushed powder and shards of mirror and tap the brush on her arm before sweeping it over her nose. When she had finished, she checked herself in the mirror again and thought she looked surprisingly good, considering where she'd started. Turning her face to see her profile, she opened her mouth slightly as she always did in photos.

Jusuf was out front talking to a man with a South African accent. Ann searched her chest of drawers for something decent to wear and settled on a white button-down dress that would look good against her tanned skin. She picked up Richard's book from the bedside table and took one last look in the mirror before going outside.

The pilot was waiting on the front steps, so Ann had to go around from the back. "Ann," he said when he saw her. She was holding the book open in her hand as if she'd been reading it.

"Hello. James, is it?" she said. They shook hands.

"The Bergmans asked me to stop in to see if there's anything the hospital needs while I'm here."

"I wouldn't know about that," she said.

"No, I didn't mean to ask you. I wanted to ask your husband, but he wasn't at the hospital."

Ann felt suddenly nauseated. After she'd found out about Maria she had checked on Richard obsessively, listened in on phone calls, visited his office unexpectedly, looked through his wallet. She had felt a visceral thrill every time she thought she might have caught him in another lie, but once she had accepted that she wasn't going to leave him, instead of praying that she would find something, she started to pray she wouldn't.

She brushed her hair away from her face, wondering if the pilot was thinking whatever men thought when they saw women they wanted.

"Am I interrupting?" he asked, looking at the book in her hand.

"Oh no." She put the book, which was a grease-stained, taped-together mess, on the railing outside. "I'm...no."

She invited him to have a drink with her on the top balcony, and as she followed him up the stairs she pictured Richard with a beautiful young patient splayed in front of him. But why young and beautiful? Why not old and ugly, like Maria? Like Ann herself? She hated to be thinking that way, but that was what he had done to her. She hadn't seen other woman as enemies before. Or maybe she had, but she just hadn't noticed because in the past she had never doubted that she was the most beautiful woman in any room she entered. Now she couldn't even be sure that this pilot found her attractive.

"So, how's it going?" He leaned back in his chair and sipped his gin and tonic.

It had started to rain gently, and scanning the trees through the mist, Ann remembered that the rainy season was ending, and maybe in the dry season the house would be better. She had a feeling that the pilot wouldn't approve of her complaining, so she said, "I'm starting to prefer it to Canada, in some ways."

He arched an eyebrow. "Will you be at the Sandis' house for dinner tonight?"

"We don't see much of them any more."

He seemed about to say something more but sipped his drink instead.

"How is your work?" she said. He shrugged. "I would love to go up with you some time."

"I don't know if you could afford it," he said.

"How much would you charge me?" she asked playfully. They were both holding their glasses on the table, and their pinkies were almost touching. Again she imagined Richard with that patient, bringing home some new disease to kill her with.

"A lot of people like the idea of flying, but when they get up there, they change their minds," he said.

"My father was a pilot. In the RAF. He fought in the Battle of Britain."

"You mentioned that the last time we met," he said.

"Anyway, I would like to go up with you. It's so beautiful here, I'd love to see it from above. Sometimes I think it's hard to see a place when you're in it, you know?" She took a sip of her water, pursing her lips suggestively on the outside of the glass. He was staring at her. Could he see her huge pores and uneven skin through her makeup? Was he disgusted by her dry, lank hair? The bags under her eyes? She felt so self-conscious that she stood and started to ask if he would like another drink, even though his glass wasn't empty. He stood too, and she thought he might be about to leave, but instead he put his hand on her stomach.

She stayed there for a moment, wanting to prolong the feeling of having his hand on her but unable to pursue it further, because she would never do that. He stepped back, and she turned to face him.

"Sorry," he said.

"No," she said. "It's ... I could never do that to Richard." She meant this. She never intended to have sex with James or anyone else. She just wanted him to want her. She wanted to push to the edge of his desire for her and then stop him. It wasn't fair, but she needed what she needed from him more than he could ever want whatever he might want from her.

"I understand," he said. She took a step toward him, staring at his broad chest. He took her by her forearms, leaned down and kissed her. His lips were rough and chapped, and they pressed against hers gently at first, then harder. Suddenly his tongue was in her mouth and he was breathing heavily and fiddling with the buttons on her dress. She was furious. A gentle kiss, maybe some innocent touches were all she had expected, not this desperate groping.

He grabbed her by her bum and pressed himself up against her. "Stop it!" she said. She tried to step back, but he held her close, his mouth to her ear.

"We don't have to fuck," he said. His breath reeked of alcohol. She pushed him away, and he groaned. "You know I didn't come here for this," he said.

"What's that supposed to mean?" she said.

He shook his head. "I have to go. Thanks for the drink." He was already on his way downstairs. He hadn't even said goodbye.

She sat down, feeling ashamed and angry, and sipped what was left of his drink. She wondered if he would go to the hospital now and talk to Richard as if he hadn't just tried to have sex with his wife. Men were snakes, she told herself. Absolute snakes.

She went back to the hammock and tried to read her book, but nothing could distract her from the memory of the experience. She'd made a fool of herself, and for what? Because she needed everyone to be in love with her? How deluded could a person be? She was pathetic, unable to accept the invisibility of middle age, hopelessly looking in every reflective surface for her old self, who was gone forever. As if she could cover that up with some powder and a wrinkled old dress.

She put down her book, and instantly the thoughts rushed in. *Where the hell was Richard? What was he doing?* She groaned aloud at the memory of her uncontrollable rage in those first days after she found out about his affair, when she pulled all the books off the shelves in his study and destroyed everything she could get her hands on. She turned on her side in the hammock and remembered how a stranger at the supermarket in Nova Scotia had looked at her with the exaggerated bottom-lip-out face of pity people make at children when they hurt themselves. Through the railing she could see women bathing in the river, their perfect, flat stomachs. She touched her own stomach, flabby and disfigured by stretch marks. *Where is he? What the hell is he doing?* She pictured the pretty nurse she'd seen at the hospital once. *Why would he want you if he could have her?*

She was looking down at her unshaven legs, feeling like the most unlovable person in the world, when Maggie and Aminata arrived. Ann asked if she could come back to the orphanage instead of staying home with Aminata. "I need to get out of this place," she said when Maggie hesitated.

"I have to pick up Pastor Mark first," Maggie said. "He's doing some evangelizing."

"Let me change my clothes," Ann said.

"Alright," Maggie said. "But hurry up."

Maggie drove to a busy market at the edge of town. Ann had dressed herself in the kind of frumpy outfit she thought would befit a missionary — ankle-length skirt, long-sleeved blouse, wide-brimmed hat, closed shoes — and she felt embarrassed to be seen like that by the young men hanging out around the stalls.

"Where are we going, exactly?" she said.

Maggie pointed to a collection of thatch huts to one side of the market, from where Ann could hear music and laughter. "The lost boys," Maggie said. "Mark visits them every week."

Aminata stayed in the truck, and Ann followed Maggie to the huts. Maggie peered into several doorways before she found Mark talking to a group of men sitting on bamboo benches and smoking. When Maggie and Ann came in, the men greeted them, and two of them stood to offer their seats.

"But why wine, Pastor? That is my question," one of the men said. The smell of his joint reminded Ann of dark times with John in the cold, miserable house they lived in when they first got married. "If Jesus says that wine is not good, why did he produce it?"

"It's not alcoholic wine, it's fruit juice," Mark said.

"So they should not have called it wine. They should have said juice."

The other men agreed.

"Also, Pastor, in Genesis God says that he gives all the plants and seeds for our use. What about cannabis sativa? Did he not give us cannabis sativa for our use?"

"The seed represents the word of God," Mark said. "It is not an actual seed." Ann hated Mark's arrogant way of talking. As if he had all the answers. He so reminded her of Mr. Carter, who used to punish her by forcing her to walk him home from school. He would make her walk ten paces in front of him, and from behind her he would shout, "We all, like sheep, have — *finish* it! *Finish* it!" and she would have to say, "We all, like sheep, have gone astray."

"Pastor, does God condemn people who play with fetish?" one of the men said.

Mark opened his Bible. "Exodus 20:4–6," he said. "Thou shalt not make unto thee any graven image, or any likeness of any thing that is in heaven above, or that is in the earth beneath, or that is in the water under the earth. Thou shalt not bow down thyself to them, nor serve them: for I the Lord thy God am a jealous God, visiting the iniquity of the fathers upon the children unto the third and fourth generation of them that hate me."

This was exactly what had driven Ann away from Christianity. That judgmental gangster God who burned people in hell because they were human and made mistakes.

"I do not bow down and serve them, but I can play with them," the man said.

"Why play with it if you don't believe in it?" another man said.

"Well, who made devils? Didn't God make devils? It's a gift to us," the first man said.

"The gift of juju?" Mark said. "No. Jesus says, 'Why do you call me Lord and not do the things which I say?' If he tells you do not play with fetish, you do not play with fetish."

"The difference between Christian and Muslim is that Christians believe Jesus is the Son of God and he *is* God, not so?" one of the men said. "But if Jesus is God, who is almighty Allah? Me, I can't believe that Jesus is God. I believe Jesus is a prophet like Mohammed is a prophet. God sends the prophets for them to teach we and for we understand the word of God." Ann completely agreed, but she knew that Maggie would never forgive her for saying so.

"Jesus himself says that He is the Son of God!" Mark shouted. "In John 10:30, Jesus says, 'I and my Father are one.' It is clear!"

"And now it's time for the Pastor to go," Maggie said.

"Thank you for coming to visit we, sister," one of the men said to Ann. He stood to shake her hand. "You are always welcome." The lost boys seemed really nice, Ann thought, and she wished she hadn't dressed like a nun to meet them.

"That was *such* an interesting conversation," she said as she followed Maggie and Mark back to the truck.

"That was Satan speaking," Maggie said.

ANN HAD ONLY BEEN to the orphanage once before. Right after the Berringers had arrived, Sandi toured the three of them around town, introducing them to every official and small-town politician he could find while Ann tugged on Richard's hand and felt about ready to collapse from the heat. When they got to Maggie's, Tor had been excited to see another white person, but he was disappointed to learn that Maggie had nothing good to eat or drink, and the best she could offer him was a cup of Ovaltine and powdered milk.

The orphanage was a mint-green concrete structure built on one level with a courtyard in the middle, shared rooms for the children along two sides, two bedrooms and a bathroom along the third side, and a kitchen, dining room, and common area on the fourth. Mark and Emily and their children lived in a small house next door. When Maggie, Ann, Aminata, and Pastor Mark arrived, all the children were seated on the ground in the courtyard, and one of the older ones was leading them through their times tables. As soon as they saw Ann, several of them ran to her and held onto her legs and hands. She picked up a toddler, and he slapped the hands of the other children, who were trying to pull him down from her arms.

Maggie said they should let the kids get back to their lessons, so Ann took the baby boy with her and followed Maggie into her bedroom, a tiny space with a small window, a single bed, one chair and a shelf full of religious books. The two women sat close to each other, Ann on the chair with the baby on her lap, Maggie on her bed poking out her tongue as she painted in a children's colouring book.

"Do the children usually do lessons by themselves?" Ann asked.

"No," Maggie said. "Emily usually teaches schoolwork when Mark's on evangelizing trips, but Emily's not here, so we had to do it different."

"Where is she?"

"I kicked her out," Maggie said.

"Why?"

"She got in a fight with Mark. She went wild. She was attacking him, throwing stones. I locked her outside, and she started throwing stones through the windows. I was scared she was going to hurt the kids. Finally her brother came to take her away, and I told her she can't come back for a week."

"Why did she do that?" Ann asked.

"She wanted 500 more leones for the market, and I told her there was no more money this week, so she threw the money I had given her on the ground and Mark slapped her face and she went berserk."

"That's terrible," Ann said.

"I know," Maggie said. "She's real hard to live with. Her family is deep into witchcraft, so that's why. These things are passed down through families. Mark wants to leave her, but I say to him, 'you want to marry someone else and get all of their curses too? No. You have to pray.'"

"I mean it's terrible for Emily."

"Well, sweetie, you weren't there, so you don't know."

"I don't think it's fair to label her like that," Ann said. She knew how dangerous labels could be if they stuck. Mr. Carter had called her a prideful know-it-all, and although it was clear to her now that he had probably been a common pervert, that didn't make his words any less indelible.

Marian — Mark and Emily's daughter — brought Ann a glass of water and a bread roll. "Mayonnaise and banana," she said.

"That's our specialty," Maggie said. Marian watched as Ann drank the water and bit off a corner of the bread. Ann offered some of the banana to the baby on her lap, and he ate it, then used his sticky, wet fingers to brush the hair away from her forehead. "I'd like to take you home, you little monkey," she said. She turned to Maggie. "What are you painting?"

Maggie showed Ann and Marian the page she was working on — a black and white Cinderella sweeping by a windowsill where a meticulously painted bird was singing. "I shouldn't use their books, but I love to colour," Maggie said. She turned to Marian. "Go back to your lesson," she said.

"Yes, ma." The girl left.

"How are you feeling?" Maggie asked Ann.

"The same," Ann said. "Good days and bad days, but the same." She suddenly realized that she had forgotten about Richard not being at the hospital. If she had been at home she would have thought of nothing else.

"When I came to this place, I was a mess," Maggie said. "I came here thinking it was gonna solve all my problems, but then my husband left me and went back to America. I had no money, no friends. My kids refused to visit me. My son said that all poor people are lazy and should be shot. I started to seriously doubt my purpose here, but God gave me such a heart for the lost, and that's what healed me. Through these kids He healed me. And if you trust in God He will heal you too."

Ann was crying. Something about the baby stroking her hair and what Maggie was saying, which she wanted so much to believe.

"I got rid of the masks," she said. She was sure all the stuff about curses was pure superstition, but she had removed them anyway just to be safe. She wasn't sure what to do with them — giving them away hardly seemed right, and the idea of burning them frightened her — so she found a quiet place by the river and threw them into the rapids.

"That's good," Maggie said. "You really don't want to have things like that around." She put down her brush and shifted to the edge of the bed. "You said you've been sick for a long time, though, so that probably wasn't the reason. Do you want me to help you to find the reason?"

Ann was incredibly touched to have someone not only believing that she was sick, but genuinely trying to help her to find a solution. "Can you do that?" she said.

"Through prayer and fasting, God reveals things to those of us who have the gift of discernment. When I pray and fast, God opens my eyes to see things."

"So if it's not the masks, what is it?"

"I don't know. It could be an ancestral thing or an evil spirit or some cursed possession. It could be Satan out there just throwing his garbage around to mess up someone's life. It could be a malfunction of your body."

"Have you seen demons before?"

"Of course."

"What do they look like?"

"Unless you have spiritual discernment, you can't understand. I can't tell you what it looked like. You'd have to see it yourself."

"But I can't see it, can I?"

"Look, the spirit world is real," Maggie said. "Jesus cast out demons, unclean spirits. So did Paul. Lots of so-called Christians seem to skip over that part of the Bible."

"But it's the mould that makes me sick."

"Or is it Satan *using* the mould to make you sick? Because that's not the same thing. If it's a physical reaction to the mould, you gotta respond to the problem using physical ways, but if the mould is a spiritual attack, then the only way to fight it is spiritually. Some people believe that everything is a curse and that's not always right, but sometimes it is right, and you have to find out what it is. Fear causes us to perceive things wrong, and that's the enemy's main tool — fear."

Ann wanted to say *You're the one who's using fear as a tool,* but her resistance to this idea about demons was breaking down, partly because she had little resistance left in general and partly because she was so desperate to get well she was willing to try anything.

"So what do I do?" Ann said.

"If it's about demonic oppression, you have to do deliverance," Maggie said. "It's the only way. But first you have to believe, that's the first thing, and then you have to repent for anything in your life that might have opened a door...."

"Like what?"

"Well, for example, have you used drugs? Have you broken the law? Have you ever participated in the occult?"

"What do you mean?"

"Astrology, palm reading, psychics, séances...."

Check, check, check, check, Ann was thinking. She had experimented with all of that stuff when she was living in London with John. "Meditation, yoga..." Maggie continued.

"Come on, what's wrong with yoga and meditation?"

"If you're meditating on God, fine, but if you are trying to remove all thoughts from your mind altogether, well you might as well throw down a welcome mat for Satan."

"I *am* meditating on God," Ann said. "Or I'm trying to, anyway. It's Christian meditation."

"So you don't try to clear your mind?"

"No. I focus on the word *Maranatha*. It means *Come, Lord.*"

No need to tell Maggie that she sometimes used the transcendental meditation mantra she had been given or pictured that Hindu goddess with all the arms who wore severed heads around her neck.

"And yoga?"

"It's exercise!"

"It is anti-Christian self-worship, and it leaves you wide open for the Enemy and his deceptions."

"You can't be serious," Ann said.

"I am very serious," Maggie said. "All that Eastern mumbo jumbo, it's all deeply evil. And also, and I'm telling you this because I love you, Jesus said, "No one comes to the father except through me," so as a Catholic when you're praying to Mary or angels or saints or bowing down to images of Mary, that's idol worship."

"I don't pray to Mary," Ann said. "I pray to God, and to Jesus."

"And all that New Age hooey. *I create my own reality. There is no good. There is no evil.* There *is* evil, sweetie, and it is not some abstract concept. It is right here in our midst, and those New Age seductions are a perfect example of Satan trying to lure people into his trap."

"So what do you want me to do?" All Ann wanted was an answer.

"If we pray and fast together, God will...."

"I don't want to do that," Ann said. No way was she going to spend days on end starving herself and hearing Maggie go on about how she was a sinner and going to hell.

"Okay, so just pray," Maggie said. "Ask God to reveal the source of your illness. Would you like to do it now?"

"No, thank you," Ann said. "I'll do it on my own, later."

Despite her misgivings, when Ann got home she did give some thought to what might have opened a door in her life for something evil to enter through, and that night she had another nightmare about George. She was supposed to marry this small, old Indian man that she knew was George, and her sister was dropping her off at the church. Ann wished she could call it off, but everyone was inside waiting for her. When she walked in, her mother was by the doors arguing with someone about the catering. George was at the altar, and all Ann could think about was that he was going to want to have sex with her, and how disgusting it would be, because he was old and emaciated. He came down the aisle and took her arm, and everyone was smiling at them like, *look at the happy couple,* but she felt like a child being led away by a killer. He took her to the side of the building next to a dumpster and started reaching up her dress and trying to grab at her crotch. She wanted to scream and fight him off, but she knew she couldn't stop him. He lifted her dress all the way up, and his bones were bashing against her pelvis so hard that when she woke up she thought she could still feel it.

The next time Ann saw Maggie, she told her about George and the dream. "It's a very, very, very dangerous thing to own something like that," Maggie said. "Did you ever ask yourself what kind of person has their skeleton sold on the street? And don't you know that India is the homeland of witchcraft? Witches and sorcerers from Africa travel there in the spiritual realm to increase their powers."

"I didn't want it in the house. It was Richard...."

"Is it your house?"

"Yes."

"Then it's your problem."

"So what do I do?"

"You have to do deliverance, but before you do it, you have to trust Him one hundred per cent if not one hundred and fifty per cent. Doubt is a spirit. When you doubt and you say okay maybe I believe, maybe I don't, God show me, I want to see. God is not a God to be mocked."

"If I do this deliverance, do you think I will get better?"

"Yes, I do."

"And do you think it could help me and Richard to have another baby?"

"I knew a woman once who wanted a child but couldn't conceive." Maggie said. "She had been to a jujuman already, and he gave her a fetish doll and told her to feed it and bathe it and when the gods were satisfied she would get a baby. Thank God it didn't work, because those babies you get that way do not come from God. Anyway, she told me her problem, and we prayed and fasted together, and on the third day we were in her room and God opened my eyes. There in the corner of the room was a demon. I looked at the woman's hand and I saw that she had two wedding rings, but one was real and the other God was revealing to me. I told that demon to leave this woman alone, and he said, 'No, she belongs to me.' I told him she belongs to Jesus Christ, and I rebuked him in Christ's name. I held out my hand and I said, 'Fire of the Holy Spirit upon you!' and he started to scream, 'I'm burning, I'm burning!' And then he was gone. After that, the second ring disappeared, and she had a baby nine months later."

"Okay," Ann said.

"Okay what?"

"I'm going to try."

"Trying isn't enough. You can't hedge your bets. You can't have dual allegiance. A lot of people will say, 'Oh Jesus, Jesus help me,' and then they'll go, 'Oh jujuman, what do I have to do?' The lady up the street from us, she's at church on Sunday, then on Monday when her child gets sick she's slitting the chicken's throat and putting blood on the idol. She doesn't understand that Jesus is all and in all."

"Okay. I won't try. I *will* believe," Ann said. She did believe in God. She believed in Jesus. And there was no harm in trying to believe in the other stuff, because if Maggie was right, Ann was much better off believing, and if Maggie was wrong, what difference did it make?

"You have to be prepared, though, because Satan doesn't usually disturb people who belong to him already," Maggie said. "Once you start believing, and once you let him know that you are prepared to wage war against him, he is going to become very angry, and he is going to attack you more than ever before, because he doesn't want to lose his grip on you. Do you accept that?"

"Yes. I accept," Ann said.

"Do you want to call out to God now and renounce any occultist activities you were involved in and commit your life to Jesus?" Maggie said.

Ann had no intention of renouncing anything, but she told Maggie she would do it in her head.

"All you need to do is say, God, have mercy on me, a sinner," Maggie said. "Can you do that?"

"I will. Later."

SINCE THAT DAY, Ann had been reading the Bible Maggie had given her, and Maggie was right. There were exorcisms all over the place. She found it fascinating that before Jesus drove out a deaf and mute spirit from a child, the boy's father said, "I do believe; help me overcome my unbelief!"

"Help me overcome my unbelief," Ann whispered to herself.

"What?" Richard was next to her in the bed, half asleep.

"Did you know that Jesus cast demons out of people?" Ann said.

"People believe all kinds of crazy things," Richard said.

"But this is in the Bible. Did you know this was in here?"

"I've never read the Bible, and I don't feel a need to." He turned away from her.

"Don't be ridiculous. You've gone to church your whole life."

"Have you read the whole Bible? Honestly?"

"They read it in church every week."

"Don't get too caught up in this stuff, Ann. Please don't. Maggie is a fanatic. You said it yourself. Think of the harm religion has done...."

"Spare me this part." It was typical of his whole approach to life. He toed the line, he went to church every week, sat through the sermons, sang all the hymns, but he didn't believe in any of it. Not like Tor, who had refused to take communion and was even angry that his parents had baptized him, since he felt that he should have been allowed to make the choice himself.

When Tor was six, Ann had enrolled him in catechism class, but he ran away during the second lesson and showed up next to her on her walk home. She asked him where he had gone, and he told her he'd been climbing trees.

"You have to learn about God," she said.

"I'll learn that boring stuff when I grow up."

"If you wait until then, you might never do it. Are you going to wait until you grow up to learn about math?"

"It's not like math," he said. "They just make it up to make children be good." He was quiet for a while and then he said, "And anyway, God's rude."

"What do you mean?" she said.

"It's rude to ignore someone who's speaking to you, and God's never answered me, so he's rude."

She marvelled at his independence of spirit even though it scared her. She thought that he must have brought it with him when he was born, and she decided not to worry about catechism class, because faith was only worth having if you came to it freely.

But now she wondered if she'd been dangerously laid-back with Tor and with herself. After all, the demons in the Bible didn't seem to be metaphorical. And if Satan was real, why wouldn't he try anything he could to break her down and make her lose her faith? It made so much sense, and in a strange way gave her hope, because it meant there was a solution. She'd had enough. She wanted her life back, and if there was any chance that believing in this could help her, she had to try.

CHAPTER

14

RICHARD DIDN'T LET HIS suspicions about Tor's motives for
showing him the burrow diminish his satisfaction at finally knowing
where it was. This was something like giving Tor the benefit of the
doubt — assuming, hard as it was to imagine, that Tor was simply
trying to be helpful. Of course, it was far more likely that the whole
thing was a trap designed to harm or humiliate Richard in some
way, but Richard was at least open to other possibilities, the most
compelling one being that Tor had finally started to feel remorse for
everything he had put Richard through, and this was his small way
of apologizing.

In this spirit of skeptical receptivity, Richard decided that he
would let Tor help him to destroy the burrow according to the plans
outlined in Collins-Bridge's book. First Richard would use steel wool
and plaster to plug both entrances, and after giving the rats a few days
to either die or escape, he would let Tor help him to dig up the burrow
and dismantle the pile of mess it was built under so that, with any
luck, the rats wouldn't come back.

Richard had Jusuf buy the supplies at the junction, and he filled
the holes himself before he went to work one morning. When he
came home in the afternoon, Tor was waiting for him with a length
of hose. "Dad! I got this on my way home from school," Tor said.

"All we have to do is connect it to the tail pipe and then put it in the hole and then Billy can just wait by that other hole that you found and...."

"Stop, stop," Richard said. Tor's excitement at the prospect of killing—that vulgar, animalistic energy, which reminded Richard of every imbecilic thing the kid had ever done—brought out a reflexive inflexibility in Richard that left him without the patience to explain the wisdom of following Collins-Bridge's careful instructions instead of trying out a hare-brained farm trick Tor had heard about, which would probably end with the truck blowing up and Billy being infected with some muroid virus. "We won't be doing that," he said. No use saying it was impossible because the holes were already filled.

"But!" Richard expected Tor to launch into an argument, but instead he turned and walked back to the house with his hose looped around his wrist. On the way, he dropped his arm, letting the hose fall onto the ground, and Richard heard him say, "Bullshit" under his breath but decided to let him get away with it, just once.

That night Richard set up all the traps he had, and over the following three days he caught four rats, which he took as a sign that the disoriented rodents were being driven to recklessness. He had planned to wait a few more days, to be completely sure that any rats left in the burrow were dead, but on the fourth morning he came down from the top balcony and found a huge rat standing between him and the door. He kept going, expecting the rat to run away, but instead it leapt toward him. He shrieked and retreated up the steps to the landing, where he stood shivering for a while before going back up to the top balcony and climbing down the air bricks like a criminal. After that, he decided it was time to finish what he had started.

Jusuf got some rubber gloves and a couple of black plastic bags while Richard used a spade to move aside the rubbish from around the first hole. He was surprised how deep he had to dig before he found the nest cavity. He reached in with his gloved hands and brought out handfuls of rotting material: twigs and leaves, chunks of plaster, bits of plastic and shreds of paper, several pink rat babies, presumably dead of starvation. Once the worst of the nest was in the bags, Richard dug a bit further to make sure there were no more bodies, then left Jusuf to clean up the mess while he got ready for work.

Walking to the hospital with Billy in his arms, Richard felt profoundly satisfied. He'd discovered the root of the problem, he'd exterminated a whole generation of vermin before they'd even had a chance to open their eyes, and he'd done it all in the space of a few days. But he wasn't even halfway to the hospital before he started to feel anxious. He thought of the dead rats he'd found in his water traps, the pink bodies in the nest that he'd thrown away like garbage, and he wondered if he was feeling guilty — after all, the rats were only following their nature, not intentionally antagonizing him — but then he realized he was anxious not because he had killed them, but because now there might be none left to kill. This struck him as so depraved a thought that he tried to muster an accompanying sense of shame but was only able to manage a secondary kind of shame — a shame at his lack of shame — which he forgot about quickly, but which remained at the periphery of his awareness throughout the day, so that he was repeatedly troubled by the sense that there was something to feel bad about, if he would only stop and remember what it was.

JUSUF WAS WAITING on the steps of the house when Richard got home.

"What's wrong?" Richard said.

"Mrs. Berringer," Jusuf said. "She is not . . . herself."

"What's the problem?"

"I don't know."

"Where is she?" Richard went inside, and when Tor saw him, he looked relieved — not a good sign. He could hear Ann moaning from the bedroom. He found her in bed, covered in sweat and heavy blankets, gasping shallowly and speaking tenderly to the ceiling.

Without moving her head, she turned her sunken eyes toward him. He sat next to her and checked her pulse. Tor and Jusuf were standing in the doorway. "Jusuf, what happened? How long has she been like this?"

"I don't know," Jusuf said.

"Was she bitten?"

"I don't know."

"Was she upset? Did she say she felt depressed? Anxious?"

"I don't know."

"You can go home," Richard said to Jusuf. "Tor, go and get some clean water…please."

Richard tried to remember what state of mind she had been in when he'd left in the morning. It occurred to him that she might have had pills hidden somewhere. She had just come back from a shopping trip with Aminata, and she'd spent all the money they had for the rest of the month on stuff for Maggie's kids. Maybe she'd bought pills, too. Maybe she'd been planning this for a while. It wouldn't be the first time, although it had never gone beyond threats. Maybe she'd come up with some crazy story about him having another affair and this was her way of punishing him. She'd been cross-examining him about being away from the hospital. She probably assumed that he was with another woman. Then it came to him. The night before she had been talking again about having another baby, and he'd reminded her again that he'd had a vasectomy five years earlier, while she was on holiday with Torquil. She said he could have it reversed, and he told her that he didn't want to discuss it any more. They'd had this conversation many times, and he was expecting it to end with her attacking him somehow, as she had in the past, but instead she turned away and went to sleep.

The bedclothes were tucked under her armpits. Richard drew them back a bit and felt her belly to check for peritonitis. When he lifted her nightgown, a wave of foul air came with it, and he pulled back the blanket to find that the bed was soaked in diarrhea.

"Dad...."

"Don't come in." Richard met Tor at the door and took the water. "Go to the junction and get a few bottles of Sprite," he said.

"I have some in my room," Tor said.

"Great, get that."

Richard took off Ann's nightgown and bundled it into the corner along with the soiled sheets. He carried her to the shower and gave her a bucket bath while Tor, who had returned with the Sprite, put clean sheets on the bed.

"Now I want you to open all of the bottles and bring me a spoon," Richard said as he carried Ann back to the bed.

"Is that hurting her?" Tor said.

"No."

"What's wrong with her?"

"I don't know yet." He looked at his son and had the horrible thought that he would be incapable of taking care of him on his own. "Go and get the spoon now, please."

"Is she going to be okay?" Tor asked.

"Yes," Richard said.

He tried propping her up against some pillows, but she blacked out, so he put her on her back and gently slapped her cheeks.

"Where am I?" she said.

"You're at home." She looked so young. Sometimes he was surprised by how young they still were.

Tor brought him an opened Sprite, and Richard tried to spoon some into Ann's mouth. "Drink this. It'll make you better," he said. He parted her lips with his fingers and poured the liquid between her teeth. When it seemed like she was going to be able to keep it down, he found some Tylenol to give her. The next time he checked, she'd had diarrhea again, so he carried her back into the bathroom and washed her carefully, holding the back of her head, dipping the cup into the bucket of water and pouring it over her body.

It took another two hours of spooning Sprite into her mouth a tiny bit at a time while she mumbled to herself before she finally passed some urine. In the meantime, her diarrhea continued in waves, and after Tor went to sleep, Richard decided to try and make her comfortable in the bathroom so that he could wash her easily, since there were no more clean sheets. He stripped her naked and laid her down so that her bottom was near the drain in the middle of the room. He sat on the floor, rested her head on his lap and listened to her mumbling about oranges.

He couldn't remember when he'd last been free to gaze at her naked body, and although it was strange given the state she was in, he was struck, for the first time in a long time, by her beauty. Her looks had been so important to him in the beginning, but now he usually found it impossible to see either her or Tor's bodies as separate from the creatures that inhabited them.

He held a cloth to her forehead and thought about one of the last times he could remember having sex with her. It was in the new house, the night before Tor's birthday. She had done nothing about presents, so he'd suggested wrapping one of the pieces of luggage they had bought when she decided that she and Tor would come with him to Sierra Leone. He had reached for her when she came to bed that night, his hand resting on her hip. When she didn't push it away, he lifted her nightgown, stroked her soft belly and smoothed over the ripples of skin. She didn't react at all, so he kissed her neck and turned her over. He knew she was awake, but she lay beneath him like a corpse until he pulled away, the sweat between them making a sucking sound as their bodies came apart. She followed him to the bathroom, and they performed their toilet-paper ablutions in silence, except for the sound of the rough paper against their skin.

Richard poured a few more cupfuls of water over Ann, got another bottle of Sprite and began spooning it into her mouth. It occurred to him how fortunate she was to have him, because she was the kind of woman who could have convinced almost any other doctor to take out all of her spare parts before she accepted that her discomfort did not stem from anything physical. And who else would have stayed with her, he wondered. Who else could she have possibly found to endure everything she had put him through and then on top of it be told what a bastard he was in front of the marriage counsellors, in front of his son?

He imagined their marriage as a frozen lake. They had survived the thin ice at one side and made their way to the relative safety of the middle, but a fissure had opened up, and they had become prisoners of this predicament: the ice was just as thin on the other side, and they couldn't go back. Meanwhile, the spectre of Richard's affair floated beneath them, appearing again and again as a gelid corpse, every detail perfectly preserved.

He hated that he'd spent so much time talking about it and analyzing it when really it was just one more unremarkable mistake in a series of unremarkable mistakes, and he'd made it not because he loved Maria or because he didn't love Ann, but because Maria had helped him and he'd felt duty-bound to repay her. This would have been impossible to explain to Ann, because to tell her how Maria had helped him would only have made things worse.

One day, Ann and Richard had a huge fight in front of Maria, and Ann threw an iron at his head and took off in his car, leaving him stranded at home when he was supposed to be on call. Maria asked if that sort of thing happened often, and Richard confided in her about Ann's crazy behaviour, which he had never told anyone about before. After that, whenever he and Maria were alone in the house she would try to get him talking, and little by little he continued to share with her, because he had no one else to talk to and she seemed to understand him. She told him that Ann was crazy and she didn't know how he lived with it. She told him that he deserved better, that Ann was a maniac who had turned his son against him.

When Maria found out she was pregnant again, he was the first person she told, although she refused to say who the father was.

She was so distraught he assumed she had been raped, and because he was grateful to her for listening to his problems and confirming that he was a sane person living in a madhouse, he told her he would help in any way he could and everything would be fine.

Then one night while Ann and Tor were away, Maria called and asked him to come over to her house. He thought it was something to do with her pregnancy, but as soon as he got there, he understood what she expected of him, and because he knew she worked so hard for nothing and she was lonely and her life was hell, he gave her what she wanted.

In a way he did enjoy that first time. There was something about the illicitness and her pregnancy, especially, that had its appeal. But as soon as he left her house that day, the guilt began, and it had never stopped. It wasn't so much guilt over how much he stood to hurt both women. It was guilt for having done something so careless and pre-dictable and for setting himself up for what inevitably came next, which was that he had two women making impossible demands on him instead of one.

To make matters worse, Ann kept inviting Maria and her chil-dren along to parties and outings, and the increasing flagrancy with which Maria tried to assert her claims on Richard made him more and more convinced that she wanted Ann to find out. It also became obvious that she was going out of her way to get closer to Ann so that she could keep being invited, and Richard felt completely trapped.

He tried to avoid her, but she always found a way to corner him, and he worried that if he refused her she would tell Ann what was going on. And meanwhile he saw all his money and all his future money sinking into Ann's money pit in that shitty little town where he couldn't believe he'd ever agreed to live his life.

When Maria's baby was born — Richard insisted that Don deliver it, not him — Ann cleaned Maria's entire house, and for the first time Richard felt genuinely guilty for Ann's sake. When they moved into the new house, he suggested they fire Maria, but Ann wouldn't hear of it and even gave her extra hours because of the new baby, so even though Richard couldn't stand the sight of her any more, Maria was a constant presence in his life.

Then one day he came home from work and found Tony and Ann at the dining room table with a letter between them. His first thought was that they were about to announce an affair of their own — it was no secret that Tony was in love with Ann, not even to Julia.

Ann passed the letter to Richard without saying anything. *Dear Ann,* it began. *I'm sorry to have to write this letter to you, but I would want someone to do the same for me....*

"We can't prove it was one of those bitches, but Tony's willing to give them a warning," Ann said.

Richard was lost. "Bitches?"

"Your secretaries. *Don's* secretaries. Who else would do this to you?"

"I'd be happy to talk to them if you want me to," Tony said. "But this letter is from someone at the hospital. They said they heard you behind a curtain, not in your office."

"Well, of course they would do that," Ann said. "They don't want to give themselves away." For once, her anger wasn't directed at Richard, and it was a more focused, sane anger than he'd ever seen in her.

"I think we should ignore it," he said. "I've got enough problems at the office without accusing the girls of...."

"This is slander," Ann said. "If they're writing this filth to me, imagine who else they're spreading rumours to."

She hadn't even considered the possibility that it might be true. If Tony hadn't been there, Richard would have hugged her and told her he loved her, something he never did any more unless in response to her asking, "Do you love me?" which made him even more resistant to saying it.

He had never felt more ashamed of himself or more indebted to his wife. That night he told Maria it was over. He thought she would cry or shout at him, but instead she said, "That's what you say now."

The next day, she rang during breakfast, and he had to pretend it was an emergency at the hospital so he could take the call in his study. She asked if he'd forgotten that he'd promised to take her to Halifax for her birthday the following weekend.

"I told you, I can't do it any more," he whispered. He wished she would just disappear.

"Richard, I've never loved anyone like I love you."

"I confessed to Father Matheson," he lied.

"You can confess again next week," she said. "Isn't that how it works for Catholics?"

"Listen . . . ."

"You promised me," she said.

"Listen," he said again, trying not to sound like he was pleading.

"No, you promised, and you are going to keep your promise," she said, and he did. Afterward, he felt disgusted with himself in a way that was entirely new to him, but when Ann finally did find out the truth, which was only a couple of weeks later, the loyalty she had shown him that day with Tony was a big part of what made him stay and try to make up for what he had done.

"Stop!" Ann wailed.

"What?" he said. "What is it?" She seemed to be avoiding looking to her left.

"Can't you see it?" she said. "Oh please, please stop. Please *stop!*" She looked directly at him. "Go away!" she screamed.

"Shhhh. There's nothing there," he said, stroking her forehead. He had let her sleep for a while, and now that she was awake, he could tell she was starting to rehydrate. He tried to prop her up against himself, to see if she could tolerate it.

"Oh, I'm going to faint," she said. She went limp again, so he laid her back down in his lap. Seconds later, she woke up.

"Why are we in the bathroom?" she asked.

"You're ill, sweetheart," he said. "You need to rest." He put some more Sprite on a spoon and fed it to her.

"Oh, John," she said.

"No, John's not here." Richard wondered why she would ask for the driver but then realized she probably meant her ex-husband. He checked her pulse again. She started thrashing her arms around, trying to get up, but he held her.

"I don't want to go to the hospital," she said.

"You're not going to the hospital." He held her firmly around her arms, and she kicked her legs. Her lower body slipped around on the tiles. After a few minutes, she went back to sleep.

Some hours later, Tor came into the bathroom, rubbing his eyes. "Is mommy okay?" he said.

"Yes," Richard said. "She needs to rest and so do you. Go back to bed."

He felt uncomfortable with his son seeing Ann naked like that, but he knew it was nothing unusual for Tor. Ann was at once peculiarly prudish and disturbingly exhibitionistic. She usually wore clothing that covered her entire body, and she wouldn't dream of sleeping naked, but she would whip off her shirt during a game of tennis in order to prove some feminist point or go around on her hands and knees cleaning cupboards wearing only a T-shirt and no underwear.

He had been warning her for a long time that it wasn't normal for Tor to bathe with her or see her naked, but their relationship had always had something inappropriate about it. Until he was nine or ten, Tor had gone with her to the women's changing rooms instead of going with Richard to the men's, and it had been the cause of a lot of embarrassing arguments, but of course Ann always took Tor's side.

Richard checked Ann's pulse again. He shook her to make sure she was sleeping, not unconscious, and she woke up for a minute.

"Richard," she said. He thought she might be coming around. "Oh," she said. She held her hand over her mouth and started to cry. "He's gone."

"Who?" Richard said.

"I thought...."

"Go back to sleep."

"I need those oranges," she said. "Please, please, please." She grasped desperately as if at something just out of reach.

"Shhh. Go to sleep." He held the cloth over her eyes, and within a minute she was sleeping again.

She woke up every five minutes or so for the next two hours, and Richard took the opportunity to move his legs, which kept falling asleep under her and giving him excruciating pins and needles. Sometimes when she woke up she talked to herself softly. Other times she was agitated and he had to hold her down. Mostly she cried, but silently.

Sometimes he thought she had been crying since the day he met her, but he knew that wasn't true. The crying started after Tor was born and became steadily worse, but it didn't get completely out of hand until she found out about the affair. She told him once that the reason he couldn't respond to her crying was that he wanted to cry himself, but she was wrong. If anything, what bothered him was that he never wanted to cry. Apart from that time with Joan, he hadn't cried since he was born, as far as he knew.

He'd always known that he was missing some of the feelings other people had, and so as a young man he'd put a lot of time into studying people and copying them. He told Ann this at the Marriage Encounter weekend. He told her things that weekend that he had never told anyone, and he repeated all the sad stories of his childhood that she loved so much. At first, it had been a concession — a necessary evil to make her get over the thing with Maria more quickly — but once he started it felt so liberating that he kept it up.

He told her about his backward heart, about how he had tried to kill his little brother. He admitted to her that he had never loved Tor like he knew a father was supposed to and that he was afraid he was becoming his own father and he was powerless to change it. Ann knew much of this already, but the difference this time was that he was telling her these things not as a series of facts, but as a story about why he was the way he was. In reality, no story could ever explain him or anyone, but he had decided to give up denying her the formula she seemed to need to make sense of all of their lives, all of their failings. When he saw how happy it made her, he wondered why he'd held out so long.

At the end of the weekend they'd renewed their wedding vows, and as they sang "I Know I'll Never Find Another You" with the rest of the participants, Richard dared to imagine that it was a new beginning and they could live the rest of their life together in happiness and peace. But of course it didn't turn out like that.

He had hoped they could to move forward in a spirit of forgiveness and optimism, but she preferred to wallow in the muck forever, writing letters to each other and rehashing what had happened, talking about their childhoods and their parents and their inner children. So thanks to that, and thanks to Tor still being the way he had always been, the sense of promise that had sprung up that weekend quickly died, and they were back where they'd started and perhaps even worse off than when they'd started.

But sitting on the cold tiles of the bathroom floor listening to Ann's breathing and checking her pulse and cleaning her body, Richard realized that some part of him still held out hope that somehow they might be okay, because they were still together, and they had finally arrived where he'd been headed when they first met. He had set out to be a physician in Africa, and now he was.

BY DAWN, Ann's breathing was less laboured and her diarrhea seemed to have passed. Richard washed her well with soap, dressed her in a clean nightgown and propped her up in the bed, and she managed to sit upright without blacking out. He got some more Sprite, put the bottle in her hand this time, and helped her to hold it to her mouth so that she could drink. After a few sips, she started to fall asleep again, so he lay down next to her on the bare mattress.

He didn't wake up until Jusuf knocked on the door. "Everything is okay?" Jusuf asked.

Richard looked at Ann, who was sleeping deeply. "Yes, Jusuf," he said. "Everything's fine."

CHAPTER 15

TOR WAS LOST. He had never been so far into the cashew field by himself before, and suddenly every tree looked the same. He could smell food cooking somewhere nearby, so because he didn't know the way home — and because the food smelled so good — he kept walking toward it.

He had gone for a walk to get away from Aminata. She was always there, banging around with her crutches and calling Ann mom, and she even slept in bed with Ann sometimes. Tor was convinced she had stolen his Guns N' Roses tape, but if he ever tried to bring it up with Ann she would take Aminata's side, because she thought Aminata was perfect.

He couldn't take it any more. He was wasting away. Richard was a liar who had destroyed the rats' nest without even telling him first. Ann still wouldn't consider going home even after getting so sick she almost died. Kelfala was a useless friend who had terrible taste in music and was always trying to fight. But Tor didn't want to fight. He wanted to eat.

The only thing he had to look forward to was watching a movie, and even for that, he had to wait. The previous Sunday, Kelfala's uncle had finally announced that he had the VCR. The Berringers were driving back from church with a bunch of the kids from Maggie's house, and Tor was stuck in the back of the truck with them all singing Christian songs the whole way. He wedged himself into a corner and closed his eyes, pretending he was a prisoner of war being driven blindfolded to a camp by the enemy, who had forced the other prisoners to sing battle songs in a language they didn't understand.

Shortly after they passed the junction, the truck stopped. Kelfala's uncle was standing in the middle of the road flagging them down.

"Kushe, Doctor," the uncle said to Richard. "Kushe Takweel," he said. Tor was jerking his head to the side to show the uncle that he should come over to the back of the truck so Richard wouldn't hear whatever he was going to say.

"I go lek for invite una for watch film nar me os dis satide," he said. Torquil groaned. At least it didn't seem like he was going to blow Tor's cover, but now Tor was worried that Ann was going to invite all of Maggie's kids to watch the movie as well.

"You get nice bohboh, Doctor," the uncle said. "Nar bohboh wae fine."

"Tenki," Richard said. "And you are?"

"Me na Kelfala ohnkul," he said. He patted himself hard on the chest. Tor and Kelfala stayed away from the house when Richard was around, so Richard would have had no idea who Kelfala was. "I don dae wait for dis VCR *long* tem. E don kam now." He held onto the truck and watched Tor with wide eyes, and Richard must have assumed there was something wrong with him mentally, because he didn't say anything about the movie, and afterward he told Tor it was nice of him to be friendly with someone like that.

WHEN TOR FOUND the tiny shack among the trees that was the source of the smell he was following, he figured it probably belonged to the crazy man from the river. He wondered if he should run away, but his hunger was more powerful than his fear. Plus he needed help getting home, and he remembered from their last meeting that the guy spoke English.

"Hello," he called.

There was some banging inside the hut, and the crazy man came out.

"Kushe," the man said.

"Kushe," Tor replied. There was a pause.

"Are you going to sit down or not?" the man said. Tor sat on the bench outside the hut, and the man went inside. He came back with two tin bowls of stew and gave one to Tor.

"Thanks," Tor said. He started to eat right away, chewing slowly, not wanting to throw it all up after five minutes.

"What's your name?" the man said.

"Tor. You?" The stew was thick and rich; big chunks of potato and meat in gravy and dark orange fat. It was the best thing Tor had eaten since the Bergmans left.

"You can call me Ibrahim," the man said. "Puss puss puss." He held a piece of meat from his bowl toward a skeletal gray cat that was watching them from behind a tree. "Meow. Meow," he said. "Puss puss puss." He threw the meat toward the animal. "That's the cat that steals all my food."

Tor wanted to be polite, but he wasn't sure what to say to the man, so he just asked what he had been wondering all along. "Why does everyone call you *oporto* when you're black?"

Ibrahim sat down next to Tor. "When I was eighteen I went to study in the States, because my brother was living there. I was only there three years, but here in Sierra Leone if you've been to America, you must have something to do with *oporto,* and *oporto* makes money. He prints money. So I am an intellectual *oporto,* you are an economic *oporto.* When I came back, they expected me to turn this place into gold. They say, 'Oh, you went to America. You have to have millions.' When you're tired you can find it hard to put up with."

"So...are you hiding from them?" Tor said.

"Ha! If I wanted to hide from them, I would stay at my house on the other side of the river. No, I work for the owner of this place. I am the caretaker."

Tor wasn't sure if the man was serious. "Is that, like, your job?" Tor asked.

"The man who built the house you live in was my friend, so I am taking care of his field for him, but no one pays me for that."

"So how do you have money?"

"Some people are kind, and they are able to share what they have. They see that I am down, and they have pity for me. But others look at me as someone to exploit. The son of the wealthiest man in the community, but I have no family left and no nothing. I'm alone, lone, I'm a lone child. Sometimes I prefer to stay here, since no one bothers me, but people vandalize my home if I stay away too long. They think that as long as you are *oporto* they can take your things. They say my brother sends me money from America, but I haven't spoken to him in almost twenty years. I tell them I didn't go to America to get money, I went to get an education, but they don't understand that. They say 'he's crazy.' They look at me as some devil amongst them. When I came back from America, do you know what they said? They said I went there on a peanut shell to destroy my brother's future. Is that for listening to music?" Ibrahim pointed at Tor's Walkman.

"Yes," Tor said. He needed to leave. His stomach was starting to reject the rich food. "Can you tell me how to get back to my house?"

"One second." Ibrahim went inside his hut. There were a lot of noises, but he came out empty-handed. "I have some cassettes. Somewhere I have some cassettes. Do you think if I brought them to you I could listen to them on your machine?"

"Sure," Tor said. "But can you tell me how to get home?"

"Yes, sorry. I'll walk with you." Tor would have preferred to go alone, but Ibrahim was already collecting his stuff.

"You must miss America a lot," Tor said as they walked.

"My experience in the States was actually very negative," Ibrahim said. "I was in a white college, and I experienced a lot of terrible things there…. This is the main path again, see? Remember this. You get to this clearing and turn off by this tree here. This was where the original house used to be. The house where you live was his wife's idea, because she wanted to be on the river, but they never stayed there because the place was so damp and there were so many mosquitoes. But anyway my experience with America was like sixty forty. Sixty per cent awful, forty per cent good. I did have a lot of good times. I lived in the ghettos with dumpsterians, I lived in the mountains with hippies and nudists. I was free and I loved that. I had a few pleasures there, and sometimes I find it was very much worth it. It was something I had to go through. Otherwise I might have believed that America's all golden. And I also learned some things there that have probably saved my life. For example, everyone laughs at me because I boil my water and I get it from a spring. They say I should drink river water, because it flows. I say because water flows, doesn't mean the germs are dead. The germs flow too! So they laugh at me because I boil my water, but that keeps me healthy. I tell them, you don't share the same cup as someone who has tapeworm or cholera, and you don't kill those things by saying *Bismillah ir-Rahman ir-Rahim*. God made everything good and everything bad, but He gave us the common sense to choose between the two. But they believe in all their superstitions. Little girls tie this thing around their waist and they believe that will stop them from getting pregnant. How can you expect that to work? But mama believes in that, papa believes in that, auntie believes in that. And then when she gets pregnant, they say, 'Oh, it was God's will,' but you could have prevented it by going to a gynecologist or masturbating."

"I think I can find my way from here," Tor said.

"Sorry, sorry," Ibrahim said. "I'm not used to talking to people so much. I'll find more thoughts next time we meet."

"Sure. Thanks for the soup. Bye!" Tor called over his shoulder.

When he got close to the house, he realized he wasn't going to be able to keep his food down, so he stopped to puke in the field, because he didn't want to do it in front of the people at the river.

He knelt and stuck his fingers down his throat until he vomited. When he was younger, he was afraid to throw up, because he thought his insides might come out of his mouth. Now he felt like it had actually happened, and he was just an empty shell. He used a twig to bury his puke under some leaves, then lay down on the ground and closed his eyes. It was time to give up. It was never going to get any better, they were never going home, and it was all his fault, because if it wasn't for him and his stupid pranks, they might have been able to stay in Nova Scotia.

TOR WAS STAYING at Andrew's house for the weekend when he got the idea that the keys he'd found in Richard's briefcase must be office keys. Andrew asked his dad to drop him and Tor off in town for a few hours so they could go to the arcade. Richard and Ann were away at some therapy thing, so Tor reassured Andrew that there was no chance of Richard showing up at the clinic while they were there, but Andrew chickened out and stayed at the arcade while Tor went to the clinic by himself.

The keys opened every single door, including the doors to the supply closet and the kitchen. Tor spent the first hour eating cookies and watching wrestling on the leather couches in the waiting room. He called Lisa Formier to invite her to hang out with him, and he imagined a whole elaborate story around what would happen when she got there, but her father answered the phone, so Tor had to hang up. He thought about making a big mess, ripping up some papers, maybe writing swear words on the walls in permanent marker or peeing on the bathroom floor, but then he had a better idea. He found some scotch tape in the supply closet and worked his way around his father's office, unplugging every device and wrapping tape around the connectors, being careful to cover all the metal without using more than one layer of tape, so that it was invisible. He stood on the examination table to unscrew the lightbulbs in the ceiling and put tape over their connectors before screwing them back on. Once all the sources of electricity in the room were taped over and everything was back in place, he left, making sure to turn off the lights and lock the door behind him.

There were still some keys on his key ring that he hadn't found matches for, so he decided to go to the hospital and see if they would open his dad's office there. He didn't want to be seen, so instead of going through the front doors, he tried one of the keys on a back door he had seen Richard use in the past, and it worked. When he got to Richard's office, Maria was outside of the door.

"What are you doing here?" she said. She was wearing her baby in a sling, and she looked as if she had been crying.

"What are *you* doing here?" he asked.

"I have an appointment with Dr. Williams," she said.

"Yeah? It's the weekend. And this isn't his office," Tor said. She said nothing. "I think you're gross," Tor said. "I know what you did, and I think you're disgusting."

"Please don't hate me," she said.

"Save it," Tor said, and he walked away and waited around the corner until she left, having slipped a note under Richard's door.

When Maria was gone, Tor unlocked Richard's office, threw Maria's note in the garbage and rigged up the lights and appliances with tape. He didn't know where the idea came from. He must have seen it in a movie or something. It wasn't nearly the most creative plan he'd come up with to get back at Richard, but it worked better than he could have ever imagined. He had expected Richard to come to the clinic, find things not working and maybe spend half an hour or so figuring it out before getting on with his day. Instead, Richard went ballistic and accused his coworkers of sabotage in front of a waiting room full of patients. When Richard found out what had really happened, the whole thing was so overblown that he couldn't even properly punish Tor. Instead, he said something like, "You're a miserable bastard child and I can't wait to be rid of you." That was it. At the time, Tor couldn't believe his luck.

WHEN TOR GOT BACK to the house, Kelfala was waiting for him on the steps with a ghetto blaster.

"Where did you get that?" Tor said.

"My uncle is bringing it from Freetown. Oh, oh, oh. I get fine boom box."

"It's called a ghetto blaster," Tor said.

"I get fine ghetto blaster!"

Aminata was in the kitchen hut, stirring something on the fire.

"Dinner is almost ready," Ann shouted from the top balcony.

"I'm not eating anything that mutant made," Tor shouted back. Kelfala laughed.

"Shut up!" Aminata shouted as she came out of the kitchen hut on her crutches.

"Comman-do!" Kelfala said. He saluted her.

"Bo, set you mot," she said.

"I have a new song!" Kelfala said. "Let us make a recording."

"What are you doing?" Aminata said.

"You need a tape to make a recording," Tor said. Kelfala opened the machine and showed Tor a blank tape. Tor shrugged, as if he wasn't impressed.

"What are you doing?" Aminata said again.

"None of your damn business," Tor said, but she came over anyway and pushed in between the boys.

Kelfala pressed Record and spoke into the machine. "My name is Kelfala Kargbo, and I . . . ."

"My name is Aminata Kanu . . ." Aminata said.

"Bo wait, no." Kelfala said, pushing her away.

"No fighting," Ann said from the doorway. In her pink dress, with her hair pulled back in a ponytail, she looked almost like her old self. "Take turns," she said.

"It's not hers," Tor said. "It's Kelfala's."

"Everyone can have a turn," Ann said.

"Let her say something so she'll leave us alone," Tor said.

He didn't care about hearing Kelfala's song anyway.

Kelfala gave Aminata space, and she leaned forward so that her lips were almost touching one of the speakers. "My name is Aminata Kanu," she said. "I am a girl."

"Nanananana," Kelfala said.

"Shut up!" Aminata hit him and continued. "I am thirteen years old." Kelfala pushed her. "Leave me! I am thirteen years old. I love to read books. My best friend is name Miss Ann Berringer. I love Miss Ann because she is my friend."

Kelfala moved the machine toward himself. "My name is Kelfala Kargbo," he shouted. "I am a boy. I am fourteen years old. Fourteen years of age. I want to continue my studies so that I can be a US Marine. I am speaking beautiful English."

"No! This boy don't know how to speak English," Aminata said. "Me, I know. I am the chairman for speak English."

Jusuf came to sit on the steps with them.

"Your turn, Jusuf," Tor said.

Jusuf leaned in close to the machine. "My name is Jusuf," he said.

"What else?"

"I have thirty-one years of age. I have three pikins."

"What else?" Tor said.

"I love Mr. and Mrs. Berringer and Torquil. They are my friends, so I love them for that."

"And I too I love Miss Ann because she is a beautiful lady," Aminata shouted.

"I am a beautiful boy," Kelfala said.

"I am beautiful. I am God's daughter," Aminata said. "I love Miss Ann because Miss Ann too is beautiful. Miss Ann fine pass me. Miss Ann fine pass all."

"Okay, she had her turn," Tor said to Ann. "Can you take her away now?"

"Come on, sweetheart," Ann said to Aminata. Aminata went back inside with Ann, and Tor and Kelfala recorded Kelfala's new song and listened to Tor's music on full blast, blaring AC/DC and Twisted Sister to the people in the river.

Later, Jusuf hitched a kerosene lantern to a metal pole. Tor and Kelfala stood on the steps and waited. In the distance, they could hear "Bam Bam" playing. The moon was behind the clouds. Jusuf held his finger to his lips. The boys stayed perfectly still. They could hear sounds under the tin roof. Chirps, claws scraping. Tor clenched his fists. "Do it Jusuf," he said. Jusuf walked to the other end of the house. He lifted the pole up to the roof, and the black bats flew out from the other side, over the spot where the boys stood barefoot, dancing. Tor squealed with delight like a much younger child, forgetting himself.

CHAPTER 16

We thank you, Lord Jesus, for bringing us together this morning. We ask your blessings on this food, Lord Jesus, and we plead your blood over our sins and the sins of this nation. We ask that you will bring peace to this land. We ask that this new ceasefire will work and there will be an end to the rebel war and to ignorance and darkness everywhere.

It was four-thirty in the morning. Ann had expected to stop for two minutes to pick up Aminata, but when she arrived everyone at Maggie's house was awake, and the table was set. She and Aminata needed to get going if they wanted to be to be in Freetown before the shops opened, but Maggie convinced Ann to stay for a quick breakfast, and Ann forgot that nothing was ever quick with Maggie, because of her constant praying.

When Maggie finally finished, Mark and the kids said, "In Jeeeeeeeeeeeesus' name, Amen," and Mark's son Daniel dragged on Jesus' name until Mark gave him a look that made him shut up. They sang "Nothing but the Blood" and "Tell God Tenki," and Emily passed out banana and mayonnaise sandwiches. Ann didn't take one. She didn't remember much about the night when she almost shat herself to death, but her intestines were only just starting to get back to normal again after Richard gave her some medication, and she planned to be extremely careful about what she put into her mouth from then on.

Maggie, who was fasting, asked Emily to get her some dry bread and water. "I can get it," Ann said, but Emily was already on her way to the kitchen.

"Get me mayonnaise," Mark shouted.

"Shouldn't we wait for her?" Ann asked.

"No," Maggie said.

Ann was appalled. "So she makes food for us, and we're all going to eat without her?"

"Bring me mayonnaise," Mark called again.

"I will fetch it," Aminata said.

Daniel rolled his eyes. "I will fetch it," he mimicked, and Ann assumed he was jealous because Aminata got to go to Freetown while the rest of the kids stayed home and did their lessons.

Seeing Aminata at Maggie's, Ann had realized her affinity for the girl might have something to do with the fact that they were both elective outsiders, although Aminata didn't have any of the status that Ann had gained by choosing to be a misfit. The other kids clearly didn't like her, and Ann often saw them pushing and hitting her when they thought the adults weren't looking. Ann wondered if they resented the special relationship Aminata had with her, but Maggie said that it had always been like that. Aminata had trouble getting along with the girls, Maggie said, because she was too rough and she always thought she knew best. "No one likes a know-it-all," Maggie said, and Ann said that she liked Aminata very much.

Aminata had just stood up when Emily came back with the mayonnaise. Ann touched Emily's hand. "Come and sit with us," she said.

"I am not finished," Emily said. She pulled her hand away and went back to the kitchen.

MAGGIE AND MARK came outside to say goodbye to Ann and Aminata. Maggie put her hand on the truck. "Please, God, watch over Ann and Aminata on their journey to Freetown today," she said. "God, we plead your blood over the truck, over the road, over each checkpoint." Ann looked at her watch. "Please, Papa God, protect them and watch over them and bring them home safely —"

"Amen," Ann said. She tapped the driver on the shoulder, but he didn't respond until, after a few seconds of silence, both Maggie and Aminata had said, "In Jeeeeeeeeeeeesus' name, Amen."

On the drive to Freetown, Aminata rested her head on Ann's shoulder and Ann looked out the side window into the darkness and thought about the Suppressed Ambition Party, the only fundraiser she'd ever held in the new house, where Maria came as a sexy nurse and Ann thought she was asking about the "whore divorce," because she didn't know how to pronounce hors-d'oeuvres. She thought about Maria's stringy hair, her ugly, ill-fitting clothes, and wondered again how it was possible that this woman had been her undoing.

She had called Maria once in an especially dark moment and said, "He told me he hated you. You were a burden to him."

"I know," Maria said. "I'm a piece of garbage." Ann hung up on her, refusing to feel pity. She had chosen to make Maria the focus of all her rage, to believe Richard when he said that Maria had manipulated him. Julia McCann tried to tell Ann she was a useless feminist for doing that, but in fact, Ann had never felt greater solidarity with other women. Every day all over the world wives were being betrayed by their husbands and taking the pathetic route of blaming the other woman. Now Ann, who had spent her whole life thinking she was so extraordinary and unique, had joined them.

The truck slowed down, and in the headlights Ann saw a bamboo and oil drum barricade manned by very young soldiers carrying big guns.

Going through the checkpoints was the only thing that made her question how safe they were in Sierra Leone. The soldiers were usually young and jittery, and sometimes she suspected they were drunk or drugged as well. But they weren't malevolent. They were probably just people, like her, who were trying to get their needs met in a less than ideal situation.

The truck came to a stop, and Ann pulled Aminata close to her. One of the men talked to the driver for a minute, then shone a light at Ann and Aminata. Ann smiled at him, but he didn't smile back.

"He want your ID card," the driver said. Ann pulled her passport out of her purse and gave it to him. He looked at it quickly and gave it back to her but kept his hand out and made a beckoning motion.

"What does he want?" Ann said.

"He want Aminata ID card."

"She doesn't have one," Ann said. "She's a child. He can see that."

The driver talked to the man again. "Don't you want to give him something?" the driver said.

"My husband and I are volunteering our time to help this country. Tell him that," Ann said.

"I think it is better if you give him something," the driver said. Ann scowled at the man, reached into her purse, and pulled out a bill. He took it and turned away, making an upward motion with his hand to indicate that the pole should be raised.

"It is much easier for you if you give them something in this case," the driver said once they had gone through the checkpoint.

"Well, that's easy for you to say. It's not your money."

"If you don't have ID card and if you don't want them to delay you, you give them something to let you go."

"They are supposed to be doing a job, not making themselves rich by intimidating people. I should have given that man a Bible, like Maggie does. He could have learned something from it."

"Bible does not say anything about checkpoints," the driver said. "These men are on high alert because of rebels, and your fate is on their hands in these cases."

"We're not rebels," Ann said.

"They don't know that. You have to satisfy them. They can even kill you if they are not satisfy with you."

"They cannot!" Ann said.

"They can," the driver said. "They are soldiers. They can do what they want. Sometime people are fired with rifle. Some are beaten to die with pains. Your fate is on their hands."

Ann pulled Aminata closer. She had decided to bring Aminata instead of Tor because it was horrible going shopping with Tor, and he needed to be punished for being such a bully to Aminata, blaming her for taking his tape when it was probably lost or stolen by that hoodlum kid he was spending all his time with lately.

Ann was sensitive to accusations of theft. When her father was alive, she used to sneak into his room and raid his pockets, which were always full of money or mints. She told herself he wouldn't notice, or if he did, he wouldn't mind. After he died, her stealing became more brazen. Her mother made her work at the general store, and at least a few times a week Ann took some sweets from the bins or money from the till. As a teenager, she was caught shoplifting and had to do community service, and even now she was terrified that people would find out about it. She had made the mistake of telling Richard, hoping to encourage him to be more forgiving about his own mistakes, but he only used it against her. What she had never told him, what she was too ashamed to fully admit even to herself, was that her shoplifting had continued long after she married Richard and had the means to buy whatever she liked, because she did it not out of any material need, but to fill some huge emptiness inside her, which could never be satisfied.

ONCE ANN HAD FINISHED her errands in Freetown, she had the driver take her and Aminata to a fancy hotel, where they had Coke floats and cheesecake for lunch. Afterward, they went to the beach, and Aminata put her feet in the ocean for the first time in her life.

Their last stop in the capital before they went home was the British High Commission. Waiting for Ann was a package of blue airmail envelopes, brown letters from the Foundation, a few white businessy things from Canada, and two boxes from Julia McCann.

Ann opened the letter from the Foundation, which she knew would have a cheque in it, and asked if there was some way the Commission could cash it.

"It would be highly irregular," said the man behind the desk.

"We've just come from downtown," she said. "We can't go back."

"Don't you think you oughtn't to have thought of that earlier," was his stiff reply as he took the cheque and went somewhere out of sight. While he was gone, she remembered that Richard had told her to use the Visa to get some money at a travel agency as well, because the Foundation cheque probably wouldn't be enough for the month, and now that the Bergmans were gone and Richard didn't seem to be on very good terms with Sandi any more, there might be no one to help them if they ran out.

"I need you to give me some cash from my Visa as well," Ann said when the man came back with her money and a piece of paper for her to sign.

"I'm sorry, madam, but that is not possible," he said.

"But…."

"I've already stuck my neck out cashing the cheque," he said. "And we're not a mail service in the first place. You can go to the bank or a travel agent's if you want cash from your Visa. Good day."

"But they won't do it at the bank where we live!" Ann said. He turned and started to walk away, and she leaned over the counter and shouted, "Thanks for all your help!" before he was out of sight.

She dozed most of the way home, her head banging against the metal door of the truck. When she woke up, she decided to try and read the mail in the car, even though it made her feel ill. Sorting through the pile, she put the airmail envelopes on top of the boxes from Julia and the white envelopes from Canada, including one from the Canadian government, on the bottom, under the letters from the Foundation.

Ann loved getting long, newsy letters. The first was from her friend Helen, who had opened a coffee shop in Scotland and was back together with her useless ex-husband. Reading it, Ann enjoyed a guilty kind of satisfaction along with the disappointment she always felt for her friend, who had never even tried to get it right. The next letter was from her sister, who wrote the kind of impersonal brag rags that were really nothing more than long lists of the accomplishments of her painfully ordinary children and gossip about people Ann no longer knew in a place she had spent most of her life trying to forget.

The third letter was from Tony, who wrote about the weather and hospital news and assured Ann yet again that he was keeping an eye on the house. A few people had looked at it, he said, but he suspected they were just being nosy. He signed the letter *With love,* but this time there were no appeals for her to come home.

In the first box from Julia, there were two tins of Ann's favourite Earl Grey tea, a bag of Lavazza coffee, and a bubble-wrapped Bodum coffee plunger. In the second box, there were books and other papers for Richard. Someone from the Foundation wrote about some report Richard had promised to send and extended formal well wishes to Ann and Tor. Finally, after Ann had returned everything else to its original packaging, she opened the letter from the Canadian government.

Official requirement letter

Dear Dr. Berringer,

Regarding the production of books and records.

For purposes related to administration or enforcement of the Income Tax Act I hereby require you to provide within 30 days from the date of receipt of this notice of requirement information and documents as follows:

Pursuant to the provisions of paragraph 21.2(1)(b) of the Income Tax Act, all tax records for the period of 1990–1992.

To comply with this notice of requirement you should provide the information and documents hereby requested to an officer of the CRA *who will attend at your premises for that purpose.*

Please contact me in order that a mutual date within the 30-day period can be arranged.

If this notice of requirement is not complied with, you are liable to prosecution without further notice under subsection 238(1) of the Income Tax Act, which provides for a fine of not less than $1,000 and not exceeding $25,000 or such a fine and imprisonment for a term not exceeding 12 months and/or seizure of property and freezing of assets until such a time as this matter is resolved.

Your attention is directed to subsection 238(2) of the Income Tax Act, which both provide for a court order to enforce compliance where a person has been convicted of an offence under subsection 238(1).

Yours Truly,
David Corbett

"WHAT'S THE MATTER?" Aminata said, but Ann, who was trying through a series of increasingly desperate calculations to figure out what time it was in Canada, couldn't respond. She turned the letter over and checked the date. It was already almost a month old. What did that mean? Should she go back to Freetown and phone this man? See if she could make him take back that awful bit in the letter about *imprisonment* and *seizure of property* and *freezing of assets?*

She never should have written to him in the first place. She could have said she'd never received the letters, and then what could they have done? But now they knew they could reach her, and that had set a process in motion, and she had no idea what it meant.

"Stop the car," she said.

"Pardon?" the driver said.

"Stop!" She was already gagging. By the time the driver pulled over, she was vomiting out of the window and pawing at the door handle. She got out of the truck, and some men who were coming out of the bushes stopped to stare at her. She sat on the ground, put her head in her hands, and tried to breathe.

Why was this happening to her? Maggie would say it was Satan attacking her. Was it? How could she know? How could she know that the God she talked to in her head wasn't actually Satan? It would explain why absolutely nothing went right for her, no matter how hard she tried.

She had to think. She had to get a grip. It was all going to be okay. They weren't going to lose the house and she wasn't going to go to jail. She hadn't done anything she couldn't explain.

Aminata lowered herself onto the ground and put her arm around Ann's shoulders, and Ann sobbed, thinking about her house, how her dream for it had changed after Marriage Encounter — how, for a moment, she thought everything had changed. For the first time, she felt that Richard loved her. They wrote love letters to each other and read them twice, once for their heads and once for their hearts. He confessed to the priest, and Ann admitted that it was her fault, too, what had happened, because she hadn't recognized the child inside Richard who needed to be loved without conditions.

That weekend brought out the very best in both of them, and Ann imagined all the amazing things they could do together. They didn't have to have a big house to themselves. They could sponsor a refugee family and hold meetings and workshops that would help people to grow and connect. They didn't have to have another baby. They could take in a foster child. Together they could meet their full potential — to be magnificent, giving, loving human beings.

In the final session, Richard said, "When you married me, you didn't look me in the eyes."

"I hardly knew you," she said, and she felt then that she was meeting him — the real him — for the first time. He asked her if they could say their vows again, and when they did, she looked into his eyes and thought this was their new beginning, and this time it wasn't a fantasy for children, it was real.

But once they got home, it all fell apart. He refused to keep up the journalling. He didn't want to communicate any more. Soon he returned to his abuse, his criticisms, his shunning, and everything else his father had taught him. Still, he didn't leave her, and what they had experienced together during that weekend at Marriage Encounter made it impossible for her to leave him.

Thinking about these things was only making it more difficult for Ann to breathe. She closed her eyes and tried to do a meditation in which you were supposed to imagine your body from the outside, as separate from yourself. Not *your* body but *the* body. *The body is on the ground. The mouth is open. The lungs are empty. The body is struggling. The body might die, but you will not die. You are not the body.* Her heart rate slowed, and for a moment she could breathe again, but once she was back in the truck with the dust and the bumpy road and Aminata incessantly talking to her, she couldn't get her mind to focus on her body's otherness, so she was trapped in it and convinced, once again, that she was dying.

By the time they arrived at the hospital, she was in such a state that she had to hold onto the driver while she looked for Richard. When she finally found him, he was examining a pregnant woman "What is it?" he said crossly. She held her throat, gulping for air.

"What?" he said.

"I can't..." she gasped.

"If you're short of breath get the nurse to give you an inhalation," he said. "As you can see, I'm busy." He turned away from her.

A young nurse tried to take Ann's arm, but Ann shook her off. Stumbling to the truck with everyone watching her, she couldn't even cry. The driver kept saying, "Are you alright?" but she couldn't respond. She pulled herself onto the passenger seat and flailed her right hand in the air to tell him to drive. Aminata was coming toward the truck on her crutches, but Ann waved the driver on.

Once the truck was moving, she was able to reflect on her situation enough to see that there were two things happening. The first and most obvious was that she was having a lot of trouble breathing and adjusting to the possibility that she had ruined all of their lives and might be going to jail, and the second was that she was feeling increasingly calm about this, and her growing calm made her wonder if she might actually be dying. She opened the window to let in some fresh air but got a face full of dust instead. By the time they got to the junction she was dry heaving on the floor of the truck, but when the driver tried to stop she banged on the dashboard to make him keep going.

When they arrived at the house, Ann opened the door and almost fell out of the truck, barely managing to land on her feet in the dirt. Leaving the door open, she made her way to the river as if in a trance. People got out of the water as she approached. Were they running away from her? And if so, why? She fell to her knees and put her hands into the forbidden water. Slowly she crawled forward, letting the water seep into her loose dress and her hands sink into the muddy bottom. When she was out far enough, she lifted her legs and turned to float on her back. Her head was almost submerged, only her eyes, nose and lips were above the water. She could hear her own heartbeat as she struggled to breathe, and she thought, *this must be what it's like to drown.* And why shouldn't she drown? Why shouldn't she drink the whole river if she wanted to? But no, she told herself, she was trapped here in this body, in this life.

She opened her eyes and asked God to help her. She told him that it was all her fault, everything that had happened, and she wanted to die, but she couldn't leave her son. She said out loud, "God, have mercy on me, a sinner." Suddenly, her heartbeat started to slow down, and everything went quiet. Her inner voices abruptly stopped their chatter, and it was like stepping out of some infernal boiler room into a cool, clear night. She was shocked to realize how hellishly loud her mind had been now that everything was so still.

She considered the world around her. The trees, the insects, whatever might live in the river. She felt her animal body — not that she was an animal, but that she *had* an animal. Her body was her animal, and she was something else outside her body, and that something else was connected with a whole other reality that she seemed to know but had forgotten, where there was nothing to be afraid of and no one to blame and nothing to lose. She held her arms out by her side, breathed in, and filled her lungs with air. She felt nothing. Emptiness. One persistent voice tried to tell her that something strange and probably quite important was happening before it too was swallowed up by that emptiness where there was nothing happening at all.

Holding her arms up above the water and closing her eyes, Ann knew in a way that she had never known before and would never be able to explain afterward that God loved her. She started to sing "Amazing Grace," and although she only knew the first verse, she sang it again and again. When she was certain that the moment had completely passed, she found her footing and waded out, shocked to discover that the water, which had seemed unfathomable moments earlier, was only a few feet deep.

CHAPTER 17

RICHARD WAS AFRAID TO GO HOME. It had been a long time since he'd said no to Ann, and God only knew what she might have done to the house or herself as a result. Then again, she might have simply taken Torquil and left, but he wasn't counting on it, and anyway, where would they go? It occurred to him that it would be just his luck if this was the one time she wasn't crying wolf, and he hoped she hadn't died out of spite.

He couldn't help feeling betrayed by the dysentery experience. To have spent the whole night spoon feeding her and cleaning up her shit only to have her be as manipulative as ever once she was better was just too much. He didn't blame her for not remembering — after all, the brain is capable of protecting us from all sorts of painful recollections — but he did blame her for not even thanking him when he told her about it. Nothing would satisfy her craving for attention, and seeing her with her fake allergies barging into a legitimate emergency so soon after he'd done everything he could to care for her made it absolutely clear to him that he had to stop trying to appease her, because it was only making her worse.

He had been about to do an emergency delivery of a breech baby. The mother's membranes were ruptured and her cervix was fully dilated, so there was no time for a c-section and he knew he would have to get the baby out within minutes or it would die. He was asking Musa to explain this to the mother when Ann came in, pointing at her throat.

In Nova Scotia she had often come to his workplace unexpectedly. She always had some excuse, but he knew that she was checking up on him, because even before the affair she had never trusted him. She was always beautifully dressed and perfumed as armour against all the mediocrities (his secretaries, for example) whom she thought hated her (and they did hate her). Sometimes she would actually barge into his office while he was with a patient, and if he asked her to leave she would say, "Just quickly, just one thing," as she checked out the person on the examination table and scanned the room for clues about what he was up to. Then she would launch into whatever excuse she had fabricated for being there while he tried to figure out what to say to get rid of her without setting her off.

She had never done this in Sierra Leone — she was too busy lying in bed all day — and he hadn't realized how pleasant it was to not have to worry about her arbitrary intrusions until he turned and saw her pointing at her throat and gasping for air like a dying fish. In front of him a woman and her baby needed his full attention to survive the next few minutes, so he asked Martha to give Ann a Ventolin inhalation, turned his back to her and got on with what he had to do, half expecting Ann to attack him from behind and bite down on the soft part of his shoulder that had always been a favourite of hers.

He couldn't feel the baby's feet, so he hooked his fingers around the hips and pulled the body out by the pelvis then did a Løvset manoeuvre, taking the lower arm from above the shoulder to deliver it before swinging the baby through 180 degrees and easing the other arm out the same way as the first. After this was the sweatiest part — getting the head out as quickly as possible to keep it from compressing the umbilical cord — and while he was doing this he noticed that the baby's left arm was hanging unnaturally. He asked Musa to tell the mother that the delivery had resulted in nerve damage which might take some time to recover or might not recover at all. When he turned around again, Ann was gone, and that was when the dread began.

After he had washed his hands, Martha took him aside. He assumed she was going to tell him some humiliating thing Ann had done in retaliation for his ignoring her, so he was relieved when she said, "Do you remember the story about that witched girl who people were saying was responsible for killing that boy?"

"The one who turned herself into a snake?"

"Yes."

"What about her?"

"I have heard she is at the herbalist's house now. Her family has brought her to him, because he said only he can fix her."

"Okay wait here," Richard said. "I'll get my bag."

They found the herbalist sitting on his front porch. After they greeted him, Martha asked in Temne about the girl, and the herbalist said he had never heard of her.

"I think he is lying," Martha said.

"Why would he?" Richard said.

She looked at him as if it should be obvious. "He doesn't want you to interfere."

"Well, tell him that we just want to see her," Richard said. "Tell him maybe we can help."

Martha translated, and the herbalist answered sharply. "He says he has never seen her himself," she said. She looked uneasy. "I think we can go now."

They thanked the herbalist and left, and Richard didn't mind letting that be the end of it. Like so many things in life, the relationship with the herbalist only sounded good on paper. Richard was still a bit disappointed, in part because he thought it was a missed opportunity to change people's minds, and in part because he had to admit that, in this case at least, Sandi might have been right.

His last patient that afternoon was a young woman in the first trimester of her first pregnancy complaining of abdominal pain.

She'd had a more drastic form of circumcision, one Richard hadn't seen before. It looked as if her labia majora had been removed and the margins sewn together, leaving her with a vaginal orifice so small he wondered how she'd become pregnant in the first place.

Since the day when the woman with the two daughters told him off, Richard hadn't broached the topic of circumcision with any more patients, but in this case he had to at least try. He sent for Musa, and while the woman got dressed, he asked the nurse who had been helping him to step out for a moment. She seemed to resent this request, but she left anyway, and when Musa arrived he and Richard sat down across from the woman.

"I want to ask her about how she is cut. Does she know why she was cut this way?"

The woman gave a long answer, and Musa listened intently, but when she finished he only said, "She is a foreigner. It's not easy to understand her."

"Okay, please make sure she understands what I'm about to say," Richard said. "Because of the way she has been cut it is very important that she come to the hospital to deliver her baby. Ask her how far she lives from here." While Richard was speaking, Martha peered in the window and seemed about to say something before changing her mind. She stayed there, listening, and Richard could see the back of her head and the collar of her uniform.

"She says it is not too far," Musa said. "She says she will come."

"Tell her she should come early. Don't wait until late in the labour."

Musa translated. "She says she will come early," he said.

"Are you sure she understands?" Richard said.

"I am sure," Musa said.

"Now please tell her that I'm sure her parents did this to her because they love her and wanted what was best for her. I am also sure that she will care just as much about her own daughters, and once she understands more about how dangerous and wrong this cutting is, she will agree that it actually isn't best for anyone."

As Musa translated, Martha marched into the room and stood between him and the patient, her hands on her hips. "Tell Dr. Berringer what you were saying," Martha said. Musa was eyeing the door. "Tell him." Musa said nothing. "Fine," she said. "I'll tell him. He told her that you said she must come to the hospital to give birth, but after that he was speaking about vaccinations."

"I don't understand," Richard said, although he was beginning to. "Why would you do that, Musa?"

"Dr. Sandi —" Musa began, but Richard was on his way out the door before Musa had finished his sentence.

He found Sandi in admissions making a little girl laugh while he held a stethoscope over her heart.

"How dare you," Richard said.

Sandi turned to him. "Can I help you, Dr. Berringer?"

"How dare you tell Musa not to translate for me!"

"He asked me for advice," Sandi said. "If you had bothered to ask me, I could have told you he was never going to say what you were asking him to say."

"You know what? I think you're a bloody coward," Richard said.

"And you're a bully," Sandi said. Ann's word. The child had started to cry, and Sandi spoke to her Temne.

"Bullshit!" Richard shouted. He turned to leave and tripped over a baby sitting on the floor. "Damn!" he said to the stunned baby, who didn't start to wail until Richard was halfway to the inner courtyard.

He found a tree to sit under while he tried to calm down. He looked at the patients hanging around waiting, waiting, waiting. For what? They could rot in hell for all he cared. They didn't want what he was offering them. They wanted to continue with their traditions. They didn't want a better way of doing things, they wanted money. They wanted lunch. They wanted something for free. Because he owed them. Because he had so much. Because they had so little.

Richard hit himself in the forehead with his open palm. These were terrible thoughts, and he would not think them. He was fed up, that was all. Fed up to be going through the same things over and over again, relentlessly. Him and Sandi. Him and Don. Him and Ann. What he had learned from all of them was that trying to reason with unreasonable people got you nowhere.

Every time he had tried to talk to Don, he had only created more problems for himself. Once, on a rare trip to Toronto for a weekend conference, Richard had learned from a colleague who sat on some of the same committees as Don that those committees paid generous honoraria. This meant that while Richard was working like an idiot and covering all Don's rounds and on-call shifts for no extra pay, Don was being paid a fortune to play golf and stay in fancy hotels.

When Richard brought this up with Don, Don said, "I'm a senior member of our profession, and serving on these committees is an important part of my contribution. I'm sorry it creates extra work for you, but that's part of your contribution, and one day it will be your turn." Richard knew there was some failure of logic in this, but he couldn't penetrate it. As a result, his resentment remained at a steady simmer, and when things did occasionally flare up, Richard always ended up regretting it, both because he was never able to defend his position and because he suspected that Don was finding subtle ways of punishing his insubordination.

After Ann's freak-out about the office expenses, Richard had gone to the clinic ready to have an adult conversation and come to terms that would satisfy everyone, but instead he'd ended up worse off than ever. When he walked into reception, Pat gave him what he was sure was a sarcastic greeting. Ever since he had refused to pay his full share of the huge bonus Don gave the girls every Christmas, Richard had noticed a distinct chill in his dealings with them. All three of the girls had been working for Don for twenty-five years, but by Christmastime they had only worked for Richard for six months — why should he have been expected to give them so much money? It wasn't as if they were such stellar employees, either. Pat did seem to do a fair bit of work, but all Paige did was answer the phones, and Angela didn't seem to do anything at all.

"Pat?" Richard said. "Please tell Dr. Williams that I need to talk to him before he leaves today."

"Uh huh," Pat said, without looking up from her magazine.

There was a chart waiting in the slot on Richard's door. Barb Arsenault. Don had written PF on the top right-hand corner of the first page. Ever since Richard had talked to Don about the honoraria, he'd found himself spending more and more time reassuring the PFS and arguing with the PITAS and holding the hands of the newly divorced or the chronically depressed. This wasn't the worst thing in the world — after all, unlike Don, Richard was on salary instead of fee-for-service, so he had no incentive to get people in and out of his office as quickly as possible, and he actually found some satisfaction in unburdening people of their worries, no matter how much Don pressed him to keep visits under fifteen minutes.

The problem was that the PFS and especially the PITAS were the highest litigation risks. Half the job was to convince them that while you acknowledged that their symptoms were real, there was no evidence, after multiple investigations and treatments, that there was anything wrong with them. That part, while tiresome and time-consuming, was fine. The stressful part was managing the risk that you might be wrong — after all, even hypochondriacs get legitimately ill — and end up getting sued as a result.

Barb stood up when Richard came in, and for a second he thought she was going to hug him. It wasn't fair to call her a PF. She was just worried.

"Hi Barb," he said.

"Hi Dr. Berringer, how are you doing? How's the house coming along?"

"Great, yep."

"Ann is doing a lovely job."

He opened her chart on his desk. "So what seems to be the trouble, Barb?"

She sighed and moved her hands to her belly. "It's only that this pain hasn't gotten any better. I tried, you know, the teas and that, and I stopped eating dairy, but it gets worse and worse."

"Let's have a look," he said. "Hop up here for me." She winced as she got up onto the examination table.

"Any changes in your stool?" he said as he examined her abdomen. She shook her head. "And you say you cut out dairy and that didn't help?"

"Not at all. If anything it got worse."

"Okay, you can hop off now," he said. He sat in his chair and flipped through page after page of lab reports, pretending to read them. There was nothing wrong with her. She just needed some attention and reassurance, and he needed to resist the urge to practice defensive medicine. Don had his pen to the prescription pad the moment they walked in the door, and he had them in and out in five minutes every time, but Richard refused to conduct himself like that. He took the time to assess what was wrong with people, and if there was nothing wrong with them, he took the time to explain that to them instead of passing the buck to the specialists at an enormous cost to the taxpayer.

He put his hand on Barb's shoulder. "Barb, I believe that you have these symptoms, but the specialists you have seen over the years have excluded any serious causes for them, so I don't want to subject you to any more tests. Now you can see this as the glass being half-empty because the stupid doctors don't have enough brains to figure out what's causing your symptoms, or you can see it as the glass being half-full, because there is nothing seriously wrong with you."

"But it's getting worse," Barb said. "It affects my work. I can't exercise. It even hurts to bend over."

"I can give you something for the pain you're feeling," he said. "But it's not a long-term solution. I believe that the less you worry about your symptoms, the less troublesome they will be." He wrote her a prescription for Tylenol 3. "Come and see me in two weeks," he said. "We'll see how you're doing then." She sighed loudly and made a big production of getting up and out the door. Richard went to call in the next patient, but before he could pick up the chart, Don came into the hallway.

"The girls said you want to see me?" he said.

"Yes, do you have a minute?"

Don came into Richard's office and leaned against the desk.

"I wanted to talk to you about the bill for the office expenses," Richard said.

"I asked Pat to send that to you ages ago."

"I know. We have it, but I have to tell you, Ann and I were both quite shocked at the number."

Don nodded. "I know. It's incredible what it costs to run a clinic these days. It's more than I made in a year when I started out. *Before* taxes!"

"It seems disproportionately high to Ann and me," Richard said.

"What do you mean?"

"Well, I guess I assumed that some of those expenses would be included in the rent for the building, because it's already so high."

Don snorted. "This is a purpose-constructed building, and it includes all of the extremely expensive equipment that's at your disposal. Are you saying you're not happy with the quality of the building?"

"I'm saying I can't afford it. I don't think you were clear with me about how much...about what this bill was going to amount to, and as you know I have a lot of expenses with the new house."

Don was smiling. "Is Ann giving you a hard time? I remember when we were renovating our house. Pat was a total basket case. But you know what? Eventually it will be finished, and she will go back to normal. I promise."

"No, it's not just the house, Don. It's too much money going out. We have to find a way to reduce the expenses here."

"Do you have any suggestions?"

Richard paused. Was he really going to say this? "Do we need three girls out there? Can't Paige do Angela's job as well?"

Don shook his head. Richard hated how he could do that. There were no discussions with him, only entreaties. "It's totally out of the question. Now listen. I have a staff to pay, I have the mortgage on this place, I have to pay malpractice insurance, I have to pay maintenance on all the equipment, not to mention donations, medical education expenses, vehicle expenses, Christmas parties, bonuses...." Don counted on his fingers, but unlike Ann, he only added one for every item on his list. "In July, you can switch to fee-for-service, and if the past couple of years are any indication, you will be making plenty of money and you won't have to worry."

Richard nodded, staring at the floor, then shook Don's hand and even thanked him. He had accomplished nothing. Ann would be furious and Don would tell Angela that Richard wanted to fire her and nothing good had come out of any of it.

It wasn't until later that night, when he was lying in bed reflecting on what had happened, that Richard started to feel angry, and quickly his anger had turned into determination to get some kind of revenge. First thing the next morning, Richard announced to Pat that from then on he wanted her to book his patients for half-hour instead of ten-minute appointments. This would be a great fuck you to Don, because not only did it mean that he wasn't making as much money off Richard, but it would also show everyone in town what bad service Don had been giving them all those years.

That was the plan. In practice, Don didn't even seem to notice, and Richard only succeeded in making his own life more stressful, because soon all the most difficult patients were specifically requesting him instead of Don. He told himself that the principle mattered more than the details, but his attachment to principles was starting to wear thin, even then.

On the day of the power outage fiasco, Richard had come into the office already at the end of his rope. Ann had tried to stop him from leaving the house by holding onto his leg, and when he finally got to the hospital, already very late for a full morning of appointments, none of the lights or outlets in his office worked, though the rest of the hospital wasn't affected. He cancelled his appointments, called in an electrician and went over to the clinic, only to find that there the power was also out in his office, and only his office. He took his desk lamp to the waiting room to see if it would work there, and when he was plugging it in, he saw the tape.

He couldn't think of any other possible explanation than that Don or the girls had sabotaged him. Or maybe Don *and* the girls. Who else had access to both his offices? The only question was why. Because he didn't want to pay their ridiculous bonuses? Because he'd suggested they fire Angela? Because he'd had an affair, as if that was any of their business? He knew the girls had sent Ann that letter, and he also knew that they did it not to help her but to hurt him.

Richard demanded that Paige arrange an emergency staff meeting, and her response, the bitch, was, "I'm on the phone. That's why I'm holding it next to my face?" Richard stood next to the counter fuming. They had worked on it together. He knew it. And Don too, of course. But they wouldn't get away with it. They wouldn't get away with it! When Paige hung up the phone, Don came out of his office, and Richard finally lost it.

"I am fed up to the back teeth with you and your henchmen here making me … undermining me every day is one thing, but this is just bloody stupid, and…. No!" Don was trying to lead Richard away from the waiting room, but Richard shook him off. "You should all be ashamed of yourselves… just, childish!" he shouted.

While he would have been perfectly justified in confronting Don and the girls about any number of other things, of course he had to choose the one they'd had nothing to do with and in the process lose all credibility forever, since the five or six people in the waiting room managed to get the story out to everyone in town within twenty-four hours. It was so unfair. It was so unbelievably unjust, and he didn't know what any of it meant any more. He didn't know what he could be doing better or if there was any point in trying.

RICHARD FOUND THE TRUCK parked in front of the hospital with the keys in the ignition and John sleeping under a tree in the driveway.

"John, if you leave the keys like that, anyone can take the truck," he said.

John opened his eyes. "Sorry-o," he said.

"Usai Abdul dae?" Richard asked.

"My son is learning to be a soldier," John said. Richard almost envied how much simpler life was for people like John and Abdul. They couldn't afford to think too far into the future, so they didn't have a chance to make plans that would only crumble to dust if they had.

When the truck pulled up to the Foundation House, Richard was first relieved and then disturbed to see no signs of trouble, no signs of anything. In the past when he'd come home after a fight, he'd heard Ann wailing from the sidewalk or found her burning his belongings in the fireplace, but now there was nothing, and it unnerved him. Of course, there was so much less she could do to embarrass or harm him in Sierra Leone. He didn't care any more what theatrics she got up to in front of Jusuf, and they didn't have anything of value for her to destroy.

He smelled food cooking. Something other than rice and *plassas*. Normally he didn't take much interest in food — he saw it as a means to an end — but this was different. He followed the exotic aroma upstairs, where he found Ann, Tor, and Aminata at the table. Aminata was smiling at him. Ann was pouring water into glasses, Tor was holding his fork and knife and licking his lips. Between them was a huge bowl of spaghetti. Music was playing somewhere nearby.

Ann dug two forks into the spaghetti and let it fall onto a plate in sensual coils. It was coated in thick tomato sauce and strong cheese, which stung Richard's nostrils. Everything was fine, it seemed. Ann was happy to see him. She was smiling and chatting about her day like nothing had happened. Tor was waiting for him to sit down so they could eat.

CHAPTER 18

WHEN TOR REALIZED he wouldn't be able to keep down more than a few bites of pasta, Ann agreed to save him some for the next day, but she kept putting more and more onto Richard's plate, and because Richard kept eating everything she gave him, soon there was nothing left, and Tor had to ask to leave the table because he thought he might cry.

Ann had been acting really weird. When Tor got home from school, she'd given him a long hug, rubbing his back and saying that she loved him. Usually this meant she was about to have a meltdown, but instead she'd clapped her hands and said, "How would you like a pasta dinner?" On the surface, this seemed like a good thing — she was happy, she was cooking actual food, he was getting what he wanted — but Tor knew there had to be more to it than that.

After leaving the table, Tor went to his room and looked at his Playboys under the covers. It was the opening night of the cinema, and Kelfala would be coming to get him soon. Tor had collected a stash of candy, and he and Kelfala had designed special outfits — T-shirts on which they had written Wolverines in charcoal and bandanas made from a Hypercolor T-shirt that Tor didn't wear in Sierra Leone because the heat made it turn pink instead of blue. But as he lay in bed thinking about going to the movies in Canada with fresh popcorn, Milk Duds, and bottomless Coke, Tor started to lose his enthusiasm for the idea of eating gross gum and watching a movie in a hot room with a loud generator and probably lots of annoying people talking the whole time.

Ann came into his room, and he could tell she was going to do the *Your father and I* routine.

"Go away," he said.

"Sweetheart, your father and I are worried about you not eating."

"Why don't you tell that husband of yours that if he cared about me eating he wouldn't have eaten all the spaghetti *himself?*"

Ann sat down on Tor's bed and ran her fingers through his hair. He wanted to curl up in her lap and have her rub his back until he fell asleep, but instead he showed her the cut on his leg, which was too old to be a legitimate excuse for his tears. She tried to pull him over to her.

"No," he said.

"Yes," she said. "Even me, when I hurt myself, I sometimes still cry and want my mother. She never comes, but I still want her."

Recently, Tor had been on his way back from school when he saw a white Land Rover parked outside the bar by the hospital. There were four white people sitting at one of the tables, three men and a woman. Tor was going fast, so when he hit the brakes, his bike skidded sideways, and he was so focused on making it look like he was doing it on purpose that he didn't notice the chainring had cut into his leg.

He bent over with his hands on his knees and panted, holding up his index finger to the white people. He was aware of how pathetic he must look to them, so skinny and desperate and covered in sores. One of the men offered him a beer but took it back when Tor reached for it. They invited him to sit with them and ordered him a Fanta. They were journalists, and they all spoke English, but the woman and one of the men had accents Tor didn't recognize. They asked him what he was doing there.

"I'm on vacation," he said. They all laughed, but Tor didn't.

"Are you serious?" one of the guys said.

Tor shrugged. "My mom wanted to go to Disneyland, but I was like, you know what, mom? I got a better idea."

"What do your parents do?" the woman said.

"They suck," Tor said. "Cigarette?" He offered them his pack of 555s, but none of them took one.

"Are you a missionary kid?" one of the guys asked.

Tor shook his head and lit a cigarette. "My dad works at the hospital. How long are you staying here? You could come to our house for dinner."

"As long as it takes for us to finish these beers," one of the guys said.

"You're bleeding," the woman said. Tor looked at the blood running into his shoe.

"That's nothing." He crossed his legs away from her.

"We should get going," she said. "And so should you. Your mother's going to think you've been taken by the rebels."

"Sure you don't want a smoke first?" He offered his pack around again, but they got up to leave. "Hey, kid, God bless," said one of the men as he got into the Land Rover.

Tor gave them a thumbs up and said, "One love."

When he got home, he took out his notebook and turned to his list of white people. He crossed out the Bergmans and added *Those jernalists,* and somehow it made him feel more hopeless than ever.

WHEN KELFALA ARRIVED, Tor was kneeling in front of the toilet wearing his backpack and his Wolverines outfit. "I don't feel good," he said. Kelfala knelt next to him on the bathroom floor.

"So sorry, my friend," he said. He put a hand on Tor's shoulder. Tor looked up at him. He was wearing his pink bandana and Wolverines T-shirt. There was a rusty knife slung through his rope belt. "You can be Matty," Tor said.

All the way to Kelfala's house, the boys pretended they were approaching an enemy village, and if anyone saw them, they would be shot.

"This is called pre-emptive attack," Tor said. They were both crouched behind Kelfala's neighbour's kitchen hut. "You keep them on their toes, so they won't attack you first." Tor peered around the side of the hut, and in the moonlight he could see several men hanging out drinking *poyo*. "You're doing covering fire," he said.

"Boom, boom, boom," Kelfala said, pointing an imaginary gun in the direction of his own house.

"That's a fifty calibre. You have an AK47. It's like...." Tor showed Kelfala how to do the sound, and Kelfala copied him. Tor peeked around the corner again. "They're drunk," he said.

The boys decided to forget about the ambush and find out how Kelfala's uncle had set things up for the cinema. At the door of the house a boy was asking for money. He was dressed in fatigues and a black woollen hat, and it took a second for Tor to recognize that he was the driver's son. Tor said, "We're part-owners," and tried to push his way inside.

"One thousand leones," the driver's son said.

"Ask...Kelfala's uncle. We're part-owners!" Tor said. The uncle came to the door. "Ask him!" Tor said. The uncle said something to the driver's son and then beckoned Tor to come in, so the driver's son had to stand aside.

A small black and white television and a huge VCR were set up on a table in the corner of the main room. A few men sat on mats on the floor drinking milky *poyo* from tin cups. The uncle was sitting on the only chair. "First of all," Tor said to the uncle, "what the hell is this piece of crap?"

"Panasonic television," the uncle said.

"It's a black and white piece of crap. And what is this shitty VCR? You paid two hundred bucks for this? And where are people going to sit?"

The uncle pointed at the mats on the floor.

"No, no, no," Tor said. "You have to put chairs in rows facing the TV."

The uncle laughed. "We no get enough chair."

Tor had a brilliant idea. "Okay," he said. "If it's going to be like this, let's make it like the place where the Wolverines live in when they're hiding in the woods."

Kelfala said something in Temne to the uncle, but when the uncle responded, Kelfala's face fell.

"What?" Tor said.

"He don't want to watch *Red Dawn*," Kelfala said.

"What? Didn't you tell him about it? Didn't he tell you about it?" Tor turned to the uncle.

"Me padi get one fine film wae we go watch," the uncle said.

"What film?"

"*Top Gun*," the uncle said.

"Are you kidding me? That movie is crap. Are you...okay, okay, okay. Listen, okay, *Red Dawn* is the most awesome movie ever. What happens is, these kids are in school and they look out the window and there are all these bad guys parachuting down and all these kids are watching and the bad guys shoot the school and kids are shot in the head, like right between the eyes, and these guys, these cool kids, they run out and they go to the store and get all the bullets and guns and camping gear and a pickup truck and they go to the hills and escape the bad guys and when the town is captured they stay in the woods and hunt animals and they become the Wolverines and they do raids and attack the bases and the bad guys come looking for them and they fight them."

"Yes," the uncle said. "But *Top Gun* na fine film wae all dem people ya want for watch. En den dae pay we for see am."

Tor suggested they could watch both movies, but the uncle said they only had enough fuel for the generator to show one film. When Tor offered to pay for the fuel to watch both, the uncle said they couldn't show two films in one night because they wanted people to come back again and spend more money.

"But we've been waiting forever to see *Red Dawn*," Tor said. Kelfala said something in Temne, and the uncle got up and hit him on the head.

"What did he say?" Tor asked.

Kelfala was holding his head. "It's okay," he said. "We go watch *Top Gun* now ehn we dae watch *Red Dawn* next tem."

"No," Tor shouted. "I paid for half of this piece of shit VCR and I am going to watch my movie!" Kelfala was edging toward the door. When the uncle shouted something at him in Temne, Kelfala shook his head.

Some of the drunk men had come inside, and they were standing behind the driver's son near the door.

"Alright, fine," Tor said. "We'll watch *Top Gun* tonight, but next week, *Red Dawn*, okay?"

The uncle nodded, and Tor sat down on one of the mats. "One thousand leones," the driver's son said.

"Are you kidding me?"

"One thousand leones," the boy said again. Tor looked at the uncle.

"Tell him I don't have to pay," he said. The uncle barked something at Kelfala.

"It's not fair," Kelfala said. "They want to take all your money."

"Screw you," Tor said. "This is my VCR, and you can all go to hell." He picked up the VCR. The uncle leapt up and tried to take it away from him, and just when Tor was about to lose his grip, Kelfala jumped on the uncle's back.

Before this, the other men hadn't been paying much attention to what was going on, but now they were shouting at Kelfala in Temne. The uncle pushed Kelfala onto the floor. The driver's son took a swing at Tor, and Tor held up the VCR to block the boy's fist, which hit the bottom of the VCR. The driver's son pulled his hand into his chest and shouted "Why!" Kelfala was still on the floor, and his uncle was holding him by the throat. Tor held the vcr under his arm and kicked the uncle in the balls from behind. The uncle screamed and fell onto his side, giving Kelfala a chance to get up. "Run for your life!" Tor said.

Kelfala pulled aside the curtain and both boys dove out of the open window, landing on the porch. Tor clutched the vcr under his arm and the cord trailed behind him as he and Kelfala ran. It was completely dark. The only light came from a lantern that Tor knew must be on the steps of his house, and he went toward it, unaware of the ground under his feet. He could hear the men shouting behind him.

When they got to the house, the back door was locked. Tor ran around to the side of the house, Kelfala following, and climbed the air bricks with the vcr still under his arm.

"Hey!" he heard Richard shouting. "What's going on?"

"Dad, it's me," Tor said. He pushed the vcr under the railing and pulled himself over it.

"What are you doing?" Richard said. Ann was sitting next to him at the table.

"Mommy," Tor shouted.

"What the hell do you think you're *doing?*" Richard said again.

"Dad, they attacked Kelfala and they were choking him and I had to fight them off him," Tor wheezed. There was banging at the front door, and Tor could hear Jusuf shouting at the men to go around to the back.

Richard went downstairs, and Tor clung to his mother. "Mommy, you can't let them in. They'll kill us."

"Tor!" Richard yelled. "Come here right now." Tor and Kelfala looked at each other. "Tor!" Richard called again. Ann went with the boys to the back door, where Jusuf and Richard were talking to the men through the bars. "You little shit," Richard said. He took Tor's arm and hauled him toward the door. There were five men outside, including Kelfala's uncle, who was holding his crotch.

"These men tell me that you tried to get into their cinema for free, then you attacked this man when he asked you to pay, damaged Abdul's hand and stole their VCR."

"That's a lie! They're liars."

"Dis bohboh don beat me padi ehn tif we video machine," one of the men said.

"They're lying mommy," Tor cried. "He was choking Kelfala."

Ann held up both hands. "Tell me what happened, sweetheart," she said.

"We went to the movies at their house and we wanted to watch a movie I brought but they wanted to watch some other stupid movie and so we were discussing that and they said I had to pay more than everyone else so Kelfala got upset and stood up for me and they attacked him and tried to kill him."

"So you didn't hurt anyone?"

"Yeah, but I had to because they were choking Kelfala."

"Yes, yes," Richard said. "How noble of you to protect your friend."

"And you didn't steal the VCR?" Ann said.

"I didn't…" Tor said, and then he knew he was screwed.

"Of course, your son would never *steal*, right Ann?" Richard said.

"I can't protect you unless you tell me the truth," Ann said. "Is this the truth?"

He couldn't tell her the truth, because then she would want to know how he got the money for the VCR. "I did take it, but it's not their VCR," Tor said. "Mrs. Bergman gave it to me, and that guy tried to take it from me and Kelfala tried to stop him and he was choking Kelfala so I kicked him and we ran away."

"Why didn't you mention that before?" Richard said.

Richard pulled off Tor's backpack. Tor tried to stop him, but Richard already had the zipper undone, and he was taking out Tor's copies of *Red Dawn* and *Rambo*. He opened the plastic casing on one of them and looked at the VHS.

"Rated R," he said. "What a surprise." Ann took the film from

Richard and shook her head. The uncle was talking to Jusuf now. The driver's son was holding his hand through the bars. "Wiggle your fingers," Richard said. "You'll be fine. Tor, you are going to apologize to these men, you are going to pay them one thousand leones out of your pocket money and you are going to give them back the VCR."

"Mommy, they're lying," Tor said.

"You're lucky I don't put you outside and let them deal with you," Richard said.

"Mommy." Tor could see that she wasn't going to help him. "No," he said. "I won't apologize because it's not fair."

"Okay," Richard said. "Don't apologize, but until you do, you are not allowed to play with this boy any more." Kelfala was wiping away streams of tears with his bandana. "You are not to come around here," Richard said to him. "And if you do, I will tell your uncle. Do you understand?" Kelfala made a whining noise when Richard opened the gate and pushed him out. One of the men grabbed him by his shirt, and Jusuf said something in Temne through the bars. Tor guessed that he was telling the men not to hurt Kelfala, but it wouldn't make any difference. They would just wait until later.

Richard told Jusuf to go and get the VCR from upstairs. "I'm sorry about all of this," he said to the men. "I say padin. Tor go be punished until he say padin too. We go bring you some money tomorrow for the ticket." Tor watched his father speaking his stupid, wrong version of Krio, and he wanted to punch him in the throat. Jusuf came back downstairs with the VCR and gave it to the uncle.

"Well done as usual, Tor," Richard said.

"Fuck you," Tor said. As soon as it came out of his mouth he knew he had to run. When he got to his room, he thrust a chair under the door handle, ran to the far corner and cowered on the floor. Richard was trying to force open the door, and Ann and Jusuf were begging him to calm down. When the door opened, Tor covered his face, waiting for Richard to beat him, but nothing happened. He looked through his fingers and saw Richard standing in the middle of the room with Jusuf's big arms around him. Richard's whole body was tensed. The tendons in his neck were strained, and he was staring at the wall. Tor studied Richard's face, wondering what he was thinking. No one moved or made a sound. When Richard finally relaxed, Jusuf let him go, and Tor was afraid that he would pick up where he left off, but he just walked away. Ann followed him, and Jusuf also left. Once they were gone, Tor cried for a long time. Later, his mother came to kiss him and rub his back, but he pretended she wasn't there.

CHAPTER 19

THE EXPERIENCE IN THE RIVER was like a distant dream. Ann knew it had been profound, and she could remember the feelings she'd had, but she didn't feel them any more. It didn't matter, though. She knew that reality was real, and she could never doubt again that there was a God, and that God loved her.

When Ann came soaking wet up the riverbank, the driver, who was waiting in the truck, had driven her back to the hospital. Aminata was still sitting on the steps, so they picked her up and went to the orphanage, where Maggie was giving the children a Bible lesson in the common room. Ann and Aminata waited near the door and listened.

"Our duty is to know that God is there in the midst of our suffering," Maggie said. "Any situation that happens in our life, God allowed it and he trusted that we can bear it. If we trust him, he will help us to go through it. I'm not saying it will be easy, but he will be with you."

Ann, still wet, still half under the spell that had been cast on her in the river, felt that the message was clear: This was God's plan for her. If they lost the house, that was what God wanted, and she could trust that God wanted the best for her, because he loved her and he forgave her. He knew every bad, shameful thing she had done. He knew she had stolen. He knew she had lied. He knew all the mistakes she'd made with Tor, what a hypocrite she was. He knew the truth about the taxes. God knew all of it, and he still loved her and forgave her, and if he could forgive her, she might even be able to forgive herself.

A radical thought came to her then: she could be happy in Sierra Leone. She looked at the children sitting on the floor in a circle. Maggie and Mark and Emily loved them, but they lacked the warmth those children so desperately needed. Maggie read to them from the Bible and taught them religious classes and told them they were all sinners, but she didn't cuddle them and sing them songs and read them stories until they fell asleep. She didn't tell them they were all special and perfect in her eyes. That could be Ann's role. That was something she knew she could do well.

Surely the Foundation would love to have Richard stay on longer. Maybe they could move into the Bergmans' old house and have enough money to run a generator and get some air conditioning. They could contact that pilot about finding some better food for Tor. Maybe they could stay for a year, and then move to England. Maybe everything was still possible. Maybe they were exactly where they were meant to be, and this audit was an answer to her prayers, a way to get rid of that that albatross, that white elephant, once and for all.

There was no way they could get their money back — as if anyone else who could afford such a house would choose to live in that town — and renting it out would only bring in a fraction of the mortgage. The only way they could keep paying for it was to go back and submit to that life, which seemed worse than hell. She understood then that she'd taken so long to finish the house not because there was so much to do, but because she hadn't wanted it to be finished. Once they moved in, that was supposed to be the beginning of their life, the culmination of all her striving, and she would have had to admit that it would never be enough. But maybe now they could wash their hands of it, walk away, start over. If the government didn't seize it, someone would buy it for something, or the bank would repossess it, or maybe it would end up like the Foundation House, the sad relic of someone's hubristic dream, left to rot as a warning to anyone tempted to make the same mistakes.

Maggie looked up at Ann and smiled, and Ann felt such love for the strange, brash Texan. Here, with Maggie, she could do something meaningful. She could become the person she had realized she was capable of being during the Marriage Encounter weekend — someone generous and peaceful, someone capable of real love and forgiveness and service. Just thinking about it made her quiver with happiness. She had to go home. She had to dry off and go home to her family and tell them she loved them.

WHEN SHE GOT HOME she'd made a spaghetti dinner, which was nice, but then there was that dreadful scene about the VCR, and that night she had a nightmare that she was pregnant with a demon fetus and had to try and starve it to death. She woke up the next morning feeling worse than she had in a long time. Her eyes and tongue felt swollen, and she was congested and dizzy. Tor left for school crying after Richard told him that they might have to put Billy to sleep and if they did it would be his fault.

"How can you be so cruel?" Ann said when Tor was gone.

"I'm cruel?" Richard said. "Have you forgotten what he did?"

"What do you mean?"

"I mean that he spun Billy in an onion sack and shot rocks at him with a slingshot."

"He didn't mean to hurt him," Ann said. Richard didn't respond, just picked up the dog and left.

When Maggie and Aminata arrived, Ann was in the hammock crying. "What's wrong, sugar?" Maggie asked. Ann was sure Maggie must be sick of her crying. Everyone must be sick of her. She was sick of herself. She wanted to tell Maggie about the river, but Maggie would probably say it was a demon communicating with her. And maybe it was. It had been such a beautiful experience, and she had thought it was the answer to everything, but here she was back in the hammock with all the same problems.

"I need your help," she said. Aminata sat in a chair beside the hammock, and Maggie knelt next to Ann and held her hand.

"Let's pray," Maggie said. "Lord Jesus, we want to thank you for bringing us together here this morning. We just love you so much, and we ask you to continue to open Ann's heart. You know she is a sinner, but because of your precious blood, she can overcome her bondage. We ask for your guidance, Lord Jesus, so that she can identify any spirit that is trying to harm her, and claim authority over it in your blessed name. Amen."

Maggie's praying left Ann cold. It had nothing to do with what she had experienced in the river. That experience wasn't about being delivered from some invisible evil. It was a perfect, wordless knowing. And her God didn't love her as a lender loves a borrower or as a landowner loves his serf and certainly not as a shepherd loves his sheep, but as a father loves his child — not because he forgives her sins, but because he understands her and doesn't count her mistakes as sins at all.

When Ann opened her eyes, Maggie was staring at her, as if waiting for some reaction. "Have you placed your whole faith in Jesus Christ?" Maggie asked.

"Yes."

"And have you renounced those occultist practices you were involved in before?"

"I said, 'God have mercy on me, a sinner,'" Ann said.

"Have you been reading the Bible?"

"I was."

"And?"

"I can't concentrate."

"That's Satan," Maggie said. "He doesn't want you to read your Bible."

"Uh huh," Ann said.

"You have to know Satan is trying to attack you every chance he gets, but you can't be afraid. Fear is a spirit. I told you that. It's how the devil enters your life."

"If I believe that I'll feel more afraid than ever," Ann said.

"Not if you have the peace of knowing that Jesus is with you. Through the Bible, you can prosper. Many people try to use other means, and they may prosper on earth, but they die and perish in hell."

No, no, no, Ann thought. God was loving and compassionate. He wasn't holding the threat of hell over her.

Maggie stood up and reached into her bag. "Can I read to you from my Bible now?" She opened the book without waiting for an answer. "In the beginning was the Word," she read in an artificially calm and soothing voice. "And the Word was with God, and the Word was God. He was with God in the beginning. Through him all things were made; without him nothing was made that has been made. In him was life, and that life was the light of all mankind. The light shines in the darkness, and the darkness has not overcome it."

Maggie reached down and put her hand on Ann's head, which made Ann feel incredibly angry. She desperately didn't want to be angry, but she couldn't seem to help it.

"He said to them, 'Go into all the world and preach the gospel to all creation. Whoever believes and is baptized will be saved, but whoever does not believe will be condemned. And these signs will accompany those who believe: In my name they will drive out demons; they will speak in new tongues; they will pick up snakes with their hands; and when they drink deadly poison, it will not hurt them at all; they will place their hands on sick people, and they will get well.'"

Ann tasted something bitter that made her screw up her face. Then a thought came into her head. *He never loved me. He never loved me.* The first time she thought it, but the second time she heard it, as if someone was saying it in her ear.

"Who never loved you?" Maggie said. Ann was confused. Had she said it out loud? Could Maggie read her mind? "Your husband?" Maggie said.

Ann lips trembled. "Must be," she said.

"Your daddy?"

"No!" She felt like she could beat Maggie for having said it. "He's the *only* one who ever loved me."

Maggie put a hand on Ann's shoulder, and Ann wanted to throw it off and run away, but she couldn't move.

"What's your name?" Maggie said. *Oh fuck off, you know my name,* Ann thought. The anger was growing. She was losing herself, overwhelmed by the thoughts that she never let herself think because she was supposed to *forgive* and *let go* but *fuck that* because they had ruined her life, those *fuckers. That bitch, that fucker, that bitch, that fucker, that bitch, that bitch, that bitch.* She would never, *ever* forgive them.

"Is there someone you can't forgive?" Maggie said.

Ann held the sides of the hammock. "Don't you dare say her name," she said. She couldn't bear to hear it from Maggie or from anyone.

"I don't know her name," Maggie said.

"I'm not going to say it either! I never want to fucking hear it again!" Part of Ann was horrified by what she was saying, especially in front of Aminata, but she couldn't seem to stop herself.

"Who else can't you forgive?" Oh yes, Ann saw what Maggie wanted her to do. List all of the people she couldn't forgive — Richard, her mother, her stepfather, John, Maria, her perverted high school teacher — and then at the end, when she thought there was no one left, Maggie would deliver the clincher: *What about...yourself? Can you forgive...yourself?* But she wasn't going to play Maggie's game. She wasn't going to sit in that hammock with Maggie standing over her like the big judgmental God telling her what a stupid sinful, unforgiving, angry loser she was. She tried to get up, but Maggie pushed her back down with surprising force.

"Is there anyone else you can't forgive?" Maggie said. She was totally calm, which only made Ann more angry.

Ann made her hands into fists and held one by her chin as she bit the other one and growled. She took her fist out of her mouth and held her flexed fingers in front of her. She looked up at Maggie. "What do you want me to say?" she shouted. "My father? Is that what you want to hear? I can't forgive my *fucking* father for dying and leaving me with my bitch of a mother!"

"Do you feel like your father doesn't love you?"

When Maggie said this, a rage like Ann had never felt before came over her. "He *never* loved me!" she screamed in a high-pitched voice that was not her own.

Suddenly she felt overwhelmingly tired. She yawned, and her head shook *no,* and she was trying to keep her eyes open but they kept closing. She lay back down in the hammock, and Maggie held the Bible to her head and shouted, "I command you to come out of her in the name of Jesus Christ! You spirit of unforgiveness, you have no right to hold her any more! In the name of Jesus!" Ann's body was rigid. She wouldn't have been able to move if she tried. "You spirit of anger, you have no right to hold her any more! In the name of Jesus I renounce you! Any unclean spirits that have entered her through Catholicism or occultist activities, I renounce you! In Jesus' name!"

Ann felt split through with exhaustion and rage and relief, and yet there was still that calm part of her watching the scene and her riot of opposing emotions with detachment and even amusement. "In Jesus' name! I bind and rebuke you!" Maggie shouted. "Come out of her and never enter her again!" A wave of relief passed through Ann's body, and her muscles relaxed. Maggie stopped shouting and brought her face close to Ann's. "Come, Holy Spirit, and fill Ann. Come, Holy Spirit," she whispered. "Thank you, Lord Jesus. Thank you, Lord." She stroked Ann's face gently, saying, "Peace, peace," until Ann fell asleep.

When Ann woke up, she was in her bed, and Maggie was sitting next to her, sipping a drink and reading by lantern light. It was dark outside. Ann tried to lift her head, but she didn't have enough strength, so Maggie helped her to sit up.

"How do you feel?" Maggie said.

"Tired." Maggie gave Ann her cup. As Ann drank the sweet, milky coffee, the events of that afternoon came back to her, and she laughed nervously and thought how strange it all was. "I'm sorry for those things I said. That terrible language, and I didn't...."

"That wasn't you," Maggie said. "You received a miracle from God." Maggie took out her Bible and started to read, and Ann closed her eyes and went back to sleep.

She didn't wake up again until Richard got into bed next to her. She turned toward him, and he put his arm under her neck and held her, which he hadn't done in ages. When she next opened her eyes, it was morning, and he was gone. She could hear Aminata's crutches. She sat up slowly, expecting her body to feel heavy and weak, but she felt surprisingly good — better than she had in a very long time. Her breathing was clear and easy. Her tongue and eyes felt normal.

Aminata came into the room and sat next to Ann on the bed. "Good morning, mom," she said. She looked so pretty — her lovely, innocent face, her smile, her awful golden dress, which she kept wearing even after Ann had bought her two new ones. Ann felt a surge of love for the child. She reached out to take Aminata's hand and had a vision of herself holding her own mother's hand when her mother was dying.

In the last days of her life, Ann's mother had been transformed. All of her entrenched grudges and judgments seemed to fall away. A devout Catholic all her life, she wouldn't let anyone speak to her about religion at the end, and when her priest came to visit she told him to go play with marbles. She told Ann and her sister Dot that she loved them. She called them "my beautiful girls," which made Dot laugh and Ann cry. She pointed at Ann's pregnant belly and said, "I remember when you and I were like that." Dot told the priest that their mother wasn't herself, but Ann believed that her mother had never been herself *before* then, and that brief breach in the seemingly impenetrable wall that had always stood between them helped Ann to let go of years of bitterness and pain.

"What happened to your mother?" Ann asked Aminata. The girl stared at her lap as she told Ann that her mother had been in a car accident, but she hadn't seemed to be injured, so she came home and went to bed. Aminata got into bed next to her, and when Aminata woke up in the morning, her mother was dead.

"Did you love your mother?" Ann asked.

Aminata nodded.

"And did she love you?"

Aminata nodded again, and tears fell down her cheeks.

"And now? Does anyone love you now?" Ann asked, her own eyes filling with tears. Aminata shook her head no.

"I love you," Ann said.

WHEN ANN TOLD RICHARD she wanted to adopt Aminata, he said, "Sometimes I wonder if when you do good it's really for yourself."

He hadn't said no, so she brought it up again later and he said, "It wouldn't be easy," which was as good as yes.

Maggie wasn't as happy about the idea as Ann had imagined she would be. Her first response was: "She's not a puppy."

"I know she's not a puppy, but she is an orphan, and we have always wanted a daughter."

"Well that's nice for you," Maggie said.

"Yes, it would be nice for me," Ann said. "And it would be nice for Aminata, too. To grow up in a family, with love and security."

"And you think *your* family is going to give her that?"

"I do."

"Honey, I'm not saying she doesn't like being with you, but I don't know if adoption is what's best for her. I want her to grow up with the right influences...." *Of course,* Ann thought. Maggie was worried that Richard and Ann would raise Aminata as a Catholic, or worse.

Since what Maggie was calling Ann's "deliverance," Maggie had been pushing for Ann to do deep Bible study and keep on rebuking everything and building up her "spiritual armour." Maggie had also told Ann she had to get rid of *A Course in Miracles* — which Ann was finally getting into — after Ann made the mistake of explaining that it was actually Christian, because it was channelled from Jesus. Maggie said that if Ann didn't study her Bible and renounce all of her *ungodly* possessions and *demonic* books, the spirits that had been oppressing her were going to come back, bringing with them even more unclean spirits, and then she would be worse off than before.

For Ann, what had happened was a continuation of the miracle that had begun in the river. Her inability to forgive had been making her sick, and through God's love — expressed to her directly in the river and later through Maggie's care — the anger she was carrying had been purged. The way she saw it, the whole experience was meant to teach her that God worked in many different ways, and she didn't have to have a mystical encounter to feel connected to him, because he was present in everything that happened to her and everyone she met.

Now, miraculously, she seemed to be getting well. She could breathe! Every morning she woke up expecting the old symptoms to be there, and every morning she was amazed to find them gone. Something inside her had shifted, too. It was as if she had taken a step back, and her problems didn't seem so incredibly intense any more. Not that they didn't matter, but that on some level nothing mattered, or at least not in the way she'd thought it did. *A Course in Miracles* said, and this was perhaps her favourite sentence from any book ever: "Nothing real can be threatened. Nothing unreal exists. Herein lies the peace of God." She had been trying to hold the world together with her judgments and opinions for so long, and she was still trying, but a part of her had completely and perhaps irreversibly let go.

When Ann asked Aminata what she would think about being part of the Berringers' family, Aminata was quiet for a while, then repeated what Ann had asked her. Once she was sure she understood, she said she would like it very much and then spent the rest of the day acting like a drunk, being an insufferable brat and speaking rudely to Ann one minute, crying and apologizing the next, then sitting sullenly on her own.

Tor was the only one whose response to the adoption idea Ann could have predicted. He screamed in her face that she was stupid and he hated her, then he ran to his room and cried and wouldn't let her come in. She knew he would get over it, so she let him cry. He had been crying a lot and behaving horribly in general. Richard had announced that he was grounded until he apologized for stealing the vcr, and Tor was as likely to apologize for something he wasn't sorry for as Richard was to go back on a punishment once he'd said it out loud, so there was no way out for either of them.

Almost overnight, a new impossible dynamic arose to replace the old impossible dynamic. Before, Ann had been struggling with her breathing problems and trying to protect Tor and herself from Richard's cruelty, but now all of her problems centred on Tor, whose behaviour was becoming more and more disturbing. He still refused to eat, and he looked ghastly with his gaunt face, leaking wounds and the filthy bandana he insisted on wearing everywhere. He antagonized Aminata all the time, stealing her crutches, calling her names, trying to trip her. Whenever Richard entered the house, Tor started up with his rap noises and continued until he got a reaction, so Ann had to give him a smack herself before the situation got out of hand, and each time she did she felt further from her experience in the river.

She tried to encourage Tor to come to Maggie's house to play football with Daniel, because she thought they would get along well, but he said he wouldn't be caught dead with "that bunch of losers." Once, Ann caught him touching Aminata's breast and saying, "You've got nothing there." She had barely managed to stop herself from acting on her anger, which was actually fear he would turn out to be a sexual pervert or a criminal and it would be all her fault. "You will *never* touch Aminata like that again," Ann said in her most severe voice, but Tor just laughed and pulled a face.

Maggie told Ann that when she was overcome with anger toward Tor, she must say out loud, "I rebuke you in the name of Jesus," to let the spirit of anger know it had no authority over her, but all too often it did. Sometimes she wondered if Tor was demon-possessed. After everything she'd been through, now when she was finally feeling better, her son had to choose that moment to become a little devil.

Once while he was running around the house chasing the dog with a cutlass, she prayed out loud, "God, please, can't you make this kid be normal? Please!"

"You know there's a name for people who talk to themselves," Tor said. He chased Billy up and down the hall and back into the kitchen, where Billy cowered behind Ann. Tor peeked around the corner, and for a moment Ann had this wild idea that he was going to say sorry, but instead he said, "There's a name for people who sleep with men for money, too."

It took her a second to understand what he meant, and by then he was at the end of the hallway. When he saw her coming toward him, he started laughing, as if they were playing a game of hide and seek, and when she caught up to him she fell on him and hit him, and he kept laughing the whole time. Later, when the crushing remorse set in, she imagined that behind Tor's laughter she had seen such sadness in his eyes, and she felt like the worst mother in the world, the worst *person* in the world, thinking she was so different, thinking she'd learned something and been healed, but still doing all of the same terrible things as before.

"WE HAVE TO BE patient with him," Ann said to Richard. She was sitting on the dockhouse balcony with her book in her lap, talking to him through the broken window. "He's feeling threatened, because of Aminata."

Richard sighed. "You didn't tell him about that, did you?" Ann had been working on a new exercise. In this one you looked around and told yourself that you didn't understand anything you saw. *I don't understand this chair. I don't understand that glass. I don't understand that woman in the water.*

"I didn't see any reason not to tell him," Ann said. "He's part of this family, and it would affect him too."

"Did you take the time to explain it to him, or did you just blurt it out like you always do?"

"I don't think I *always* do anything," she said.

"There's paperwork to be done. We don't even know if we're allowed to adopt her yet, and if we are, it could take years. And I don't know if I *want* to adopt her. She might already *have* a mother somewhere."

"I told you her mother is dead."

"So she says."

"Are you saying she's lying?"

"I'm saying she's a kid who knows how to get what she wants."

"Have you noticed that I'm better now?"

"What does that have to do with anything?"

"Look, I know you don't believe in this, but I truly believe that I was healed by God, and I feel that part of my purpose now is to take care of Aminata."

Richard rolled his eyes. "Seriously?" he said. "So I'm supposed to accept this because, what, God said so? God wants us to adopt her? Well, how can I argue with that?"

Ann felt sorry for him. "That's not what I said. I had a profound experience that I'm not ready to share with you right now because you are so antagonistic. And because of that experience, and because of Maggie's help, I am *better* now. Can't you see that I'm better? Don't you care?"

"I care that you're better, yes. And I have my own theories about why that is, but we don't need to get into those. As far as I'm concerned, you can believe that you're better because of God or Maggie or Santa Claus or whatever you like, but I'm not going to adopt a child into our already struggling family because of what you believe, because it wouldn't be fair to her."

"Richard, it was your idea to bring her into this family, and I am not going to just walk away from her when she needs us."

"She doesn't need us, Ann. You need her. You need a project to make your life feel worthwhile, but Aminata is a person, not a project."

For the first time in a long time, Ann felt above his judgments. Instead of crying or fighting back, she simply resumed her exercise. *I don't understand my dress. I don't understand that tree. I don't understand my husband. I don't understand myself.*

CHAPTER 20

RICHARD HAD ASSUMED that the argument about Musa was the end of his friendship with Sandi, so he was surprised when Sandi came into his office one morning, sat down opposite him, and said, "You're an outsider here, Richard. You have a good heart and you want to help, but you have to understand that other people's faith in what they believe in is as real to them as your faith in Western medicine is to you."

Richard would have liked to object to the use of the word "faith" when referring to science, but he wanted to repair the bridge he had burned by swearing at Sandi in front of the patients, so instead he said, "I know, Osman."

"If you just start lecturing them about how wrong they are you will only end up alienating the people we want to help."

"So what do you recommend?" Richard said.

"As I told you, if we keep offering good services, people will be more and more likely to come to the hospital first. That's already happening. And as for the herbalist, you know, I talk to him freely, I'm not afraid of him, but to be honest, I think he has some mild form of schizophrenia, and he's quite powerful in this community and has a lot of influence with the Paramount Chief, so I don't want to end up in conflict with him."

"Maybe we should offer him some Haldol," Richard said. "Put him out of business that way." Sandi smiled, and Richard decided to drop both topics — the herbalist and the circumcision — for good.

THAT AFTERNOON, Martha pulled Richard aside in the middle of his clinic. "Can you come somewhere with me?" she asked.

"Right now?"

"Yes. It's quite important. And please bring your bag."

"Okay," he said. "But quickly. Sandi's not here, and I've got people waiting."

He followed her behind the hospital, down a dirt road and through a field. They arrived at a shack in a treed area. An elderly woman was sitting on the ground outside and stood up when she saw them coming.

"This is Mammy Fatu," Martha said. Richard shook the old woman's hand. Martha said something in Temne, and the woman opened the door of the shack. When Richard looked in, he was confronted with the horrendous smell of rotting flesh and human waste. A little girl lay in a fetal position on the floor, coughing. The parts of her body that were visible were covered in lacerations, and liquid oozed from wounds in her neck.

"How long has she been here?" he asked. Martha talked to the old woman.

"Since yesterday," she said.

"Is this the witch girl from the herbalist?" Richard said. Martha nodded.

"And why is she in here?"

"Many people want to do her harm."

"It looks like they've had a go at it already."

Richard knelt next to the child. Her neck was swollen and scarred, and she had bruises on her face. The smell coming from her was stomach-turning.

"You can see that she's emaciated," he said over his shoulder to Martha, who was standing behind him holding a scarf over her mouth and nose. "Her neck is swollen and red. It's hot and tender to the touch." He gently pressed on the girl's neck, and she cried and coughed roughly. "These scars are probably from previous abscesses which have drained spontaneously. She's drooling, probably because she can't swallow her saliva." He looked back at Martha. "Rubor, calor, tumor, dolor, functio laesa." He pronounced each word carefully. "Redness, heat, swelling, pain, loss of function. These are the cardinal signs of inflammation. I assume it's caused by an abscess. Can you ask granny how long she's been like this?"

There was a drawn-out exchange between Martha and the granny, and Martha seemed uncharacteristically frustrated with the old woman. Finally she said, "The girl has been sick for many years, but the difference in her neck is…the past day or so."

"Sick how? These sores on her neck, have they been here for a long time?"

"She has had those sores for a long time, but over the past day or so her face and her neck have changed and she can't talk."

"Ask her if there's anyone else in the family who is thin and has a chronic cough."

Martha spoke to the granny and then said, "The uncle."

"Tell her…what's her name?"

"Rugiatu."

"Tell Rugiatu I need her to open her mouth as wide as possible," Richard said. Martha came closer and spoke to the child while Richard pulled on some gloves and found a tongue depressor and flashlight in his bag. Martha helped the girl to turn her head, and when Richard brought the tongue depressor toward her, she opened her mouth a bit. "Her tongue is very swollen," he said. "So it's unlikely that the swelling in her neck is the result of trauma."

Richard put the tongue depressor in her mouth and she gagged, so he got a quick glimpse of the diffuse swelling at the back of her throat. "It's not a quinsy," he said. "That would be on one side or the other. I think she has tuberculosis, which explains her emaciation and swollen lymph nodes, so I suspect this is a retropharyngeal abscess, or an abscess in the back of the throat, which might be related to tuberculosis in her cervical spine."

"What can we do for her?" Martha said.

"It needs to be drained, but it has to localize first, and it's still in the process of developing, so it's just a matter of waiting for it to localize, and in the meantime we need to keep her under observation to make sure that her airway isn't obstructed and she doesn't aspirate the pus if it bursts in an uncontrolled way."

Richard bent down to pick the girl up. "What are you doing?" Martha said. The girl didn't resist, but her face contorted in pain as he arranged her wasted body in his arms.

"We'll make her comfortable at the hospital, and by tomorrow we should be able to drain it."

"We can't."

"We have to. If we try to do it now it'll be a bloody mess."

"No, we can't take her to the hospital."

"Surely you don't think I should leave her here." Richard looked at the granny for support, but she had understood nothing. "No one will bother her," he said.

Richard took the girl to Sandi's office in order to avoid the people still waiting outside his own. He didn't want to draw attention to the girl, so he needed her washed and admitted before Sandi got back. She was increasingly panicked and wouldn't cooperate when he tried to examine her abdomen and check again to make sure that her airway wasn't obstructed, so he left her with her granny and went to look for Martha, who he found in admissions. "Matron," he said. "I've left the girl in Sandi's office with her grandmother. I want you to wash her, check her airway, and make her comfortable in the ward. I'll come back and examine her later, when she's more relaxed."

"I have no time," Martha said. "I'm on duty."

"Exactly," Richard said, trying not to show his surprise at her reaction. "Wash her, please."

When Richard had finished his last appointment for the day, he tried to talk to the girl and the granny through Martha, who was inexplicably annoyed about being involved, even though she had been the one to involve him.

"Why did she take her to the herbalist and not the hospital?" Richard asked. The granny, who was crouched on the floor by her granddaughter's cot, answered almost inaudibly, looking back and forth between Richard and Martha.

"People wanted to hurt the girl, so she was hiding her," Martha said. "She says when some people found out where she was, they came and took her to the police station, where they were beating her and not giving her food. Her uncle went to the Paramount Chief, and the herbalist said he could help her, so the Paramount Chief said let her go there."

"Where are her parents?"

Martha asked the granny. "The parents are dead," she said.

"And why was she in the bush?" Richard asked.

"The herbalist was keeping her there."

Richard tried to examine the girl's belly again, but she did every-thing she could to stop him. He assumed she would be even more distressed if he attempted a pelvic examination, and since she was too young to be sexually active, he decided to forgo it for the time being, because he was in a rush, and because he felt scrutinized by Martha, whose careful attention to his actions now took on a differ-ent meaning.

He had only seen the abscess for a second, but he was sure his diagnosis was correct. After it had ripened, he could drain it, if it didn't drain spontaneously before then, and then he could test her for tuberculosis and get her on treatment. In the meantime, he would make her comfortable with painkillers and keep her safe.

He heard raised voices and went outside to see the herbalist shouting at two nurses. The man, who suddenly seemed huge, was wearing a long blue robe and holding a lit cigarette in his right hand. He jabbed his left index finger forward and leaned his torso back, as if he was pronouncing curses that he didn't want to get too close to himself.

"You see!" Martha hissed in Richard's ear. She had never spoken to him like that, and he wanted to placate her somehow, but there was no time.

"What's he saying?" Richard asked. The herbalist turned, and Richard found himself smiling nervously and stepping back into the children's ward as the man advanced on him and Martha.

"He says you took his patient," Martha said. The herbalist stopped in the doorway to the ward, casting Richard and Martha in shadow.

Richard tried to make his smile look deliberate and confident. "Tell him she's my patient now," he said, but Martha didn't translate. The herbalist took another step toward Richard, and Richard, who was now looking up at the man, had to force himself not to look away.

"He says you have been on his private property," Martha said.

Richard stopped smiling. "The girl's granny brought her to me," he said.

"I will not tell him that," Martha said. "It was your idea."

"No it wasn't!"

"Yes it was," Martha said. "I wanted for you to help her, not take her away."

The herbalist spoke again. "He says you will not be able to cure her," Martha said. The herbalist said something then that made Richard shudder, even though he didn't understand it. "What did he say?" he asked Martha. She didn't answer.

"How much does he want?" Richard asked.

He couldn't bear to have her turn against him, too. He wanted to say, *Please understand me, Martha,* but instead, he said, "Tell him I'll give him five thousand leones. It's all I have. And tell him there's no smoking in my hospital."

Richard went to find his wallet, praying that the herbalist wouldn't follow him and that Sandi wouldn't show up until the man was gone. When he gave the herbalist the money, which really was all he had, the herbalist left, cigarette still burning, but Richard had a feeling that wouldn't be the last he would see of the man.

He decided it would be better if he told Sandi about what had happened himself instead of letting him hear about it from one of the nurses, but before he had a chance to find Sandi, Sandi found him in the corridor outside the children's ward.

"For goodness' sakes, Richard," Sandi said.

"Before you...."

"Some of the nurses are extremely upset. A few of them have threatened to leave."

"That's their problem if they want to leave," Richard said. "I did what my professional responsibility required, and this is a great opportunity to prove to people that what we have works."

"I've spent the last ten years trying to do that," Sandi said with disgust. "Did you give her antibiotics?"

"Not yet."

"Don't you dare let anyone know if you're giving her free treatment. We'll never hear the end of it. And don't you dare let her die."

BY THAT EVENING, when Richard sat down with Turay for a drink, he was feeling extremely uneasy about what had happened. "Are you afraid of the herbalist?" he asked Turay.

"This one behind the hospital?"

"Yes," Richard said.

"No. My God is greater than anything he has," Turay said.

"Do you think I should be afraid of him?"

"Oh no," Turay said. "He won't bother you, as long as you don't interfere with him."

"I took his patient away today."

Turay peeled a strip off the label of his beer. "Well...let me say if he was going to harm you, he probably would have done it already." This was little reassurance for Richard, who was starting to think he might have unleashed a dragon.

"We usually say that when you go to these traditional healers you fall into more trouble, because you start seeing different evil things," Turay said. "Also some of them don't tell the truth. Even if they know that they will not be able to treat this illness, as long as the patient will pay, they will pretend as if they will be able to treat that case."

"So you don't think they can help people at all?"

"Some can, of course," Turay said. "God made herbs for our use, so they can help, and there are healers who have great success with them. But those that work with demons are not good, and after the treatment with them when you come home, you start behaving in a different way, the way you would not even like to see yourself. So in my opinion some of them are good and some are bad, but there are people who behave badly in every profession, not so?"

"He said he worked with the good demons," Richard said.

"Demons are always there for bad," Turay said. "They are seriously against the peace of this world. When he treats people with his demons, he will put more demons in them, so he can get more money and grow the demon kingdom."

"What if I told you I don't believe in demons?"

Turay shrugged. "If you don't believe in them, does it mean they don't exist?"

"So you think that demons can cause diseases?"

"Yes, I believe in that."

"So what are we doing at the hospital? We should all be exorcists, not doctors and anaesthetists."

"If we look at the life of Jesus, he usually did not heal two people in the same way," Turay said. "In one case, he spits and puts his fingers into the deaf man's ears. In another case, he heals the centurion's servant without even having sight of him. In another case a woman is healed by touching his garment. I believe he did his healing differently each time so that we would understand that as a healer you have to ask and pray and wrestle, and then something good comes, but there is no formula to follow."

"I agree there isn't only one formula, but you have to adapt your approach according to scientific and technological advances, not messages from some voice in your head."

"Okay," Turay said. "I cannot oppose your beliefs because I belong to another way of thinking. No one knows anyway. No one has ever died and come back to tell us this is the right way to go. We can only pray that God will give us the right direction."

On his way back to the hospital, Richard saw a stray dog sleeping in a pile of dirt at the side of the road. He bent down to pick up a stick to throw for it, and when he stood up again, it was peering out at him from behind a concrete wall, as if expecting to be beaten. Richard thought of Billy. The wound wasn't healing. He was in constant misery, getting weaker and weaker. As much as Richard didn't want to admit it to himself, it was time to face facts. He had to end the dog's suffering. But how? The kindest thing would be to give him ketamine to knock him out and a paralyzing agent to stop his breathing, but Richard still couldn't justify giving a dog drugs that were in such short supply. Of course, this was the same logic that had kept him from repairing the wound in the first place, which might have saved everyone a lot of pain and trouble. Another option would be to just take the feeding tube out and let him starve, which wouldn't take long, but if Richard had the heart to do that, he would have done it a lot sooner.

In the children's ward, the granny had fallen asleep under the girl's cot, and the girl seemed to finally be resting comfortably, so Richard decided to wait until the morning to examine her. He gave the night nurse instructions to give her penicillin and feed her water through a straw, and he went home with John, who was for once there when Richard needed him.

Normally he would have been keen to go to the dockhouse when he got home, but the rats were gone, so there was nothing to do but try to write more depressing fundraising letters. He was feeling more morose and generally anxious without his traps to take his mind off things. Even his book was destroyed, having been left out in the rain by Ann, so now he would have to wait until he got back to Canada to find out what had become of the main character, although it had seemed obvious for some time that he was planning to off himself, a conclusion Richard had started to look forward to as the man became increasingly whiny and fanatical.

Considering the possibilities for how he might distract himself from his growing anxiety, Richard was surprised to discover that he wanted to be with Ann, so he was disappointed when he got home to find that she was out. She had been so strange lately, talking constantly about God and demons. He wished she could see that those beliefs were just invented as a way of surviving. Powerless people needed to believe in a supernatural being who could intervene on their behalf. People whose lives were incredibly difficult needed to believe in an afterlife where they would be rewarded for all their suffering. But none of that was true. There was no hereafter. There was no God, at least not how people like Ann imagined. If God existed at all, he was a scientist who, having placed some cells in a petri dish, was watching impassively to see how they behaved.

But the good news about Ann's new beliefs and her new friendship with Maggie was that her behaviour had improved considerably. She wasn't complaining about smells at all any more, which made her much easier to be around. She seemed to love playing with the kids at the orphanage, and she always came home excited about some new project she was doing with them. The only troubling part was that she was spending a lot of their personal money on these projects, and they really didn't have any to spare.

She had also finally started taking a harder line with Tor. Predictably, this made his behaviour even worse, but he couldn't keep it up forever, and besides, Richard didn't see much of him except for mealtimes, when Tor tried his best to push all of their buttons. As for Aminata, she was growing on Richard, and her behaviour was a good example for Tor of how respect begets respect. This didn't mean Richard wanted to adopt her, but if that was what it took to keep Ann happy, he was prepared to at least consider it.

When Ann finally came home, dropped off by Maggie, Richard told her about the girl with the abscess, and her horror made him feel vindicated. "That poor child. Let's pray for her," Ann said. He lay in silence and let her pray. Normally he would have been ashamed on her behalf to hear her speaking out loud to some imaginary entity, but at that moment, he was glad to be distracted from his other feelings, which were becoming increasingly difficult to ignore.

He couldn't understand why he felt so anxious. Nothing had happened, really, but he was full of worry and even dread. He remembered how when he was a boy and his mother sent him out at night to deliver messages to his father at the pub he would tell himself, *I am the danger here,* so that he wouldn't be scared.

"You know what's really interesting?" Ann said suddenly, and Richard startled. "People think of barbarians as savages, but originally it just meant someone who isn't Greek. That's a really, really interesting fact, I think. It's amazing how often we think of people that way."

"What way?"

"I still have all my classics books somewhere," she said dreamily. "I might read them again." He turned to speak to her, but her eyes were closed.

He lay awake for hours, missing the calming sound of the rain on the tin roof as he listened to the rowdy soldiers at the bridge checkpoint and the neighbourhood dogs howling. When he did fall asleep it was fitful and brief, and he held on to Ann for comfort.

WHEN HE ARRIVED at the hospital in the morning, he found two women and a nurse arguing with Martha in the courtyard.

"Wetin na di problem?" Richard said.

"They are upset about the girl you brought here," Martha said. "They want to discharge their children."

"What happened?" Richard said.

"This one says she saw the girl walking backward through the ward at night," Martha said.

"What rubbish. She can't even walk."

"And this one said she had a dream that the girl was trying to initiate her child into witchcraft. I told her it is just her imagination because she has it in her head that the girl is a witch."

"All of the children were crying throughout the night," the other nurse said.

"So what?"

"She should not be here," the nurse said. "There are a lot of sick people. There are a lot of kids, and witches can easily manipulate kids."

"Listen to me," Richard said to the nurse. "That girl is not a witch. She is a sick child, and she needs our care. If you don't want to care for her, you are free to find another job, and if these patients don't want to be here, they are free to leave, but if you want to stay working here, you will not repeat anything that has been said here this morning. Do you understand?"

The nurse said nothing.

"Dis titi no dae witch, no need for make palaver...."

The nurse held up her hand. "I understood you," she said. "I am trying to digest what you said."

After some more grumbling, the women went back to the ward and the nurse went back to work. "She cannot stay here," Martha said.

"Well, you have to tell people that she's not a witch," Richard said.

"I did!" Martha said. "I told them they shouldn't talk, because they are making people afraid that she is going to transfer the witch

290

to them, but they told me not to listen to you because you only know the medical side and you don't know about our tradition. I am the one going close to her. I gave her crayons to crayon. I tried to tell people that she is not a witch, she is a normal person like they are, go close to her, talk to her, but they won't listen to me."

"So what should we do?" Richard said.

"We shouldn't be bringing patients to the hospital if we can't protect them."

"Well, it's too late now," Richard said. "I'm not taking her back."

WHEN RICHARD CAME to check on the girl in the afternoon, he found an orderly shouting in her face. "Dis nor to you witch place. If you do am again, I go kill you!"

"What on earth are you doing?" Richard said.

"This child attacked me in my dreams last night," the orderly said. "Now I'm telling her not to try that with me again, or she will be sorry."

Richard was furious, but he knew that making a scene would only create more problems for the girl. "Go back to work right now, please, and do not come in here again," he said. The orderly left, and Richard sat down at the end of the girl's bed. She was awake, staring at the wall. He had absolutely no idea what to do with her. He couldn't keep her at the hospital, but he couldn't return her to the herbalist either. *What do I do? What do I do?* he said over and over to himself, but no answer came. Just when he was starting to seriously consider the possibility of uttering some sort of prayer, he heard Ann's voice and turned to see Ann and Maggie walking toward him, looking for all the world like a pair of door-to-door missionaries.

"What are you doing here?" he said.

"I wanted Maggie to meet her," Ann said. She gasped when she saw the girl. "Oh! Poor thing!" she said, and Richard had his answer.

CHAPTER 21

TOR WAS STARING AT Aminata's plate. She had more than him. One whole extra piece of meat, and much more sauce. It wasn't fair. This was his family, his food. And she didn't even know it was special. She wouldn't appreciate it. He was so angry he couldn't even eat what he had.

Ann came upstairs with a tiny pan of cheese sauce and poured some over Tor's bread. "Aren't you going to give Aminata some?" Richard asked.

"She wouldn't like it," Ann said.

"How do you know if you don't let her try?"

"She's got more meat than me," Tor said.

"I've told you a hundred times to take that filthy thing off at the table." Richard reached for Tor's bandana, but Tor moved out of the way.

"I don't want to be at the table anyway," Tor said. He tried to leave with his plate, but Richard caught his arm and forced him back into his chair. A piece of his meat fell onto the floor in front of Billy, and Billy sniffed it. When Tor tried to kick it away, he accidentally kicked Billy in the nose. Richard banged his fist down on Tor's hand, which was resting on the table.

"Ow!" Tor screamed. He turned to his mother, but she was ignoring him.

"Go to your room," Richard said. There was no way Tor was going to go downstairs and have them all up there eating his food, so he grabbed the tablecloth and pulled on it. Richard held the tablecloth with one hand and with the other hand pushed Tor's chest.

Tor fell onto the floor, and Ann got up and dragged him by his arm toward the stairs, saying "What is wrong with you?" At the top of the steps he yanked his arm free and ran to his room. She followed him, and he slammed his door in her face, but she came in anyway and sat on his bed.

"Why can't you be good?" she said.

"Why did you give Aminata more than me?"

"Don't be ridiculous. I always give you more. I gave you all of the cheese, because I know it's your favorite. Now come upstairs and finish your meal."

"I'm not going back up there with them," Tor said.

He expected her to offer to bring his food to his room, but instead she said, "Okay, it will be waiting for you upstairs if you want it."

Tor took off his shirt and lay on his bedroom floor for a long time. He had been stuck in the house for too long. Not only was he not allowed to hang out with Kelfala or take the bike out except to go to school, but Ann had also forbidden him to go into the cashew field ever since Richard told her about the secret society bushes. Tor could have gone out anyway, because there was really nothing his parents could do to punish him any more, but there would have been no point, because there was nowhere to go that was better than the cool tiles of his bedroom floor.

Home, school, home, school. That was his life, and his only friend was Jusuf, and Aminata had stolen his mother. He hated Aminata. He couldn't believe Ann would even consider bringing her back to Nova Scotia. She would be the biggest loser in the whole school, and he would have no choice but to be associated with her. Richard didn't want her either. Tor could tell by the way Richard treated her.

Sometimes he would be nice, but that was only when he was trying to teach Tor a lesson. The rest of the time he ignored her.

Once Ann got mad because Richard said they shouldn't talk about something to do with money until after Aminata had gone home. Ann said Aminata had every right to be involved in family conversations, and Richard said, "Well Ann, I'm not sure you're right about that. I think that both you and Aminata have to understand that it will take some time for Tor and me to get comfortable with this new dynamic you're trying to create."

They had a big argument about it, and afterward, when Richard left to go to the dockhouse, Tor followed him.

"What do you want?" Richard said when he saw Tor behind him.

"I wanted to say I thought you were right. She's not being fair to us."

"You should mind your own business." Richard said.

TOR GOT UP OFF THE FLOOR, used a chair to barricade his door and took out the tin of Canadian dollars hidden in his mattress. Next to the money was the letter he'd taken from Richard's garbage can. He sat on his bed to read it.

Dear Joan,

I'm sorry it's been so long since I've written. Then again, maybe you don't want to hear from me. I have never written a letter like this, and I don't know how to begin. It seems so artificial to write it down and send it through the post to a place that seems so far away, a place where I'm not sure it will find you.

You once told me you were an Acadian witch, and that if I ever hurt you, you would put a curse on me. Sometimes I think it was true. When we were together, I appreciated nothing, I knew nothing, and you gave me everything and asked for nothing in return. I don't think I will ever experience such selflessness again.

I want to tell you the shameful truth about why I left you, so that you will know what an absolute shit I was. I hope it will help you, somehow, but maybe you won't care. I hope that it will make you smile, at least, to know that however much you suffered when I left, I have suffered ten times as much since.

I would like to be able to say that I left you because I was a coward. That I loved you, but I didn't know how to give and receive love, so I ran away because I was frightened and didn't want to hurt you. You accused me of that once, and all I can say is that I wish I were capable of such nobility. I did love you, Joan, as much as I believe I am capable of love. I loved you best when things were going badly in other areas of my life. When I felt like a bad person, when I felt inferior, small or stupid, you could be counted on to restore my confidence. But when I was happy and feeling good, I could only see your overwhelming unsuitability.

The truth, Joan, is that I left you because you were not beautiful. You and I were a pair of comfortable old socks, familiar and warm, but suited only to a night in. With Ann, I felt like I could go anywhere and everyone would immediately see how important I was. She elevated me the in esteem of others, while you only elevated me in my own esteem.

I began this letter telling you I was sorry, but now that I'm at the end I can see that it is only myself that I owe an apology to, since you are so much better off without me. I wish there was some way to go back and make things right between us. I wish I could be close to you again, and feel the way only you have ever made me feel. Mostly I wish for you to be happy.

With love,
Richard

TOR PUT THE LETTER in his pocket and went outside to look for wasps' nests. He found one at the end of the weird hallway on the side of the house, and he was about to knock it down with a broom when he heard Ann and Aminata outside.

"Hey, Aminata, do you want to help me with something?" Tor called through the air bricks.

"Where are you?" Ann said.

"In the hallway thing. Tell Aminata I need her help."

Tor heard Aminata coming on her crutches. "I'll make you a snack!" Ann said. Tor met Aminata at the door to the hallway. She was smiling.

"I dare you to go in there and knock down that nest," he said. She looked at him skeptically.

"It's fine. Jusuf and I do it all the time." Tor handed her the broom, and she put down one crutch to take it. "Let's do it together," he said.

She followed him to the end of the hallway. He took the broom from her and held it up. "Ready?" he said. Aminata nodded. Tor hit the nest and ran, and Aminata did her best to run after him, but she only had one crutch. Tor didn't have a chance to plan it, certainly he hadn't intended to do it in advance, but when he got outside he turned around, and something about Aminata's panicked face, her legs buckling under her, gave him the idea that he should close the door.

He didn't lock it. All she had to do was turn the handle. But instead, Aminata lay down on the ground and howled. Ann came outside to see what was going on, and Tor hid behind the mango tree and listened while Ann helped Aminata out of the hallway and tried to calm her down. "Oh my goodness," Ann said as she checked Aminata's body for stings and Aminata tattled about Tor locking her in.

"She's lying!" Tor said. He came out from behind the tree. "I didn't lock her in. The door closed behind me." Ann ignored him. "Why don't you tell Dick? Why don't you send me to my room? Why don't you send me there for the rest of my life so you and Dick and Miss

Perfect here can live happily ever after?" He wished Ann would look at him at least, yell at him, hit him, but it was like he wasn't there.

"Mommy, don't ignore me," he pleaded. She continued to check Aminata for stings. "Mommy, please!" She didn't respond. He kicked at Aminata's foot, and Aminata moved it away. Feeling desperate, Tor picked up the cutlass from the top step and started hacking at the trunk of the mango tree. Ann led Aminata inside, saying something about getting ready to go back to Maggie's.

Tor kept hacking at the tree, and when he was worn out, he went down to the river's edge and sat by himself. He wondered what was wrong with him. He didn't mean to do those things. He didn't want to hurt Aminata. He just wanted to go home. How much time had he spent listening to his mother talk about the mould and Richard, and now that she seemed to be getting better, he felt like he was losing her.

It had started with a huge house cleaning. She'd had Jusuf bleach the house from top to bottom, and after that she'd stopped spending whole days in the hammock. Instead, she went to Maggie's or read and did lessons with Aminata on the dockhouse balcony or even on the sofa in the living room, which she'd suddenly decided was safe. This should have been a relief to Tor. She was well, she wasn't crying all the time. But instead it frightened him, because it meant that either she had surrendered to some even deeper depth of despair or, much worse, she had accepted things the way they were.

Tor heard people near the water hooting and looked up to see Ibrahim coming toward him with his oar.

"Hello, Tor," Ibrahim said. They shook hands. "I've found my cassette tape. Can I listen to your machine?" Tor didn't want to let Ibrahim use his Walkman, but he'd said he would, so he went inside and got it from his bedroom.

Ibrahim needed help with every step of the process — opening the Walkman, putting the tape in, pressing Play, figuring out how to wear the headphones — and as soon as the music began, he started crying. Tor felt incredibly awkward, but he couldn't leave Ibrahim alone with the Walkman, because he might steal it or break it, so he had to sit next to this crying man until enough time had passed that he could say he had to go back inside. Meanwhile, he ripped Richard's letter into small pieces and dropped them into the water.

"Thank you so much," Ibrahim said after a while. He wiped away his tears. Some people were still hooting.

"Why do people make that noise at you?" Tor asked.

"Where are you from again?"

"Nova Scotia."

"Aha! That's close to New York. Come with me."

Tor had nothing else to do, so he followed Ibrahim toward the cashew field. "I found this rock the other day, and I'm sure it's something very special. I want you to take it to the Smithsonian. There's a man there named Peter or Patrick Smith, I think."

Ibrahim wandered through the trees for a long time before finally stopping at one that looked like every other tree on the plantation. He rested his hand on the trunk. "I left it here," he said. "I'm sure I left it right here."

Tor rubbed his eyes. "I can't take a rock to Canada," he said.

"I know it was here," Ibrahim said.

"How big is it?"

"About the size of an American football. You just look at it and you think, what is *in* there?"

"Why do people make that noise at you?" Tor said.

Ibrahim sat on the ground. "I used to have a son. I found him in a rubbish pit, and I raised him. That was the only noise he could make. And those people love to make fun. They think I'm cuckoo because I don't do like them and become like a dodo, the birds in Madagascar, they can't fly, they push around go dockadockadocka. What we have here is called retrogressive development. It might look like development, but its bringing people backwards. Somebody gets educated, he knows good and bad, he goes back to his village and says it's what I believed in as a child that works, because that makes everyone else happy. You know it isn't true, but you promote it anyway, to please them. As soon as you do something like I did when I took care of my son, you have a number of spectators and evaluators with different types of interpretation of the action you're doing."

"I don't understand," Tor said.

"I don't know if my son was already retarded when he was born, or if it was somehow because of deprivation. Anyway, he made that noise, and that's why they make it at me."

"Where is he now?"

"Someone drowned him. I never found out who. I'm waiting for death myself, but I'd like to die in peace, enjoying the sound of the water, the beat of the rapids, but it's obstructed by these people. They always want to see you suffer, drag your belly on the ground, even if you have the chance to live in a skyscraper. So it mellows my own ambitions."

It was the worst thing Tor had ever heard. Could it be true? And if so, how could this guy not take a flamethrower to whoever did it? Maybe that was why Ibrahim was crazy, Tor thought, and he wondered if the same thing would happen to him eventually — if he would lose his mind because he couldn't make things fair. "I have to go home," he said. "My mother will be worried about me."

"I'm worried about your mother," Ibrahim said. "You people need to leave. This place is going to be bloody, man."

"Anyway, I should go," Tor said.

As he was heading back to the house, he heard a whimpering noise. He stopped and waited until he heard it again. It was the sound Billy made when he was in pain or afraid. Tor wished that the dog would disappear. He felt really sorry that Billy was suffering, and he knew it was partly his fault, but he didn't want to be reminded of it any more.

He followed the sound to the riverbank, where he found Billy stuck in the mud. He trudged in to help the dog, but when he reached out, Billy tried to bite his hand. "Relax," Tor said. Billy's cone had come off, and his wound was full of dirt. Tor tried to pick him up again, but Billy kept snapping at him.

"I'm helping you, you idiot!" Tor said. He went around behind the dog to try to pick him up him from a different angle, and he managed to get him out of the mud, but Billy twisted his body around by digging his hind legs into Tor's arm and pushing the weight of his upper body into Tor's chest. He bit at Tor's face, Tor flung him away, and he landed on his side with his legs at strange angles.

"Stay still!" Tor reached down to pick the dog up again, and this time Billy tried to slither through the mud into the water. When Tor pursued him, the dog turned and snapped at him again. Tor pushed Billy's face down into the mud with his foot, picked him up, and threw him into the river, reasoning that the dog would be freed at least, and could swim back to the shore on his own, but instead Billy thrashed around in the water, looking like he was drowning. Tor waited a few seconds to see if Billy would start swimming, but he didn't, so Tor waded into the water toward him.

Now Billy should have let Tor help him. Instead, he tried to swim away from Tor, and Tor had to chase him. "You moron, come back," Tor yelled. He grabbed the scruff of Billy's neck, and Billy tried to bite him again, but choked on a mouthful of water.

Tor pushed Billy under the water and held him there, waiting for him to calm down. When he let him back up, Billy was still fighting, so Tor pushed him under again. A bird that had caught some kind of rodent in its beak flew low over the water. The bird was almost dragged down by its prey, and it seemed as if it would have to drop the other animal or crash into the river itself, but at the last second, the bird raised itself up, its wings beating the air in powerful, audible thrusts before it disappeared in the trees.

Billy had stopped moving, so Tor carried him out of the river and dropped him on the shore. He sat next to Billy to catch his breath, and after a couple of minutes he realized the dog still wasn't moving. "Come on!" he said, shaking him. He pushed on Billy's chest a few times, but still the dog didn't move. "Come on!" he said. One of Billy's legs was at a weird angle, so Tor moved it to make it look more normal. He opened Billy's mouth and pushed on his ribs again to try to make him breathe. "Please, Billy!" he cried. Billy's tongue was blue. Tor shook him again, but again, nothing. He sat down next to Billy, weak with horror, and put his muddy hands over his eyes. He hadn't held Billy under that long. Maybe he'd had a heart attack? Then Tor remembered the wound, and it made sense. He must have filled up like a bottle held under water.

Once, in a movie, Tor had seen some dead person being sent off on a raft in a farewell ceremony, so he decided to make one for Billy. He started by gathering sticks and breaking them so that they were the same length. He lined them up in a row and found some long stalks of elephant grass to tie them together. His plan was to tie the grass on at one end, loop it around each stick until he reached the other end, and tie that end, but the grass kept breaking before he'd made it from one end to the other. Next he tried to weave the grass only halfway across the raft, working inward from each side and tying the two middle sticks together with a separate piece of grass. This made the wood stay together, but it was flimsy, and when Tor checked if it would float, he could see that it was already coming apart.

He scanned the riverbank looking for something stronger to hold his raft together. Jusuf was calling him. Out of the corner of his eye, Tor saw the tail of his Wolverines bandana, which had turned blue from the cool water. He took it off and wound it through next to the elephant grass. The material was strong and stretchy, so it worked well. When he'd finished, he tried to pull some of the pieces apart, and they stayed together.

He collected some more grass, made a nest, and placed Billy's body on it, curling him up carefully as if he were asleep. He knew that Jusuf would come looking for him if he didn't go back to the house soon, so he quickly lifted the raft into the water. Before he pushed it away into the current, he touched Billy's nose, which was still warm, and knew that Richard had been right about him all along.

22

MAGGIE SAID SHE KNEW as soon as she saw Rugiatu. She looked at the girl's face and saw a demon instead of a child. She said this was revealed by the Holy Spirit.

The idea, as Ann understood it, was that Maggie was going to counsel and testify to Rugiatu until Rugiatu was ready to confess and be redeemed. After that Maggie could do deliverance on her. Maggie warned Ann that witches can be cunning, and they shouldn't fall into any of the girl's traps. "You have to get to know them," she said. "Make them feel accepted and loved. Satan never shows love. It's always violence. When you come with a gentle hand, they see what God's love is like."

Rugiatu couldn't speak, but she could respond to questions by nodding or shaking her head. When Maggie asked Rugiatu if she was a witch, Rugiatu nodded yes. When Ann asked if anyone else had told her to say that, she shook her head no. They asked more questions. Had she harmed people? Had she killed people? Was she in communication with the devil? To all of these she responded yes, but Ann doubted she really understood what she was being asked.

When Ann came back to Maggie's later that evening, Rugiatu spoke for the first time, and although it sounded like her mouth was full of marbles, Emily's translation of what she'd said was perfectly clear: "She said she turned herself into a snake and went into people's houses to drink their blood."

"Was she working with anyone else?" Maggie asked, eyeing the grandmother. The girl said nothing.

"Emily, why don't you and Aminata take granny and show her how to make a Christmas wreath, and ask Mark to come in here, please," Maggie said.

When Mark came in, Maggie told him to ask Rugiatu if her grandmother had helped her to become a witch. Rugiatu said nothing.

"Tell her it's okay," Maggie said. "She won't be in trouble." Still Rugiatu said nothing, just touched her stomach and groaned.

Mark held his hands over the girl. "We pray against the spirit of witchcraft and darkness and anything in this child's generation that might have caused it to attack her," he said.

Emily came back and sat on a chair in the corner. "Go and see about the children," Mark said, and Emily immediately got up to leave.

"She should stay and pray with us," Ann said.

"It is their bedtime, and they need supervision," Mark said.

"Why are you always so rude to her?" Ann said. "Doesn't the Bible say love your wife as Christ loved the church?"

"You don't have to speak for me," Emily said crossly to Ann. "I can speak for my own self." She left, closing the door behind her.

"Let's pray," Maggie said, but Ann was concentrating on not crying. She had only been trying to stick up for Emily, because Emily never stuck up for herself.

As Maggie prayed, Ann remembered how, on the last day of grade twelve, Mr. Carter had come into the room where she was having a detention and said, "What are you doing here?"

"It's pretty obvious, isn't it?" she said.

"What did you say?" he shouted. "Come here right now."

She walked over to where he was standing by the door. He grabbed her upper arm. "We are going to your house right this minute to speak with your mother," he spat.

"She'll like that," Ann said. "She doesn't get many male visitors."

He took her other arm and shouted into her face while he shook her. "All we, like sheep, have — *Finish* it! *Finish* it!"

"Let me go! That hurts," she said. She pulled away.

"Finish it!" he shouted into her face.

"Get lost," she said, and she walked away and never looked back. She thought she was ruined. He would tell her mother. She would be failed and have to repeat the year. But nothing happened, and she never heard from him again.

THAT NIGHT IN BED, Richard let Ann read him the newest exercise from her book: *God did not create a meaningless world.*

"The world you see has nothing to do with reality," Ann read. "It is of your own making, and it does not exist.'"

"Mmmhmmmm," Richard said. His eyes were closed.

"You are supposed to think of all the most horrible things in the world, and say, *God did not create it, and so it is not real.*"

"Mmmhmmmm."

"This is your personal repertory of horrors at which you are looking," Ann read. "Some of them are shared illusions, and others are part of your personal hell. It does not matter. What God did not create can only be in your own mind apart from His. Therefore, it has no meaning."

"Ann, please don't let Maggie bother that girl too much with her praying," Richard said.

Ann didn't mind that he wasn't listening to her. She was thinking about Maria, which was the worst thing she could think of, and telling herself that the whole chaotic, attacking world she used to see around herself had been her own invention, not the reality of God. *God did not create betrayal, and so it is not real.* Richard turned in the bed and looked at her. She knew he wanted to have sex, and some mixture of gratitude for him at least trying to care about the book and the blossoming hope she'd had ever since she started to feel better allowed her to not turn away long enough for him to take it as an invitation.

There was something desperate about the way he pulled up her nightgown that made her feel queasy. He was stroking her face and staring into her eyes, but she had to turn away. It was like he was trying to engage her in some kind of simultaneous self-soothing, and it seemed dirty, as if they were two children doing something unnatural and wrong. She let him continue to touch her, and she was so relieved when he suddenly stopped that she didn't even ask him what was wrong.

After he fell asleep, she lay in the darkness and felt sorry. He was being kinder to her. He was leaving it mostly to her to discipline Tor. This was what she had wanted, and she should be happy and care more about his needs. But caring only about Richard and Tor wasn't enough for her any more — it never had been. Looking back on the last ten years of her life, she realized that every effort she had made had amounted to nothing, and she couldn't believe how foolish she had been to think that it could have been any different. If Richard hadn't had the affair, if the house hadn't been full of mould, she would have lived the rest of her life in that little town obsessing over what he was thinking and doing while she fought a losing battle to maintain her body and her sanity. This was how God worked. The mould, which had seemed like a curse, had actually turned out to be a blessing. And even the affair had been a gift. She and Richard had been cracked open by it, and for the first time they had seen each other nakedly, the best and the worst. Now God had given her Maggie, and through Maggie the chance to help two children, Aminata and Rugiatu, and who knew how many others. This could be her purpose, and she would never have discovered it without the suffering that had brought her there.

Richard would call her a bleeding heart if she told him these thoughts. Every time he saw her try to reach out to someone, he found fault with her way of doing it. Once, when they were leaving church, a woman on the street had asked Ann for her shoes, and Ann had given them to her. Richard said it was embarrassing, but Ann couldn't understand why. She told him she had other shoes, and the driver was there, so she didn't need them to get home. "John! His name is John!" he shouted at her in front of Maggie and Emily, and she was so hurt that she didn't even respond.

While Richard slept with his back to her, Ann considered what he had said about people doing good for selfish reasons. It was true. She wanted to feel useful, she wanted love, like everyone else. But that wasn't the whole truth. She didn't do anything for only one reason. Probably no one did. And she wasn't even fully aware of her own motivations most of the time, so how could she expect to understand anyone else's? It was such a simple insight, but for Ann it was revolutionary. She tried applying it to Richard and Tor, admitting that she would never know all of the reasons why they were the way they were. She tried it with Maggie and Mark and then with Maria, but that was too much for her, so she came back to Richard and focused on breathing love into the mystery that lay between them.

WHEN ANN ARRIVED at Maggie's house the next morning, Emily and the kids were making wreaths out of scraps of *lappa* fabric, and Mark was using characters on a felt board to illustrate a Bible story. "Mom, mom," the kids shouted when they saw Ann. They crowded around her, all trying to show her their wreaths, which she admired, one after the other.

Daniel stood next to Ann, and once the other children had gone back to what they had been doing, he took her hand, put something in her open palm and closed her fingers around it. He watched her face as she opened her hand to reveal a coin.

"Is this for me?" she said.

He nodded. "God gave it to me," he said. "I said 'God, I need money,' and he gave me this. He loves me."

This touched Ann almost to tears, because Daniel was usually such a tough little boy. "Yes, he does," she said, and she knelt and hugged him.

When Mark had finished his story, he left, and Ann called the kids to come and practise their carols. She was planning a fabulous Christmas celebration for them, despite Maggie's initial reservations. Maggie said it would cost too much, and they would be disappointed if it didn't happen every year, but Ann said she didn't mind paying, so Maggie couldn't argue. Ann was going to have a separate celebration for Tor and Aminata as well. They would drink Ovaltine around the fire and get some sort of tree to decorate and play cards and maybe even have Kraft Dinner if she could get to Freetown in time.

Ann told the kids to sit in a circle on the floor. Aminata pushed her way in to sit next to Ann. She was always trying to get Ann's attention, but so were all of the kids, and Ann spent much less time with them. Aminata wrapped her arm under Ann's and held it tightly.

Ann assumed that Aminata was going to ask her about going to buy second-hand clothes from the junk market. She had promised this to Aminata but changed her mind when Maggie said it was unfair to the other kids if Aminata got something they didn't. Ann knew this meant she should buy clothes for all of the kids, and Maggie too, but Richard was becoming more and more strict about money, so she couldn't. Once the holidays were over, she planned to contact her friends in England and organize a fundraiser for the orphanage, and then she would be able to help out more and make some badly needed changes.

"Emily, why don't you join us?" Ann said. Emily smiled tightly and said no, and Ann felt like asking what her problem was. She had never been anything but nice to Emily, and all she got in return was rudeness and rejection. Still, it must be awful for Emily to be judged and ordered around by Maggie and Mark all day, so Ann couldn't hold anything against her.

"Ann, can I speak to you for a minute?" Maggie was standing in the kitchen doorway with her arms crossed. Ann pulled her arm away from Aminata and went over to Maggie.

"Is everything okay?" she said.

"I just want to know what you're teaching the children."

"We Three Kings," Ann said.

"Honey, I am real grateful if you spend time with them, and I know they love you, but I don't want anything to compromise the fundamentals of their Christian education. If you want to teach them something else, though, you are welcome. English, for example."

"You know, I'm a Christian too, Maggie. And what you're talking about sounds a lot like indoctrination to me. Not letting them have access to any other perspectives than your own."

"It's not my *perspective*, Ann. It's the Holy Bible. Everything I teach those children is directly from scripture. And if you want to talk about indoctrination, you are the one who grew up in a belief system that encourages people *not* to read the Bible so they won't notice how unbiblical their beliefs are. Add to that all this New Age stuff and Eastern mumbo jumbo and you don't know which way is up. It's your choice if you want to continue to do that after the miracle that God did in your life, and I love you no matter what you believe, but I don't want it affecting these children."

"Wow," Ann said.

"And that goes for Rugiatu as well."

"Uh huh," Ann said. She was angry, but she also felt sorry for Maggie, because as hard as it was to live with doubts, it must be even harder to live with a certitude so feeble that you had to defend it all the time.

"Mom?" Aminata called. A toddler was pulling on Ann's dress, and Ann picked her up.

"Is that all?" she said to Maggie.

"That's all," Maggie said.

"Mom?" Aminata said again as soon as Ann sat down.

Ann checked to make sure that Maggie was gone. "Okay, let's hear 'We Three Kings,'" she said. "Daniel, you lead." Daniel picked up a pencil and used it as a conductor's baton, singing the song in a high-pitched voice that made all the children laugh.

"Come on, Daniel. Be serious," Ann said. Daniel put down the pencil and sang with his hands clasped behind his back. The other children followed along, and Ann imagined starting her own orphanage, one where she could teach the children whatever she wanted — meditation and evolution were the first examples that came to mind — without being treated like a corruptive element.

"Mom," Aminata said again.

"What is it?" Ann looked at Aminata and saw that she was trying to hold back tears.

"What is it, sweetheart?" Ann said. She put her arm around Aminata's shoulders, but the crying had gone too far, and Aminata couldn't get out whatever she had wanted to ask.

After the carol practice, Ann went into Rugiatu's room. Maggie was sitting on the bed showing Rugiatu an illustrated Bible story, which Mark was translating. When Maggie and Mark had first started reading the Bible to Rugiatu, the girl had stared at the ceiling, but now she was turning her head to listen. Maggie probably thought this was because she was ready to receive the Word, but what she didn't know was that Ann had been left alone with Rugiatu the previous evening, and instead of reading to her from the Bible, Ann had sung her a lullaby and caressed her hands and feet and looked into her hideous face with love.

The girl turned onto her side and held her stomach. "Where's the grandmother?" Ann said.

"I asked her to leave this morning," Maggie said.

"Why?"

"At first she wouldn't go, but then I told her we couldn't help her granddaughter with her here."

"Surely it was better for them to be together," Ann said.

"Rugiatu got this from her grandmother, and that's why she isn't saying how she became a witch, because she's afraid of getting her grandmother in trouble," Maggie said. "One of the nurses told me that Rugiatu and the grandmother slept in the same bed at the hospital, and the granny was whispering evil things to her in the night. I also think she put incantations in Rugiatu's food. That's why she has a stomach ache."

Ann wondered if she should tell Richard about all of this, but she didn't want to undermine Maggie, so instead she resolved to pray for the child's pain to go away, knowing that she would be having her operation soon enough.

Maggie put down her book and held Rugiatu's hand. "Jesus loves you," Maggie said. "He wants what's best for you. Do you know that?" Mark translated and Rugiatu nodded. "This is not what Jesus wants for your life. You are his child, and he wants to know you. Would you like to invite him into your life?"

Rugiatu nodded again.

"Yes?" Maggie said. "Do you want to confess your wickedness and repent of your sins?"

Rugiatu nodded.

"Can she kneel?" Maggie asked. Together they helped the girl to kneel on the floor and stood in a circle around her. Mark put his hands on her head. "God, we ask you to have mercy on Rugiatu in the name of Jesus so that she can become a real person of good potential," he said. "She knows that she is a sinner, and she has repented. Lord Jesus, we love you and glorify your name. We plead your precious blood to cover Rugiatu. We just...." Rugiatu clutched her throat and started gagging. Ann was about to pat her on the back when the girl opened her mouth and white liquid and blood gushed out onto the floor. Maggie was saying, "Jesus, Jesus, Jesus." The girl spewed out more of the liquid while looking at Ann with an expression so grotesque it made Ann back away. Whatever was coming out of her mouth smelled unimaginably vile, and Ann started to retch, too.

"Oh my God," she said. "Oh my God."

"Speak the name of Jesus," Maggie said. Pus and blood kept coming out of the girl's mouth. Maggie put her hands on the girl's head and shouted, "Out! In the name of Jesus, I command you to come out! Fire of the Holy Spirit upon you! Fire of the Holy Spirit!"

Ann had to run outside to get away from the smell. When she came back, the girl was lying in bed. Her whole face had changed. She was talking to Emily, and Ann understood the words *thank you, thank you, thank you.* She realized that the girl's expression, which had seemed so sinister while she was puking and choking, was actually a smile. The girl was *smiling.* She was a completely different child. She was transformed. It seemed too literal and immediate to be possible. You just talk about Christ's blood and people puke out their demons?

Ann's thoughts were interrupted by the sound of a vehicle coming up the driveway and the children calling, "Doctor, doctor."

"You won't believe it," Ann said when Richard came into the room.

"What's happened?"

Maggie held out her arms toward Rugiatu as if she was presenting him with a prize.

"Oh, it's drained, has it?" he said.

"This child was deep into witchcraft. She admitted it to us, but now she has given her life to Jesus, and he has released her from the grips of the demons that were binding her," Maggie said.

"No," Richard said sternly. "I told you the abscess in her mouth could drain on its own at any time." He turned to Ann. "Don't you remember I said that if it happened you must get her in a head-down position and call for me?" Ann didn't remember that at all. "Look in her mouth," he said. He tried to open Rugiatu's mouth.

"Stop it," Maggie said. "Can't you see she's afraid of you?"

"Fine. Fine!" he said, letting go of her jaw. "But if you looked in her mouth you would see that there is a hole in her throat that is draining pus. I appreciate you taking care of her, but this is not a miracle. It's exactly what was expected, and I don't want to hear one more word about this poor kid being a witch. I cannot believe you two are talking like that."

"Did I force her?" Maggie said. "Do you think I told her to say that? No. You can't force someone to say they are a witch, but all witches confess at some point."

"No, no, no," Richard said. "She's mentally disturbed. She's been abused."

"Yes they do," Maggie said. "Either because they feel guilt or because they are so proud and they want recognition." Ann wished they could all just work together and support each other, and she was about to say so when Maggie said, "Ann's right about you. You can never admit when you're wrong, can you?"

"Where's her granny?" Richard said.

"She's gone," Maggie said.

"Where?"

"She was influencing the child. It was necessary to separate them."

"You had no right to do that," Richard said.

"The grandmother was the one who trained the granddaughter, and the granddaughter had become more powerful even than her, but now she is free from that," Maggie said.

"Do you honestly think that's what made her better?" Richard said.

"You are so dang arrogant," Maggie shouted at him. "I suppose you have some explanation for how your wife got better too, don't you? You can't once give God the glory, can you? You think you've got it all figured out and you're so dang pleased with yourself."

"My wife getting better has nothing to do with your superstitious claptrap," Richard said.

Ann had no idea what to think about any of it any more. No more clever opinions. Every time she thought she understood, she found out she didn't. But still she trusted that there was an order somehow, and that it had to do with goodness and love, or God, and maybe that was the best she would ever do.

Richard was pulling the blankets off the girl. "Pastor Mark, will you please help me to get her into the car?" he said. The girl held her stomach and groaned.

Mark turned to Maggie. "Go ahead, Mark," she said. Mark picked the girl up and took her away. Richard paused at the door on his way out, and without turning to face Maggie he said, "She's not a witch. But thank you."

"I'm sorry," Ann said to Maggie when Richard was gone.

"You don't need to be sorry, honey," Maggie said.

"I'm sorry for Richard," Ann said.

"You can't make someone see what he doesn't want to see. Only God can do that."

"I'm sorry I've judged you sometimes," Ann said.

"I thank the Lord that you came into my life," Maggie said. She embraced Ann.

"I'm sorry I thought I would be a better mother to Aminata than you are," Ann said into Maggie's hair.

"I think you would," Maggie said.

CHAPTER 23

THE DOG WAS ALWAYS UNDERFOOT, but the one time Richard went looking for him, he was nowhere to be found. It had been a brutal afternoon at the hospital, and he had come home to find Aminata sleeping in his bed, which he assumed was Ann's way of punishing him for what had happened at Maggie's. He had decided to write some letters in the dockhouse, but when he sat down at his desk, something felt wrong, and he realized it was because Billy wasn't there.

He searched for the dog until dusk, then went back to the dockhouse and sat down at his typewriter, but he couldn't concentrate. He hated the thought of Billy lost, wandering in the cashew fields alone, but he couldn't bring himself to go back outside. He could hear the secret society drums in the distance, and he told himself that if he were a braver person he would go and find the source of the sound and see for himself that it was just a bunch of people bonding over old rituals that none of them really understood. It was no different than what he did when he went to church — eating flesh, drinking blood, and singing songs to a God he didn't believe in, all in the service of feeling like he was a normal person who was part of something.

He stared at the blank piece of paper he had fed into the type-writer. There was nothing to write. He wished he had never allowed

Maggie to get involved with the girl, but how could he have guessed that she would believe the child was a witch? Now she'd probably take credit for the child's recovery and make him look like a fool, but he was too tired to care. In any case, the girl *was* getting better, and Richard was relatively confident that she was going to be okay. She'd tested strongly positive for tuberculosis, and Martha had agreed to hide her in one of the storage rooms at the hospital on the condition that first thing in the morning Richard would start looking for somewhere for her to stay during her treatment. He could only hope that once the girl was gone things would go back to normal, but under the circumstances he wasn't sure what that meant any more.

Not so long ago he'd spent all his time in the dockhouse trying to get away from Ann, and now that all he wanted was to get into bed next to her, he'd been replaced. Just weeks earlier she'd spent her days crying and complaining about mould to anyone who would listen, and now she was happily caring for orphans with Maggie, singing them lullabies and giving them math problems and joking about taking them all home and calling them *little monkeys* — God, he wished she would stop that. Now she was devoted to Aminata, or the idea of Aminata anyway, and as much as he suspected she wanted to bring the girl back to Canada as some sort of trophy — an exotic new character in the story of her life, an emblem of her new mission — he doubted she would figure that out before it was too late.

His only hope was that she would be too disorganized to arrange the paperwork, but already she was talking about a trip to Freetown, a visit to the High Commission. On the other hand, maybe if they came home with an African orphan — a crippled one at that — it would give people something to talk about other than his affair. Richard felt disgusted with himself for thinking this, and he wondered if his disgust was real or only a reflex, the scolding voice of the person he knew he ought to be.

He heard a vehicle approaching and looked out the window to see the hospital truck pulling up in front of the house. For a second he considered hiding. Whatever it was, he didn't want to know. It gave him a thrill, the thought that he could hide. He would be leaving soon, and they would have to manage without him then, so why not now? Why did he have to fix everything? Why not Sandi?

Waiting for John to find him, Richard was certain for the first time that he wanted to go back to Nova Scotia. Don and the house and the scandal, all of that seemed so much easier to deal with than this nonsense. He would switch to fee-for-service, he would patch things up with Don and the girls, he would do whatever it took to make the house livable for Ann, and in time people would forget.

John was coming down the jetty. "Doctor Berringer, I come to take you to the hospital," John said.

"Why can't you get Sandi?" Richard called out of the window. "He's in charge of the hospital, isn't he?"

"Martha say only you must come," John said, and Richard was so glad to know that Martha had asked for him that he got his bag and went with John without any more questions.

When they arrived at the hospital, Martha was with Rugiatu in the storage room. The girl was lying on her side, unconscious. At first Richard thought she might be dead.

"How long has she been like this?" he said.

"I don't know. I sent John to get you as soon as I found her."

The girl's skin was clammy, her pulse thready, her belly distended and rigid. Richard tried to talk to her, but she was unresponsive. He must have missed something, but what? He tried to remember if he'd done an abdominal examination when he first brought her in.

"Get Turay right now," he said. Martha left, and he heard her shouting at John. When she came back, she asked him what was happening.

"We're going to need to do a laparotomy. She must be bleeding from somewhere."

"Why?"

"I don't know, but we need to find out and fix it...."

"Where's the granny?" Martha said.

"Shit!" Richard said.

"Where is she?"

"That woman sent her away."

"Where?"

"I don't know!"

"We need permission to operate."

"We have to do it anyway. She could die within the next few hours if we don't."

"But no one has given consent," Martha said.

"There's no one to *give* consent," he said. "We'll do it now and explain later."

"We should ask Dr. Sandi...."

"Never mind Sandi!" Richard shouted. "Where's Turay?"

Turay arrived fifteen minutes later, and Richard could smell alcohol on his breath.

"Why not treat her with antibiotics," Turay said. "If she's going to die, why make her die with an operation?"

"It's my responsibility," Richard said.

Richard gave Turay permission to use whatever drugs he needed, saying he would pay for them himself. Martha acted as the scrub nurse, while another nurse on duty, the actual matron, filled in as circulating nurse. While Richard was scrubbing up, Turay tried to intubate the girl and struggled to bypass her still swollen throat. When the girl's lips started to turn purple Richard was about to step in, but Turay finally seemed to sort it out.

Richard opened the girl's abdomen. Her belly was full of blood and blood clot. He scooped it out by the palmful, getting it out of the way so he could find the source. A fly was bashing itself off the ceiling of the operating room. "A fly," he said. Once there was less blood in the peritoneal cavity, he could see that the source was above his incision, so he extended upwards. He was reaching up into her left diaphragm to find her spleen when he noticed Turay giving her cardiac massage behind the curtain.

"Is there a problem?" he said. Her blood was much darker than it should have been. The fly landed on Richard's shoulder.

"Her heart's not too strong," Turay said. Richard had to act quickly. He found the spleen and squeezed around the hilum, stopping the blood flow. He scooped the organ and its blood vessels forward so he could see the root, and he noticed that the girl's stomach was expanding and contracting. "Turay. You can't have your tube in the right place," he said. There was no answer. "Turay!" he said.

"I'm moving it," Turay said.

"Will someone kill that *fucking* fly!" Richard shouted. He heard a choking noise from above the curtain. The blood was getting darker. He asked for catgut, which he used to tie across either side of the spleen before using scissors to cut through the vessels. Her heart rate should have slowed, the bleeding should have become red, but it was still dark. "Damn it all, Turay! What's happening?" Richard said. Her blood stopped flowing altogether. The blood vessels stopped pulsating.

"I told you," was the first thing Turay said once Richard had confirmed the girl was dead, and it took Richard a moment to understand that Turay was blaming him.

"You put the tube in her esophagus," Richard said. "You were pumping air into her stomach the whole time."

"She didn't rupture her spleen just now," Turay said. "She's been bleeding for days."

"She asphyxiated because you didn't intubate her properly," Richard said.

Turay didn't respond.

Once Richard had sewn the girl up, he helped Martha carry the body to the morgue, a small brick building at the back of the hospital. When they returned, Turay was gone.

Martha picked up her bag. "I'll be making a report on this in the morning," she said.

Richard put his hand on her arm. "It wasn't our fault."

Martha moved away from him. "Goodnight, doctor," she said.

After Martha left, Richard fell asleep on his examination table. He woke up some time later — hours or minutes, he couldn't tell — to the sound of a vehicle pulling up outside. For a moment, he forgot what was causing him such crushing anxiety, but then it all came back to him. The girl was dead, and he was going to be blamed. Martha had turned against him. Turay had accused him of misdiagnosing the girl. Apparently he'd admitted it himself while he was operating, although he couldn't remember that.

He heard Sandi talking to the night nurse outside his door, and he sat up, preparing himself for a shouting match. Sandi came in without knocking. When he saw Richard, he closed his eyes, as if trying to spare himself the sight of this man he used to respect waiting like a child to be beaten.

"Tell me," Sandi said, "in Canada, do you operate on children without the consent of their guardians?"

"You would have done the same thing," Richard said.

"You would have been up for some form of disciplinary hearing," Sandi said.

"And I would have had no trouble explaining myself," Richard said. He was surprised to find that he actually wanted to draw this conversation out. He wanted to be lectured and even threatened with punishment, because that was so much less frightening than being left alone with his other, more murky fears.

"You probably think this doesn't matter," Sandi said. "This is just one more dead African kid and no one will notice. Well, you'll see. Even here there are repercussions for this kind of negligence." Sandi turned and left.

He's just trying to scare you, Richard told himself, but his imagination was already running wild. What did Sandi mean about repercussions? Under whose authority? Richard thought of the Paramount Chief. He'd visited the man once, when they first arrived. He'd been led into a room filled with lace and knick knacks where the

Paramount Chief sat with an advisor on either side of him. Richard had brought a bottle of rum and a sack of sugar as a gift, as Sandi had instructed, and he could tell by the way everyone was acting as he presented them to the Chief that the man's power was more than symbolic. What, he wondered, would the Chief think if Sandi or the herbalist told him about what had happened? What would he do? Probably nothing, but how could Richard be sure? He didn't know the rules. He had no idea how things worked. He understood then how appealing it was to think that God was protecting you in a place like this, because no one else would.

Outside, there was only the thinnest crescent moon, and Richard could hardly see at all. He found the truck sitting empty in the yard with the keys in the ignition. He could hear music and laughter from Nene's bar. Turay was probably there, telling everyone what had happened.

Richard called for John, but there was no reply. He checked around the hospital but couldn't find him. There were no other vehicles in the yard, so Sandi must have left. Maybe John went with him. But no, John wouldn't leave Richard stranded. He must be sleeping somewhere in the hospital, or maybe waiting at the bar.

It was so dark, Richard couldn't see the road in front of him, so he had to hold onto a wall that ran along the edge of the road and walk slowly to avoid twisting his ankle in a pothole. The generator was running at Nene's, and there was loud music playing, so he couldn't pick out any of the voices.

His plan was to sneak in and tap John on the shoulder to let him know that it was time to go. Instead, as he blinked into the bright lights of Nene's bar, Richard saw Sandi, Turay, John, and two policemen sitting together at one of the white plastic tables. Sandi was leaning back in his chair drinking a beer, and Turay was leaning forward, talking intensely to the police officer next to him.

"They're probably talking about football," Richard told himself. John said something to Sandi then that made Sandi drop his head back and laugh, and all at once, Richard understood. There was no other vehicle at the hospital because Sandi had come to the hospital in the truck with John. Either Turay or one of the nurses — God, not Martha — must have sent John to collect him so that he could save the girl from Richard or the hospital from Richard or Richard from himself or whatever. That explained why Sandi had happened to show up so late at night. It also explained why John was at the bar now — not waiting for Richard at all, but finally finished with him.

Richard held onto the wall all the way back to the hospital gate. When he reached the yard, he got into the truck and turned on the engine, hoping that the sounds of the music and the generator would be loud enough that the people at the bar wouldn't hear. He couldn't take the main road past Nene's, because there were so few vehicles in town that if a truck drove past, people would notice. Instead, he went straight ahead through the hospital gate and took a long, winding back road that was deserted apart from the white eyes of dogs that appeared like phantoms in the headlights.

When he got home, he parked the truck behind the house in case John or Sandi came looking for it, went inside, and locked the door behind him. He was halfway to the bedroom before he remembered Billy. He lit a lantern and stood on the front steps calling Billy's name. The dog didn't come, so Richard walked around the outside of the house, trying not to think about what could see him out there in the darkness.

He was about to check around the dockhouse when, from the jetty, he saw something by the river's edge. "Billy," he called again. He walked along the bank holding his lantern in front of him. Among the long grasses in the shallow water near where the boats docked, he found the dog's body curled up on a small raft. The body was already partly eaten, and beneath it was a bed of grass whose arrangement looked ceremonial.

Richard retched as he scrambled up the embankment. There was no question of burying Billy, no time to wonder who had killed him and what else they might be capable of doing — his only thought was to hide. Walking toward the house, he felt a naked chill along his back, but he forced himself not to run. Once he was inside, he locked and bolted every door, and doing this made him feel more frightened than ever, because it was an admission, finally, that there was something to lock out, even if he wasn't sure yet what it was.

The top balcony was impossible to block off, because anyone could climb up the air bricks, so he tried to cut off access to the inside of the house by jamming a chair under the door handle in the kitchen, but he doubted it would work if it came down to it. When he'd finished securing the house as well as he could, he sat down on Ann's side of the bed and gently shook her out of her sleep. "What's wrong?" she whispered. She sat up and stroked his arm, and Aminata stirred beside her. "What's wrong?" she said again. He thought he might be about to start blubbing, so he turned away. She held him from behind and rested her head on his back.

"Tell me what happened," she whispered.

"Your girl died," he said.

"Who?"

"The girl from Maggie's. I tried operating, and it might have worked if Turay....". He closed his eyes and focused on the comforting feeling of his wife's arms around him, her hot breath on his back.

"If he what?"

"It doesn't matter. She's dead. Everyone will blame me."

"I won't blame you," she said.

He hunched forward and sobbed. "I'm so sorry," he said. He turned to face her. She was wearing a white nightgown, and her sleepy face looked angelic in the lantern light.

She touched his cheek. "I love you, Richard," she said.

"We have to go," he said.

"Go where?"

"Back to Nova Scotia. We have to leave here."

She rubbed her eyes. "You can't let this one thing...."

"It's not one thing. Honestly, I don't think we're safe."

"Come on," Ann laughed, and he shushed her. He didn't want Aminata awake and asking questions. "Of course we're safe," she said.

"We're in a *war*, Ann."

"It's nowhere near here."

"You don't know that. You don't know anything about it." She looked hurt, not angry. "Look...I don't believe we're safe."

She took his hand. "Is it really the war you're worried about? Because if that's it, I could understand, but I don't think that's it." He said nothing. "You're being hard on yourself because you want to be perfect, but no one is perfect."

"Ann, it's over," he said.

"But I finally feel like I can be happy here. I think part of the reason I was so miserable before is because I spent all my time trying to be better than everyone else...."

"Ann, I know it's hard for you to see this right now, but I think that you're still doing that, just in a different way."

"That's not true. Look, we've planned a Christmas celebration and...we can't go back now."

"We can, and we will," Richard said. "I'm not working with Sandi any more. He's threatened to bring some kind of legal action against me." His lips trembled. "And someone killed Billy."

"What?"

"I found him by the river."

"That doesn't mean someone killed him," she said.

"It looks like it was part of some fucking ceremony or something," Richard said.

"Oh God," Ann said, and then her expression changed. "I have to tell you something."

Richard had said this enough himself to know that it was the worst thing a person could say. If there'd been anywhere else to go he would have run out the door, started the truck and driven away. Instead he closed his eyes and said, "What?"

"We can't go back," she said.

"Why?"

"We were audited." He opened his eyes. She seemed to be waiting for a reaction, but he was only confused.

"So?"

"So...there's no money to pay...and I...."

"To pay what? You show them your records. You don't have to pay when you're audited."

"I can't show the records," Ann said.

Richard understood immediately. Once a thief, always a thief. And of course she would have been so obvious about it that she was begging to get caught. How could he ever have trusted her? "Did you respond to them?"

"Yes."

"And? Damn it, Ann, tell me what happened." He was speaking at full volume now. He didn't care if Aminata woke up.

"They wouldn't back off. There was nothing I could do from here. I tried to fix it, but I couldn't, and now they say we could...it could be very bad."

"So, what did you do?" She looked at him helplessly. "What did they say?" he said.

Ann got up and headed toward the kitchen, and Richard followed her. She reached into the back of a cupboard and pulled out a letter. Richard scanned it quickly. Their assets would be frozen, she might go to prison. *He* might go to prison.

"Did you tell the truth when you did the taxes?" he said.

She didn't respond.

"Did you even pay all our taxes this year?"

"How could I?" she said in a sudden explosion of emotion. "You gave all our money to Don!"

"I didn't give it to him. I paid a bill that we owed, and I trusted you to do the same."

"You paid it with the tax money!" she said. She started to say something else, but he wasn't listening because he had looked at the date on the letter and couldn't think about anything other than the urgent need to find out if their bank account was frozen.

"We have to go to Freetown," he said. "What day is it?" Her mouth was open. "Shit, it's Thursday," he said. It was too dangerous to travel at night. They would have to leave first thing in the morning. "We have to get to a bank before they close for the weekend," he said.

"We don't have to go all the way to Freetown to go to the bank," she said. He thought about his insurance medical cash, which he'd deposited in a separate bank account in Canada before they left, in case of emergency. Would that account be frozen too? And did he even have a way to access it from Sierra Leone?

"Didn't you hear what I said, Ann? We're leaving. Pack everything we need. We're going to make it look like we're going on a vacation. I'll tell Tor." He started to walk away.

"Richard..." she said.

"What?"

"What about Aminata?" Where once she would have demanded that Aminata come with them, now she seemed to be asking.

"It's not that simple," he said. "There's paperwork...."

"We could do it in Freetown."

"We would need Maggie to sign the papers," Richard said.

"So let's invite her to come."

"There will be a process. It could take months. Years."

"But we have to try," Ann said.

"Maggie probably knows by now, about the girl...."

"Let's ask her."

"Ann, Aminata doesn't belong with us," Richard said. "She belongs here, in her own country with the people who love her." It may have been true, but the greater truth was that he didn't want another burden in his life, and Ann's colossal mistake had given him a way out.

"I love her," Ann cried.

"Okay, okay. We'll invite Maggie to come," Richard said. This was not the moment for an emotional scene. "But we have to stick to our story that it's a vacation, alright?" If Maggie came she would be able to take the truck back to the hospital when they had finished with it, a problem Richard hadn't thought of until that moment. It would be better for everyone if they just got it over with instead of postponing the inevitable and toying with Aminata's emotions, but he could worry about all of that later. Now he had to go and tell Tor he was finally going to get what he wanted.

CHAPTER

24

TOR STARED DOWN THE BARREL of the gun at the checkpoint
boys. "There can be snakes here," Kelfala said.

"You wanna go home, go ahead," Tor said. He aimed at one of the
checkpoint boys and made a firing noise from the back of his throat.

Earlier that night, Tor had been lying in bed thinking about
Billy. He had been doing everything he could to distract himself,
but Richard was outside calling Billy's name, so there was no way
to escape it.

When he heard the driver come and take Richard away, Tor
thought he might finally be able to sleep, but he couldn't stop thinking about the dog. *So this is how it will be,* he thought. He might forget
about it for a while, but it would be with him forever. He had killed
his dog. He was a dog killer. He couldn't explain it away, and there
was nothing he could tell himself to make it better.

He heard hissing outside his window, sat up and saw Kelfala
peering through the bars. "What?" he said. Kelfala beckoned for him
to come outside.

"Why should I?"

Kelfala held up something black and shiny, and it took Tor a
second to realize he was looking at a handgun.

Tor picked up the lantern by the door of his room on his way outside. Kelfala was waiting for him on the steps, holding the gun toward him. "Holy shit," Tor said when he had it in his hands. He'd never held a real gun before. It was heavier than he had expected. The barrel was short and fat. He pulled down a release on the side, and the barrel flipped open. Inside was a single shell. "Whoa! This bullet is huge!" he said. "It must be a Magnum."

"DARE ME TO shoot their ghetto blaster?" Tor aimed the gun at the machine, which was on a bench next to the barricade.

"You cannot do that," Kelfala said.

"Wanna bet?" Tor said.

"Please," Kelfala said. "It is my uncle gun." Tor pulled back the hammer.

"No," Kelfala said. He wrapped his hands around Tor's and shoved him. Tor fell backward, and Kelfala fell on top of him. They struggled over the gun, and there was a loud pop followed by a rushing sound as a white star shot up into the air. Kelfala and Tor lay on their backs, mesmerized by the flare's ascent. The music stopped. Shouts came from the checkpoint. Kelfala snatched the gun from Tor's hand, took Tor by his collar and tried to pull him to his feet.

"No! Stay down," Tor said. He put his arms around Kelfala's neck to hold him down.

"We must run." Kelfala strained against Tor's arms. A bullet ripped into a tree next to them. Kelfala fell back with his hands over his ears. Tor helped Kelfala up, and the boys ran through the cashew field. When they got close to the house, Tor stopped to catch his breath and heard Richard shouting his name.

He had only ever heard Richard call for him in the voice of blame and punishment, but now there was something in Richard's voice that was more frightening to Tor than any punishment could have been. It was this voice that made Tor take Kelfala by the hand, run toward the light of Richard's lantern and tell Richard what had happened in the field. It was this voice that made him obey when Richard told him to take Kelfala to his bedroom, hide the flare gun, and wait there for him in the dark. It was this voice that made him certain, beyond any doubt, that they were leaving.

It wasn't until Richard came into Tor's room with his lantern that they saw the blood on the tiles. Richard looked Kelfala over. "Go and get my black bag and a towel," Richard said to Tor as he closed the curtains.

"What's wrong with him?"

"He's got something in his scalp," Richard said.

"What is it?" Tor said.

"It looks like wood."

"But is he okay?"

"Do as I said."

Tor was surprised to find Ann awake and stuffing clothes into a suitcase. Aminata was asleep in Ann and Richard's bed. "What are you doing?" Tor said.

"Shhh," she whispered. "We're going to Freetown."

Tor picked up Richard's bag. "Don't touch that," Ann said.

"Dad needs it."

"For what?"

"Kelfala. He hurt his head. Dad's fixing it."

"What? He's here?" Ann followed Tor down the hall to his bedroom and gasped when she saw Kelfala's blood on the floor.

"Just a little accident," Richard said. "Scalp wounds can bleed a lot, but we're fine here. Go and finish packing."

Tor sat on the floor next to Kelfala and held his hand while Richard picked the pieces of wood out of his head with a pair of tweezers.

"Now lie down and apply pressure with this," Richard said, passing Kelfala a towel. "Tor, pack your things. We're going to Freetown for the weekend."

By the time Tor had finished packing, Kelfala had fallen asleep in his bed, so Tor had to push him out of the way to get to the

331

mattress. He knew his parents weren't telling him the truth about where they were going, so he decided to take all of his money and he spent a long time finding different places to hide it in his clothes and his bag.

When he was ready, he went to his parents' room. "I want to know what's going on," he said.

"Shhh," Ann said. "Aminata's sleeping."

"I know this isn't a vacation."

"Come here." Ann held out her arms. He went to her and let her hug him. "We're leaving," she whispered.

Tor pulled away. "Where are we going?"

"We're going to stay in Freetown for as long as it takes to sort out Aminata's papers, and then we're going to England," she said.

"No way," Tor said.

"Shhh," she said, looking at Aminata.

"You can go to England if you want to, but I'm going home."

"It's wonderful in England. We can have a house in the country with a garden, and you'll be with your family there, all your cousins."

"Do you think I care about those stuck up losers?"

"You don't have a choice," Ann said. She went back to folding clothes. "None of us do."

"What does that mean?"

"We can't go back to Nova Scotia," she said. "We have some problems with money that we have to sort out, and your dad hates it there."

"No he doesn't. You do! You think you're too good!" Tor got up and ran to the living room, where Richard was sorting through some things on the bookshelf. "Mom says we're going to England," he said. "Is that true?"

Richard turned to face him. "No, we're not going to England. We're going back to Nova Scotia. We're going home." Richard didn't say it, but Tor knew that whatever had happened was Ann's fault.

He also knew that Richard would fix it, and that as much as he hated Richard, he would be much worse off without him.

"When?" he said.

"We're leaving first thing in the morning, and we'll get the first flight we can."

Tor nodded.

"Go and get some...." Richard was cut off by a thunderous banging at the front door. He held his finger to his lips and stayed crouched on the floor looking helplessly at his son.

CHAPTER 25

THERE WERE SO MANY POSSIBILITIES, none of them good. The police. Rebels. John looking for the truck. The herbalist. Sandi. The family of the girl who died. The banging came again.

"Dr. Berringer! Ann!" someone shouted.

"Who is it?" Richard said.

"Pastor Mark."

Richard exhaled. He got up and opened the first front door but didn't unlock the second barred one.

"I'm sorry for the late hour," Mark said through the bars. "Is Maggie with you?"

"No," Richard said. "We were going to come and get her in the morning. We're taking a vacation to Freetown and we thought…." There was an eruption of shouting in Temne. Three men grabbed Mark and pinned him to the side of the house.

"Lef me!" Mark shouted.

"Hey," Richard said. "What is going on?"

"This man is a rebel," one of the men said.

"I can assure you that this man is not a rebel," Richard said. In the beam of the soldiers' flashlights, he could see dark footprints and smears of blood on the white steps. Kelfala's blood.

One of the soldiers came toward the bars. "He was shooting at us at the checkpoint, and he ran away this side," he said.

"He is a pastor," Richard said. "I am a doctor, and he is the pastor at my church." There was a pause. He tried not to look at the blood on the ground, but his gaze kept returning to it.

"Your identification," one of the men said.

"Ann," Richard called. He couldn't leave the men there with the blood. "Ann," he called again. Tor came. "Tor, get my passport from your mother."

Ann was in her bedroom going through a bag. "I need Dad's passport," Tor said.

"I'm looking!" she said, as if he had already been badgering her.

"I need it now!"

"What's going on?" she said.

"I don't know. There are men here." Tor knelt next to her and tipped the bag upside down on the floor.

Ann shouted "No!" as a heap of papers, toiletries and clothing fell out.

"Where do you keep them?" Tor said.

"Now I have to put this all back!"

"You are so disorganized!"

"Is that Mark?" Ann said. She stuck her head out into the hallway to listen.

Tor picked up the empty bag and opened every zipper and clasp. He had just found an inner pocket when Richard came into the room, pushing Ann away from the door. Tor pulled out three passports and gave them to his father. Richard ran back down the hallway, Tor and Ann following. He handed the passports to one of the soldiers. "Okay. Thank you doctor," the man said after he had looked at them. "We are only trying to make everyone be safe."

"I know. Thank you for that," Richard said.

Another voice shouted from a distance, and the men called back, then left.

Richard opened the barred door and helped Mark up off the ground. "I'm sorry, Pastor. Are you all right?" Mark came inside, and Richard locked both doors.

"What are you doing?" Ann said. "Why did you lock him out? Who were those men?"

Richard remembered the blood and wanted to clean it up, but he was too afraid to open the door again.

Mark was rubbing his neck. "Maggie is missing," he said. "She went on an evangelizing trip, and she has still not returned. My wife is with her."

"What do you think happened?"

"Maybe they had problems with the motorcar," Mark said. "Or maybe they have run into troubles with the checkpoints. I have heard reports of some problems at thirty-eight checkpoint, but when I went looking for Maggie and Emily, I was allowed to pass there unmolested, and the soldiers claim they had not seen a white woman there today."

"Who were those men?" Ann said.

"They were soldiers," Richard said, realizing that for once something was working in his favour, because now Ann would believe in the danger. "They said there were rebels in the area." He turned to Mark. "I'm sure they're fine," he said, but all he could think about was how he and Ann were going to get through the checkpoints with no cash.

As if reading his mind, Mark said, "You should not be going to Freetown for holidays at this time. It might be dangerous. The situation is not stable in the country, as you can see." He turned away and rubbed his neck again.

"Well, we have to do some banking as well," Richard said. Suddenly it seemed foolish to lie. "To tell you the truth, we might not be coming back."

"In that case, I advise you to go north, to Guinea," Mark said. "It is much more safe to go in that direction, and Conakry is closer than Freetown also."

"How would we get there?" Richard said.

"In the truck," Ann said.

"But how would it get back? It would be easy to arrange it from Freetown, but I don't know how we would do it from Guinea."

"You have the motorcar from the hospital?" Mark said.

"Yes," Richard said.

"I know someone who can help with bringing it back. I will give you his details."

"Great," Richard said.

"We need to find Maggie and Emily first," Ann said. "Where could we look for them?"

"They probably just had car trouble, right Mark?" Richard said.

"We'll help you find them," Ann said.

"Mark, do you mind if I talk to my wife alone?" Richard said.

"Of course," Mark said.

Richard led Ann into the kitchen and Tor followed.

"Tor, go to sleep please," Richard said. "Your mother and I need to talk."

"I want to know," Tor said. "I have a right to know, too." This was where the normal Richard would get up, drag Tor to his room, and kick him in the butt for being disobedient, but instead, Richard sighed and whispered, "Okay. We need to leave today, as soon as it's light out."

"But we have to help Mark look for Maggie. Why don't we go tomorrow, when she's back," Ann said.

"Didn't you hear Mark? There are rebels in the area. It's not safe."

"But maybe it's safer not to travel if there are rebels around," Ann said.

"It's now Friday morning, so this is our last chance to get to a bank before the weekend, and it's only a matter of time before John comes here looking for the truck, so we need to be gone before that happens."

"But…."

"No buts, Ann. I don't know who is going to come knocking on that door next, and I don't want to wait to find out."

338

"But what if they won't let us in to Guinea? Don't we need visas?"

"It's not far to the border, so we'll know soon enough."

"Do we have enough money to pay if they ask for a bribe?" Ann asked.

Tor got up and left the room, and while he was gone, Richard suggested the possibility of taking some money from the hospital and paying it back later. "We raised it in the first place, and we've already given thousands of dollars of our own money to the hospital," he said.

"If we do that, it means we haven't learned anything," Ann said.

He was surprised by this reaction from her, and he realized that he would have no problem defending himself if Sandi reported him for what happened with the girl, but stealing money on top of it would look very bad.

"You're right," he said. He closed his eyes and knocked on his forehead with his knuckles. There had to be another solution.

"Here," Tor said, tapping Richard's arm. Richard opened his eyes. Tor was handing him a small stack of Canadian dollars. He took the money and was about to ask where it had come from but changed his mind and started to count it instead.

"But…" Ann said. "What about Aminata?"

"Six hundred and eighty dollars," Tor said.

Richard looked at Ann and shook his head. "I'm sorry, there's no way," he said.

ANN WENT TO THE BEDROOM and woke Aminata up by kissing her on her forehead.

"Wake up, darling," she said. Aminata opened her eyes. "Richard and Tor and I are going on a trip in the morning, and you are going to go home with Pastor Mark."

Aminata sat up and held Ann around her waist. She pressed her face into Ann's breast, and the fierceness of it made Ann wonder if she already knew what was going on. "No," Aminata said.

Ann pulled the girl's hands apart. "Mark has come to take you home," she said. "Maggie is lost, and he needs you to help him look for her."

"Don't left me," Aminata cried.

"I'm not leaving you," Ann said, but she knew she had to tell Aminata some version of the truth. It wasn't fair to lie to her. "The situation in our country isn't good for us right now, but we're going to go home and sort it out, and then we're going to send for you. I promise I'll do everything I can, okay?" Of course Aminata would feel abandoned, but Ann didn't have the power to change what was happening, so she just wanted it to be over. "I'm so sorry about this," she said. *God did not create abandonment, and so it is not real.*

Aminata's poignantly tacky dress was bunched up around her chest, and she tried to pull it back down. "You are such a beautiful and talented and special person, do you know that?" Ann said. Aminata nodded. *God did not create guilt, and so it is not real.*

Ann got up to go to the living room, and Aminata held onto her waist and limped along next to her. Mark and Richard were sitting on the sofa, talking solemnly. "I'm sure you'll find them," Richard said. When Ann and Aminata came into the room, Richard turned away from the sight of the girl holding onto his wife. "I'm sure you'll find them," he said again.

Ann asked Richard to bring Aminata's crutches from the bedroom, but Aminata was so distraught that she couldn't negotiate them, so Mark had to carry her to his truck. Ann looked as though she was about to fall apart too, but as soon as Aminata and Mark were gone and the doors were locked behind them, she went straight to sleep with Tor curled up next to her.

Richard spent the rest of the night sitting at the foot of the bed, listening and waiting. By the time the neighbour's rooster crowed, he had become so attuned to the slightest sound — a cockroach in the bathroom sink, the breeze scraping the leaves of the mango tree gently against the house — that the rooster's call had the effect of an electric shock.

He woke Ann and Tor and told them to get dressed. He was bringing the bags to the front door when Jusuf arrived. Richard felt grateful for Jusuf's presence, which made everything feel more normal, but then he remembered Billy's body left exposed by the river for anyone to find.

"Jusuf, we're going away for the weekend," Richard said. "Can you go and help Ann with the bags please?" Jusuf went inside, and Richard walked down to the place where he'd found Billy. The body was a mess of gore and bones, but the face was mostly intact. The raft was made of sticks and held together with elephant grass and a piece of dirty blue fabric. Richard suspected that he would have some strong feelings about it all later, but for the moment he could only think about getting out of there as quickly as possible, so instead of burying Billy, as he would have liked to do, he pulled the raft into the long grass and covered it with branches and leaves.

While Jusuf and Richard finished packing the truck, Tor went to his room and divided his remaining cash between his shoes and pockets. Once his money was organized, he shook Kelfala awake. "We're leaving," he said. "You can stay and sleep if you want."

"I dae go," Kelfala said. He put on his bloodied T-shirt, took the gun from the chest where they'd hidden it at night and stuffed it into the waistband of his shorts. Tor followed him outside.

Richard was closing the tailgate. "Let's have a look at you," he said. He checked Kelfala's head. "If it's still paining on Monday, have one of the nurses at the hospital look at it, okay?"

"Yes, doctor," Kelfala said.

Richard went inside.

"So, let me know when you're a Marine," Tor said to Kelfala. "I'll come and visit you in America and we can try out some real guns."

Kelfala smiled, but Tor already regretted the joke, because he suspected that Kelfala knew and had always known that he would probably never be a Marine or go to America or do anything else that he said he was going to do.

"Goodbye, my friend," Kelfala said.

Tor held out his fist. "Wolverines," he said.

"Wolverines." Kelfala pressed his fist against Tor's.

By the time they were ready to leave, the day had already begun to heat up, and Ann had dark sweat marks up the back and chest of the long-sleeved dress she had chosen for the journey. Tor gave Jusuf one last hug goodbye. "You are my good boy, Tor," Jusuf said. "You are a real gentleman." Tor wondered if Jusuf knew they were leaving for good.

As Tor was getting into the truck, Jusuf touched his arm. "Can you give me your knife?" he said. Tor shook his head no. He felt like Jusuf was ruining everything at the last moment. Jusuf shrugged, rubbed his hand on Tor's head and said, "Goodbye, troublesome."

"We go see back," Tor said, although he knew they would probably never see each other again.

"And Billy?" Jusuf said to Richard. Tor's chest tightened.

"He'll turn up," Richard said. "Please take the bike to the hospital today."

None of the Berringers turned to wave goodbye to Jusuf, but Tor touched his knife in his pocket and felt some regret.

RICHARD WAS slowing down at the bridge checkpoint when Tor recognized the driver's son wearing an AK47 strapped over his shoulder. "Dad!" Tor shouted, but it was too late. The boy had seen them.

"Don't say anything," Richard said.

"Good morning, doctor." The driver's son leaned into Richard's open window.

"Good morning, Abdul," Richard said.

"Usai una dae go?" Abdul asked.

Richard wiped his forehead with the back of his sleeve. "To Guinea. Just for a quick visit. We've never been there!" Ann put her hand on his lap.

Abdul peered at the luggage in the back of the truck. "You have tif my father motorcar. He tell me last night it is missing."

"I am using the truck, yes. But it is not your father's. It belongs to the hospital. It belongs to me, actually."

"My father is the only person driving this motorcar," the boy said.

Richard eyed the barricade, which was just a rope. He pulled a twenty-dollar bill out of his pocket and gave it to Abdul.

"Tenki, doctor," Abdul said. "But I no go make you pass ya."

"I paid for this truck, damn it. I did. Not your father. Your father has done nothing but...." The other soldiers were watching the exchange.

Tor felt desperate. If they didn't get through, his parents might change their minds and decide to stay. They might never leave. Or they might go looking for Maggie and get themselves shot. He wished he'd kept more of his money instead of giving almost all of it to Richard, but then he reminded himself that it was actually Richard's money, and he'd had no choice.

"Abdul, this is not your father's truck. You have no right to stop us passing here." Abdul turned toward Tor and twirled his finger to indicate that Tor should roll down his window. Tor locked his door.

"This boy need to pay me for my hand," Abdul said, holding his hand up for Richard to see. Richard pulled out another twenty.

"Do you think you can buy a soldier?" Abdul said as he put the money into his pocket.

"Now lift the barricade," Richard said.

"I no able let you pass," Abdul said. "I go take this motorcar back to my father."

"It's not his motorcar!" Richard snapped. The other soldiers gathered around Abdul.

"Fine!" Richard said. He threw the truck into reverse, and the soldiers started shouting.

"Okay, okay, okay," Richard put the truck in park and took his hands off the wheel. "We no get money," he said. "We no get money. I na doctor."

The soldiers laughed, and one of them pushed past Abdul and bent down to look into the truck at Ann. "Dis nar you wehf?" he said. Tor flipped his Swiss Army knife open in his pocket and held it in his sweaty palm.

Abdul spoke to the soldier in Temne. "You must come down," the soldier said to Richard.

"Who?" said Ann.

"All," he said.

"Go," Ann said to Richard.

"No," Richard said to the soldier.

"It's a piece of rope. Just go!" Ann shouted.

"No!" Richard said.

"We have to get out," Tor said.

"What do you mean?" Ann said.

"We have to get out, get our bags and start walking."

The driver's son reached in through Richard's window, unlocked Tor's door and opened it. "Come down," he said. He had his hand on his gun.

Tor gripped his knife. The driver's son spoke to the other soldiers. "Wetin a don tehl dis bohboh ya for do?" he said.

"You don tehl dis bohboh ya for kam dohng," one of them said.

"So?" he said to Tor.

"Walk away, Tor," Richard said, but Tor still had to reach into the truck to get his bag, and he wasn't going to turn his back on the driver's son.

"Leave him alone," Ann said. She started to get out of the truck, but Richard held her hand to stop her. "Let me go, Richard!" she said. "Get away from him," she screamed at the driver's son.

"Now you see me, I am a soldier, and you are a little boy," the driver's son said to Tor.

Richard let go of Ann's arm and opened his door slowly. "Tor, don't do anything stupid," he said.

Abdul horked and spat a thick slug of phlegm into Tor's face.

Tor used the back of his arm to wipe it away, then reached behind himself without turning around and pulled his bag out of the truck. Abdul and the rest of the soldiers were laughing at him, but Tor didn't care. He put his bag on his back and started to walk toward the barricade. Ann got out and ran after him, and one of the soldiers stood in their way. Tor tried to go around the soldier, but the soldier pushed him back, and Ann held him.

Richard got out of the truck and started taking the bags out of the back. "We're going to Guinea. If you won't let us take our vehicle, we will walk and find other transportation in Pamalap." Richard wasn't sure if this was possible, but it sounded plausible.

"Your papers?" Abdul held out his hand.

"Come back here," Richard said to Ann and Tor. He wanted them all close together. "You mean our passports?"

"*Laissez-passer.*"

"We can get them at the border," Richard said, although he had no idea what they were.

"And how you go do that?" Abdul said. He spoke to the others in Temne, and they all laughed. "Guinean they love money, and you think you can buy all man, eh doctor."

"Look, it's none of your business. I will sort it out with them."

Abdul crossed his arms. "I no go make you pass ya," he said.

"WHAT ARE WE GOING to do now?" Ann said. She and Richard were following Tor toward the cashew field, all of them laden down with their belongings.

"I don't bloody well know, Ann!" Richard was wearing two backpacks and struggling to pull a wheeled suitcase through the dirt while carrying a second suitcase on his head. "Why the hell do I have to come up with all the solutions?"

"I know what to do," Tor said. "Stop arguing and follow me."

Tor told them about Ibrahim, how he had a boat and a house on the other side of the river and could help them get to Conakry.

345

"Go up to the house. I'll be back in ten minutes," Tor said.

Ann and Richard found the house locked, Jusuf and the bike gone. Ann went to wait on the front steps, but Richard insisted they hide, so they were crouching behind the kitchen hut when Tor came back, followed by a man in rags. "Mom, Dick — Dad — this is Ibrahim," Tor said. Richard recognized the man. From the dockhouse window he'd seen him coming and going in his boat, ignoring children who threw stones at him and called him names. Was this really someone who could help them?

"How do you do?" Ibrahim said. He shook hands with Richard and bowed to Ann.

When Ibrahim brought out his boat, it was clear that the Berringers wouldn't be able to bring half of what they'd had in the truck.

"Once we get to the other side it's about six or seven kilometres to the border," Ibrahim said. "We might be able to find transport, but there's no guarantee, so you must take only what you can carry."

Richard, Ann and Tor quickly went through their belongings, picking out what they absolutely needed. Ann brought *A Course in Miracles*. Tor brought his movies, his Swiss Army Knife, and a few cans of sweetened condensed milk. Richard brought his papers, his doctor's bag, and his money. Meanwhile Ibrahim paced back and forth, talking about the CIA, New York City, male chauvinism.

Tor got into the boat first and knelt at the front. Ibrahim helped Ann to get comfortable near the back. Richard passed Ibrahim his bag and wedged himself in behind Ann. "Here religion gets mixed with tradition and male chauvinism," Ibrahim said as he began to row. The boat, weighed down with the Berringers and their belongings, sat perilously low in the water, and the river lapped up against the sides and sloshed in each time Ibrahim pulled on the oar. "I might be a chauvinist myself. I'm not exonerating myself from that. But it's good to give the woman the choice about her body and even the property that you have, that she has the same right to it."

They were cutting across the river at an angle against the current. Tor was at the front bailing with a plastic bucket tied to a hook. He bailed mechanically, in time with Ibrahim's oar strokes, pausing now and then to look up at the shore in front of them, telling himself that this was it: they would be allowed to cross the border, they would get tickets and go home and never, ever, *ever* look back.

Richard felt wetness seeping through his shoes and looked down at the water in the bottom of the boat. *What are we doing?* he wondered. Crossing a dangerous river in a tiny boat with this strange man. And why? What had actually happened? Nothing. No one had tried to harm them. Maggie probably had a flat tire. If they waited until Monday they could pack and say goodbye properly and have John drive them to Freetown to spend a week at the beach before flying home. They didn't need to leave like this. But thinking of the alternative, of staying one more moment in that house, locked up in hiding from some indefinable terror, from whoever had killed Billy, Richard couldn't do it.

Maybe what he was most afraid of was losing his chance to have a reason to leave other than fatigue and disillusionment and shame. He had a way out, a way to feel like he was escaping rather than giving up. In Nova Scotia, he could go back to being himself again, a better him, even more devoted to his ideals because he wouldn't have to defend them every day. He would keep writing his proposals for the Foundation, he would extend the mortgage on his house, he would pay back whatever he owed the government, and he would work for Don for the rest of his life, if that's what it would take. That was the kind of heroism he was capable of. He wouldn't keep running away, and he wouldn't allow Ann to, either. He would pay for her mistake, because that was so much easier than paying for his own. He was grateful to her for that. He was grateful to her in general. He reached forward and drew her toward him, and the boat tipped slightly until they shifted their weight.

Ann turned to look back at the house. From that distance, in that light, it almost looked beautiful. It was as though she was going across the river for some sightseeing and would be back later that day, ready to go to Maggie's to read stories with the children and tuck them into their beds. She imagined Maggie dead on the side of the road, killed by rebels or soldiers. How awful it would be. But actually it wouldn't be awful. It wouldn't even be real. *God did not create a meaningless world.*

She felt profoundly serene. After all their struggles, her family was still intact, and they had come to the kind of peace that becomes possible when everyone is equally wrong. It was so strange and sad to be leaving this way, without even saying goodbye, and she hoped that they weren't being foolish and running away from nothing, but she trusted that it was all for the best. She turned again for one last glimpse of the house she had hated so much looking perfectly safe and inviting behind them, and she was sure that someday it would make sense that it had ended like this, and in the future, when they looked back, they would understand.

EPILOGUE

Dear Mrs. Berringer,

I am writing to you once more even though it has been a very long silence. I hope that this letter will find you and you will get some information about what has happened to Sierra Leone in your absence. Of course, I know that if you get this letter it will be such a nightmare to you, because you thought that what you are reading could not happen in a country you know to be peaceful and full of friendly people such a short time ago.

Today we in Sierra Leone are living in an era of tragedy and doom. All civilians, excepting those responsible for the calamity that has befallen us, are mourning and wailing. When the rebels reached our town, they burnt down twenty-two buildings, including the orphanage and the hospital, killed an equal number of people amongst which were three school children: one girl and two boys, and abducted sixty-five schoolboys and girls and Miss Maggie herself (she was later released and sent home to Texas).

Amongst the abducted children were my son Daniel (eleven years) and my daughter Marian (fourteen years). They were taken away, and we do not have hopes that we will see them again. Later the rebels attacked Port Loko, where they abducted about two hundred children that went to take the O level exams, burned down thirty-five houses, and killed four Lebanese businessmen.

349

Now Sierra Leone, a once poor but lively state, is today in terrible tears. However, there is some hope. A trained military group was hired from South Africa, and since they came the war has tempered down. They have killed hundreds of rebels using helicopter gunships, and according to their promise they will end the war by December. Sanity is gradually returning, and we look forward to the change to civilian rule as elections are around the corner. The ban on political parties has been lifted and fourteen parties have already been registered. Soon we have the National Registration of eligible voters, and I am sure we will have foreign observers. We are keeping hope alive if nothing else.

Dear Mrs. Berringer, I hope you are well and that if you receive this letter and you are not too busy you will write to let me know your news and perhaps to let us know that you are thinking about us also. I know Torquil has grown too much. Give my love to him and to your husband. The children miss you, especially Aminata, who speaks about you often. My wife sends greetings to you. She was captured but managed to escape with six kids.

Best wishes.

Your friend,
Pastor Mark Sesay

Dear Miss Ann,

How are you, and how is the family?

I'm sad, and feel sick. What is your feeling about? Please, Miss Ann, don't forgot me. I'm alway thingking about you and Mr. Berringer. Up till now I have write several letter but you are not replying me, why?

Miss Ann, I would like you to send a family picture and other one of you and Mr. Berringer. Please so that I will show it to my friend. How good you are and how lovely you are.

Our country is in mess we are not in peace. Things are so terrible for us in Sierra Leone in this rebel time. Please keep on praying for us in Sierra Leone for peace.

Greetings to all, Torquil and Mr. Berringer.

With lots of love,
Aminata Juliet Kanu

Please reple me I will have it through Pastor Mark.

God bless you all!

THANK YOU

To my teacher, Terence Byrnes, whose suggestion that I develop one of my short stories into a novel led me to write this book, and to my parents, Eleanor Harper and Phillip Cooper, whose loving support helped me to write it. I am particularly grateful for my father's enduring patience and generosity in assisting me with the medical details and my mother's constant encouragement and sharp editorial eye. Many thanks to my friend, co-brainstormer, and travel companion, Paul McNeill. Thanks to my siblings Rebecca, Alex, William, and Sam, and to my love, Jonáš Koukl. Miluji tě.

Thanks to my wonderful research assistant, Imran Mark Sesay. To Dan Kelly and Bailor Barrie for inviting me to spend time with them in Kono, and to Nyani Quarmyne for joining me on that journey. To Abdul Karim Kebe Kamara. To my dear friend Michael Redhill. To my agent, Martha Magor Webb, and to Kelsey Attard, Anna Boyar, and everyone else at Freehand for believing in my book. To Barbara J. Scott, my brilliant editor, and to Natalie Olsen for her beautiful jacket design.

The guidance that I received from other authors was enormously helpful to me while I was writing this book, and I am so grateful for their generosity and kindness. I would especially like to thank Nino Ricci and Shyam Selvadurai, my mentors through the Banff Centre's Writing Program, and Carol Bruneau, my mentor through the Writers' Federation of Nova Scotia's Mentorship Program.

I also want to acknowledge some of the many teachers who have inspired and encouraged me over the years, especially John Baxter at Dalhousie University, and Josip Novakovich and Mikhail Iossel at Concordia University.

I would like to express my heartfelt appreciation and gratitude to the friends I met Sierra Leone, who taught me so much, especially Bassey Akpan, Daniel Bangura, Sherry Andrews Browne, Lesley Buffington, Helen Clark, Peggy Cummings, Ernest Dugbartey, Ann Fleming, Gary Parker, Alusine Kamara, Alpha Kargbo, Daniel Kargbo, Edwin Alpha Sesay, and Clementine Tengue.

Thanks to everyone who read and commented on this manuscript, especially to Mary Katherine Carr, Sarah Faber, Carolyn van Gurp, Peter Heron, Kathleen Martin, Tracy Monaghan, Susan Paddon, Jocelyn Parr, Rebecca Silver Slayter, Tiffany Steel, Jane Warren, and Michael Wuitchik. I also want to thank all those who offered their time and expertise to help me with my research—especially Lansana Gberie and Paul Richards for their advice on the depiction of the Sierra Leonean civil war; Fuambai Sia Ahmadu, Ann-Marie Caulker, Bríd Hehir, and Tom Obara for their advice on the depiction of female circumcision; and Phil Tunstall for his help with the rat extermination storyline.

Thank you to the Canada Council for the Arts for supporting this work through the Grants for Professional Writers Program and to the Nova Scotia Department of Communities, Culture and Heritage for supporting this work through the Grants to Individuals Program. The support I have received from both of these agencies has played a vital role in my development as a writer, and I'm grateful to all those who fund, administer, and advocate for them.

Finally, and especially, thanks to Jusuf Bangura, who my family will always remember with deep affection and gratitude.

The book Ann is reading is the "Workbook for Students" section of *A Course in Miracles*. The letters written by Torquil to his grandmother and to Mrs. McCann are based in part on letters and journal entries written by my brother, Sam Cooper, when he was a child. The conversation that Richard and Sandi have about circumcision on the dockhouse balcony is based in part on a report written by my father, Dr. Phillip Cooper, for an academic course at McGill University, entitled *Regarding Cultural Factors Influencing Maternal and Perinatal Mortality and Morbidity in Rural Sierra Leone*. The "rebels are fighting" song that Torquil sings is taken from "The World," written and recorded by Thomas George. The "goat" song that Kelfala sings is one that I remember a boy at my school in Sierra Leone singing, which I assume he made up. Aspects of the storyline about the herbalist are inspired by experiences I had while in Sierra Leone researching a story about mental health, which was published in *Guernica Magazine*. The two letters that make up the Epilogue are based on letters my mother received from friends in Sierra Leone.

CATHERINE COOPER is a Nova Scotian writer with a Masters degree in English Literature and Creative Writing from Concordia University. Her fiction and non-fiction have been published most recently in *Brick Magazine* and *Guernica Magazine*. Her first book, *The Western Home: Stories for Home on the Range*, is a collection of short stories published by Pedlar Press in 2014. *White Elephant* is her first novel. She lives in Prague, Czech Republic.